He Loves Me Knot

ANNABELLE McCORMACK

Para mi prima, Raquel, casi-hermana. The Beth to my Amy. <3

...and for anyone who has ever felt the sting of being rootless. May you find a home in someone safe, and in the strong bonds of friendship. I know your loneliness—and this one's for you.

He Loves Me Knot

CHAPTER ONE

Two Years Ago

"Bollocks!"

Lydia Winnick startled to a stop on the sidewalk, nearly slamming into the back of the swearing man in front of her.

Oh crap. Poor guy.

He had one foot in a puddle, and water clearly seeped into his sock and dress shoe.

"Bloody—"

A few feet away, a woman leaving the Notting Hill Bookshop gave the man a sharp, disapproving look.

The man probably hadn't meant to scandalize the exiting woman. Actually, he'd only stepped into the puddle to allow her to pass.

Which worked out for me. Liddy was just inches from the puddle, and she hadn't noticed it either.

But as the offended woman continued her scowl, the man

laughed. "Shite weather we're having, am I right?" He pushed past her into the bookshop and let the door swing shut behind him.

Liddy snickered to herself, then ducked her chin as the lady's withering look transferred to her. If only she could come up with something as clever. Instead, she hurried into the bookstore, happy to get away from the irritated lady.

She shook out her rain jacket by the door, wishing she'd brought an umbrella. When she'd packed her apartment in Nashville to move to London, she'd accidentally shipped her umbrella instead of packing it in her suitcase. Four days after arriving, her mistake was glaring.

And that carry-on full of books isn't doing me much good in this weather.

On the other hand, books were nice to have in her empty apartment.

Books had always been one of her comforts, no matter where she went or what life threw at her. When she'd been in grade school, there had been few problems she couldn't solve—or avoid—by turning to a book.

This was why, when the CEO of Camden Enterprises, Aiden Camden, had told her they'd be holding her "welcome" dinner in Notting Hill, she'd left extra early to visit the bookstore she'd heard about in the movies. Whether it was a tourist trap.

The smell of books was comforting—a perfume that reminded her of home.

Heading for the nonfiction section, she heard her stomach growl as she passed the cookbooks, the glossy photos of delicious food a reminder that she hadn't eaten all day. She'd spent most of the day filling out forms online for her new job. After she'd gotten her master's degree in the spring, she'd applied for a job at Camden Enterprises without telling her sister Elle or her future brother-in-law, Quinn. Quinn's family company specialized in defense contracting, and it was a perfect fit.

And more importantly, the company was in London, where she could get a fresh start.

Her surgery five years ago was supposed to be her fresh start, then college.

But somehow, neither had been.

But maybe moving across the Atlantic will be.

As she drew closer to the section that held travel guides, she caught sight of the man she'd seen outside. He faced the bookshelf and was on his phone.

"And I don't really care what she thinks. You wouldn't be asking me to be there if it were anyone else. She wants to impress me? Then she can start by proving she deserves to be there."

Liddy stepped back. She shouldn't eavesdrop on his conversation, but he stood in the way of the books she wanted to look at.

"As a matter of fact, I had plans . . ." The man's voice dropped. "No, not Natalie. I saw her two nights ago. Vivienne." The man glanced over his shoulder, then noticed Liddy, his eyes locking with hers for a moment. *Whoa, hottie.* He had short, wavy dark hair and unique ice-blue eyes. A shadow of stubble was on that sexy jawline, and the finely tailored suit he wore couldn't hide his broad shoulders.

No wonder he has so many dates lined up.

He lowered his voice even further and stepped closer to the books.

She almost turned in a circle and did another lap around the bookstore.

She wrinkled her nose. Then again, he was still in her way and taking up valuable floor space in a small store while talking.

His voice went up a notch with irritation. "Well, you're

never going to convince me of that. What was all that *'I will not interfere with your team'* shite? And now you want me to accept some twat without blinking an eye?"

"Excuse me," she finally murmured.

He scowled and stepped back to let her pass, not glancing her way.

Too bad. Hottie was quickly losing points. *Maybe he's just rude, after all.*

Her gaze focused on the travel guides lining the bookshelf in front of her.

"Yes," she murmured, spotting the book she'd come for. Elle had recommended it as a quirky, off-the-beaten-path guide to London.

"It's just the sort of thing you'd love," she'd said on the phone. "It has lots of fun little tidbits that you'd never know. Right up your alley."

She reached for the book, and her hand bumped into the outstretched hand of the man on the phone.

Their fingers collided, and for the briefest moment, his fingers enclosed hers rather than grabbing the book. Startled, they both dropped back nearly at the same time.

Her eyes locked with his again and widened.

A blush heated her cheeks as though he'd caught her trying to steal something, and her hand darted back to her side.

God, he really is gorgeous.

"Let me call you back." He hung up and shoved the phone away, grinning at her. "Normally, I don't hold hands until the second date, but in your case, I'll consider it."

And there's that charm that has the dates lining up. She rolled her eyes, hoping he'd notice.

"You know, I would, but I really don't want to upset Natalie. Or Vivienne."

A hint of startled amusement lit his eyes and then he

released a chuckle. "It isn't polite to eavesdrop, you know. At least not in British society."

She shrugged playfully. "Then the rules don't apply to me. I'm American."

"Everyone here is American. Or a fan of Julia Roberts."

"I'm more of a Hugh Grant kind of girl." She gave him a grin of her own, tilting her head. "But what about you? You're English, and you're here."

"Who says I'm from here?" He gestured toward the worker behind the register. "And I'd venture a guess he's English, too."

His answer was intriguing.

"What does that mean? You sound English."

"Maybe. I've moved a lot. Been in London since I was eighteen. But I spent long stretches of my childhood elsewhere, too."

Equally evasive.

I need to stop being intrigued by the hottie and just get my book. He has enough women to keep him busy.

She quirked a brow. "Interesting." She grabbed the book she'd come for.

He held out a hand. "Actually, I was going to get that book."

Seriously?

"Then get another copy."

"That's the only one." He pointed at the space on the shelf. "And I was here first."

She bit her lip.

I can just let him have it. Order one later.

She set the book back slowly, then crossed her arms, settling her weight on her back foot. "Now you're calling dibs?" She lifted her chin in a defiant dare.

"Yeah, I think I am." He smiled. With full lips and straight teeth like that, he could be a model. He also had the slightest cleft in his chin. *Ugh. He probably is a model.*

But random men—even hot ones—didn't normally get her attention like this.

Random strangers aren't normally so effortless to talk to either.

"What are you getting the book for?" she asked.

He searched her gaze as though he didn't quite believe what she was saying each time she opened her mouth. "As a matter of fact, as a gift."

"For Vivienne?" She'd already admitted to eavesdropping. She may as well have some fun with it.

"No." He sighed. "For some glorified intern I'm being forced to work with. It's my attempt to pretend to be nice when, really, I'm an arsehole and will do my best to see her fired in the first month."

"Ah . . . the *twat*." She tried not to laugh at how forthcoming he'd been. "I appreciate your honesty." She tugged the book closer toward her. "I'm going to have to go with no. Because my sister recommended this book, I just moved here, and I need to find my way around town. Also, why waste your money on someone you hate and who might not even appreciate it when I will?"

This time he guffawed. "Well, my sister *also* recommended this book." He scanned her face, contemplating the situation. Then with a choked laugh, he ran his fingers through his hair and said, "And despite my protests, I've been asked to be nice. Books are the only thing I can think of as a neutral gift that won't cause her to get any ideas about my motivation."

Her lips pursed. "Hmm." No doubt, women questioned his motivation for lots of things.

I really should just take the book and go.
But I'm also having fun.

She sighed and let go of the book, then reached into her purse. "All right, we'll flip for it."

"Beg your pardon?"

Pausing in her search for a coin, she smirked. "You know. Flip a coin." She pulled out a quarter. "Heads or tails?"

He crossed his arms. "But I was here first."

She shrugged. "I didn't see you holding it. Until someone buys it, it belongs to the store. Heads or tails?"

What am I even doing right now?

Am I flirting?

Yeah, I think I'm flirting . . . with the guy who has at least two girlfriends.

Yet something about him made her want to keep talking to him.

Grudgingly, he nodded. "Fine. Heads."

She flipped the coin, but it tumbled to the floor between them, then rolled to a stop. They both ducked down to look.

Oh great.

He'd won.

Not that I'm going to give up that easily.

"Heads, I win!" She fist-pumped in victory.

The guy snatched the coin. "In what universe does calling the correct side mean you lose?"

"The one where you're stealing my book." She laughed. "We didn't define what heads means. It could mean you lose."

"I say best two out of three," he grunted back. "You completely lost, and this is me being merciful."

She held out her hand for her coin. "Fine, best two out of three. But my rules. And I already won the first round."

He placed the quarter in her hand, his fingertips brushing hers for the second time. Their eyes locked, and goose bumps rose on her arms. *What the hell is going on here?* Besides the complete absurdity of the two of them squatting on the bookshop floor for this.

An unsmiling man approached, and they both looked up.

Just when Liddy was sure he was about to scold them for being on the store floor, he instead reached past them, sniffing in disdain, and lifted the book in question from the shelf.

The hot guy exchanged a look with Liddy.

They both scrambled from the floor as the man started away, the guidebook in his hands.

The guy caught up with him in a few steps. "Excuse me." He touched the man's elbow, and the older man stiffened.

"Sorry." Hot guy raked his fingers through his hair. "Sorry —I—uh, I was going to buy that book."

"And so was I," Liddy added as she reached them.

Not an ounce of sympathy appeared on the man's face. "Well, have a chat with the owner. Perhaps there's another copy." The man started forward again.

Liddy groaned. *Why is this the most popular book here?* "But we were there first—"

"Not now, love." The hot guy put his arm around her shoulder and gave her a squeeze. She gave him a baffled look, and he dropped his hand, winking.

"Sir, if I could just have a moment of your time." The hot guy stepped in front of the man once again. "It's my girlfriend's first time in London. And I promised her I'd buy her this book and that we'd follow it from the first page to the last. I have a whole thing planned for it, but it's all based on this book. Which I need."

Why was he trying to get this book so much?

Maybe he deserves it.

Or he's just really competitive.

Either way, he amused her.

Then the hot guy blurted out, "I'll give you twenty quid if you let me have that copy."

The man gave him a baffled look. Then his lips drew to a line. "Fifty."

"Done." The hot guy reached into his pocket.

Sixty dollars?

To win a guidebook? *Hot guy is insane.*

After he'd retrieved the book, the hot guy gave her a victorious smile as he paid for it at the register.

But she smiled and held out her hands, palms up, and shrugged. "All right. You win. The book is yours. Nice job."

She looked down at her watch. Damn. She had that welcome dinner in—*shit—twenty minutes.*

She was never late. And if she wasn't early, she considered herself late. "I have to go. Nice to meet you."

"I have a boring business meeting first, but you wouldn't want to get drinks later, would you?" the hot guy said in a rush.

She gave him a tight-lipped smile. "I can't. I have plans tonight. Soon actually." She walked backward toward the door. "And anyway, you already have plans with Vivienne."

He followed her. "They're not important."

"Well, mine are."

"Boyfriend?" He took another step toward her.

She shook her head and stopped.

She wasn't the girl who purposely went for the jerks in life, but it was nice to be *desired* by the hot guy. Even going for drinks would be fun. New city . . . maybe a new friend.

He reached into his breast pocket and pulled out a pen. Flipping to the end of the book, he wrote his phone number on the last page. Then he closed the book and held it out to her. "I'm only giving you this book under the condition that we take a rain check on the drinks. My number's in here."

He's asking me out.

Even though she was flattered, she was determined not to make it easy for him. After all, he didn't seem like the sort of guy who was told no often.

She hesitated, then nodded and took the book, sharing a

warm smile with him. "What if I have a rule against writing in books?"

"Do you?"

"Yes." She held his gaze. "But I'll make an exception."

"You sure I can't convince you to cancel your plans? Go out with me instead," he said, his voice a rough scratch, his piercing gaze almost commanding it.

And if I didn't have that welcome dinner, I completely would.

For which she really needed to get going.

As smoothly as she could, she slipped the book into her purse and said, "I should go."

Liddy left the bookshop, willing herself not to go back as she hurried toward the restaurant. Two blocks later, she realized she'd never asked the hot guy his name.

Idiot.

She paused, then pulled the book out of her bag. On the last page, she found the black ink and bold scrawl with his phone number and his name, *Cal*.

She closed the book, holding it to her chest for a moment before she gave an excited squeal.

Maybe London would be a fresh start after all. And it was *such* a good first meeting. He definitely had a bad-boy side, no doubt, but he'd also made her go weak in the knees. And that wasn't *nothing* either.

The restaurant where she was supposed to meet Aiden and her new coworkers from Camden Enterprises loomed close by. Aiden had told her he'd rented the event space upstairs, but he waited for her near the doorway.

Aiden gave her a giant smile as she approached. "Has anyone ever told you that you have an uncanny resemblance to an American country singer?" Aiden teased.

She laughed. "Has anyone ever told you that you look like

some Goody Two-shoes English viscount who is well-known for his international nonprofit endeavors?"

"Oh, touché." Aiden winked. As the younger siblings of overachieving and successful older siblings, Aiden and Liddy had bonded over their shared woe at having been born second. No matter what they achieved, Elle and Quinn would both outshine them. Although they both tried to avoid stroking their egos, Liddy knew how lucky she was to have such an amazing sister.

"Ready to meet the team?" Aiden asked, adjusting his collar as he walked inside. "They're all really lovely and keen on meeting you. Mason's girlfriend, Rebecca, is in your department. She's a good one to get to know and show you the ropes. And I hear one of the other women, Miranda, is looking for a new flatmate if you still need someone to share the costs of your flat."

"Oh, wow. That would be great, Aiden. Thank you for that."

"No problem. Let's go."

The news that Mason Camden had a girlfriend who would be working with her was welcome. All the Camden brothers were equally nice to Liddy, and if Aiden liked Mason's girlfriend, it was a good sign. And that there might be a flatmate, too. *Today seems to be my lucky day.*

They went through a busy bar area and then headed up a stairwell. A flutter of nerves rumbled in Liddy's stomach, reminding her once again that she probably should have eaten. The scent of food hung heavily in the air, but she couldn't identify it—though Granny had once told her that a fried onion could be just as alluring in smell as a five-star dinner, and she wasn't wrong about that.

The event space was crowded, and Liddy picked out the familiar faces of Quinn's brothers, Mason and Logan, near the front. They all looked alike, really. Quinn's parents were also there, but that's where the familiar people ended.

As Aiden introduced Liddy to the strangers in the room, her head spun. She could hardly keep up with the names, let alone the polite inquiries and who she'd already told about how her flight went or when she'd moved over from the States.

Anxiety bloomed in her.

Moving to a new country is more terrifying than I thought.

She didn't know anyone outside of the Camdens.

Feeling slightly ill, she excused herself from an introduction, made a beeline for the bar, and then set her hands on it. "I'll have a glass of white wine," she told the bartender.

Beside her, a man shifted and turned to give her a smile. "You're the guest of honor, aren't you?"

She nodded, and he turned, holding out a hand. "Luca Harris. We'll be coworkers. Different departments, though."

"I'm Liddy Winnick." She shook his hand.

He had a kind smile, his sandy-blond bangs sweeping low over his eyes. He pushed it back to reveal soft blue eyes. "You're a brave one, working for Scott. Don't tell Aiden I said so, but Scott's the toughest sod at Camden Enterprises."

"Oh, that's a relief," Liddy said with a sarcastic laugh. She shook her head. "And here I was feeling overwhelmed with just meeting people."

Luca smiled. "I'm sorry. I'm not doing a good job at helping you relax when clearly you just need a drink. Let's try again." He held out a hand. "Luca Harris. Always with my foot in my mouth and perpetually in the wrong place at the wrong time. I also tend to make an arse out of myself."

Somehow, his self-deprecating humor *did* make her feel better.

Maybe because I can relate to it.

"Nice to meet you," she said with a more genuine smile this time. "I . . . have social anxiety and always feel like an outsider."

"Perfect." Luca winked and took a swig from his beer. "Just what we need at Camden Enterprises. You'll fit in perfectly with us nutters."

She laughed, feeling immediately more at ease.

"Liddy, there you are," Aiden said from behind her. "I wanted to introduce you to the head of your department." *Yikes. Her boss.*

She turned toward him, and her smile froze at the sight of the man beside Aiden.

The hot guy from the bookshop.

Her heart gave a heavy lurch.

What are the chances?

And then she thought about his words, causing a seed of dread to form in the pit of her stomach.

"*. . . she can start by proving she deserves to be there . . .*"

"*. . . And now you want me to accept some twat . . .*"

"*. . . for some glorified intern I'm being forced to work with. I'm an arsehole and will do my best to see her fired in the first month.*"

She blinked, swallowing hard as she searched the guy's handsome face. Red had crept into his neck, but his eyes were like flint now, not an ounce of the friendliness from before.

I'm the twat.

I'm the one he doesn't want working for him.

Aiden looked from Liddy to her boss. "Liddy, this is Callum Scott."

Callum offered her a cool smile, a warning in his eyes. "Welcome to Camden Enterprises, Miss Winnick." He held out his hand toward her.

That piercing, confident gaze that had ordered her before

to cancel her plans and go to dinner with him seemed to command something else right now: *Don't say a word.*

Acid burned in her throat.

If he'd been anyone else . . .

Despite her anger, she could handle this gracefully.

She shook his hand. "Nice to meet you, Mr. Scott," she said in a monotone voice.

He gave a nod as though to say, *Good job.* Then he turned and went farther down the bar without another word.

Aiden gave her a sheepish look. "Callum's been one of Quinn's best mates since grammar school. But he's not the most social. Don't worry, he'll come around. Hi, Luca."

As Luca and Aiden struck up a conversation, Liddy's head throbbed. Bitter disappointment seeped into her lungs, and she snuck a glance at Callum.

She wished she was the sort of woman who could just march up to him and tell him to fuck off. But he was her new boss. And she *was* the outsider.

Gritting her teeth, she felt the sting of tears in her eyes.

A twat?

A glorified intern?

Because . . . why? He didn't even know her.

Asshole.

She dashed the tears away. *This is just a minor blip on the radar of moving to a new country, Lid. Do not let his assholery get you down.*

She would prove him wrong. This was her new start, and she would not let Mr. Scott destroy this chance.

Even if he pushed her hard at work and tried to make her quit, Callum Scott would never, ever make her want to cry again.

That's for damn sure.

CHAPTER TWO

Now

Retrospectively, Callum should have known this would have happened the moment he'd seen her walk into the bar.

To begin with, his sole purpose for coming out tonight had been to get completely, obliterating, blindingly sloshed before stumbling back to his flat. And when he was going through these moments, he liked to drink alone *and* avoid situations like this.

She'd been coming onto him for months.

It had been subtle at first—a flash of too much leg here, a low-cut top and careful dips as she'd set assignments on his desk there.

Now, with her whisky-flavored tongue shoved down his throat and her hand down his waistband, stroking his hard-on, the subtlety was gone.

And there was the fact that, even when she wasn't throwing

herself on top of him in the back alley near his flat, Miranda Kaster was sexy. He'd always had a thing for brunettes and Miranda had long, dark tresses that were currently draped across his face.

His brain blanked for a moment, lost in the sensual pleasure of her fingers wrapping around him.

Fuck, yes.

Except . . .

He never, ever slept with women he worked with.

Ever.

Especially not women who worked *for* him. His father had told him a long time ago never to "dip his pen in the company ink," and if he'd listened . . . *maybe everything would be different.*

At the very least, he would have had no reason to get drunk tonight.

The hell with all that.

His head pounded from the effort to slog through the dizzy thoughts. He'd been fine—he thought—until he'd started the walk back home, and she'd followed him.

"Oh my God, Callum. I want you to fuck me," she whispered against his lips.

Focus.

He didn't respond, his fingers feeling numb as he caressed her breasts—under her shirt—but not below the bra.

Sex. That's all this is. That's all it ever is.

And Miranda would probably be good.

But taking a woman he worked with back to his place? That was another rule he'd never broken.

"Here?"

"It has to be your place. Surely, you know my flatmate has a crush." She nibbled on his earlobe, leaving it wet with moisture.

Her flatmate.

Callum closed his eyes, trying not to lose his mind as she knelt in front of him. The whole alley seemed to spin, which wasn't a good sign either.

Her flatmate, Lydia Winnick.

Callum set his hand over hers as she reached for his zipper.

"I can't." He cleared his throat, drunken desire screaming at him. He'd let the kiss spiral wildly out of control, and that was a regret he'd have to live with. But he could put a stop to it at least.

Miranda looked up at him, then laughed lightly. "You might be the first man who has ever said no to a jobby." She tugged on his zipper, ignoring his hand.

"I'm serious." Callum moved her hand again, then helped her stand despite his unsteadiness. "I'm going to request an Uber for you." He pulled his phone out and opened it.

Miranda stared at him as though she couldn't process his words. "You must be joking." She took one more step toward him, and when he continued on to the app, she knocked his phone out of his hand. It clattered dully on the pavement. "Bastard."

She started out of the alleyway, her heels clicking as her hips swayed with her flight.

Just let her go.

Not that it was entirely responsible either. But this wasn't an unsafe area.

Gritting his teeth, he collected his phone and then followed her.

"Miranda—"

"I can get my own Uber, thank you."

He wouldn't be pathetic and apologize. She'd initiated the kiss. Found him in the bar and sat beside him to flirt.

Though, it wasn't as if you didn't know what she was after.

And, maybe in a small way, he'd been after it, too. Her

company, while unexpected, hadn't been entirely unwelcome. With each drink, he'd told himself to go home, and now he was here, dealing with a furious woman.

This won't go over well at work either.

"I shouldn't have allowed it to happen."

Miranda whirled around and threw him a glare. "Don't you dare bullshit me with some ridiculous attempt at 'values,' Callum. You may be discreet, but you still have a reputation. You arrogant wanker."

Her words hardened his resolve, and he drew his core in. "I don't fuck women I work with. Especially not if I'm drunk."

"I've felt the energy between us. We could be good together. I wouldn't tell anyone we're together if that's what you're worried about."

He nearly choked at her suggestion. *Together?* She was getting ahead of herself. "I don't do relationships either. Unless you'd like to hand in your resignation to me, I'm at a bit of an impasse."

She flinched, then stalked closer. "I'm not going to give up my career for a one-night stand, Callum. No matter how good it might be."

"And I wasn't asking you to." He narrowed his gaze at her. "Good night."

Miranda didn't move. "Or you could recommend me for a promotion. To the position Luca Harris vacated last month. Then I wouldn't be working directly under you anymore, anyway."

He didn't want to believe that this was what her attempt to seduce him had been about . . . *but could it be?*

Chuckling, Callum shook his head. "Or I could just tell you no. Like I already did."

Fury lit her eyes, and her hand rose. He stepped back before she swung to slap him. *That* was something he didn't want to deal with tonight. "Good night, Miranda. If you're lucky, I may even forget this happened."

He went the opposite way down the alleyway, away from her, the spins hitting him hard. As he reached the other side of the alley, he stepped out of it, then threw up on the pavement.

He hoped Miranda had gone on her way and hadn't heard him. Not that it mattered.

Right now, the only important thing was getting back to his bed.

He had an early flight to catch the following morning and only a few hours to sleep.

Pulling out his phone, he dialed his sister.

Isla picked up after the first ring. "Why are you calling me so late?"

"Because I'm sloshed, and I want you to keep talking to me. Make sure I don't wind up deciding to take a nap on the tarmac and get run over."

"Callum." Isla's scolding tone was gentle. "You promised me last night you were fine."

"I lied." The taste of vomit hung in his mouth, and he suppressed the urge to throw up again. Too many nice rose gardens on this street for that.

"That's it. I'm changing my flight. I'll come with you tomorrow."

"And miss the audition you have on Saturday? Don't you dare. Besides, the flight is probably booked."

"You know, right now I feel like the elder sibling. And I don't like feeling like the elder sibling. It makes me cranky. This is going to be fine, Cal."

"I doubt it. Did I tell you Mum sent me photos of Sophia today? Not new ones, of course. Old ones. She took photographs of old photographs with her phone. Live view and everything. And not one or two. Over twenty of them."

"She lays it on so thick." Isla groaned. "I'll talk to her and tell her to give it a rest. But I really think she wants you to forgive her. So everything can just go back to the way it used to be."

"The way it used to be is that I was going to marry Sophia and *that's* what Mum wants. Hold on." Callum pulled the phone away from his ear and retched again, this time behind a parked car.

I'd hate to be the owner of the car in the morning.

Wiping his mouth with the back of his hand, he returned the phone to his ear. "I'm back."

"That was disgusting. And I *meant* Mum wants you to forgive *her*, not Sophia."

"Well, I don't see either of those options happening." His building swam into view, and he crossed the street toward it.

"You know I support you no matter what, Cal, but . . . listen to you. You're miserable. And I can't remember the last time I saw you truly happy. You won't find what you're looking for in a bottle of scotch or between some random woman's legs. Your solutions aren't working, and I'm genuinely worried about you. It's been five years. If you're still so hung up on Sophia—"

"Fuck, no. There's a difference between dreading seeing her *and* Mum and being hung up on her."

Seriously? Is that what she believes? This had *nothing* to do with Sophia and everything to do with not wanting to see Mum. Sophia being there made it worse, but not by much.

"Yes, because you've moved on so brilliantly."

"I'm fine." Callum scowled, his words sounding slightly slurred even to his own ears. The last thing he wanted was one of Isla's lectures right now. "Listen, I'm home now. I'll text you tomorrow after I land."

"You'd better. Let me know how things go with Mum."

He punched in the code on the building's security keypad

as he hung up, then started up the stairs. Whatever idiotic idea had possessed him to live on the top floor now taunted him as he gripped the rail, feeling as though he might fall back at any moment.

He hadn't been this drunk for a long, long time.

No wonder he'd almost slipped up with Miranda.

Reaching his door at last, he unlocked it, then headed straight for the loo.

Morning would be here, unforgivingly, soon enough and he still had a flight to pack for.

At least the flight would be uneventful.

CHAPTER THREE

In the grand scheme of things, the lack of coffee made everything worse.

Lydia hadn't worried about it when Elle had let her know the flight time had been changed. Five thirty in the morning wasn't so different from six thirty. *In theory.*

But an international flight meant she had to be *at* the airport at three thirty at the latest.

And security was a breeze at that time of the morning, so by four, she was already in the departures gate waiting for her flight, which wouldn't be boarding for another hour.

And no coffee shops in London Heathrow were open at four.

But really, that had seemed like less of a problem until she'd seen *him*.

Liddy's grip on her carry-on bag tightened, and her eyes bored at his bent, dark head. He appeared to be dozing in his seat, his long legs spread out in the aisle.

Callum freaking Scott.

Of all the damn luck in the universe.

Not that this was a coincidence, or even bad luck, really. They were both in the wedding party. Both heading down to Costa Rica for her sister's wedding. And, thanks to Elle and Quinn's generosity, the happy couple had even arranged and paid for travel and accommodations for their bridal party.

But if Liddy had known Callum was going to fly down at the same time as she was, she would have begged for another flight.

God, he even sleeps like a cocky asshole. If that was possible. Liddy gritted her teeth.

She would just sit at the other end of the boarding area, hoping he wouldn't see her or sit near her. She could handle this. It wasn't like she didn't deal with him every day.

But never before coffee.

And also never when she was looking like this.

She'd worn yoga pants and a hoodie for the early morning flight and didn't have a lick of makeup on. Normally, she wouldn't care if anyone saw her without makeup . . . *but everyone else isn't Callum.*

Callum was an exception to that.

Because she'd decided two years ago when she'd met him that she would never, *ever* let Callum see her at anything less than her best. Everything she did for him was perfect. Precise. She'd never turned in a deliverable or project to him that wasn't polished to the extreme.

If she was honest, she had largely put their first run-in to the back of her mind. She'd worked hard, and at no point in the past twenty-four months had he had any cause to fire her—or even suggested anything like that. Not that he ever really gave out compliments.

But as his presence still sometimes rattled Liddy—*he really is nice to look at*—and even though he wasn't the most communicative boss, she was so glad that she'd moved to London. It wasn't home, per se, and she still missed her mom, dad, and brother, but she'd found her routine, a community, and true job satisfaction. *On her own.* Which was what she'd set out to do.

She lifted her carry-on so that the wheels wouldn't drag behind her and risk making any sound on the tile floor. First, she'd make a beeline to the restroom and throw on some makeup with whatever she had in her purse. She really should have packed her makeup bag in her carry-on, but since she had decided to carry the bulky garment bag with Elle's wedding dress onto the plane rather than risk letting anything happen to it, she'd been forced to take her smaller, more lightweight carry-on.

The strap on the garment bag was cutting off the circulation to her right arm, as it was.

Rather than continue forward, she stepped backward, hoping to slip behind the safety of the restroom wall just before the boarding area.

Crash.

Lydia whirled around in time to see a bright yellow plastic Do Not Enter sign tumble to the floor behind her.

But that wasn't the worst of it.

As she turned, she tripped on a janitorial cart, which had been behind her. She hadn't noticed the restroom being cleaned before, or the cart, and as she tried to catch herself against it—clutching the top of the cart—the wheels skittered forward, taking her flying forward.

The cart slammed against the restroom wall, rolls of toilet paper spilling from the top. A mop bucket attached to the side of the cart gave a *slosh* and gray water splashed onto her thigh on her pants leg, just narrowly missing the garment bag with Elle's wedding dress.

Oh, eew. But also, thank God.

"Lydia?" a familiar, deep voice sounded beside her.

Shit.

Of course.

Cheeks flaming, Liddy cringed, then straightened, both of her hands still on the janitorial cart. She turned to find Callum approaching, his strong, dark eyebrows knitted with proper concern. "It is you. I almost didn't recognize you with that dark hair. Are you all right?"

"Oh—" Words got stuck in her throat as she scrambled for what to say to him. She'd nearly forgotten that she'd gotten her hair dyed to a pretty chestnut last night after work, not that she needed to explain that to him. Her natural roots had been showing, and she had figured she may as well go with her base color for the wedding. *Look different from Elle.*

She stood there, trying to remember how she'd even started thinking about her hair, then she relived Callum's approach a minute earlier. After a few awkward seconds, she gestured to her wet pants leg and blurted out, "Mop water, not pee."

He furrowed those brows further, but now amusement hinted at his light blue eyes. "What's that?"

Really? That's the first thing she'd said to him? Her embarrassment increasing by the second, she cleared her throat and tried again. "I hit the cart and covered myself with mop water. You know. Um . . . just in case you thought I didn't make it to the bathroom on time."

This had to be a nightmare.

"I wasn't." He took three quick strides toward her, then grabbed a stack of paper towels from the cart. "You look like you could use these, though." Handing her half, he squatted beside her, then wiped the spilled water on the tiles by her feet.

She stared at him suspiciously. In what universe did Callum ever do anything nice for her?

Liddy dabbed her pants, wishing she'd packed a change. If it wasn't for the sign, she'd dash into the bathroom and seek shelter. But considering the succession of unfortunate events that had just happened to her, she'd probably slip on the floor and hit her head or something.

She frowned down at the garment bag, still resting against her body. This wasn't the sort of luck she ever had.

This is Elle's luck.

Clumsy, wouldn't-believe-it-if-I-told-you, doesn't-happen-to-anyone-else luck.

Her big sister had the craziest things happen to her. While people who didn't know her often watched with astonishment, Liddy had grown accustomed to it by now. And it wasn't just bad luck, either. The love of Elle's life, Quinn, had stumbled across her sleeping in a closet. Elle had also had a brush with fame and was still a recognizable face in the country music world because she'd won a Grammy for the best new artist after being discovered while singing at karaoke in their hometown of Nashville.

Liddy, on the other hand, had missed the luck bus.

As Callum straightened, he grimaced. He wasn't in his usual expensive, bespoke suit. He wore a jumper and trainers with jeans. *Sweater. Sneakers.*

She'd been living in London for too long if their verbiage was sneaking into her thoughts.

And dammit if he doesn't look good in his "casual" as opposed to my hot mess.

But then again, Callum always looked good. Half of her coworkers were infatuated with him. Miranda often referred to him as "dishy." That he ignored them all and seemed to regard them with equal contempt made no difference.

"Thanks," she mumbled as Callum tossed the used paper towels in the bin. Her brain was still feeling like unstirred molasses, and she blinked to clear her thoughts. *I've barely said anything to him.* "I guess you're on the way to Costa Rica this morning, too."

She gave a tepid glance at the waiting area. Who knew how long the restroom would be closed—not that she needed to rush and put some makeup on now.

"Elle didn't tell you we were on the same flight?" Callum appeared surprised, then followed her gaze. "Here, let me help you carry something. That garment bag looks heavy."

"Um . . . sure. It's Elle's dress. I had to pick it up from Logan in Littleton a couple of days ago." His politeness threw her off guard as she handed the bag over to him.

And no, Elle knew better than to mention the travel arrangements. *Speaking of which, I'm going to kill Elle for not telling me.* Elle was probably asleep in the comfort of her resort bedroom in Costa Rica. An irritated text would roll off her like water on butter.

"You're bringing the dress all the way from London yourself?" Callum raised a brow. "Impressive. They should have just made Logan do it."

"You know, maid of honor duties." Of course, he *was* right. Elle could have asked Quinn's youngest brother to bring the dress, but she'd asked Liddy because she didn't think Logan was responsible.

Why was Callum being *so* polite? Because he felt sorry for her after the mop water incident?

If there was anything she hated in the universe, it was Callum Scott feeling sorry for her.

"And to think all Quinn asked me to bring was a good bottle of Glenfiddich." Callum set her bag down on a chair, then gave her a thin-lipped smile.

"I'll leave you here. See you on the flight." He nodded goodbye and then headed back to his seat.

That's when it hit her. He hadn't taken her bag over to

where he sat. He'd dumped her several rows away, as if . . . he didn't want to sit beside her either. Her eyes narrowed at his receding form.

Oomph.

And there it is.

That was the Callum Scott she knew. The one who seemed to hold the world in contempt.

She visualized the smirk on those full lips and tore her gaze away as he sat. Out of the corner of her eye, she saw him don headphones.

Liddy sat and pulled out her phone. Rapidly, she fired off a text to Elle.

Liddy: *You could have told me you booked me on the same flight as Callum.*

Irritated, she wrinkled her nose at the wet spot on her pants. She shifted back, trying to get comfortable in the airport chair—a losing battle. Sitting was never particularly comfortable, especially for any length of time. International flights were the worst, but the trip to Costa Rica could never be as bad as the one to Australia had been.

But that was the price to pay with a fused spine.

Most days, she didn't let it get to her. The pain she'd been experiencing since she was first diagnosed with scoliosis as a child was something she'd grown accustomed to. Like a constant hum in the back of her mind that came to the forefront only when the world was quiet enough for her to notice. But on the cusp of a flight she knew would give her trouble, with damp pants, and Callum as a burr in her boot . . . this was going to be a long day if she didn't get some coffee, stat.

Surprisingly, her phone buzzed in her hand.

Elle: *Oh nooooo, I didn't realize. Quinn's travel agent handled all the arrangements. I'm sorry, I'm sorry. I feel horrible.*

And just like that, Liddy felt any frustration with Elle vanish.

Maybe if it hadn't been so early, the travel agent thing would have occurred to Liddy. Elle was easy to forgive—she was frequently harder on herself than anyone else was—and she'd been the best big sister imaginable.

Liddy: *It's fine. Just didn't realize. It's the ass crack of dawn here. What are you still doing up?*

Elle: *All the things. Hotel wasn't quite what we expected. We've been scrambling to find accommodations for some of our guests. And Mom and Dad and Quinn's parents in the same space . . . shoot me now. I can't wait for you to be here already.*

The thought of their country-loving, very Southern parents in a hotel with Quinn's posh and upper-class British parents was enough to make Liddy chortle. Elle had been worried about it so much that it was partially why she'd settled on a destination wedding—someplace out of both sets of parents' comfort zones.

Not that the Camdens were that bad. Ironically, Liddy had spent more time around the Camdens since she'd gotten the job with Camden Enterprises than even Elle had.

Coming to live in London had been a dream—as had working with Camden Enterprises. Even though Mr. Camden was retired, and Quinn's brother Aiden was in charge of the company now, Elle's future parents-in-law still came to many business functions. And she also saw Mason Camden with even more frequency since he was dating one of her best friends at work, Rebecca.

Poor Elle, though. Liddy couldn't imagine—as in *would never*—do something like have a destination wedding. The thought of it went so against Liddy's sense of meticulous planning that it seemed more like the plot of a horror movie than a romantic escape.

Liddy: *What's wrong with the hotel?*

Elle: *You'll see when you get here. And if you talk to Callum, tell him I have a bone to pick with him. He's the one who suggested this place to Q.*

Interesting. The idea of Callum having a close friendship with Quinn still felt so weird to her. Of course, she'd never seen them interact, but that was because Elle and Quinn lived most of the year in Nashville, only coming during the summer and around Christmas to spend some time at Quinn's estate in the country, Littleton.

Whatever was going on in the hotel in Costa Rica, though, she'd let Quinn and Elle make their complaints directly to Callum.

Liddy: *Yeah, I'll let you handle that. See you soon! XO*

Liddy's gaze slid over the top edge of her phone toward Callum, her lips twisting. Elle wasn't normally the best person for Liddy to vent to about him. Maybe now if Elle was irritated about the wedding, she would finally understand what an ass he was. Sure, he could be charming and even seemingly likable at first glance. But he was like that perfect bowl of oatmeal that only became more congealed and gloppy and cold and gross with each bite.

And even if she'd sometimes wondered why her first, favorable impression of him had felt so real, the past two years had given her more than enough of his detached, unfriendly demeanor to solidify her poor opinion.

She couldn't understand why the Camdens held him in such high regard—everyone else at the office seemed to dislike him as much as she did. The only time she'd even seen him smile at work was when Aiden came by Callum's office.

Checking the time again, she wrinkled her nose, then dialed her flatmate, Miranda. Miranda picked up after a few rings. "Do you realize what time it is?"

"Yes, but this is worth it. You'll never guess who is on my flight down to Costa Rica."

Miranda yawned. "Rebecca and Mason?"

"No, they're on a later flight."

"Bono? Or Prince William?"

"Hilarious."

"Well, I was dreaming about Bono and Prince William a minute ago. And let me tell you, it was the type of dream that I'm furious at you for interrupting."

Liddy guffawed. "Really? They do it for you, huh?"

"It was *a dream*. I was horny. And it was fantastic." Miranda cleared her throat. "All I'm saying is, this better be worth the interruption."

"Callum."

A long groan sounded. "You woke me up to tell me that Callum is on your flight? I thought it would be juicy, not someone we literally see every day. I'm already bored."

"I just needed to vent."

"No, you told me because you still have a crush on him. Not that I'm blaming you."

Liddy wrinkled her nose. She never should have told Miranda about the first time she'd met Callum. Miranda had been teasing her about "nearly hooking up with" Callum ever since.

"Fine. Go back to your orgy dream."

Miranda chortled. "I'm just teasing. It's a rotten bit of luck. But so is an entire trip with him around, if you ask me. Although, promise me you'll take a picture of him for me on the beach if he takes his shirt off. I have a bet going with Dean that Callum is hiding a six-pack under that suit."

"Only you can simultaneously loathe and lust."

"I maintain that he's probably a secret Christian Grey. The

ones who treat everyone with as much apathy as he does are always the best lovers."

Miranda loved to give copious details about her love life, but Liddy did *not* want to imagine Callum that way. Not that he wouldn't be an attractive Dom, but—*okay. Stop. Not going to let my imagination get the better of me.*

"Yeah, well, I just almost knocked over a janitor's cart in front of him and spilled disgusting mop water on my pants. Then when he came over to help me pick up the toilet paper from the floor, I told him I hadn't peed myself."

"Oh, wow—"

"I'm so embarrassed."

"I know what it's like to embarrass myself in front of that man. I'm so sorry. I'm still kicking myself."

When did Miranda embarrass herself in front of Callum? Liddy frowned. "Why, what happened?"

"Ugh. Nothing. I'd rather not relive it. Are you excited about the wedding?"

Weird. Miranda rarely hesitated to share anything that happened to her. Their friendship was practically built on TMI. Liddy hung up a few minutes later, wishing Miranda was coming with her on this trip. She was excited to see her family, but they didn't understand her life here in England.

Switching to a social media app, she scrolled mindlessly, trying to forget the morning's irritating events. By the time the gate agent announced boarding, the waiting area had filled with sufficient people to block her view of Callum. Lydia stood and moved toward the gate.

To her dismay, Callum joined her in line.

Dammit.

She maintained her silence as she handed her passport and ticket to the boarding agent, then hurried onto the plane. The plane was still empty as she boarded, then she stowed her carry-on above her seat. As she glanced around for a place to put the wedding dress, Callum came up behind her.

"Need help?" he asked, pausing at her side.

"I got it." She gripped the garment bag with both hands.

Callum continued to stand there. After a second, she raised a brow at him. "What do you need?"

He nodded to the window seat in her row. "That's my seat."

"Oh." *Shit.* She forced a smile, then stepped to the side, gritting her teeth. *Seriously?*

Because, *of course.* Quinn's travel agent didn't know they didn't get along.

Callum slipped past her, then slid his carry-on bag under the seat in front of him. He sat and pulled down the window shade.

"Guess we don't want to see out the window today."

"Guess not." Callum drew his lips to a line, then once again tugged his headphones out of his bag. He plopped them on, then leaned back in his seat, eyes closed once more.

Was it too late to see about switching seats?

"Excuse me," a voice said from behind. Lydia glanced over her shoulder to see a line of passengers forming in the aisle, waiting impatiently to get in their seats.

She stepped into the row, resting the garment bag against the seat. Once there was another break in the boarding, she scooted into the aisle and tried to fold the bag into the overhead bin.

Struggling with the weight of it, she stepped on her tiptoes, wishing she was taller. The garment bag covered the top of her head, blocking her view, when it suddenly went weightless. Jerking her head over her shoulder, she locked eyes with a set of light brown eyes—and the ridiculously handsome man who had helped her push it into the bin.

He threw her a megawatt smile with perfect teeth. "You have a body in that bag?" he asked with a laugh, a soft Spanish accent to his voice.

Lydia grinned. "No, it's my sister's wedding dress. I'm on my way to her wedding."

"And bringing it all the way from London?" He raised his brows. *God, he was . . . hot.* No other way to put it. Sexy tan, the slightest bit of dark stubble on his jaw. Short silky black hair.

"It's an heirloom. Been in my brother-in-law's family for generations. He's a viscount. I have to guard it with my life."

What on earth, Lid? He didn't want to know all of that. I blame the lack of caffeine.

"Ah, so . . . expensive." The man's eyes glittered with laughter. "You're a good sister." He thrust his hand out toward her. "Sergio. Nice to meet you. It appears you're my seat mate."

Sergio. She wanted to roll his name off her tongue, but then she'd just seem like a weirdo. Lydia had the aisle seat, which meant he'd be a buffer between her and Callum.

Perfect.

"Liddy Winnick." She gave him her best smile, feeling lighter as he scooted past her and sat.

Sergio leaned past Callum, then pushed up the window shade and smiled back at her. "I always love to watch the sunrise, don't you?"

A happy dance might be obvious, but her stomach gave a cheerful flip. She pulled out her phone and snuck a picture of him when his gaze returned to the window. Then she sent it to Miranda.

Liddy: *Check out my seat mate.*

Miranda: *Oh, yum. Yes, please.*

Liddy grinned and put her phone away.

Maybe this won't be such a terrible flight after all.

CHAPTER FOUR

CALLUM KNEW two things about the man in the seat beside him.

He was one of the fakest, most insincere tossers Callum had been in the company of in a while.

. . . and Lydia is completely enamored with him.

Suppressing the urge to roll his eyes, Callum attempted to tune Sergio out and dug his knife and fork into the quiche he'd been served moments before. He needed a fucking Bloody Mary rather than the coffee he'd asked for—his head was still pounding with a headache from his decisions the night before. Getting that drunk had not been the best idea when he had an early morning flight.

Then again, arriving at the airport still half-drunk made this flight more tolerable.

". . . merengue is the most exquisite form of dance. And you have the perfect body for it," Sergio was saying. "There's a bar in Samara that I'd love to take you to."

What was that? The fourth thing Sergio had invited Lydia to do in Costa Rica?

Callum's eyes narrowed. *Why is this man flirting so hard with her?*

"That would be amazing," she said with a smile, sipping on her mimosa. A pink blush lit her cheeks.

Of course, from the way she was glowing, if Sergio invited her to join the mile-high club with him, she'd probably take him up on the opportunity.

He swallowed the dry quiche, then took a swig of his coffee.

Quinn owed him—big time—for this destination wedding.

The timing couldn't be worse, to begin with. Work was full-on right now, and the last place he needed to be was on holiday.

But that wasn't the worst of it.

Not only had Quinn ignored Callum's protests and booked out *La Hacienda Tropical* but now Callum would also be around two of the women in this world whose company made him want to join a monastery that offered perpetual silence— his mother and his ex-fiancée, Sophia. The Camdens had invited his father and stepmother to the wedding, too, but fortunately they had declined the invite.

If Isla hadn't been coming later in the week, he might have called Quinn and begged out of groomsman duties. But his sister's presence could only do so much. Even Isla's presence wouldn't help him avoid his mother's disappointment in Callum.

He hadn't married Sophia. Yet . . . Mum had practically adopted her anyway. Even after five years, Mum was relentless about what a wonderful wife Sophia would have been. *Could be.* How beautiful she was. How helpful. How intelligent. The "kindness of her gaze."

Which meant Callum kept his contact with Mum to a minimum.

To make matters worse, Quinn let the damn travel agent

book Callum's trip with Lydia Winnick—a woman who drove him nuts in a completely different way.

It had bothered Callum, at first, that things had gone so awry with her two years ago. Because his anger at her appointment had never been about her. Aiden had made him a promise and then broken it—and Lydia had fallen into the crosshairs of their disagreement.

Callum's pushback on Lydia had worked, and Aiden had also gotten the clue. Apologized even. Told him it wouldn't happen again. More importantly, the rumors that Aiden would transfer Luca to Callum's department had all vanished.

Not that he could complain about Lydia. Everything she did was excellent.

She could have made a brilliant manager for the department, too.

But she was content to fade into the banal camaraderie of her workmates, which was her biggest flaw.

The upside was that it kept her as his staff, rather than a colleague with whom he might work with more closely on a project—and that made things easier for him. From the moment they'd met, his attraction to her had been visceral, almost a reflex. Keeping her at arm's length was helpful.

A beam of sunlight pierced through the window, and Callum pulled down the shade once again. The arsehole next to him kept opening it, and the sunrise had been chasing them the entire trip over. *Prick.* Callum would have let it go if it wasn't for the sun right in his eyes. He wasn't about to pull out his sunglasses and be even more uncomfortable on this infernal flight.

"I would say . . . the thermal hot springs at Arenal, hiking at Rio Celeste, and Tortuguero, if you can manage it. The night sky in Tortuguero es *increíble.* The turtles come up from the sea and lay their eggs there. A beautiful experience. And Rio

Celeste—" Sergio kissed his fingertips and pulled his hand away in a passionate gesture. He winked at Lydia. "The only blue I've ever seen that's as beautiful might be your eyes."

Callum nearly choked on his quiche.

Is she really buying this?

He'd hoped Lydia had a good head on her shoulders with men—not that he really cared. Or had a clue about her love life. They discussed business only. And since he'd been so badly burned by Luca, he'd made it the habit never to mistake work friends with real friends.

"Those sound like an amazing top three. I would love to go," Lydia said.

"I would love to take you there. I'm a tour operator. Maybe we can spend more time together."

Callum couldn't help but choke back a laugh.

Both Sergio and Lydia looked at him expectantly.

He cleared his throat, then lifted his coffee cup, giving them a tight-lipped smile. "Quiche is a bit dry."

Lydia stared at him. "Don't mind him, Sergio. He wouldn't know anything about beautiful vacation spots," she said. "I'm not even sure he leaves his office. Or has seen the sun in the past two years."

Clearly, the mimosa was having an effect. She wasn't usually so bold. Then she gave an awkward shift as though she'd realized she might be crossing the line. "He's my boss," she added sheepishly.

"Ah, a *vampiro*," Sergio said with a chuckle.

Callum set his cutlery down and held Lydia's gaze, then raised a brow. "Werewolf. But our community prefers the term 'Lycan,' thanks." His tone was flat and Liddy shrank back, clearly unsure of his mood, which was fine. No reason to pretend, even on this trip, that they wanted to be around each other.

Sergio looked between them with uncertainty. "I didn't know you were friends. Would you like to sit next to each other?"

Friends?

"No." Their answer was in unison.

Sergio excused himself a few minutes later to go to the bathroom. *Thank God for that.* The tense silence that always seemed to hang between him and Lydia quickly replaced that relief.

As the silence mounted, he felt word vomit burning his throat. She was glaring at him. They were rarely in any social setting. Work he knew how to navigate, as she knew her place there, but this was far more difficult.

He uncovered a blueberry scone on his tray. "Having fun with Sergio?"

Lydia swiveled her gaze at him, her expression growing even more frosty. "Excuse me?"

Don't provoke her. The corner of his mouth twitched back with a grimace. "You know he's full of shite, right?"

"You would be an expert on that." Then she wrinkled her nose. "I'm sorry. I didn't mean to say that out loud."

Callum sipped his coffee. *Disgusting.* He'd read more than one article about how coffee was the last thing anyone should order on an airplane, but he needed to sober up. "Yeah, yeah, I know. I'm full of it, too. But I just thought I'd give you a friendly warning."

"I don't need your warnings, but thanks." Lydia flipped her long hair over her shoulder, settling back into her seat with a cringe.

"What reason do I have to lie?"

"I don't know." She frowned. "I know it's impossible for you to believe, but I'm pretty likable."

Yes, I know that, actually. Before he could think of a worthy retort, she shifted in her seat again, and a flash of pain crossed her features. She straightened fully in her seat, stretching.

"You okay?" He scanned her face.

"Fine. Sitting for this long is always uncomfortable."

I know that, too. He tried not to think about the cramp in his right thigh. Of course, she was nearly a foot shorter than him and in the aisle seat, so she was faring far better than he was. But he hated to point out anything else that would irritate her.

He cleared his throat. "Look, I know . . ." *What do I want to say, really?* "*It's none of my business but this fellow is just playing you. Trust me.*" But again, why should he care?

"You don't know, though, do you, Callum? You don't know me, and you sure as hell don't know Sergio. And you know what? Since we're not at work, I don't have to pretend to care about your opinion. I'd really appreciate it if you could keep your snide remarks—and chuckles—to yourself."

Wow, she speaks up for herself occasionally.

Maybe I should make mimosas a part of the workday.

"Right." He pushed his food tray away, then pulled out his headphones again. If she wanted to be ignored, then he would do that. *Easy enough.*

He turned on the screen for the selection of in-flight movies and found a thriller he'd never heard of to watch. He needed something loud if he was going to drown out Sergio's voice beside him.

Two hours later, as the movie was hitting the action sequence of the climax, the screen clicked off, and the captain's voice took over the sound on his headphones, announcing their impending arrival in Costa Rica and the need to move all seats to a full and upright position.

Callum pushed the window shade open himself this time and glanced out over the lush green vegetation below. Wavy tin and occasional terra cotta rooftops populated most of the build-ings. Every time he'd arrived here, he'd thought about how different Costa Rica looked from the air. He rarely noticed the wealth disparity of structures from the other places he'd lived when he was on the ground.

But now, the familiar sight of those tin roofs brought a wave of nostalgia, of lying awake in bed at night in his grandparents' home, listening to the falling rain. A singular rhythm. He didn't notice rain in England when he was inside. To begin with, there was too much of it throughout the year to be bothered by it—but also the walls and the roofs absorbed the sound.

He hadn't thought he missed coming here.

He'd stayed away for six years, after all.

And now that he'd been dragged here . . . he wasn't sure how to feel.

Callum clenched his jaw, then pushed away all memories. He didn't want to feel. Didn't need it. The painful past could stay buried for another ten days. Then life would go back to normal anyway and he could go right back to forgetting.

He ignored Sergio and Lydia's continued flirtation as the plane touched down and quickly passed them both when they disembarked.

Off the plane, it took him a moment to orient himself. He'd never flown directly to Liberia before. He always flew to the capital city of San Jose, which was in the Central Valley and farther from the coast.

His leg felt stiff and painful, and, combined with his headache, it meant he should take some pain medication before hopping in a rental car for *La Hacienda*.

After stopping at the restroom, he made his way toward immigration, bypassing the long line for foreign nationals and getting into the citizens' line. He'd only brought his Costa Rican passport so he could skip the line here, but the immigration area seemed to have triple the number of officers for foreign nationals than for citizens.

A couple of feet in front of him in line, a regrettably familiar voice caught his attention. "Aló," Sergio spoke into his mobile phone.

Callum narrowed his eyes at the back of Sergio's head.

"Mae, suave. Acabo de llegar." *Dude, hold up. I just got here.*

Digging his passport out of his laptop case, he searched for the customs paperwork he'd been given on the plane, trying to ignore Sergio's conversation.

"¿Cuándo? No, no me dijeron. ¿No ves que tuve que comprar tiquete por Liberia? Ojalá llegue a tiempo!" *When? No, no one told me. Believe it or not, I had to fly through Liberia —hopefully, I'll get there on time!*

Despite his best efforts, Callum couldn't help translating in his head. The Spanish he'd grown up listening to—spoken the way a true Tico would—oddly comforted him.

"¿Mañana?" *Tomorrow?* "¿En Tibás centro o Cuatro Reinas? ¿A qué hora? . . . mae, qué tarde. Bueno, vamos a ver si puedo llegarle." *In central Tibás or Four Queens? What time? Dude, that's late. I'll see if I can make it.*

Sergio moved out of earshot as he was called up to the immigration officer.

Callum followed a few minutes later.

The officer frowned at Callum's photograph, which was from when he had been nineteen—ten years ago now. He'd clearly changed a lot since then. No teenage acne. And he'd grown several inches in university—filled out a lot, too. Thank goodness his passport hadn't expired, though it was about to later in the year.

"Scott Reyes?" The officer raised an eyebrow at Callum's last name. Costa Ricans always used both the maternal and paternal last names together—though typically they flowed together better than Callum's did.

He gave one curt nod.

"Tenés mucho tiempo de no venir." *You haven't been here in a while.*

Callum nodded again. "Estaba estudiando." *I was studying.* At least, that was how it had started. Not that Costa Rica had ever been home either.

Home felt as foreign as it sounded in his mind.

Not Costa Rica, not Connecticut, not England. None of them were *home.*

The officer gave him a wary look, then stood with his passport and paperwork and went to a booth a few feet away.

As the officer consulted with a colleague, Callum felt a cold slick of sweat break out on the back of his neck. He had no reason to be nervous, but the irony that they might question whether he belonged here—or was who he said—wasn't lost on him.

A few minutes passed before the officer returned, a leisurely swagger to his step. He clearly wasn't in any sort of rush. By now, the airline might have already unloaded his luggage into the baggage claim area, right before customs. Callum's chest tightened at the thought of it sitting there unattended. Maybe he could text Lydia and ask her to keep an eye out for it?

"Entonces . . . bienvenido," the officer said, stamping his passport. *Welcome back.* He slid the passport back to Callum, then waved him off.

Yeah, what a welcome. Costa Ricans, known as *Ticos,* were known for their friendliness. This bloke had been anything but.

Callum stashed his passport in his bag, then hurried toward baggage claim.

He expected to find his bag still on the conveyor belt, probably the lone bag still left unclaimed.

What he didn't expect? Lydia, standing by the baggage claim, crying.

A sick feeling crested in his stomach at the sight of her tearstained cheeks, and he pushed aside any of their history, striding up to her instead of looking for his bag.

"What happened? You okay?"

"No," Lydia answered, shaking her head. "It's gone. He—"

Dark thoughts entered his mind as the image of *who* she was talking about swam in his memory. "What's gone?"

"Elle's wedding dress. Sergio stole it."

CHAPTER FIVE

*T*HIS CAN'T BE HAPPENING.

Liddy blinked numbly as Callum stood beside her, talking to the customs agent. She hadn't known he spoke Spanish, but it was proving to be a useful skill.

How could I have been so stupid?

She'd replayed the scene in her mind several times, trying to think straight. After getting through immigration, she'd had to use the restroom but had found nowhere to hang the dress. She'd even tried draping it across the top of the stall, but it had fallen ingloriously on the floor, which had made her nervous.

So she'd exited and bumped into Sergio, waiting by baggage claim.

Sure, maybe she didn't *know* him, but they'd spent the entire flight talking and flirting. He'd seemed trustworthy, and she'd asked him if he could keep an eye on the dress while she went to the restroom.

And when she'd come out, he was gone.

Along with Elle's dress.

Callum turned away from the customs agent and scanned

Liddy's profile. "He says they can try scanning the video security footage and calling you if they find anything but that's about the extent of it. He suggested we talk to the airline."

"Did you tell them we already did that?" *Or that the airline told us they couldn't do anything since I gave the guy my bag to hold?*

Ugh, I can't believe I'm so dumb.

She'd even exchanged phone numbers with Sergio—or thought she had. She'd tried the number he'd given her when she'd first come out of the bathroom, but it had gone right to a generic voicemail.

The panic she'd felt as she searched for him, feeling helpless, returned.

"Yeah, I did." Callum's deep voice was soft. He pressed his lips together as though deep in thought.

"That's it, then?" Liddy tried to control the urge to burst into tears again, wiping her nose with a tissue. "I just have to face my sister and tell her I lost the wedding dress that's been in her fiancé's family for forever? The dress that she's supposed to wear in a week?"

"Well, you are in an airport. You could just catch a flight to Bali and hope no one finds you." The corner of his mouth twitched, but his eyes were sympathetic.

Somehow, the ill-timed joke made her feel a little better. At least he wasn't being a jerk about it. He'd helped her, even filling out the paperwork for the customs agent when her hand had been shaking so badly.

But what in the hell am I going to tell Elle?

Would she ever forgive her?

Elle deserves to be mad at me. I messed up—big time.

"Come on," Callum said, taking the handle for her carry-on. "I'm sure we can soften the blow."

Yeah, right. I'm sure my sister will take the news super well.

But her greatest concern was the Camdens. How on earth would she explain that she'd lost their irreplaceable, much-loved family heirloom? *And they'd thought Logan was irresponsible.*

He tilted his head toward the exit from customs, and they started walking. "How are you getting to the hotel?"

She released a slow breath, her chest feeling tight. "Elle said a shuttle goes to the beach town."

Callum gave her a curious look but didn't comment on her answer. After a moment, he said, "I rented a car. If you want, I can drive you there. It's about a two-and-a-half-hour drive."

A two-and-a-half-hour drive?

Elle had *not* mentioned that. Maybe she hadn't known, though. She'd only arrived a couple of days earlier, and Liddy hadn't talked to her much since then.

The idea of riding in a shuttle that long was awful. Her body already hurt from the plane trip. Buses weren't known for their comfortable seating.

Ordinarily, she wouldn't have considered traveling with Callum, but somehow, there was a strange comfort in the notion right now. Her palms ached, and her chest was so tight she had to fight for more than just a shallow breath. *Like Sergio took more than that damn dress.* Callum might be an asshole, but at least she knew him.

He's a familiar asshole.

And that thought made her smile to herself.

THE WHITE KIA Sportage SUV rental hadn't looked especially promising as they'd loaded their luggage into the back, but almost an hour and forty minutes into their trip, Liddy worried more about the way the back bumper was bouncing every time they hit a pothole in the road—which was often.

Even though she and Callum had barely talked, and she'd mostly used the trip to take in the rugged Costa Rican terrain around her, as Callum dodged yet another bump, she asked, "Did you see the back bumper is hanging loose on this side?"

"Yeah, I noted it in the inspection. It looks as though someone went off the road with this one."

Liddy ran her hand over a questionable stain on the fabric. Whatever Callum had paid for this jalopy, he'd paid too much. It surprised her he'd been cheap about the rental, given that Elle and Quinn were covering so many of the travel expenses. Callum seemed to have expensive taste, but then again, what did she know?

She frowned at the air coming through the vents. If she had regretted the choice of clothing in the morning, now it was torture. The air hadn't appeared to work the entire time.

She twisted her long hair into a bun and clipped it at the back of her head, then fanned herself, sweating in the humid, sweetly scented warm air of the car. She put her hand near the air-conditioning vent. "I keep hoping this will work."

God, their conversations were pathetic.

Callum frowned and flipped the air to full blast. Hot air poured out with force. "I guess not."

Maybe I should go back to silence. He certainly didn't seem to mind it. But given that he'd been helpful in the airport after Sergio had stolen the dress *and* the fact that he'd invited her to ride with him, she felt awkward not attempting to be nicer.

"I thought Costa Rica was supposed to be milder. The website I checked said to bring jeans and sweatshirts." She was glad that she'd worn a short-sleeved shirt underneath her hoodie. Otherwise, she would be frying by now.

"The valley is. The coast is hot."

Lydia gave him a curious look.

The way Callum spoke about this country and the fact that he spoke Spanish were interesting. *Almost like he's spent a lot of time here.* Yet she'd never heard him talk about Costa Rica during the time she'd known him. Not that he took vacations.

Or had any life outside of work that she knew of. She'd heard him speak of women he was dating two years ago on that day they'd first met, so she assumed he dated, but she'd never seen any woman come to the office or attend a business function with him—if he bothered to attend.

And given his short, clipped answers all the time, trying to get a conversation going with him was painful.

"Have you spent a lot of time here?"

"You might say that."

Typical.

She could leave it at that. Since she'd started working for him, she'd learned to drop questions she had when he gave an evasive answer. But they still had forty-five minutes to go of this drive, and she was already uncomfortable enough. "You speak Spanish fluently."

"Yes, I do." His icy-blue gaze settled on the road, his expression blank.

Just give up already.

Glancing out the window, she focused her gaze on the lush green terrain. Costa Rica was an adventurous destination—filled with mountains to climb and treks, zip lines and white water, volcanoes, and fishing. And whereas, once in her life, she might have longed to take part in all those things, she'd learned after a lifetime of being told that her body couldn't handle intense sports that it was better not to let herself dream of them.

Not that lying on a beach in a bathing suit appealed much either.

Sweat dripped down the backs of her knees, and she rolled

the window down for relief. This trip was proving to be a disaster, and she closed her eyes, envisioning her cozy couch in her flat surrounded by bookcases. She was proud of that little place, even if it wasn't fancy and the rent was outrageous. Miranda helped offset that cost. But when Liddy had first struck out from Tennessee to move to London, her parents had acted like she wouldn't survive two days.

And I wasn't entirely convinced I could either.

Despite her parents' concerns, she'd built a life in London, though. And she had real friends.

For the first time.

The fresh start had been exactly what she'd needed.

Until now, Mom and Dad would have agreed.

Trusting Sergio was not the sort of slip-up she really needed.

She pulled out her phone and pulled up her text messages with Miranda. The picture she'd taken of Sergio taunted her, and she gritted her teeth.

Liddy: *It turns out the hot guy was a thief. Stole my sister's wedding dress.*

Miranda: *What?!*

Miranda: *Did you at least get to shag him first?*

Much as she usually appreciated Miranda's sense of humor, something about it right now was . . . disheartening. She ignored it instead.

Liddy: *I have no idea what I'm going to do.*

Miranda: *Can you file a claim with the airline?*

Liddy: *Technically, I gave it to him to hold, so they won't do anything.*

Miranda: *Ooof. That's awful.*

Liddy: *Yeah, it's been the worst. Fortunately, Callum helped me talk to them. Did you know he speaks fluent Spanish? I caught a ride with him to the hotel.*

***Miranda:** Wow, how did that come about?*

***Liddy:** Idk, he just asked if I needed a ride. He was weirdly nice about the whole stolen dress thing.*

***Miranda:** That *is* strange. So . . . what has he told you? Any interesting office gossip?*

***Liddy:** Nothing. Once he started driving, his normal lack of conversational skills came back. Cat got his tongue, apparently.*

***Miranda:** Eye roll. I'm sure he can do a lot with that tongue. He's just an arsehole who thinks everyone who works for him isn't worthy.*

A phone ringing broke into her conversation and she glanced over as Callum picked it up. He frowned at the number on the screen, then answered. Actively lowering the volume on the side, he set it to his ear as though he didn't want the speaker to be overheard.

That's interesting.

"Hey there."

Callum's deep voice had always intrigued her. He had an English accent, but used more American slang and terms than the average Brit would—like a strange amalgam of an American and an Englishman. Or something. Maybe he'd just spent a lot of time with Americans.

"I've just arrived . . . yes . . . on my way."

She snuck a look at his profile, and his eyes darted away from the road toward her. He shifted his body away slightly.

He's clearly not happy with the thought of me eavesdropping.

Why am I not surprised?

Her gaze refocused on the windshield. Who might he be talking to? And why was he so discomforted?

"Look, we've been over this. This isn't the time or the place for that. I'm only here for Quinn's wedding—"

A brief silence followed, as though he'd been interrupted, then he burst out, "Enough. I wish I could trust you not to bring it up again, but since I can't, this conversation is over. See you shortly." Callum hung up the line, tossing his phone into the console with a thud.

Well.

Ladies and gentlemen, the charming manners of Callum Scott.

A thick, awkward silence hung between them, and Liddy clasped her hands in her lap, unsure what to say.

Why did I decide to ride with him again?

After several tense beats, Callum cleared his throat. "Sorry about that."

She gave him a sidelong glance. "Everything okay?"

"Yeah, it was just my mother."

Oh.

She tried to conceal her surprise. *He hung up on his mother like that? "*Okay."

He released a slow breath, his shoulders bunched with tension. "It's a long personal story. My mother and I don't get along."

Obviously. She bit her lip. "I'm sorry to hear that. It's none of my business, don't worry." *And you don't do personal stuff.*

"It's not that—" He ran his fingertips through his short, dark hair, his jaw clenching and unclenching.

For several moments, he appeared to be struggling, his level of agitation clear that Liddy couldn't help wondering why a simple phone call would get him so angry. But she didn't want to ask either. Callum had made it clear that he didn't fraternize.

She twisted in her seat, trying to get comfortable. She needed a break to stretch her legs, but the end of this car ride couldn't come fast enough. "I get it. Family is complicated."

He rolled the window down. "My mum—she owns the

place where Elle and Quinn are having their wedding. Co-owns it. With my ex-fiancée, who Mum would still like to see me get back together with."

He has an ex-fiancée?

Wow, she hadn't expected that.

Liddy stared at him, half stunned that he'd shared so much with her in a momentary burst. No wonder he seemed to know his way around Costa Rica. If his mother owned property here, he'd probably been here often.

And no wonder Elle said something about Callum suggesting to Quinn to have the wedding there—not that it entirely makes sense. She frowned, then asked, "Why does your mom co-own it with your ex?"

He sighed. "My ex . . . her mum was my mum's best friend. They bought the place together in Samara after my parents got divorced. It was their dream to run it. But then my mum's best friend died, and the ownership went to her daughter."

She cringed. He'd probably broken more than just his ex-fiancée's heart when things had ended. Callum's mom had probably dreamed of him marrying her best friend's daughter.

"Making your mom business partners with your ex."

"Yeah. Basically. And my mum adores her, so there's that." His voice was terse as he turned off the main road.

Before she could say anything else, he said, "It doesn't matter. That's the short story. And that's why I was curt. That's all." He reached over and flipped on the radio, a burst of Spanish music cutting the conversation off abruptly. Apparently, he was done sharing.

She turned back to her own phone to find a message waiting from Elle.

Elle: *You on your way to the hotel yet? When can we expect you?*

Liddy had avoided texting Elle after the whole thing with

Sergio. She'd fired off a message when she'd landed, but then fear had stayed any further communication. No doubt her sister was worried.

Liddy: *Yeah, I caught a ride with Callum. Let me ask him.*

The phone rang in her hand—Elle must have tapped the dial button immediately.

Liddy answered, and Elle started speaking before Liddy could. "You're driving with Callum?" she asked, surprise in her voice.

"Yeah." Liddy tried not to look at him, then turned the music volume down. Between the wind rushing in through the open window and the noise in the car, she could barely hear Elle. "It's a long story."

"Put him on speaker, I want to talk to him. We both do."

"We?" Liddy asked and rolled the window up. The noise eased, but the heat seemed to smack her instantly.

"My favorite sister," Quinn said as though he and Elle were on speaker. "How was the flight?"

The flight. *Sergio.* Liddy made a face, and that horrible feeling came back. *I won't be Quinn's favorite sister for long.* "It was . . . interesting."

"Are you on speaker yet?" Elle pressed again.

Liddy groaned and reached over to turn off the music. To Callum's questioning look, she said, "My sister and Quinn want to talk to you." She turned on the speakerphone.

Callum smiled—a genuine smile that dissolved his usually stern expression. "Hi, Elle. Quinn."

"Callum Scott, I'm going to murder you. You're lucky you have family here who might report you missing. Because otherwise, when you get here, I would definitely kill you."

Wow, Elle sounds . . . frustrated.

Callum raised a brow.

"She didn't understand that when you said rustic bungalows, you meant rustic," Quinn explained, his tone apologetic.

Elle spoke up again. "It's not that I didn't get what rustic was—believe it or not, I can do rustic—but full-sized beds in all the rooms? Not to mention the size of the rooms. My closet at home is bigger than what most of our guests have to work with. And none of the ceremony amenities that were on the website appear to be here. I didn't want to complicate anything—with Jasper here to perform the ceremony, I figured we didn't need a lot—but there are no chairs for people to sit and watch. And the caterer we hired closed up shop without telling us, so now I have to find food for the reception."

Yikes.

Just how much planning had Elle put into this wedding?

She was a fly-by-the-seat-of-her-pants person, but not Quinn. Then again, knowing Quinn, he'd do whatever Elle wanted without questioning her.

I should have reached out and asked if she needed more help.

But every time Liddy talked to Elle about the wedding, Elle just said how much she wanted things to be relaxed.

"Isn't there an on-site coordinator to handle the wedding details?" Liddy asked, avoiding looking at Callum. This was his mother's place, after all, and she didn't want to step on his toes if Elle was implying things were being shoddily run.

Elle gave an exasperated grunt. "I don't even know. Everything just feels so chaotic. Grandma brought Leo with her, and now she's claiming there's not enough room in the room she booked for the both of them—which there isn't—but I don't have any place to put her. And don't even get me started on the monkeys."

Callum chortled. "You're in Costa Rica, Elle. You should have expected monkeys."

"Oh, yeah?" Liddy could practically hear Elle's glare as she continued speaking. "Should I have expected to find a three-inch-long roach in my tennis shoes the first morning I arrived? *After* I put my shoe on?"

"Is the room dirty?" Callum asked, without reacting.

"No, everything is spotless, but—"

Quinn said, "Darling, I think you'll have plenty of time to air your grievances with Callum—"

"Roaches are pretty much par for the course for this part of the world. No matter how much you try to keep bugs out, they'll find a way in." Callum flexed his arm, then casually set it on top of the steering wheel. "And I never tried to sell you on *La Hacienda*. It's no luxury hotel—just a low-key place for people who don't mind roughing it a bit."

Elle's voice grew tearful. "Yeah, well, joke's on us because Quinn's mom is threatening to stay at the Four Seasons, which will make the entire schedule even more of a nightmare because it's apparently several hours away. I had this dream of a wedding on the beach here and relaxing in hammocks and doing all the fun adventures people talk about, but . . . I just don't know how much more I can take of this." She sniffled loudly. "I'm so stressed out, guys. I'm sorry. I'm a mess."

Oh God.

Guilt ate its way up Liddy's core. As though she hadn't already felt horrible about what she had to tell her sister about the dress.

"Um . . ." Liddy cleared her throat. She should just confess and get it over with. "Look, there's something I have to tell you, Elle. It's about your—"

Callum turned toward her sharply and took the phone from her hand.

Liddy startled. *What the hell?*

"So sorry about everything, Elle. Listen, I'll do what I can when I get there. See you soon." He hung up almost as quickly as he had on his mom.

Her jaw dropped open. "Did you really just hang up on her?"

"Are you mad? Your sister tells you she's stressed, and you think it's a good time to tell her you lost her wedding dress?" Callum dipped his chin. "I may not know anything about women, but I know enough to know your timing couldn't be ghastlier. Elle doesn't need that right now."

Liddy frowned. That Callum might care about her sister's feelings was . . . strange. *And he's also right.* Her cheeks warmed at his scolding. "I just didn't want to wait and drop the bomb on her when we arrived. Let her think I was pretending everything was fine."

Callum's eyes were deep in thought. He turned, pulling the car into a small town. Nothing here was over two stories. The buildings—which appeared to be a mix of houses and shops—were close together, built on rows facing the street. Bars covered the windows, small patios with flowers, and verdant green tropical plants hid behind gates—some of which were topped with razor wire.

Liddy rolled the window down again, her body relaxing some in the rush of cooler air that came in. "What's with all the bars and gates?"

"Theft can be a problem here." Callum pulled the car up to the curb, letting the engine idle. "It's not likely someone will come up and mug you while you're walking around in the resort areas or towns like this or beach towns, but the towns near San Jose and the city itself can be dangerous."

Why was he being so negative about a place so many described as paradise? "What about *'Pura Vida'* and all that?" The Costa Rican slogan seemed to be everywhere and appeared on all the guides she'd picked up about the country.

"It's all shite." He nodded to her open window. "Also, I wouldn't leave windows down. You staying in the car?"

Callum's dislike for his surroundings clearly had a personal edge to them, which didn't surprise her, given what he'd revealed about his mother. She let it go rather than question anything he said, and closed the window.

"Are we going somewhere? We're not here yet, are we?" They didn't appear to be anywhere near the beach.

"Not quite. About thirty minutes away." He killed the engine and rolled his sleeves up to his forearms, revealing a tattoo there. An emblem or crest of some kind. She'd never seen his arms bared before, and somehow, she never would have expected him to be tattooed.

She'd never cared for tattoos, but it looked good on him. Suited him, even. Or maybe it was the fact that his surprisingly tanned forearm was well-muscled and spoke to the care he took of his physique. He looked *fine* in a suit, and the women at work had admired that about him on more than one occasion.

"I'm hot, and I could use a cold drink."

Yeah, you are.

She moistened her lips. *Where had that thought come from? And . . . ugh. I'm really having an off day, aren't I?*

He pointed toward a little shop on the corner of the street. "There's a *pulperia* there—a convenience store. You want something?"

Her eyes flicked back toward the razor wire on the gated house they'd parked next to. Given her experience with Sergio and what he'd just explained, a clammy feeling broke out on her palms again. *And my back needs a break from this seat.* "I'll go with you. I wouldn't mind stretching my legs. Will the luggage be safe?"

"Yeah, it's fine. We won't be inside that long." Callum opened the door and swung his long legs out. She tore her gaze away and hurried after him since he hadn't bothered to wait for her.

They crossed the street, and Callum breezed into the small shop, which had the door already propped open. The interior was cluttered but clean, with shelves of packaged goods and food, newspapers, and even baked goods like loaves of bread near the register. Callum went for the refrigerated drinks and grabbed something. "Soft drink or iced tea?"

"Iced tea, I guess."

He took another bottle of what he'd grabbed and handed it to her. Starting toward the register, he paused at the freezer of ice cream bars. A hint of a smile came to the corner of his mouth. He grabbed two and took them up to the register as well.

After they'd paid, he handed her one. "I loved these as a kid."

"Oh—" *He bought me ice cream?* "Thank you."

They started back toward the car, and she unwrapped the ice cream. It didn't look too different from chocolate-covered ice cream bars from back home—but maybe the nostalgia of it had made him suddenly generous. "I take it you spent a lot of time here as a kid?"

He bit into the ice cream, and his features softened. He chewed and swallowed, then nodded as he opened the car door. "Yeah, my mum is from here. I spent every summer here as a kid. Was born here, too."

He's part Costa Rican? She never would have expected that.

She settled back into her seat and took a bite of the ice cream. *Delicious.* Nothing particularly unusual, but even so, it was amazing for a simple ice cream from a convenience store freezer.

"What do you think?" Callum asked, glancing at her.

"So good."

He smiled, then started the engine. "It'll melt too fast with the windows down if I drive." Giving her a thoughtful gaze, he licked some chocolate off his lip, and Liddy focused on the ice cream. Costa Rican Callum seemed different somehow.

"You know, we might still be able to track down Sergio." He settled deeper into his seat, then rolled down his window.

Liddy's brows drew together. *What?*

That came out of nowhere.

"How do you mean? Airport security said they couldn't do anything."

"Yeah, but airport security doesn't know where Sergio might be tomorrow. I do."

Liddy turned in her seat as sharply as she could, wishing this was one of those times that her fused spine didn't make it difficult to move like that. "What in the hell are you talking about?"

Callum's expression was blank, and he shrugged. "I heard Sergio talking to someone on the phone while we were in line at immigration. He said something about some event he was invited to in a church in the middle of the country tomorrow."

She gaped at him, her mouth parting. *What. The. Fuck.* She wanted to beat him with the rest of her ice cream bar. "Why didn't you say something about that sooner?"

He polished off his ice cream, then set his hand on the shifter. "I didn't think it would be worth mentioning."

"Not worth mentioning . . ." How in the world would it *not* be relevant? He knew how upset she was and what that wedding dress meant. "And now you do?" Lydia asked, baffled by his logic.

The ice cream no longer tasted as good with his words. Was that why he bought it for her? To butter her up? Without the ability to dispose of it, she finished it, then opened the iced tea to wash it away.

He pulled away from the curb. "Yeah. Well, after hearing Elle so upset . . . I might try to look for that bastard. But seeing as nothing may come of it, and it's a monumental task, I have a favor to ask of you in return."

She should have known Callum was being too pleasant.

He's still the same jerk from London.

"What sort of favor?"

Callum gave her a deliberate look, up and down. "You won't like it. And to be honest, neither do I, but it's the only chance I have of escaping the next week with my sanity intact."

She crossed her arms. "I already don't like the sound of this."

"My mother is going to be driving me mad about Sophia for the next week . . . unless I show up happily attached to someone else."

Oh. Man . . .

He wants me to pretend to be in a relationship with him?

She almost barked with laughter. *Her* with Callum?

"I don't know if Elle would buy it. She knows . . ."

"How much you loathe me? Yes, I assumed." He turned a palm up. "You're welcome to tell her, but then—"

"You mean, if I agree to it. Because I would have to be out of my mind to agree to that." *Also, I clearly haven't been that great at hiding my dislike of him.*

His smile indicated he was losing his patience with her. "Of course, if you explain to her why you feel the need to repay me a favor, you may have to explain about the stolen wedding dress. Or, you could do things my way, potentially find Sergio, and attempt to get the dress back without her knowing a thing about it being stolen."

Son of a bitch.

Was this even a tenable plan? Sergio wouldn't hold onto the stolen dress that long, would he? But if they tracked him down in a day, it narrowed the window of time he had to get rid of it. And how easy could it be to get rid of a priceless heirloom wedding dress?

Or I could not do this ridiculous plan, then face telling Elle that I lost her dress and didn't try the only ludicrous idea to get it back.

Elle. Who was clearly stressed as it was. Who would do anything for her.

Who had done everything for her.

When their mom had gotten into a terrible car wreck while Elle had been in college, her older sister had quit school—sacrificing her career plans—and come home to take care of Liddy and their younger brother, Kyle, because they'd both been in high school and needed the help.

Elle had also used the money she'd gotten from her career as a country singer to buy their parents a better house and get Liddy started in London—as well as paying off Liddy's loans from college.

Acid rose in Liddy's throat. That Callum had a way to help her and would only do it in return for a favor was despicable. "You know, as Quinn's friend—*and groomsman*—you should help with no strings attached. Sorry that your situation with your mom sucks, but that's not my problem. I could just as easily tell Quinn about how you're trying to bribe me, you know."

Callum's face darkened. "I didn't have to say anything about what I overheard with Sergio. Trying to find this fellow—which might not even be possible—means giving up my time to go scrambling halfway across the country to fix *your* mistake."

Ouch.

Lydia scowled at him. "Yeah, well, I reject your offer.

You're a real piece of work thinking you could twist and use this horrible situation to your advantage."

Grabbing a pair of sunglasses from the console, Callum slipped them on, his expression hardening. "All right. Forget I asked." He turned the radio back on, his jaw clenching.

As if. Once Quinn and Elle heard about this, he'd have to tell them what he knew about Sergio anyway. And then, maybe, once and for all, everyone would see Callum for the asshole he was.

She tugged her phone out of her pocket again, her stomach clenched, then fired out another text message to Miranda:

Liddy: *I think our boss just sank to an all-time low.*

CHAPTER SIX

LYDIA DIDN'T SPEAK to Callum for the rest of the drive, which was fine with him.

I don't know what the hell I was thinking.

Except that wasn't entirely true. He'd wanted a way to tell Quinn about that arsehole from the plane without making Lydia look like a complete flake. Whether he liked Quinn's new sister-in-law, he didn't want the animosity between them to impede his friendship with Quinn. He'd warned Lydia about Sergio, after all, and maybe that was why he hadn't been able to stop himself from eavesdropping on the man while they'd been at immigration.

And then, after their respective phone calls, Callum had been thinking that maybe Lydia might just be as desperate as he was.

He'd picked up that phone call from his mother, against his better judgment, and one of the first things out of Mum's lips had been, *"We have to talk about Sophia."*

Mum hadn't even had the courtesy to wait until he'd

arrived on the property to start with her relentless pushing. His anger had flared, and he hadn't been rational.

You're a damn idiot.

As he pulled into a space at *La Hacienda Tropical,* he blinked at the nicely paved car park—and the new sign for the hotel. The last time he'd been here it had been a hand-painted sheet of plywood. Sophia had painted it, though, so he hadn't told her he didn't like it.

The dense canopy of trees above the car park threw shadows onto the windscreen, cloaking him with a darkness similar to what he felt deeply inside him. The beaches on the Guanacaste Coast were often hilly and wild, with rainforests jutting right out onto the mixed sand beaches. His favorite beach in Costa Rica, Ostional, was a black sand beach north from here, a sight that made the land feel otherworldly.

La Hacienda was in Samara, a small beach town that still retained local charm. Even the foreign nationals who lived here were all ex-pats who'd fallen in love with the Costa Rican life-style. The hotel itself was on a quiet, more private area of the beach, closer to Puerto Carillo, about a twenty-minute walk from the main street of Samara.

Everything that his mother had loved, and why she'd wanted to live here.

He opened the trunk and helped Lydia get her bags out, then she hurried away without another word, leaving him staring at his own suitcase.

This is going to be a long trip.

Rubbing his burning eyes, he set his suitcase on the pavement, then put his laptop case on top of it. A line of ants made their way just past the wheel of his suitcase toward the edge of the pavement, and birds chirped and cried overhead. Funny how these minor details of everyday life here had receded far back into his memory.

He had no desire to catch up with Lydia or go to the office, but he had little choice, unless he wanted to sleep outside. Given that Costa Rica had more venomous snakes per square meter than almost any other country, he'd pass on that option.

As he dragged the suitcase toward the office, the hibiscus bushes brushed against his trousers. The bushes needed trimming, but he could also understand why they hadn't been—they were exotic and beautiful, just as his mother liked.

He reached the office and saw a hand-painted sign on the path that led down the steep stairs to the beach. *Morning Yoga: This Way*.

Some things never change.

Steeling himself for the encounter with his mother, his hand tightened around the handle of the suitcase. He wished he'd had the guts to tell Quinn about why he hadn't wanted the wedding held here, but it had been a bit too personal. Too deep. If Quinn had known, he likely wouldn't have pushed through with the idea. But once Quinn had booked the place, Callum hadn't wanted to change his mind.

Callum pushed the door open. He'd expected to see Lydia inside, but she wasn't here. Maybe Elle had told her to meet her somewhere else.

A footstep sounded, then a shadow passed through the back doorway. "Un momento," a female voice called, and Callum stiffened.

Bollocks.

Should he just go and come back later when his mum was in the office?

Seconds later, Sophia breezed through the back door, a warm smile on her gorgeous face. Her feet faltered for a split second, then she pushed on toward the counter. "Callum."

She's just as beautiful as ever. Five years had done nothing to change that. She had curves in all the right places, long, dark, and glossy hair—that she appeared to have highlighted—and tanned, olive skin that spoke to long days in the sun. Her dark eyes shifted over him, and she raised her chin. "I—um." She cleared her throat. "Let me get *Tía*." Her English was near perfect, though she had an accent. Like his mother, Sophia had not only learned English in school but had plenty of practice speaking it now.

Maybe it was strange that his ex still called his mum by the affectionate "auntie" nickname, but she always had, so he'd never thought twice about it. When they'd been engaged, Sophia had switched to calling her *"Mi suerte"* a slang term for "my mother-in-law" or *suegra*. But that, at least, appeared to have stopped.

"It's fine." Callum crossed the space toward her, determined to dispense with the awkwardness. He'd have to see her many times during this trip. She meant nothing to him now, and he wouldn't pretend he still harbored old wounds. "I just need to check in and get my room key."

"Tía!" Sophia called out, ignoring him. She gave him a taut smile. "It's so good to see you, Callum. How are you?"

"Fantastic." He could do without the chitchat. He avoided looking her in the eye, reaching into his pocket for his phone. "I think my reservation is—"

"Callum!" His mother came around the corner and rushed toward him. She threw her arms around his neck, tears in her eyes. "Cuánto deseaba verte." *How I longed to see you.* She held him tightly, as though nothing had ever changed between them.

In a small way, this was preferential to the other Latina mum way of handling a contentious situation—resentment and guilt.

When Callum pulled away, she framed his face in her

hands, holding his cheeks. "You're even more handsome than you look in photos. I can't believe how tall you are now."

Callum groaned inwardly. *This spectacle is ridiculous.* He hadn't seen his mother since he was twenty-three—and he certainly hadn't grown since then, though he'd filled out. He'd been much leaner and lankier before. Before he'd traded endurance training for lifting weights.

Sophia had slipped away. *Thank God.*

"Good to see you, Mum." He forced the lie out through his teeth. Funny how the "mum" title had stuck. Dad had used it, so Isla and Callum had used it. That his Costa Rican mother was stuck with a British term for mother set by a man she'd divorced so long ago was sort of . . . *ironic?* He didn't know what it was.

"I kept praying you would come back here. Every day, I prayed." Mum wiped her face, leaving behind a streak of mascara on her cheek. She was smaller than him, by about a foot, only about five foot two. He'd taken after his father, while Isla was only a couple of inches taller than Mum. "I have your room at the house ready to go. Come, I'll show you." She spoke in a mixture of English and Spanish to him, sometimes blending so much "Spanglish" that Callum didn't really keep up with what language she'd said. He typically responded in English, regardless.

Callum didn't care to remind her of why he hadn't come back. Why he avoided her calls most of the time or had scheduled work trips for the couple of times she'd come to London to see Isla. And that Mum kept acting as though he should just forgive her already and just go right back to "home sweet home" was the only evidence he needed not to bring it up. They would never see eye to eye on what had happened with Sophia.

"I actually booked a room." He grimaced and took another step back. "But I appreciate the offer."

"Yes, I saw the reservation come through." Mum frowned. "But I canceled it and gave that room to someone else. There's no reason for you to pay good money to stay here when I have a place for you to stay for free."

Fuck, no.

Anger flushed through him, his gut churning.

This is why I should have told Quinn about my mum.

She would do something like this. He gritted his teeth, taking another step back as he tried to calm himself. He rubbed his jaw, feeling the stubble of the morning against his palm. "This—this is just *classic*, Mum."

His voice had come out louder than he'd intended, and Sophia poked her head through the doorway, a concerned expression on her face.

Mum shrank back, any visible joy in her demeanor vanishing.

The door to the office opened, and Lydia breezed through, a burst of fresher sea-salt air coming with her. "There you are!" Lydia sidled up to him.

Uhh . . . what?

Lydia hugged him from the side and whispered in his ear, "I couldn't tell her."

Callum stiffened, trying not to react. *What the hell?*

Elle and Quinn were just steps behind Lydia.

"Callum!" Elle's voice came through the door. She wore a confused look, her pretty face already tanned, her long blond hair cascading in perfect waves over her shoulders. Even her sundress seemed to shimmer as she made her way toward them even though they were inside the office.

Where did all her anger on that phone call go?

Quinn trailed behind her and gave Callum a jaunty smile.

He shook hands with Callum. "You sod. You didn't breathe a word to me about this."

"I had no clue you two were together." Shock was written on Elle's face as she looked from one to the other.

Callum blinked, trying to catch up. He hadn't expected *this*. Given how adamant Lydia had been in the car about how much his proposal had disgusted her, he considered, for a split second, giving her away.

Now she wants my help? Fuck that. He wasn't in the mood to put himself on the line for anyone.

They hadn't had time to talk any of it through. He hadn't even given more than half a thought to the potential consequences.

But his mother was right there watching. As was Sophia.

Lesser of two evils.

He recovered as swiftly as he could and slipped his hand into Lydia's, interlacing their fingers.

A mischievous feeling rose in him despite it all.

She wants to play games . . . so be it.

"We wanted to surprise you, didn't we, darling?" He tugged Lydia closer. She glanced up, and those full, gorgeous lips parted.

Then he dropped a kiss to her mouth, his free hand curling around her waist.

He'd intended it to be nothing more than a playful peck, a small moment of revenge, but her lips were unexpectedly soft and pliant against his, and a jolt of electricity passed through him as they connected.

Lydia stepped on his toes—hard—leaning her weight against them.

Ouch. Right.

He pulled back, then turned back to see the surprised looks being leveled at him from everyone else in the room.

Then Elle's open jaw closed and she pulled Lydia into a fierce hug. "I can't believe you didn't tell me. My sister and Q's friend? That's amazing. Why didn't you say something at Christmas?"

Wow, Elle . . . is surprisingly happy. Is she being sincere?

Lydia's cheeks had turned pink, and she ran her fingers through her hair, giving Callum a nervous glance. "Yeah—um, well, it all just sort of happened recently."

"And we didn't want people at work to know yet, of course," he added.

Fuck. Work. With Aiden and some of his coworkers here, he couldn't just make this vanish after the trip. This was going to get overly messy quickly. They needed ground rules. Which was why he would have preferred to discuss this in the car rather than this last-minute show.

"Well, they're going to find out if you're staying together here," Quinn said with a smirk.

Together.

As Lydia's eyes widened, Callum glanced over at his mother and fought—hard—not to laugh. *Or cackle.*

This is perfect.

Yes, there was no reason for him *not* to be staying with his girlfriend, was there?

"You're staying with a woman? It's completely inappropriate," Mum muttered in Spanish. Callum silenced her with a hard look, and her lips pursed. His mum had an irritating habit of using Spanish to communicate secretly, as though other people couldn't read body language.

"I think Callum booked his own room, though, just for appearance's sake," Lydia was already saying.

Oh no. You wanted to do this. We're doing this. Liddy wasn't about to get the benefits without the work.

He squeezed Liddy's hand. "Actually, it turns out my

mother canceled my reservation. But you're right, Quinn, this would be a good chance to let the cat out of the bag. I can just stay with Lydia." He turned toward his mum. "Mum, I was going to introduce you later, but since we're all here together, I want you to meet my girlfriend, Lydia Winnick."

Lydia narrowed her eyes at him. *She's not happy about this rooming arrangement. At all.* After a second, she released his hand and extended it toward his mother. "Call me Liddy. Nice to meet you, Señora Scott."

His mother's face grew less friendly as her gaze swept over Lydia. "It would be Reyes," she said in her accented English. "Señora Reyes. But you can call me Lety, like your sister does."

Mum doesn't like her.

Probably because she's ruining Mum's plans to have me stay with her. And get back together with Sophia.

Then his mother seemed to catch herself and smiled a bit more warmly. "Es un placer, amorcito. Anyone my Callum loves is welcome here."

Two-faced bullshite.

Callum's eyes darted toward the doorway where Sophia had been. She was gone once again.

The smidge of satisfaction he'd felt kissing Lydia faded.

"So you really don't have a room for Callum?" Lydia asked, her voice faltering.

Watching her squirm was surprisingly . . . satisfying?

"No, but he's welcome to stay at my house with me. I wouldn't want to upset your parents by—"

"That won't be necessary, Mum. Lydia and I can stay together." Callum put his arm around Lydia's shoulder, then looked over at Elle and Quinn. If Lydia was doing this, then he needed to remind her of why before she got cold feet. "Speaking of which, I have some bad news to break, mate."

He sought Quinn's face, specifically, hoping the blow would be softer on his friend. "This morning when we were leaving Lid's flat, she put me in charge of grabbing the wedding dress, and I fucked up—"

"Díos mío, Callum, do you have to use such ugly words?" Mum gasped.

Elle's eyes widened, and she stepped closer. "W-what do you mean, Callum?"

"I didn't bring the dress. We didn't realize until we were at the check-in desk, and by then, it was too late to go back for it. But I've already spoken to Isla, and she's going to bring it with her when she comes in a few days." Callum reached for Elle's hand with both of his. "Please forgive me. I'm so sorry. It's not Lydia's fault. She thought I had it and was so worried to tell you. But I promise I'll make it up to you both."

Lydia had paled. But the hard part was over. They'd told Elle about the dress not being here.

Elle looked over Callum's shoulder toward Lydia, the wheels of her mind clearly turning. "It's fine," she said at last, then looked back at Quinn. "Isn't it? It'll be fine, right? Your mom won't flip out?" In an unconvincing tone, which Callum wasn't sure showed if she was more upset than she was letting on, Elle laughed and added, "It's only my wedding dress."

Quinn slipped his arm around her shoulder and kissed her temple. "My mum will be fine. I don't even think we need to tell her."

Elle relaxed against him. "Yes, I agree. She doesn't need to worry about one more thing."

Callum turned back toward Lydia.

If he didn't know any better, she looked guilty.

But also maybe a little thankful?

She met his eyes, and his mouth twisted in a smirk.

We're in it together now.

All that was left was to figure out how to handle this situation—and fast.

CHAPTER SEVEN

Elle gripped Liddy's forearm the moment Callum and Quinn were out of sight on the pathway to the bungalow she'd be sharing with Callum. "What the hell, Liddy? Tell me everything. When did this happen with Callum? I thought you hated him."

Oh God, what did I get myself into?

Shit.

Liddy scanned her sister's wide blue eyes, considering, for the eight hundredth time, to just tell the truth and get it over with.

This was crazy, wasn't it?

Even if they tracked Sergio down, there was no guarantee they'd get the dress back—and then what? Were they supposed to blame Callum's sister?

Whatever plan Callum had, it didn't seem like a good one.

And now I'm stuck with him during this entire trip.

But Elle had burst into tears when she'd seen Liddy, something that wasn't usual for her sister. Quinn whispered how glad he'd been that Liddy was finally there because everyone else was driving Elle crazy, and that had been that. She couldn't add one more thing to Elle's plate right now.

Liddy swallowed hard. "It happened a few months ago. I thought nothing would come of it at first and now, here we are."

And he just kissed me.

She'd frozen in place when his gaze had focused on her lips, then realized if they were going to play this off, she had to consent to it.

She just hadn't expected the contact to make her heart race like that.

"I mean, he's easy on the eyes, but is he treating you the way he should? You always said he was such an ass to you. I can barely forgive the way he treated you when you first met him, so I'm not sure how you got over it. And isn't that complicated with him being your boss?"

Yeah, no, I haven't forgiven that either. "Water under the bridge," Liddy said, pushing away the memory of that kiss. "But yes, the work thing is . . . complex. Which is why we haven't told anyone."

Elle looked torn. "Are you sure about this? I like Callum. He can be really charming when he wants. But Quinn also told me some stuff about his reputation with women, and I'm not sure he's the sort of guy I trust with my sister."

Ugh. This is going to be harder than I thought. Clearly, Elle's excited reaction in the office had been fabricated, probably because she'd been in front of Callum *and* his mother.

Liddy had one easy way to settle Elle's mind somewhat, but it felt so deceptive and gross. She turned toward Elle and squeezed her hand. "Well, you trust your sister, right? I really like him, Elle. Please don't make a big deal out of it."

She almost shuddered saying it. Elle searched her gaze, still hesitant, then nodded. "If you're happy, then I'm happy for you, Liddy. I always am. I know you're all grown up now. I don't want you to feel like I'm questioning your choices."

Quinn and Callum had stopped at the doorway to a bungalow, right off the stone-lined path. The bungalows, which the website described as "rustic" were tidy one-story numbers made of wood. They stood in a circular formation centered on a small kidney-shaped swimming pool. Each bungalow had three more built directly behind it, about fifteen in all, and featured a hammock on the front porch.

And down another path, beyond a long stretch of tropical plants and trees, was the beautiful beach.

This hotel was cute. *Rustic.* Just as the website had boasted.

"So what's wrong with the place?"

"It's all just a bit . . . *less* than I should have done for the wedding." Elle pulled her hair back into a ponytail. "Not the luxury my in-laws are accustomed to. The included breakfasts are tortillas, fruit, and this rice, bean, and scrambled egg mixture called *gallo pinto*—which is admittedly delicious—but Mom and Dad have been complaining they're still hungry afterward. They have to walk into the main strip and get more food. And then the bed situation—the biggest bed I've seen is a double, including mine and Quinn's in the 'honeymoon suite.' No television or internet. Cell service is spotty, and you have to go to a local café to get Wi-Fi. And when I talked to Callum's mom, she said it's designed to encourage guests to spend time together."

Lydia laughed and squeezed her sister's shoulder with a side hug. "So it's a little hippie-dippie. It sounds like something you would love. Small and intimate, a chance to spend time with your closest friends and family. Which is probably why you booked it? It seems private, given how close to the main beach it is. And that's good to keep any potential paparazzi away."

"Yes." Elle sniffled and wiped her eyes. "I love it. I really didn't want to overdo anything. Just go have a simple ceremony, have dinner together on the beach. Do some dancing. But I wasn't trying to make everyone *else* miserable. And now I don't even have a caterer."

Liddy nestled her head against her sister's. "I'm sure we can find a local place to get food. Most of what you said sounds like a *them* problem, not a *you* problem. You just ignore their complaints. Now that I'm here, tell them they can come directly to me with every issue. Have Hunter and Taryn arrived yet? I'm sure my co-maid of honor would be willing to step in and field all parental issues."

"They arrive later this morning." Elle's best friends and business partners, who owned the music and arts studio for disabled children in Nashville with Elle, Heartbeats, would surely not put up with that nonsense. Taryn, especially.

"What about Kyle? Maybe he can take the dads out for a fishing trip or something. I hear fishing is amazing here." Their younger brother was outdoorsy. He'd jump at something like that.

"He arrives this afternoon, same as Quinn's brothers. We were thinking it might be good to have a big family dinner tomorrow. Just immediate family."

Tomorrow? Liddy grimaced. When would she and Callum need to leave to track down Sergio?

Elle put her hand on Liddy's forearm and drew her to a stop. A divot showed between her eyebrows. "When does Callum's sister arrive? She won't forget the dress, will she?"

Liddy held her breath. Elle was clearly worried about this. Maybe she should just tell her. It would be embarrassing to admit the lie, of course, but it would save her from having to share a room with Callum. And an enormous weight would be off her chest. "I think she comes in a few days. I have to double-check with Callum."

"Okay." Elle let out a slow breath. "I'm just not sure if it's going to fit as well as it did at Christmas, and I need to try it on."

Scanning her eyes, Liddy frowned. *Why would it not fit? Unless . . .*

Liddy's eyes widened. "Are you pregnant?" she hissed.

Elle nodded quickly.

Oh my God.

Liddy's jaw dropped open, then she let out a muffled squeak. "Oh my God! Elle!"

I can't believe this. Elle didn't look any different. *Except she's a mom now. What! I can't believe I'm going to be an aunt.*

"Shhhhh," Elle said. "We haven't told Mom and Dad. Or Quinn's parents. And we don't want to tell them until after the wedding. They'll take the news better that way. And I'm only like nine weeks along."

How could her sister have kept this quiet for so long?

"Nine weeks!"

Callum and Quinn twisted their heads.

Quinn ducked his chin. He chuckled at Elle as they drew closer. "You told her, didn't you?"

"She's my sister. I had to."

Liddy's heart thudded in her chest. No wonder Elle seemed so emotional. *And thank goodness I didn't tell her about the dress.* Stressing out a bride was bad enough. Stressing out a pregnant woman was much, much worse.

Thank God Callum stopped her from saying anything in the car.

"Told her what?" Callum asked as he opened the door to the bungalow.

Quinn drew Elle closer to him. "It's all hush-hush still, but Elle is expecting."

Callum grinned, then offered Quinn a hearty handshake. "That's amazing. Congratulations." He hugged Elle with such genuine enthusiasm that it almost stopped Lydia short in her tracks.

Callum really seems to care about Quinn and Elle.

She gritted her teeth. She sort of hated that fact. Hated that they loved him and vice versa. But right now, it might have to be their common ground if they were going to survive this trip.

Quinn and Elle hung by the door, holding hands.

God, Elle is glowing.

Liddy pushed her discomfort to the side. She didn't want to take one ounce of happiness away from her sister right now, not if she could avoid it.

"We got married legally back home a couple of months ago because of the whole destination wedding thing, so technically this is a honeymoon baby, but in the meantime, we don't want the parents freaking out. You know, especially with Mr. Fancy Pants over here being all aristocrat," Elle told Callum. "So don't tell anyone."

Callum nodded. "The British aristocracy is hardly in a position to pass judgment, but you know you can trust me."

Really?

Yet both Elle and Quinn really seemed to.

"We'll let you two settle in. We have a few more family members coming in the next half hour, so we want to make sure everything is ready for them," Quinn said. They said their goodbyes and left, closing the bungalow door behind them.

Their absence was a vacuum in the brightly lit room. Liddy took in the room that would be her "home" for the next week. The walls were yellow, the trim around the windows was the same wood as outside, and there were frilly lace curtains over the windows. Simple, but not elegant. *It could honestly do with some work.* Not that she'd tell Callum that. Elle was right—there wasn't much space here. And the bed looked small.

Liddy gave it a pointed look. "We are *not* sharing that. This is my room, and your body parts aren't getting close to my body parts. You can get a cot."

The corners of Callum's mouth twitched. He set his bags down near a desk in the room, so narrow that Liddy doubted a laptop could even fit comfortably there. "Don't worry, my body parts aren't interested in getting close to yours. I'll happily take the floor."

Ass.

She should have expected that. But then again, she'd set herself up for it. She pursed her lips, realizing how immature she'd sounded when he'd repeated it back to her, then grudgingly said, "Thank you for your help back there."

Callum pulled out his laptop case and set it on the chair. "Thank you, too." His eyes were unreadable as he set his suitcase on the floor and crouched. "I'm going to take a shower and change, then head into the main strip to get some work done." He opened his bag. "But if I could make a suggestion, I think we should call a truce."

"A truce?" Lydia went over to the bed and dumped her sweatshirt and carry-on on the tropical-patterned comforter.

Callum nodded. "There's no use avoiding the elephant in the room, Lydia."

She sat on the edge of the bed, her back aching from the morning's adventure. "If we're going to pretend we're dating, you'll have to call me Liddy. Anyone close to me knows I like it better."

"What's wrong with Lydia?"

"Other than that my mom named me after one of my least favorite and most annoying Jane Austen characters?" She rolled her eyes. "At least it's not as bad as my sister—who she felt the need to christen Ellis."

Callum smirked. "You should talk to my sister. Her name means 'island' in Spanish. Wouldn't be such a terrible thing—if she hadn't been partially raised in a Spanish-speaking country."

"Yikes, that's true." She flexed her fingers, a shooting pain going through her limbs. "What was that about the elephant in the room?"

Callum shut the suitcase and set some clothes and a pair of flip-flops on top of it, along with a toiletry bag. "You and I . . . don't have the best relationship." He stood and came closer.

"That's putting it mildly." She set her hands on either side of her and leaned back. "But you're also my boss. This feels threatening to even discuss, if I'm being honest."

And it was weird, how refreshing it was to be honest with him. She rarely had honest conversations with him. Except maybe on the plane, and that had been because she'd been buzzed from drinking champagne and flirting with Sergio.

"You know you won't be fired, no matter what happens. You have the security of your connections."

She didn't like the implication that she hadn't earned her position, as he'd done in the past, but that was an issue for another time. "Yeah, but you can make my life a living hell. Or more of one. Because if you think I haven't noticed you giving me the worst assignments in the past year, you're naive."

His eyes flickered. "The worst?"

She held his gaze. "You give every hard job—everything that's going to require hours of overtime—to me. And I'm not the only one who's noticed."

Callum didn't respond, the seconds ticking by in deafening silence as he seemed to absorb her statement, his expression unreadable. He secured his thumbs through the belt loops of his jeans. "Right. Well, I promise I won't make your life a living hell because of anything that happens here. Good enough?"

She stood to face him and crossed her arms. "What happens in Costa Rica stays in Costa Rica?"

He nodded. "And I would expect your discretion about the circumstances as well. Particularly to do with anyone we work with. For obvious reasons."

Except . . . she'd already probably told Miranda more than she should have. But Miranda would be discreet, wouldn't she?

God, I hope so.

Also, the Camdens would be here. And Mason was bringing Rebecca. What would they think about Lydia and Callum's "relationship"? She might figure out a way to share enough with Rebecca that she would understand what was going on. Rebecca was trustworthy.

"What about the Camdens? And Rebecca is going to have a hard time believing all this."

"Convince her any way you like. Then we can explain how our relationship fell apart after the trip."

So basically, more lying. This was what she had agreed to, though. "All right. No more kissing me like that, though. Holding hands and hugging is fine, but I think it would be best if we kept all physical contact at first base."

Callum's eyes lit with amusement. "You realize that includes kissing."

"No, it doesn't."

"Yes, it does. First is kissing, fourth is fucking, and etcetera."

Her breath hitched at his words. Even talking about this with Callum was so . . . *taking my brain places I don't want it to go.* "Then . . . then, no leaving home."

"You look embarrassed."

That's because I am. Liddy shot him a glare. "I swear to

God, if you keep being this obnoxious, our fake happily ever after will fall apart sooner rather than later. We still have to work together when this is all over."

"Agreed." Callum crossed his arms. "Hand holding and light, affectionate touches it is. Anything else? Some of us have jobs to check in with."

He really was a workaholic robot. She suppressed the urge to roll her eyes. "Aren't you supposed to be on vacation?"

"I have too much to do to disconnect for ten days. No matter how good a friend Quinn is. Not to mention that one of the hardest working members of my team is also on holiday."

She frowned. *Does he mean me?*

His expression seemed to show that he did. *Is this his way of complimenting me on my work?*

She steadied herself. *Why does it feel like he just called me beautiful or something?*

Clasping her hands together, she looked down. "Um, yeah. I guess that makes sense." She cleared her throat. "Oh, just one more thing. What happens if we don't find Sergio or get the wedding dress back? I don't want your sister to get involved in something she had nothing to do with."

"I guess we'll cross that bridge when we come to it. But there's always the old 'the airline lost the bag,' excuse." Callum winked and then went into the bathroom, closing the door behind him.

That's true.

Then Liddy startled.

That had always been true. She clamored over toward the bathroom door. "Wait a second, why didn't you suggest that to me earlier? Instead of this whole relationship idea?"

Why didn't I just think of saying that earlier? I could have bought myself some time rather than say I was dating Callum.

But she'd been so distraught, and Callum's solution had been a last-minute, desperate grab to control the situation.

The shower went on, and Callum didn't respond.

Callum had clearly given some thought to her options before this. He just said nothing because it wasn't convenient for him.

And now I'm stuck.

CHAPTER EIGHT

CALLUM FINISHED his coffee and closed his laptop, rubbing his tired eyes as he leaned back from his seat. The rest of the day had gone smoothly enough—excusing himself from the Camden wedding hoopla factored largely in that.

For now, though, he had to quit working for the day and make his way back to the hotel before jet lag got the better of him. And it would probably be good for him to show his face occasionally, given he was here for a wedding. Callum wasn't sure he was ready to jump back into the chaos, but it was part of a groomsman's duty, wasn't it? He sighed, giving a wistful glance at his empty cup.

He'd nearly forgotten how much he loved Costa Rican coffee.

And the food.

Now and then, people would bring up Latin American cuisine and extol it for its spiciness. When Dad moved him with his stepmother, Diana, to Connecticut after Callum's parents had divorced, anyone who found out he was part Costa Rican would ask him if he liked tacos and burritos. As a child, it made him mad. Costa Rican food was fresh and lacking in hot spices, as opposed to Mexican.

But the less he'd cared about *being* from here, the less it bothered him.

He wound the laptop cord, glancing from his seat toward the main street in front of Samara Beach. The town had grown since he'd last been here, even though it still wasn't as developed as many of the northern towns on the Pacific coast. No resorts and five-star hotels here. Samara still retained its family-friendly beach-town vibe, which his mother had adored.

Mum had wanted to move someplace like this, where cafés and bars opened right onto the sands of the beach. Where you could walk at night and feel safe but still enjoy some nightlife. Where monkeys and tropical birds could still be spotted in the treetops.

The familiar waft of petrol from a passing shuttle made him wrinkle his nose, and he left the café and started back toward *La Hacienda* on foot. The sun hadn't set yet, and it occurred to him it'd been a while since he'd watched the sun rise or set, unlike in the days of his youth when he'd lived for those moments and spent as much time surfing or playing football on the beach as possible.

Fútbol. The same football that had started his downward spiral.

After several minutes of walking, he heard a voice behind him. "Callum." When he checked over his shoulder, Sophia was there, holding a large, reusable striped grocery bag in her hands. "I thought that was you," she said with a smile.

A mix of dread and—*what is it . . . nostalgia?*—filled his heart. "You on your way back to *La Hacienda?*"

She nodded. "Just picking up some fruit for tomorrow morning's breakfasts."

The bag looked heavy, and Callum held a hand toward her. "Why don't I help you carry that?"

She glanced down at his jeans. "Are you sure? It won't bother your leg?"

His shoulders tensed, and he took the bag from her. Large, ripe papayas, mangoes, and even a guanabana were inside. "It's been years since that was an issue."

"It's been years since we last talked, too." She fell into step beside him. "Or you would even look at me."

Touché. Then again, I invited this by offering to carry your bag.

As time had gone on after their split, he'd thought about what he might say to her. He'd start with why she had held on to being a business partner with his mother. But he knew the answer to that. In some ways, Mum was the only family Sophia had. They'd formed their own unit. A daughter orphaned by both her parents. A mother whose grown children had flown the nest and never come back.

"Your girlfriend seems nice," Sophia said, breaking the silence.

He glanced over at her profile, wondering if it had hurt her to see him with Lydia. *Do I even care?* "Uh . . . yeah. She's great." His fingers dug into the sides of the bag. He'd expected to feel some relief in her believing that he was "attached"—even if it was fake—but he felt nothing.

"And you? Are you seeing anyone?" *There, get this out of the way.*

"No, not right now." Her brows furrowed. "*La Hacienda* keeps me busy. Too busy for much of anything."

"*La Hacienda* or my mother? Let me guess, she gets to lead all the yoga on the beach and sit in the office while watching *novellas*. Mum always loved her soaps. And you get to do everything else?"

She laughed. "Don't be mean. She's a good bookkeeper, too."

He chuckled, and then silence settled between them. Strange how someone he'd known his whole life, who he'd loved and known better than anyone, was also a stranger to him now. They could talk, of course, but the past wouldn't go away. Sophia had been the first girl he'd kissed. The first . . . everything.

And *all of it—an entire lifetime of memories—*overshadowed and obliterated by one: the sight of her in Luca's arms.

Sophia tossed her silky dark hair over her shoulder, seeming to sense the shift in his thoughts. "It's good to have you back here, Callum. I was surprised Quinn booked our place." She frowned as though considering her words. "It gave me hope. That maybe if he's forgiven me, that you might forgive—"

"Quinn hasn't forgiven you because he doesn't know what happened between us. I never told him. I didn't tell anyone except for Isla and my mother." Callum hardened his expression. He didn't want to discuss this, now or ever. He should have known better than to walk with her.

Sophia chewed on her lip. The sea breeze tugged her long skirt. "Thank you for that."

"It wasn't to preserve your dignity. It was for my own," Callum said flatly. Thank God he could see the rooftops to *La Hacienda* from here.

"Cal . . ." Sophia's voice was soft. She stopped, turning toward him with a pleading expression. "I know we've both moved on, but I hate it so much that you still hate me. Is it ever possible you'll stop?"

Cal's eyes narrowed at her. *Fuck. She'll never understand what she did to me.* He shrugged. "About as possible as you unfucking my ex-best friend."

Her face fell. "Right." She grabbed the bag, then continued forward without him.

Callum watched her for a moment, his jaw locked with tension. His headache from the morning was returning. Working had let him forget about it, like it always did. Work. Workouts. Sleep. Fucking. A splash of scotch. The five things that kept him sane.

He checked his watch. Maybe there was still time to squeeze in a run before his body gave out on him for the day. *La Hacienda* wouldn't have a weight room.

He waited until Sophia was out of sight, then made his way back to the hotel. The evening shadows were lengthening as the sun dipped lower over the water. The canopy of trees and foliage were sparkling gold, the water of the swimming pool a deep blue.

Swimming was also an option for working out, but it seemed like a hassle. He'd have to get into the ocean for a decent swim—a hundred laps in the small pool wasn't great. Plus, a few people crowded the pool area, including an old lady giving him a hawk-eyed stare.

As he got closer to the bungalow, he spotted Lydia out front, staring up at the trees while holding an expensive-looking camera. Her brow furrowed in concentration as she scanned the treetops. He tiptoed up next to her. "What are we looking at?"

She startled then, and for a split second, a genuine smile lit her eyes. "There are monkeys," she whispered. She nodded toward her mobile phone, which was set up on a stone wall that separated the foliage from the path near the bungalow. "I'm recording them."

Her smile lit her entire face as one drew closer, hanging from a tree branch. "Do you know what it is?"

The dark face was almost as much of a giveaway as the noise they made.

"That one is a howler. There are white-faced capuchins around here, too, but you got lucky. The howlers rarely come down from the treetops as readily."

She snapped a picture of the monkey that had descended. It watched them with curiosity, dark eyes keenly aware of them. "It's amazing."

Moving with speed, the howler swung closer to them. Lydia snapped a few more pictures, and Callum couldn't help but be intrigued by how different she seemed here. Her hair was loose and over her shoulders—he still couldn't get used to it being dark—and she wore a long sundress that flattered the curves of her fantastic arse.

He blinked away from her figure, noticing, too late, just how close the howler had swung to her phone. "Wait, Lydia—"

Callum darted forward, but it was too late.

The howler extended a hand, scooped up the glowing phone, then scrambled back up the tree as quickly as he'd descended.

"No!" Lydia set the camera down around her neck. "Oh my God. That little son of a bitch just stole my phone."

Callum almost chortled at her words, then grimaced, shading his eyes in the bright light as he scanned the treetops. He couldn't even see where the damned thing had gone, but from the shadows up above, he imagined the howler had gone to join his friends.

Lydia took a helpless step toward the foliage. "H-how do I get my phone back? Can I tempt it back with a banana or something?"

Callum laughed dryly. "I think it's gone for good. If you're lucky, it might drop it eventually and you can use the *Find My Phone* feature to locate it."

"Why are you laughing?" Lydia slugged his bicep with the back of her hand. "This isn't funny." She stomped, looking up at the trees. "Oh my God. What the fuck am I supposed to do without my phone? And my credit cards! My credit cards are in my case."

"Why the hell are your credit cards in your case?"

"It's a wallet-case combo thing. I don't know, it seemed like a good idea at the time." She grimaced at the trees. "Can we shoot them?"

Callum rubbed the back of his neck with a snicker. "I don't know, it might be antithetical to the whole eco-tourism thing going on here."

"Stop laughing at me," she said, stomping her feet again.

"It's a little funny."

Lydia face-palmed and looked at him, chagrined. "No, no, no, it's not. It's only funny to you because . . ." Then she shook her head and let out a helpless chuckle. "Because you're an asshole. Of course you're laughing." She strangely didn't sound angry. "Of all the damn things. A monkey stole my cell phone. This has been the theme of today."

"I've seen monkeys steal passports, rental car keys . . . really, the sky's the limit."

Her eyes widened. "And you didn't tell me?"

"I didn't think it would come down here and take it. Normally, it's the capuchins you have to worry about. The howlers like to keep away."

"Buenas!" Mum greeted, and they both looked up to see her coming down the path. Callum nearly groaned. After the encounter with Sophia, the last thing he wanted was to deal with his mother right now.

"Buenas," Callum said, instead. The Spanish language had come back to him quickly enough despite years of not using it regularly. His family had lived in England until his parents divorced when he was nine. Then Mum had agreed with Dad to allow him to stay with his father during the school year, for the expensive all-boys boarding school in Connecticut. His summers and holidays were usually in Costa Rica, though occasionally he'd gone to England to be with his grandparents.

And that was why, maybe, England had been more of a comfort. His grandparents' house was the only place where he'd continued visiting regularly until he was eighteen and had gone to Oxford. Every other place had been somewhere to sleep but without roots.

Mum stopped a few feet away and smiled broadly at Lydia. "How are you liking the bungalow?"

"The bungalow is great," Lydia said, still squinting at the monkeys. "But a monkey just stole my cell phone."

Mum gasped. "Oh no! I'm so sorry to hear it." She came over and stood next to Lydia, hands on her hips. Mum had maintained her svelte figure over the years, though her short dark hair was significantly grayer than it had been. She joined Lydia in looking up at the shadowy figures above them. "Maybe it will drop it?"

"I'm not sure my phone will survive a drop like that."

"So sad." Mum grimaced. "But I'm sure Callum will share his phone with you." She hesitated then went on, "Anyway, I wanted to invite you to yoga in the morning, Liddy. I thought it would be a nice opportunity to spend time with you and get to know you better."

Shite. He should have expected this.

Deprived of the chance to spend time with Callum, Mum would go for the next best way to needle her way into his life— through his girlfriend.

"Ah . . ." Lydia shifted, taking a step back toward Callum. "Actually, I don't do yoga. I'm . . . not flexible." Lydia's voice was apologetic, but her face guarded.

"Oh, I could teach you," Mum said with a helpful smile. "I have helped many people find their flexibility."

"I-I . . ." Lydia looked from Mum to Callum, almost nervously. "I don't think you could."

"No, I insist," Mum said and reached over and clasped her hand. "I'd like for us to be friends. And I have been a yogi for thirty years. I can really help. And you have such wonderful posture. I'm certain it would take no time to loosen you up."

Poor Lydia. She didn't have a fighting chance against Mum's stubbornness.

"Mum . . ." Callum said in a warning tone. He needed to step in if Mum was going to insist.

"Callum, I really think it would be good for Lydia to spend some time with me."

A slow blush spread to Lydia's cheeks. "I have a fused spine," she said softly. "I've had scoliosis since I was five. Unfortunately, there's no way to loosen that."

Oh.

Callum blinked, trying to keep his surprise at bay.

She'd never said a word about it.

Mum's lips parted, and she gave Lydia an uncertain look as she released her hand. "Oh. Oh, I'm sorry. *Disculpe.* Look at me, just insisting like that. Callum, you should have told me." She gave him a stern look. Mum didn't like embarrassing herself.

"I-I didn't think . . ." Callum tried to collect his thoughts more coherently. "I didn't think it would come up."

Mum nodded. "Bueno, I'll think of something else. And . . . and if you change your mind, yoga is on the beach at sunrise. Have a fun night." She turned and hurried away.

Callum watched her, almost feeling sorry for his mother. But now wasn't the moment to go after her. Lydia's revelation was personal. And regardless of their history, he needed to address it. She clearly hadn't wanted to say anything—Mum had just insisted. And on the plane, when she'd likely been in pain from the condition, she'd chosen not to share.

He chose his words as carefully as he could as he glanced at Lydia. "You all right?"

"I guess." Lydia lifted her camera and started back inside the bungalow.

Then that would be a no.

Callum followed and closed the door behind him. "We don't have to talk about it. But please know I won't share anything about your private business with anyone. You should have told me though. I'm your boss. If I had known you had a physical condition, it might have made a difference in what I expected from—"

"I would hope not." Lydia looked over her shoulder, her expression darkening. She turned and leaned against the door frame that led to the bathroom. "Because I spent a lifetime trying to get away from my 'condition.' Of people hearing scoliosis and thinking less of my abilities." She stood to her full height. "Don't you dare treat me differently, Callum. You go on giving me any assignment you used to. My pain levels and what I can handle are my business."

He raised his chin, ashamed of his words. He'd been trying to be sensitive, but somehow, he'd just been a jerk again. "I'm sorry."

"Ugh." She rolled her eyes and came closer to him, sitting on the edge of the bed again. "This is why I don't tell people. People treat the word disability as though it's a negative and I don't choose that outlook for my condition. I can't bend at the waist and turn in certain directions. And yes, I have pain, but I'm used to it. After my spinal surgery, I got most of my mobility back. But ever since I was a kid, anytime anyone saw me in my back brace or noticed I moved differently, it was nothing but looking at me with a side-eye."

And she probably thinks it makes me think less of her. Hell, it was probably killing her to have told him anything like that.

She massaged her temples, not looking at him. Maybe it was her stressful day, but she seemed to be less in control of her emotions.

Yet—he completely got it. She wouldn't think he understood, but he did.

He let out a slow breath and sat beside her. "Want to go for a run? Blow off some steam?"

She cocked her head to the side. "I don't need a pep talk, Coach."

"I'm serious. When I'm having an awful day, working out is one of the few ways I keep my brain from exploding. And I was planning on going for a run anyway."

She studied his profile. "What are the other two ways?"

"Sex and scotch. But we already eliminated one of those options."

"When did I say I wouldn't drink scotch?"

He guffawed, then caught her smirk. He'd forgotten how quick-witted she could be.

But the implication that sex wouldn't be disagreeable . . . his gaze flickered over her pretty face. *Watch it, Cal.* He'd always found her attractive. Which was why he'd always kept his distance.

"So why are you going for a run? Things imploding at work without you?"

He set his hands back and leaned into his arms. "Well, since we're sharing now . . ." He took a deep breath. "I ran into Sophia on the way back from the café where I was working. Dredged up the past."

"I take it things didn't end well between you?"

"Things ended when she came to stay with me in London after we got engaged. One day I went out to an appointment, and it was unexpectedly canceled. I came back and found her in bed with Luca Harris—who was my best friend at the time."

Lydia's jaw dropped. "Luca—as in from Camden Enterprises?"

"The same."

Then Lydia's eyes widened. "Oh my God." She lay back on the bed and covered her mouth. "Oh my God, no wonder you hated him. And here we all just thought you were an asshole."

He tried not to laugh sardonically as the pieces all fell together for her. Then he shrugged. "I am an arsehole. I wouldn't dare to change your mind on that front."

"I'm so sorry."

He lay back beside her, then turned his face toward hers. They were close to each other, given the size of the bed, but oddly, it didn't feel strange. Maybe because of the day they'd had. "You had nothing to do with it. But if it makes you feel better, when Aiden hired you, he'd told me he was also trans-ferring Luca to my department. The Camdens don't know about what happened with Sophia and Luca—and I didn't want to tell them."

Callum examined the ceiling. "But when Aiden had promoted me to head of the department, he'd also promised me full autonomy with whom I hired. I protested your hiring and stopped Luca's as a result." He drew a breath, then looked at her profile. "It was never personal, Liddy. What you overheard me say about you. But I'm sorry."

She held his gaze, blue eyes blinking with tears. "It wasn't personal *to you*, Callum. To me, it was about as personal as you can get."

Right. Because she's a professional colleague. Not a friend.

Apology not accepted, then.

He sat. "So how about that run? Then we can both come back, pop some melatonin, and go to bed like old people. You can run, can't you? Even the Bionic Woman could do that. If anything, I'd say a little titanium might put you at an advantage over me."

"Yes, I can run. I actually have to work out a lot. It keeps my back stable and keeps the pain away." She cut her eyes at him, then laughed. "All right, fine, you win. But don't get too comfortable there, Coach. You start hanging motivational posters around here, and I'll quit the team. And don't forget, you get to sleep on the floor tonight."

He smiled as she padded off toward the bathroom so they could both change. This day had been nothing short of unusual.

But oddly, their fragile alliance seemed to work.

Better not get too comfortable, Callum. This was Lydia Winnick he was talking about, after all. They had to go back to a normal professional relationship after this. He couldn't let her get too close.

CHAPTER NINE

LIDDY WOKE to the sound of a knock on her door. The howler monkeys were vocal this morning, reminding her she couldn't check the time on her phone. She blinked at the room's brightness, rubbing her eyes. She rolled over on the bed and checked the floor. The comforter Callum had taken to sleep on was neatly folded on the chair, his pillow on top of it.

He appeared to have left already.

She winced.

That can't have been comfortable. The floor was tiled.

She'd tried to encourage him to get a cot, but that would mean going to his mother or ex, which would raise too many questions.

The knock sounded again, and she swung her legs over the side of the bed and sat. "I'm coming," she grunted. She didn't know where her flip-flops were, so she walked barefoot toward the door.

She opened it to find her granny and Kyle standing there. "Up and at 'em," Granny said with a wide smile. Her five-foot-nothing, spry body was swathed in pink Lycra, and her tight white curls were perfectly in place as she strode inside.

"What on earth?" Liddy said. She hadn't seen her brother since Christmas and Granny for over a year, and this was the hello?

"Where's the hot rod?" Granny said, looking around the room.

Kyle face-palmed and came in grudgingly, wincing at Liddy. "I tried to stop her. Told her to give you some privacy."

"Hot rod?"

"You know. Your personal joystick. The one you've been hiding from the whole family." Granny waved a finger in Liddy's face. "I had a whole plan to come stay in this room with you until you showed up all shacked up. Leo's snoring is keeping me up all night."

"You mean Callum?" Liddy gathered her hair into a ponytail, sitting on the bed wearily. *Jet lag is a thing.* She was sure her body thought she should still be asleep.

"No, Leo. You know, you met him at Parkview last time. He's the widower from 7B. Where'd you come up with a dipshit name like Callum?"

"She knows who Leo is, Granny," Kyle said in a voice that sounded extra deep due to it being so early. "She means her boyfriend, who is apparently named Callum."

It's too early for this.

"Oh, then, that's the one. That one's got a nice ass. I saw you two running away from here last night before I could even get over to say hello from my chair at the pool. You Winnick girls sure pick them good-looking, but Quinn's got no ass. Don't tell Elle I said so, though."

They were all used to Granny Winnick's antics, but even this seemed outrageous for her. Liddy shook her head.

"Granny, if you ever call any man my personal joystick again, I'm buying you a bark collar."

"Oh, don't pretend you don't have fun riding—"

"I'm leaving," Kyle said, holding up his hands.

"You and me both," Liddy muttered. "Why are you guys here so early?"

"Surfing lessons. On the beach. I signed us up last night," Granny said with a smile. She looked around the room again. "But I was hoping your man could join us. I'd like to meet the fellow."

"What?" Liddy rubbed her eyes again. *Surfing lessons? I am not doing that.* "I think Callum went to get some work done." Her brain was slogging through Granny's comments like a sheep walking through a bog. Maybe it was the melatonin she'd taken the night before. It helped with jet lag, but she'd never liked the way it made her feel the next morning.

"Work? What the hell is he doing working at this hour?" Granny looked like she was about to pass judgment over Callum—and not a positive one.

Did she even have time to do anything today? If she and Callum were going to track down Sergio, they would need to leave soon, wouldn't they?

"What hour is it, exactly? A monkey stole my cell phone."

"It's five twenty," Kyle groaned. He tilted his head against the door frame, closing his eyes. His hair, which was blond and tousled, looked like the epitome of bedhead. But being Kyle, he looked like he belonged on a surfboard at this hour, too.

Liddy's eyes burned. "Five twenty . . . that's like, what eleven twenty for me?"

"Exactly. You should be wide awake. Come on, get your swimsuit on." Granny started turning lights on in the room.

"Is that what you're wearing? A swimsuit?" The bright pink outfit appeared to be a one-piece.

Granny looked insulted. "It's a wetsuit."

"You look like a *Good & Plenty*." Liddy's gaze flicked to her brother, still wondering how her brother had gotten pulled into this. Of course, Kyle was probably the easiest going of the three Winnick siblings. "Are you seriously doing this?"

Kyle shrugged. "I guess."

"He sure is. And you are, too. I don't want to hear any of that 'oh, but my back, Granny.' I got the same damn issue as you. And I got a bikini to wear later at the beach, so no moping around in a muumuu either."

Liddy threw her a glare. "Thanks, Granny." But then Granny had never—not once—treated Liddy like she was frail. If anything, she had always ragged on Mom and Dad for going too easy on Liddy and letting her wear oversized T-shirts when she'd been in middle and high school.

"You tell those little shits that your back brace is none of their damn business, and you wear whatever the hell you want," Granny had always told her. She'd meant well. But Granny wasn't the one who had to deal with the cruelty of the other kids and the crushing insecurity Liddy had always felt about her body. And while Liddy might have inherited Granny's scoliosis, she hadn't inherited Granny's tendency to be a battle-ax.

Granny and Kyle were still waiting for a response, and Liddy finally sighed. Callum had said Sergio would be somewhere tonight, which hopefully meant they didn't need to leave yet. "I'll get my suit and meet you outside. But I'm not getting on a surfboard."

"The hell you aren't," Granny grunted as she pulled Kyle back out the door.

"It's too freaking early for this," Liddy mumbled to herself as she scanned the room for her suitcase.

Speaking of which, where *was* Callum? He couldn't have left so early to get work done, could he? But, then again, thank goodness he'd packed away his makeshift bed. That would have made for some awkward questions.

Liddy changed as quickly as she could, opting for a navy-blue one-piece that she'd bought because it fully covered the scar on her back. Granny might give her grief about it later, but she couldn't very well say much when she wore that wetsuit.

Ugh, I don't have time for things like this. She needed to find out what her options were for replacing her phone, to begin with. She still needed to talk to Miranda—she'd texted her the day before to ask her not to tell anyone what she'd shared about Callum's fake relationship idea on the car ride. But Miranda hadn't answered, and then Liddy's phone had been stolen.

Maybe I can borrow Rebecca's phone and call Miranda. Rebecca should be here by now.

And she needed to cancel her credit cards, which would again mean borrowing someone's phone. Maybe Callum would help.

Then she needed to check in with Elle and help her find a new caterer and settle any other wedding details that still needed tending to.

She'd just finished changing when she heard the door to the bungalow open again. "I'm coming already," she called through a crack in the bathroom door.

"Would it be terrible of me to say, 'that's what she said' right this second?" Callum answered.

Liddy pushed the door open more widely and mock glared at him. "It would be ironic, given that your last name is Scott and you're my boss."

"Oh, too true." Callum grinned, dripping with sweat. He'd clearly gone for another run, and his shirt was clinging to him in all the right places, showing off the indents of well-formed muscle under the fabric.

Oh, man.

He did have abs. Well-defined ones that rippled under his shirt as he moved.

Liddy moistened her lips, tearing her gaze away. She'd be mortified to be caught staring.

"Have a good night, sleeping beauty? You were out for like eleven hours."

"Let me guess. You woke up at five—London time?"

"Four, actually. But that's about all my shoulder could take of the comfortable bedding." Callum crossed his arms. "I hear you're going surfing."

"My granny signed us up for lessons, apparently. But I'm just planning to go watch."

"And you're going, too, sonny." Granny's voice came loudly from outside.

"Granny, you're going to wake anyone remotely close to us," Liddy said with a hiss.

Callum scanned Lydia's face. "You ever been surfing before?"

She shook her head. "And I have no intention of starting today. The ocean and I are barely friends. I don't really have any desire to tempt it to drown me." *Truthfully, the idea of surfing would be amazing, but it's also terrifying.*

"Samara's a good beach for beginners without experience. There aren't big waves here. You probably won't get any further than learning to catch waves and bellyboard in if you try. Tell the instructor . . ." He trailed off, hesitantly.

"About my back?" she filled in for him, raising a brow. "Yeah, don't worry, I'm not an idiot. I tell the people it makes a difference with. But I'm not going to surf." Then she stepped closer, slinging her beach bag over her shoulder. If Kyle and Granny were still in earshot, she needed to be careful with her wording. "And I'm sorry if I was harsh last night. I think I let everything get to me all at once."

Granny strode into the bungalow and then looked at Callum expectantly. "You going like that?"

"Gran, I doubt Callum needs surfing lessons. He practically grew up on this beach."

Granny lifted her chin at him. "You surfed here before?"

"Mostly at Playa Carrillo, a little south of here. Went to Nosara, Buena Vista, or Marbella more often. The waves are bigger there."

Granny's eyes sparkled. "Perfect. Then you're an expert. You can teach your girlfriend and leave the other instructor to us. Get your suit on. And don't tell me you need to work. You're 'on holiday' or whatever you Brits call it. Need to learn how to relax and get whatever rod out of your ass that causes your lips to stiffen."

What? Granny isn't seriously suggesting that Callum gives me surfing lessons, is she? What would that even involve?

Liddy shook her head. "No, it's fine, Granny. If Callum wants to work—"

"No, I'm game," Callum said, his eyes sparkling with amusement. "But, just so you know, I'm not entirely from the UK."

Would strangling her grandmother be a feasible option? Liddy couldn't think of anything more horrifying than having Callum give her surfing lessons. She moved outside, joining Kyle. "Gran is getting more unhinged by the year."

"I heard that," Granny said, then exited the bungalow. "Or maybe, when you're my age, you'll realize that you wasted far too much precious time and you're running out of it and need to live it up before you're worm food."

Kyle yawned and stretched. "Can we schedule the life lessons for after eight for the rest of this trip?"

"If you're sleeping that good, I may need to come in and share your room," Granny said with a wink.

Kyle put his arm around her shoulder. "Gran, you're not sleeping with me. You brought your 'man meat'—or whatever you call him—so you're stuck with him."

Dear God. Liddy wasn't sure she wanted Callum overhearing Granny's off-color remarks. Had she been on a roll like this around Elle's future in-laws? No wonder Elle was stressed. She could only imagine what the Camdens—who were an earl and countess—would think after hearing Granny.

"You're like a one-woman version of *The Golden Girls,* Gran," Liddy muttered. "And that's not necessarily the compliment you think it is."

Callum joined them a few minutes later, wearing a long-sleeved swim shirt and trunks. He looked more alert than either she or Kyle did, which probably had to do with the fact that he'd been running as opposed to being dragged out of bed.

Liddy fell into step beside him, putting a little distance between them and Granny as they made their way to the beach. "I wanted to ask you . . . if the thing with Sergio is tonight, when do you think we should leave?"

"Probably around noon. It'll take a little under four hours to get there. If we leave soon, we can be there in the afternoon and scope things out. Wait for him to arrive."

"We should probably think up some excuse for leaving for the day. Maybe sightseeing or something? We won't be back until late probably, right?"

"Yeah, I can come up with something. I wouldn't plan on being back here before ten."

The sky over the water was a light shade of pink as they walked onto the beach to where a surfing instructor was already with Granny and Kyle. The instructor introduced himself as Victor, with heavily accented English.

"You going to tell him you already know how to surf?" Liddy whispered to Callum.

Callum gave her a lazy smile. "Not yet. You going to tell him you're not planning on taking the lesson?"

She grimaced and looked toward her eighty-year-old grandmother. If Granny was willing to try it, Liddy's reluctance would just look like cowardice.

"I mean, if we're not actually standing on the boards, I might try," she managed, ignoring how sick it made her feel.

Victor had apparently already picked boards for them. He gave Liddy a smile as he brought one over to her. "*Linda*, let me show you." He knelt in front of her, then fastened the ankle strap on her, his touch light. He held her gaze. "So the board does not float away."

"What does *linda* mean?" Liddy whispered to Callum as Victor moved on to grab Kyle a board.

"Beautiful." Callum rolled his eyes. "He's flirting with you. Notice how he didn't help me or your grandmother put our ankle straps on?"

"Maybe he knows I can't bend over like that." Liddy held a smile back. Why did it make her satisfied to have Callum notice things like another man flirting with her? She'd felt similarly about Sergio's flirtations—and, oddly, that had seemed to bother Callum, too.

But once, in what felt like ages ago, Callum had flirted with her. And she'd had fun flirting with him that day they'd first met, too. He'd made her feel . . . *desirable*. She'd never had anyone pay her a lot of attention growing up. At least not in a positive way.

College had been a breath of fresh air compared to high school for her social life. She'd gotten her spinal fusion right before freshman year, which meant that almost no one knew about her scoliosis. She'd had her first dates, kisses, boyfriends.

But the experience hadn't been entirely positive, either.

After years of insecurity and feeling horrible about her body, every compliment, or if a guy hit on her, had her reeling. She'd gotten her heart broken by more than one jerk that she never should have dated.

And she'd learned the hard way that other women could be just as vicious to each other even when they couldn't find easy prey—a fact that had just about made her want to never try to seek friends again. Maybe that was why Granny had learned to be brash and tough. People didn't mess with you if they didn't see you as soft and vulnerable.

After what seemed like entirely too short of a lesson on what to do in the water, they headed out into the waves. The water was surprisingly warm, despite how early it was, and Callum was right—the waves were mild, at best.

"All right. First, we practice get on the board. No too far, not too low," Victor said, demonstrating by climbing toward the nose of his surfboard, then moving toward the bottom.

Liddy glanced over her shoulder at Callum, who was clearly doing his best not to appear bored. "How do you know if you've gone too far up on the board?"

"Here, I help," Victor said, wading through the waist-deep water toward her. He held out a hand and helped her slide onto the board. "Right here." His hand settled on the small of her back. "*Excelente.* You're a natural."

"Oh, for Christ's sake," Callum muttered, paddling past.

Liddy smirked. It could be the fact that he was supposed to be her boyfriend, but either way, she was enjoying the attention.

Then in true cock fight fashion, Callum waited for one of the larger foamy waves, before popping up on his board and riding it in toward the shore.

It could be his muscular physique. Or maybe the water dripping from him. *But my God, he looks hot doing that.*

Granny's eyes twinkled from a few feet away, where she was struggling to get onto the board. "See, I told you. Nice buns on that one."

Victor, clearly aware that Callum wasn't an inexperienced beginner now, tilted his head. "Oh, you surf?"

"*Un poquito.*" Callum responded with a shrug.

"Perfecto. Come, you can help with la *señora.*" Victor waved Callum over toward Granny.

"Oh, lucky me." Granny grinned.

Kyle waded closer to Liddy. "I'm considering going and taking a nap on the beach. Watching my eighty-year-old grandmother act like a horndog is fun and all, but I'm definitely the fifth wheel around here."

The feel of the cold board against her stomach and torso was surprisingly freeing as Liddy paddled near Kyle. "I'm oddly enjoying this more than I thought I would," she confessed, watching as Victor and Callum struck up a conversation in Spanish—who knew about what. Callum didn't entirely seem friendly, but Victor was smiling.

Kyle climbed onto his own board. She wouldn't be surprised if Kyle turned out to be naturally gifted at this—he'd played sports and been athletic his whole life. That's how it had always been in their family. Elle was the artist, Liddy, the overachieving bookworm, Kyle, the athlete. "So this Callum guy . . . isn't he Quinn's friend that you hated?" Kyle asked in a low voice.

Liddy gritted her teeth. She couldn't lie to Kyle. They'd been close all their lives. Told each other everything. Even though Liddy considered Elle her best friend, in some ways it had taken longer for them to reach that point. Elle had been popular and busy and older. Kyle was always there for her, and they'd played together from infancy, since he was only a year younger. Somehow, he seemed more mature at twenty-three than other guys she knew that were his age.

The water was so calm that they were both practically just lying on their boards, parallel to the shore. Callum was helping Granny, while Victor, who seemed intent on supervising, continued to watch over them. Liddy set her forearms on the board and leaned her chin against her arms. "Can I tell you a secret if you swear not to tell anyone?"

Kyle raised a brow. "If you tell me you're pregnant too . . ."

Liddy laughed, wondering just how many people Elle had told her "secret" to. "No, nothing like that. It's just that I was in charge of picking up Elle's wedding dress from Logan in Little-ton, who's been staying at the estate. And then I brought it here to Costa Rica—except it was stolen at the airport."

Kyle's eyes widened. "What?"

Liddy gritted her teeth in a tight, chagrined smile. "It gets worse." She summarized the situation with Callum quickly, finishing as Victor waded back toward them to resume the lesson.

"What happens if you don't get the dress back?" Kyle asked as Victor helped guide them farther out into the water.

"Okay, from here, watch for the wave. When it's about five meters away, you start and paddle toward shore. Ride the wave on your belly," Victor told them, then demonstrated.

She watched Victor, barely paying attention to what he'd instructed.

"I have no idea what happens. But especially after I found out about the baby, I just didn't feel like I could tell Elle."

"No, I get it. She's on edge. Burst into tears when she saw me last night, but Quinn says she's been doing that a lot lately. Hormones or something."

Yeah, exactly. Elle was all over the place emotionally.

"Well, I'm glad I told you," Liddy said, sighing as Victor swam back. "I might need your help covering for me today when I go try to find this guy."

"Whatever you need. I'll help any way I can." Kyle nodded toward Callum. "But I don't like that he's manipulating you. Be careful with that guy, Liddy. I don't trust him."

"You ready to try?" Victor said, paddling over toward Liddy. He stood beside her board. "I'll help. Look back toward the ocean with me. When you need to paddle, I'll tell you go and give you push. Then paddle."

Kyle winked at her as Victor positioned her board perpendicular to the shore. She took a nervous glance back over her shoulder, comforted to have Victor standing there holding her board.

Then a wave started toward them.

Shit, I should have been paying more attention to what Victor said. "Go, go, go!" Victor said, pushing her forward.

Whatever Callum had said about this being a beginner beach, now that she was on top of a board and paddling toward shore with a wave coming toward her, goose bumps rose up her arms. She kept paddling, hoping the board would just glide on top of the water and the wave would carry her to shore the way it had with Callum and Victor, but it seemed to crest behind her.

Liddy gave a horrified glance backward, then ducked her head, jumping off the board as the wave crashed down on top of her.

Water filled her nose and lungs as she tumbled with the wave, sand and shells filling her suit. She blinked, trying to find a sense of direction, vaguely aware of the board yanking at her ankle.

Then she slammed into the shore, the sand digging into her cheek painfully. She came up, coughing, only to feel the wave suck back, dragging more sand and water through her bathing suit and the board pulling her into the sea before another wave crashed over her.

A pair of muscular arms lifted her from the sand, just as deftly releasing the ankle strap. Liddy blinked back the stinging sea water to see Callum holding her against his chest, his arms around her back and under her knees. His dark brows furrowed with concern. "You okay?"

She coughed, still feeling like she was choking, the grit of sand in her teeth. "I'm fine," she managed. Water ran from her nose and she swiped it away. *Oh, I hope Callum didn't see that.*

"If it makes you feel better," Callum said, carrying her onto the sand. "The first time I wiped out, the waves sucked back my board shorts. Left me bare-arsed on the beach. So you're still doing better than I was."

She choked out a laugh. "Are you serious?"

"I never lie." Callum's eyes sparkled with amusement as he set her down. "You know, except about having a girlfriend. And knowing how to surf. And maybe one or two other things."

"So basically you lie all the time."

He handed her a towel, and she wiped her face with it.

"I'm not lying about the surfing thing, though. I was twelve years old and just hitting puberty, too. And the girl I had a crush on was watching. That moment might have haunted my nightmares for a good decade or more."

The girl he had a crush on . . . most likely Sophia. Why hadn't he just named her?

Victor came rushing from the water toward them, carrying her board. "Are you okay, senorita?"

Liddy nodded and squinted toward him with a thumbs-up. "Yeah, I think I'm just going to take a break for a bit."

"Okay. See you soon, *bella*." Victor winked and hurried back to Kyle and Granny.

Callum sat on the beach beside her. "That fellow is laying it on thick, isn't he?"

"Maybe if my boyfriend would step up instead of flirting with my grandmother, he'd lay off," Liddy said with a chuckle.

Callum brushed her cheek with the back of his knuckle. The move was surprisingly gentle and her eyes darted toward his.

Where did that come from?

He pulled his hand back. "You're bleeding a bit, Liddy."

"Yeah, I face-planted into the sand." She sighed, staring into the serene sky. "This is why I don't do this sort of thing. I'm lucky I didn't get really hurt tumbling in the water."

Callum wrapped his arms around his bent knees, clasping his hands. "We all get hurt. Sometimes by just sitting on the sidelines."

She pressed her lips together. Was he implying that she'd missed out on things by never trying? *What does he know?*

She was tempted to tell him off, but a shadow crossed over them. They looked up to see Logan, Quinn's youngest brother, stop beside them.

"Logan." Callum stood and dusted his hands off before offering it to him. "How are you? You get in last night?"

Logan nodded. "Flight was delayed for four hours. We arrived just past midnight. Good to see you, Liddy."

Liddy touched her tingling cheek and smiled up at Logan. She hoped she didn't look as disheveled as she felt, but so be it. "Hi, Logan. Good to see you again so soon."

She didn't normally see the youngest Camden brother, who had just finished his university studies the year before. Like Quinn, he'd chosen not to go into the family business. Unlike Quinn, he often stayed in Littleton, the family estate Quinn had inherited as the eldest, which was why Liddy had needed to get the wedding dress from Logan a few days earlier.

Logan nodded pleasantly at her board. "I wouldn't have taken you for a surfer, Liddy."

"I'm not." She stretched out her legs. "But hopefully that means you didn't witness my crash-landing into the shore."

"I missed that one," Logan said, then shifted. "Erm, Liddy, by any chance, could I trouble you to have a peek at Elle's wedding dress? You still have it, right? My mother asked me if I could bring it to her room for a few minutes. She said she peeked in Elle's room but didn't see it there."

Shit. Of all the people to ask to see the dress.

"Oh." Liddy's heart thudded in her chest. "Oh, uh, do you know why she needs it?"

"I didn't ask," Logan said sheepishly. "But I'll bring it back to you directly."

Ugh. She couldn't just say no, right? But why on earth did Quinn's mom need the dress?

She could tell him she'd already handed it over to Elle, which would make sense, but she didn't want to force Elle into having to fabricate something. "Um. Sure. Let me just finish up here, and then . . . I'll find you?"

"Perfect. I'm in bungalow eight."

Callum frowned as Logan left them. "That's inconvenient. What are we going to do?"

That he'd used the word *we* made her pause. What he meant didn't need to be spelled out.

We're in this together.

She swiped strands of her hair out of her eyes and held his gaze, a warm feeling spreading across her chest. "I'm not sure. Leave sooner rather than later and find Sergio, to begin with? Maybe Kyle will help me come up with some activities that Quinn and his brothers can stay distracted with."

"We can leave right away. We'll get there early, but it'll be fine. And my mum might have some good suggestions to keep the men occupied. I can talk to her."

That he's willing to talk to his mom to help is . . . huge.

She looked at him and a slow smile spread on her face. "We're not becoming friends, right? Because I'm not sure if I could live with myself if that happened."

"Not on your life. We're partners in crime, that's all."

Liddy dragged her fingers through the tangles in her hair again, the sting of salt water still deep in her throat.

The image of Callum lifting her from the water rocked her senses.

She couldn't really be feeling friendly toward him, could she?

That was quick.

Too quick.

"Be careful with that guy. I don't trust him." Kyle's words rang in her ears.

She had a bad habit of not making the best choices in the men she trusted. Just look at what had happened with Sergio.

She wouldn't make that mistake with Callum.

CHAPTER TEN

THE ROADS in Costa Rica had improved massively since the last time Callum had been here, but the general attitude of road and traffic signs being "optional" still seemed to apply to the Ticos on the street. Callum changed gears as a truck roared around him on a curvy two-lane road. Today was not a great day for driving off a cliff.

Liddy had been nervously bouncing her knee in the passenger seat. The raw skin on her cheek was pink, but she'd already collected a slight tan this morning. So had he, for that matter.

"It's going to be fine," Callum said in a calm voice, his eyes shifting back to the road. "We're doing everything we can. Even if Elle finds out about the dress being stolen, she wouldn't be able to ask much more of you."

"I mean, I gave the comfort of my own bedroom up for her," Liddy said with a chuckle. "And maybe my dignity. From now on, everyone I'm close to is going to assume we've slept together."

"Yeah, that would be the *worst*."

"Don't worry, I have a plan. If you ever try to use this against me, I'll just tell everyone you have a small dick."

Callum guffawed at her, raising a brow. "You wouldn't."

She grinned. "Watch me. And, yes, it's a threat." She gave an exaggerated sniffle. "*We would have stayed together, but I just couldn't keep pretending I was satisfied anymore.*"

"You know, I always knew you were truly evil, but this just confirms my suspicions." He shrugged. "Fine. I'll tell everyone you're flatulent in bed."

Her jaw dropped in mock horror. Then she let a puff of air out from her lips with a shrug. "At least mine might be fixable. You're screwed. Except . . . not really, on account of your itty-bitty member."

He nearly choked with laughter. *She's entertaining, that's for damn sure.* "Having met your grandmother now, I know where you get your sense of humor from."

"Oh God, I hope I'm not that bad. She makes *me* blush."

"She's hilarious. Free. I appreciate her enthusiasm and complete lack of filter."

Liddy leaned back in her seat, and the air coming in through the open window tossed some tendrils of hair framing her face. She'd tied it back and set a bandanna on her head to be more comfortable with the windows open. She looked like she belonged in the hippie town they'd just come from. "Granny doesn't know where the line is, often to her detriment. But she also never loses."

"Which you would love." Callum grabbed a bottle of iced tea from the center console, then took a swig. He hesitated, then added, "You're quite a force yourself."

Liddy swung her gaze toward him, and he felt the weight of her stare. After a moment, she said quietly, "You don't have to do that."

He swallowed some more tea. "What's that?"

"Compliment me. We both know you don't mean it." She stretched her shoulders back as though she was having trouble getting comfortable.

He winced. *I have been cold to her for the past couple of years.*

"Just because I haven't patted you on the back doesn't mean I haven't noticed the quality of your work." He frowned and recapped his tea, then set it down. "Then again, I never really thought you needed my compliments. You'd already nabbed an amazing job—one that showed your professionalism—when we first met. You don't need me to tell you what you already know."

She looked away. "Just because I think I do a good job doesn't mean I wouldn't like to hear some affirmation occasionally."

He studied her profile. "That's fair. But if it helps, I rarely give anyone praise for doing the job they were hired to do. Your best efforts are expected."

"True, but that doesn't mean praise won't elevate camaraderie on a team. Right now, the people who work beneath you are more bonded by their dislike for you than anything else."

Wow, she didn't hold back.

Callum blinked slowly, considering her words. "I'm reserved."

"There's a difference between being reserved and being unfriendly. I'm not the most outgoing person on the planet, but even I have friends at work."

I have friends.

Though Mason and Aiden might not really count. He'd known them since he was a child because their fathers had been friends at Oxford.

"We're different, then. I prefer to keep my business and

personal lives entirely separate." *I learned the hard way that was for the best.* Besides, he didn't really care for one of her friends. His disastrous lack of judgment with Miranda Kaster a few nights ago aside, Miranda had also crossed the line of innuendo on more than one occasion—an HR disaster waiting to happen for whatever sorry bastard she might set her sights on next.

"Callum, not that this is any of my business, but what personal life, exactly? The entire office knows you practically sleep at work. You never take vacations. You rarely go out to any group functions, even the annual holiday party. I'm not saying this to make you defensive, but you even worked most of the plane ride down here and then went straight to work after arriving."

Callum ran his hands over the smooth steering wheel, his chest tightening. "You're right, it's none of your business," he said in a low voice.

Liddy's mouth parted with a quick retort, but she closed it again, clearly thinking better of it. With a nod, she shifted her body away from him to look out the window.

He regretted his words almost immediately, but any apology he thought of stung the back of his throat.

What does she know about my life, anyway?

Yet she wasn't entirely wrong.

He'd purposely set up boundaries between his work and personal life. And in his efforts to achieve career success, most of his personal life had gone out the window.

Not that he cared. He wasn't looking for the same things that many people seemed to want. Domesticity. A long-term, committed relationship. Neither had any appeal. And the hours he kept at the office made it so that he was rarely home— even the fiddle leaf fig that Isla had given him to bring "cheer" to his flat had died. He couldn't keep a damn houseplant alive, which was an indictment for his ability to keep any other living creature satisfied for long.

He liked it that way, though. It was simple. Easier.

He enjoyed being the best at what he did. Enjoyed watching his bank balance increase as a result, too. Not that he had anything he wanted to spend that money on. But it was still satisfying.

Finding women to warm his bed had never been a problem, either. He was always clear that he offered nothing more. And when, inevitably, a woman started behaving as though she was special, an exception to that arrangement, he cut things off for good and moved on.

Even that was little more than an annoyance.

Somewhere, over the last few years, he'd started *feeling* less.

But when was the last time I did anything fun?

Surfing this morning had been fun.

Maybe because it was the only thing he'd done in a while that hadn't been a part of his schedule.

Liddy didn't deserve his defensive reaction. *Why am I allowing her to get under my skin?* She had said nothing he didn't already know.

"I didn't mean to snap at you," he said at last.

"We don't have to talk about it."

"Look, Liddy, I'm not . . . particularly good at this. Talking about myself makes me uncomfortable. And you're right, I've been cold to you over the years. I regret that. I think we've made a good team despite that."

"Maybe. But what if you knew I tried to get you fired one time? Because I may as well tell you about that since we're sharing."

Fired? He raised his brows. "Over the comments you overheard me make when we first met?"

She shook her head. "No, that would have involved humiliating myself. I looked into you after I was hired. And I found out you have a criminal record. I don't know how you even got past the background check, but I went to Aiden, and he ordered me not to say anything to anyone else."

"I didn't—" He couldn't argue with the facts. No one had blinked twice at his background at Camden Enterprises because, well, they knew him. But to someone like Liddy, the red flags had been incontrovertible evidence of his ineligibility for his position.

Because it was all bullshit.

And it shouldn't bother him what Liddy thought of him.

Yet it does.

But maybe he could help her understand.

Callum cleared his throat. "When I was eighteen, I moved to England to go to Oxford because my father went there. But what I really wanted to be was a footballer." He tried to block the images out of his head. "After university, I was invited to join a football club, and my chances looked good—until a game when I shattered my leg in two places. It ended any hope I had, put me in the hospital for a while, and meant I went to physiotherapy for years."

Liddy's eyebrows drew together in confusion as though she wasn't sure why he was telling her this.

"Sophia came to stay with me while I was going through this, to help me get on my feet again. My father and his wife lived in the States, my grandparents had all passed away, my sister was in university, and my mum was already running *La Hacienda.* In the middle of all that, I proposed to her." Callum's fingers tightened around the wheel. "She kept me going through that hell. In some ways, she was the only thing I had left in my life. I started working for the Camdens, and it finally appeared that my life might get back on track."

He was silent for a moment, the gut punch of those memories coiling through him. He didn't enjoy thinking or talking about it.

"And then she cheated on you?" Liddy asked. Her wide blue eyes were sympathetic, her voice gentle.

He held her gaze briefly. "Yes. You can imagine, there was —a bit of an argument that followed. And then, once she'd left, I hauled everything that reminded me of her, of my days as a footballer, down to the street and threw it in a bin. Then I lit it all on fire for good measure."

Liddy grimaced. "So the arson and disorderly conduct—"

"I deserved it. I did it. Lost my temper. And in a city like London, when someone sees you dousing a bin with petrol and lighting it on fire in the middle of the night from a flat that's close to their house—after hearing shouts of obscenities—well, it all got blown out of proportion."

"But the Camdens didn't care because they knew about the breakup."

"The Camdens were friends of mine and knew I'd been struggling in the wake of my injury. They didn't know about the breakup. They knew about the loss of football. I never told Quinn or any of them about what happened with Sophia. I was too humiliated by the whole thing."

Liddy chewed on her lip. "If you're trying to make me feel guilty for trying to get you fired—"

"On the contrary. I'm not. The fact is, the Camdens gave me a chance. Maybe I didn't deserve it. I just wanted you to know the other side of the story."

Of course, he wasn't really sure why he wanted her to know. He couldn't redeem himself entirely by telling her. But . . . *maybe she won't think the worst of me.*

The last day felt like a week in some ways. *I don't know why it matters. But it does.*

Liddy wrinkled her nose, then looked back out the window.

She rolled it up a second later, sitting straighter. "Thank you for telling me."

"I know it's not an excuse for what I did. I was able to get out of jail time, but it left a mark on my record. I have to live with people believing I have an inherently violent side. When really, I was broken and tried to burn the memories of what I had lost."

"Bent, not broken."

He gave her a curious look. "What?"

Liddy pulled her thick braid over her shoulder and loosened it. "It's a saying we have in the scoliosis community. We're 'bent, not broken.' You weren't broken, Callum. Just a little bent out of place with what happened. Maybe you turned around and put all that energy into becoming a workaholic bossy pants, but you did it with excellence. You're not broken."

Her kindness hit him deep in his chest, a strange feeling twisting in his lungs.

She's so beautiful. Inside and out.

Why had he refused to see that about her?

"You know, you don't appear to be bent or broken."

One might say you're nearly perfect.

She gave a wan smile. "That's due to a lifetime of painful braces and now titanium rods in my back. I should have gotten the surgery earlier, but it was expensive, and we didn't have a lot of money—plus I was scared. I kept hoping that if I tightened those braces enough, my spine would be straighter, and I could look like everyone else."

"And the braces didn't help?"

She shook her head, then pulled off the bandanna, shaking her hair out. "They helped but not enough. And they were painful. God, I was always in pain. Getting the surgery was the best thing that ever happened to me." Sadness lingered in her eyes.

Something about the way she'd said it made him want to reach for her hand.

His mouth twisted. "I hate that expression. Bent, not broken. It feels like . . . less. And you're not less, Liddy. If anything, I'm learning how much *more* you've been than I even realized."

As the words left his mouth, he shook his head with a smirk. "Sorry. I'm sure that sounded idiotic. It sounded better in my head."

She shared a smile with him. "If you think this is going to soften any revenge plan I may have against you, Callum Scott, you'll have to do better than that." Her wink at the end brought a smile to Callum's face. A quick one, as he couldn't give too much away.

"I'll do my best." But he was charmed. He relaxed back into his seat, feeling strangely confused. Each of their conversations seemed to open a door that couldn't be closed. Like they'd crossed some line of comradeship, and now they couldn't go back.

But do I even want to go back?

Maybe it had been easier to keep his distance. To allow her to believe the worst in him.

Liddy Winnick had become the only new person he'd shared his thoughts with in years. The more he got to know her, the more he wanted to know.

Truthfully, that's terrifying.

CHAPTER ELEVEN

LIDDY STRETCHED outside of the car, looking at the throng of people walking through the street nearby. They'd arrived in Tibás just before eleven and, failing to find a place to park near the church, they'd driven a few streets over and parked near the soccer stadium for Costa Rica's Saprissa team.

There seemed to be some sort of festival, and Liddy nodded toward the vendors lined up on either side of the street. "What's going on there?"

"Farmers' market—called *'la feria.'* I used to go to one like this with my mum when she had a house in Heredia. They do it every Saturday. Most locals will get their produce because it's the freshest and cheapest, but you can also get fish and meat and some dairy products."

"Do we have time to go look?" Liddy asked, peering at some of the local stands. "That sounds fascinating."

Callum checked his watch. "Sure. Considering we're here extra early, thanks to Logan, we have loads of time to spare."

She laughed and slung her backpack over her shoulder. "I like how you use both American and British slang. Makes you sound as mixed up as I feel, having picked up some British phrases."

"Except in this case, I learned English from an Englishman and spent part of my childhood there. Then grew up mostly in Connecticut. But yeah, it was confusing to kids I went to school with. I just sort of picked the words I liked best and used them."

"Where do you consider yourself to be from?" Liddy asked, looking at him curiously. He'd moved to London. Did that mean he liked England the best?

"Nowhere." He shrugged. "Home is a concept for people who have roots. The places I lived were always changing."

That's incredibly sad.

"Ready?" Callum locked the car, slipped the key into his pocket, and then they started toward the farmers' market.

A sweet smell hung in the air, something that Liddy couldn't identify, and she watched the locals with fascination. In some ways, she and Callum blended in with their dark hair, but she was also quickly learning that the locals weren't anything she'd consider stereotypical . . . anything. Except maybe friendly. The locals wore smiles as a feature as she passed them, making eye contact with her in a way she wasn't used to.

The stalls were a mixture of tables and stacked colorful crates with tarps and other awning materials to protect the vendors from the sun. Onions, garlic, and bananas hung from the tops of stalls, produce carefully placed in wooden boxes. Some vendors called out in Spanish.

A vendor walking around with a bag of green coconuts made his way down between the stalls, and Liddy saw him stop, then take a machete out. "Oh, what's that?" Liddy asked Callum.

"It's a pipa—a green coconut. They slice off the top, then you can stick a straw in it and drink the coconut water."

"Can I get one?"

Callum tilted his head toward her, surprise written in his handsome features. His eyes were unreadable, but he gave a slight nod, then went over to the vendor. He returned with a pipa in each hand. "One for me, one for you."

She sipped at hers and made a face. "I thought it would be sweeter."

"Don't like it?" he asked with a laugh.

"It's . . . just coconut water."

"Yeah, I mean, kids like them. I used to beg my mum for them. But they're not spectacular or anything. You want the insider's guide to amazing fruit in Costa Rica?"

That sounds amazing.

He winked. "Come on." He guided her through the crowd, and she scooted closer to him, her hand brushing his ever so slightly. The sensation made goose bumps rise on her skin, her breath catching.

No, no, no . . . I do not want to be sexually attracted to my boss. It would complicate everything.

Yet she didn't move her hand. The featherlight touch was enough for her to want to reach out and intertwine their fingers.

But that would be crazy.

The crowd thinned again, and Callum moved farther away.

She let out a slow, shaky breath. *Stop being ridiculous, Liddy.*

"Okay, these. One of my favorites." Callum stopped at a stall and picked up what appeared to be a spiky, hairy ball, no bigger than the size of a small plum. They were a mix of colors —red, yellow, orange.

"What are they?" She wrinkled her nose at them suspiciously as he held one out.

"They call them *mamónes chinos* here, but I've seen Asian

food markets that carry them and call them rambutan. I don't know if there's an English translation other than that." Callum filled a small plastic bag, then paid for them. "Try one."

Liddy frowned. "Just . . . eat it? Hair and all?"

He grinned. "No, that's not edible. You peel it." He peeled the spiky red portion off, revealing a grape-like white fruit on the inside. "It's got a big seed on the inside, but the surrounding fruit is really sweet." He popped the whole thing in his mouth.

She took another from the bag, then followed his instructions. As the sweet fruit hit her taste buds, she gave him a surprised look. It *was* good. Not too intense, just mild and pleasant. And aptly, sort of like a peeled grape. "Okay, I approve."

"See? I won't lead you astray." He wandered toward another stall. "Now these are not sweet, but they're possibly my favorite thing in all of Costa Rica. They're called *pejibayes*—the peach palm fruit. Ticos eat them with mayonnaise frequently."

They continued a tour of Callum's favorite foods, grabbing guavas, jocotes, cas, granadillas, cut sugar cane, soursop—known as guanabana—enormous papayas, and mangoes that dripped with juice when she bit into them. As the bags of fruit they'd bought weighed down Liddy's backpack, she felt a strange sort of happiness in her.

"Did you know that wandering around and doing stuff like this is my favorite way to get to know a new country? When I moved to England, I bought this guidebook—" She stopped short.

Yeah, he knows about the guidebook. He was there when I got it.

That seemed like a different Callum.

Actually, *no*, the man with her *right now* seemed like the Callum she'd met that day. Like he'd walked out of that bookshop and become someone else. And now he was back, smiling and laughing at her reactions to different foods, watching her with an unnerving fascination.

He held her gaze, then quirked a brow. "I can see you being the type of woman who likes to wander through the flower stalls on Columbia Road or the Borough."

"Guilty." She held her palms up and shrugged. "One time, right after I'd moved, I went to Paris by myself for the weekend and just spent hours by the Bouquinistes of Paris, then drank hot chocolate and ate pastries by the river, just reading. It was heaven."

"That sounds nice." He nodded toward a vendor who had hot peppers displayed. "But Costa Rica is more for the thrill seekers, you know. Or are you going to read a book while going on a canopy tour?"

"Is that supposed to be a dare?" She set her hands on her hips, arms akimbo.

"It's not a dare." He shook his head. "I'm just saying you might have come to the wrong country for midnight strolls with poetry and some hack playing *La Vie en Rose* on a poorly tuned violin."

"Hmm." She narrowed her eyes at him. "And you don't think I can hack it?"

"Can't? No. I've been around you long enough to be firmly convinced that you *can* do anything you choose to do. And the past twenty-four hours have only confirmed that fact. But *won't* is another matter."

Given she'd just spent the past forty minutes trying new foods, his words stung. For whatever reason, she wanted, maybe even needed, Callum to believe she was up to any challenge.

"Oh, you sad, sad, compensating man. We'll see which one of us can take the heat."

She didn't wait for his reaction as she marched up to the pepper vendor. "Qué es mucho spice?"

The vendor furrowed his brow at her. "¿Qué?"

Callum strolled up behind her. "What are you doing?"

She turned and looked over her shoulder at him. "Ask him which one is the spiciest."

"Why?"

"Just do it."

"You know there's no need to go mad here, Winnick. I was just teas—"

"Did you just call me crazy?" Her mouth opened with a laughing grin. "You jackass. Just ask the vendor for the spiciest pepper he has."

He gave her a distrustful look. "Am I going to find this chopped up in my drink later? Because Costa Ricans don't like spicy—"

"Ask!"

Callum's lips twisted in a frown, and he turned and rattled something to the vendor in rapid Spanish.

The vendor's face lit up. With a smile, he reached toward a small section of his cart and pulled out a bag of red peppers, each of them no larger than a dime. "Esté."

"I want two."

"If you're intending for—"

"Two, Callum." She turned toward the vendor and held out two fingers. "Dos."

The man smiled and put two of them in a small resealable bag for her. She paid, then wandered away from the cart with a smile.

Callum followed her. "And what, exactly, are you going to do with those?"

"*We* are going to eat them. You want spice. Fine. You'll get spice from me. But I'm not doing it alone."

"If I had a nickel for every time a woman said that to me . . ." Callum cleared his throat. "But seriously. Can I have *some* say in this? I meant something like . . . white-water rafting. *Not* eating the hottest pepper you can find at the farmers' market."

"Should we get something to drink first?" Lydia turned and scanned the market, looking for anyone selling refreshments.

"I do not agree to this plan."

Something about seeing him squirm egged her on, and she grinned mischievously. "I mean, if you think you can't handle my level of spice . . ."

His eyes locked with hers, and the amusement there told her he might even enjoy their banter. "I definitely can't handle your level of spice."

"That's too bad." She gave him a playful pout. "Because I like things spicy. I wouldn't want you to think I'm looking for anything else."

Oh my God, am I flirting with him?

She was definitely flirting with him.

But it was . . . *fun.*

Oh God, this needs to stop. What am I doing?

He closed his eyes, breaking eye contact, and his firm jaw clamped shut for a second. "All right, fine." He let out a slow breath and stepped away from her. "But I'm getting a beer first."

"You want to go do this in a bar?"

"Nah. It's Costa Rica. You can open carry here. We can grab some beers—if you want one—and then do your spice challenge outside."

Liddy couldn't help but feel a smidge of satisfaction. Finding a vendor selling craft beers didn't take long, and Callum purchased two.

They wandered back toward the car without a place to sit, then stopped on the sidewalk near it. Liddy sat beside him and fished out the peppers as Callum opened the beers. Nerves fluttered in her stomach.

Sure, this isn't exactly what Callum had in mind, but I can be adventurous and impulsive, too, right?

"Ready?" Liddy asked, holding the pepper in her hand.

"No."

She laughed. "Come on, you wuss."

Callum cut his eyes at her, then popped the pepper in his mouth. He chewed, then made a face of horror before spitting it out. "Holy fuck!" He coughed as if he was choking, then quickly guzzled some beer, his eyes wide. "You know what? Seriously, you don't have to do this."

She raised her chin. "If you can do it, I can do it." With a wink, she tossed the pepper into her mouth.

Heat seared across her tongue like fire a few seconds after the first bite.

Oh my God, what the hell?

As the full weight of the spice filled her, regret clawed up her chest. But she didn't want to be weak. Didn't want to prove she couldn't do it.

She swallowed instead, throat burning, and blinked.

What the hell was I thinking?

Then a wave of dizziness hit her.

She turned toward Callum, suddenly unsteady, her mouth and lips burning as though she'd sipped molten lava. "I don't . . . feel . . ."

Then the world spun around her, and she tumbled forward into Callum's arms.

CHAPTER TWELVE

I REALLY NEED *to stop getting into situations like this.*

Callum lifted his head as the curtain to the urgent care clinic room opened, and Liddy stepped out. He'd brought her directly here after she'd passed out, but by then, she'd been rousing back to consciousness.

She was embarrassed, but the doctor reassured him she was fine. Fainting was a rare but potential side effect from eating a pepper with the spice level she'd swallowed.

The doctor was steps behind her. He stopped beside Callum, then dropped his voice and whispered in Spanish, "Warn her that it . . . well, you know, what goes in must come out. Could bother her a bit."

Callum kept his expression blank, his eyes flicking to Liddy. They'd gotten closer over the last day, but she might never look him in the face again if he told her that.

As they left the clinic, Callum held her arm and guided her outside. "How are you feeling?"

"I don't want to talk about it," Liddy said, a trace of humor in her face as she avoided his gaze. "This trip has been a nightmare."

He tried to hold back a laugh. "To be fair, you swallowed the damn pepper. Why not spit it out next time?"

A wan smile crossed her tired face as she lowered her sunglasses over her eyes. "I always swallow."

He almost stopped dead in his tracks, but she kept walking toward the car without looking back.

She's . . . something else.

And he was into it.

I like this woman.

He wasn't sure how they'd gone from polite, professional discussion to sexual innuendo so quickly, but he appreciated this side of her. And not just because she was sexy as hell.

She made him *feel.*

With each moment he was around her, it was as though his heart was thawing in the tropical sun, intoxicatingly and alarmingly.

He helped her into the car, and she muttered a thank you, then he paid the parking attendant and went around to the driver's side. "You all right?" he asked as he sat. She'd leaned her seat back and rested with her forearm covering her eyes.

"I feel like an idiot, but I'm also exhausted. What time is it in London again?"

"Nine at night." They'd lost a couple of hours waiting in the clinic for her to be seen, but Callum had insisted they stay there. Her fainting had concerned him.

"No wonder. And when is this thing that Sergio's supposed to be going to?"

"Not sure." Callum started the car. "He just said it was late. But we should probably go to the church. See what we can find out about any events scheduled for this evening. It's Saturday, so I'm thinking it might be a wedding."

"Don't Catholics have Mass on Saturday nights?"

"Yeah, but . . ." Dread filled the pit of his stomach.

She's right.

Catholics *did* have Mass on Saturday evenings. And he didn't know for sure what time the event Sergio had been invited to was. What had he said? That it was "late?" What did late mean, though? The term was relative.

He typed the address for the church into his Maps app and then left the parking lot for the clinic in a hurry, worry clawing at him. What if he'd completely misinterpreted?

Whatever his fears were, he didn't want to pass them along to Liddy, who had said nothing more. His leg was hurting from driving so much, and he was hungry, but at least he hadn't passed out from eating a pepper.

But all of it would be for nothing if they didn't find Sergio.

They found the church, and Callum pulled into a space at the park across the street. The two enormous front doors to the church were open, the sanctuary visible from the park, but threatening afternoon clouds were taking shape. The weather in the rainy season here, especially in the mountainous valley near San Jose, was predictable—morning sun, afternoon rain. Cool evenings.

As a kid, his friends from school had all talked about how lucky he was that he got to go to paradise in the summer. Little did they know that most of the time it meant being stuck inside playing board games with his sister every afternoon. Or worse yet, visiting relatives with his mum and listening in bored silence as his mum and her cousins or aunts and uncles had coffee.

Boredom was why he'd started playing football. Even in the rain, you could usually find someone willing to play.

Liddy moved more slowly than he liked, but he said

nothing as they crossed the street toward the church. She blinked up at the sky. "Is it supposed to rain?"

"It rains almost every afternoon here in the summer. It's their 'winter.'"

"Did Elle and Quinn know that when they booked the wedding for June?" Liddy asked, a baffled expression on her face.

"Probably not. But Quinn didn't tell me much about what he was thinking until after they had booked the wedding." He led the way into the church and glanced around. In terms of size, it may as well have been a cathedral, with high vaulted ceilings and enormous windows all along each side. Statues and paintings depicted saints and Jesus and Mary, and candles were lit in offering in front of some statues.

He hadn't been in a church like this for a while, but it took him back to his childhood, the twang of guitars playing during the Mass, the pews so packed that people stood in the aisles.

Callum shook off the memory. Few people were in the church now. Some older women knelt in prayer near the front, but that was it.

"Should we sit and wait?" Liddy asked. "We could hide out near the back here so he doesn't see us."

Callum nodded. "Why don't you sit there for now? I'll see if I can find the priest and ask about any events scheduled for today."

She looked relieved at the suggestion. "Sounds good."

He left her in the back of the church and then crept up the side aisle, his footsteps loud in his ears. They'd hedged so much on this one chance. *But what if nothing comes from it?* He couldn't pull a magic trick out of his hat. That he'd overheard anything in the first place had been an astronomical coincidence. And even if they found Sergio, it's not as if he'd have the dress with him. It would be a miracle if they could even get him to tell them what he had done with the dress.

His shoulders bunched with tension as he walked behind the sanctuary.

He didn't see anyone.

His phone buzzed in his pocket, and he pulled it out to take a glance. Isla was calling.

He picked up, taking a subconscious step closer to a wall. "Hello?"

"Don't hello me, Cal. You've been impossible to get in touch with, and Mum is completely freaking out about the fact that you showed up *with a girlfriend*—which, by the way, when were you going to tell me about her? How serious is this? Mum said something about Quinn's fiancée's sister. The one you work with. I didn't even know you got on with her. What is going on?"

Callum smiled. His sister was always one to leap to conclusions, but a conversation with her usually was about ten percent him talking to ninety percent listening. He checked his phone log. "I don't see any missed calls or texts from you."

"Well, check WhatsApp. That's what I was using."

Right. He'd forgotten to check it.

He had a string of missed messages from her.

"Look, it's not the best time to talk."

"You're not in the middle of sex, are you? Oh God, if she's giving you head while we're talking, I might—"

"No. I'm in church." Which made her comments even more appalling. The visual she'd conjured wasn't what he needed to be thinking about either. He glanced back at the sanctuary, slightly worried that a lightning bolt might still strike him.

"In church? That's a terrible place to have sex."

He choked out a laugh. "Mum would kill you if she heard you."

"Fortunately for me, I know you won't tell her. Why are you in church?"

"Long story, *little island*. But I'll call you later. But yes, she's the one I work with, but she's not really my girlfriend. In fact, if you'd asked her twenty-four hours ago, she probably would have told you I hated her. I don't have time to get into it now, though."

"That's a terrible cliffhanger to leave me on, Cal. You'd better call me soon."

Callum hung up, his head spinning slightly. Talking to Isla always had that effect. She was effervescent and warm, outgoing and fun—totally his opposite.

A priest was in the sacristy, and he lifted his head sharply as Callum approached. "Buenas."

"Buenas," Callum responded. "Estoy tratando de averiguar si hay una boda aquí hoy en la noche." *I'm trying to find out if there's a wedding here tonight.*

The priest frowned and shook his head. "No, not tonight," he answered in Spanish.

The tightly corded muscles in Callum's shoulders seemed to swell. He continued in Spanish, "Oh, I thought there was. No, um—baptisms? First communions?"

"I did a baptism about an hour ago, but that's it," the priest said, then gave him a curious look. "Why?"

Callum scrambled for a reason. "I'm supposed to meet a friend here to . . . take some pictures. I wanted to make sure we wouldn't be in the way, that's all. Thank you."

He left just as quickly as he'd come, defeat burning acid in his throat.

A baptism.

Was that what Sergio had been invited to?

If so, they had missed it—and him. While Liddy had been in the clinic.

Shite. She's going to be so upset. With herself or with me.

Either way, it's not good.

He rubbed the back of his neck as he walked toward her. She didn't deserve this. Even if she'd made a mistake by trusting Sergio, she was clearly a wonderful sister, and had been doing everything she could to make it up to Elle since then. All without credit, too, because Elle wouldn't ever know the trouble she'd gone to for her.

I never should have bribed her.

She lifted her head, hope in her eyes as he approached, and the acid burning in him brimmed.

I don't want to let her down.

Which, in itself, is such a foreign feeling.

This is Lydia Winnick—one of my staff.

He stopped where she was sitting and set his hand on the back of the pew in front of her. Releasing a slow breath, he raised his chin.

"There's no wedding. Apparently, there was a baptism a bit ago, but it's obviously over."

Liddy's face fell. She rose from her seat, her eyes misting, and then nodded. "Thanks for trying."

Then she slipped past him and hurried out of the church.

Callum's hands balled into fists.

And that was that.

Any hope of getting the dress back was gone, and even though she had to help him for the rest of the trip, she still had to tell Elle the dress was lost. As time went on, she'd probably hate him for putting her in that position, and then any tenuous truce they'd made would be over.

Not that I blame her.

Callum turned and looked over his shoulder back toward

the altar. On the ceiling above, a lamb holding a cross with a flag was painted into a dome.

He closed his eyes for a second, his jaw clenched. *Please.*

Shaking his head, he almost laughed at himself. *Why does this even matter to me?*

He turned to go, and his foot slid back on a paper on the floor. Bending down to pick it up, he scanned it. Not just a paper, an invitation.

An invitation for a baptism.

Callum's heart rate ticked up a notch as he scanned the invitation.

Outside, the wind was stirring, and he waited as cars and buses crossed the street, scanning the park for Liddy.

She was by the car, arms crossed, defeat written on her face.

Crossing the street, he hurried toward her. She wrinkled her nose as he got closer. "Why do you look happy?"

"Because." He lifted the invitation. "Because I not only have the name of the people who were having the baptism, I know where they're holding a party for it. At the church salon, a couple of blocks from here."

Liddy scanned his face, light filling her eyes. A smattering of rain didn't seem to dampen her joy, and she stepped closer to him. "Are you saying there's a chance we still might find him?"

He nodded. "But we should go over there right away."

Liddy squealed, then threw her arms around his neck.

She probably had only intended it to be a quick, celebratory embrace, but as her body collided with his, his arm curled around her waist, and he hugged her back.

The rain started in earnest then, but neither of them let go. Liddy's face tucked in against his neck, the soft butterfly touch of her lips grazing his collarbone.

Callum closed his eyes, nestling his cheek against the top of her head. Her hair smelled like coconut shampoo, and her body curved against his perfectly. His heart pounded, his pulse in his ears as he ignored the raindrops that wet the back of his shirt, collecting in his hair.

Holding her feels . . . right.

But she pulled away. "We should probably get out of the rain," she said with a sheepish smile.

He nodded and unlocked the door. She slipped inside and into the car, and he paused as he closed her door, raising his face to the sky as the rain trickled down his face. Between Isla's mention of giving head and having Liddy's arms around him, he needed a cold shower.

But this isn't quite what I meant.

CHAPTER THIRTEEN

Liddy shivered in the car, waiting for Callum to come back outside from the church salon.

He'd gone in by himself for two reasons. He was the only one who could speak Spanish and, this way, Liddy could watch the door in case Sergio somehow spotted Callum before Callum saw him.

Not that she wanted to confront the creep herself.

Nervous energy made her want to bounce her legs, but she knew she was still reeling from the effects of that hug. That hadn't been like the kiss he'd given her to pretend they were dating. They didn't have to fake anything here.

And what I felt was the furthest thing from fake imaginable.

She'd wanted to kiss him. *So badly.*

She was probably just out of it. And tired. Jet lag was wearing at her again, and outside of the fruit they'd bought at the market this morning, she hadn't eaten. She still had fruit in her backpack, in fact, but she was craving something more.

I'm hangry. I have to be. Why else would I be thinking I might be feeling something for Callum?

She wished she had her cell phone. She really, really needed to talk to Elle. Hell, she wished someone other than Kyle knew about this mess she was in. Kyle and Liddy did *not* talk about relationships or sex, except superficially. That was what her big sister was for.

Kyle had told her to be careful, and he was right. If *anyone* had told her forty-eight hours ago that she would wander around the countryside of Costa Rica with Callum, sharing some of her deepest and most personal secrets, she would have laughed and bet good money that it wouldn't happen.

This wasn't a stranger she was talking about—it was her boss. If anyone even suspected she'd been flirting with him, she would lose the respect of some of her coworkers. Last year, an intern had started with the company—a gorgeous, busty blonde named Amanda who spent a few weeks working closely under Callum.

When the rumor had started that she was sleeping with Callum, she became the girl who was "shagging her way to the top" and a pariah.

Amanda had quit a week later.

And while these were all things she *should have* considered before she'd accepted Callum's ludicrous proposal, she was only thinking about them now because she'd felt something when he'd touched her.

The door to the church salon opened, and Liddy straightened, her hand inching closer to the door handle.

Callum came out, a plate in one hand, punch cup in the other.

She gave him a quizzical look as he climbed inside the car. A couple of pastries were on the plate, as well as a slice of cake.

"You were . . . eating?" *What the what?*

"It's a . . . Latina thing. Short story is, here's some food if you want it. The cake is amazing. The pastries are meat empanadas—sort of like a Cornish pastry." He set the cup in the cupholder. "And this is Coke."

She examined them and then took one. "It's a good thing I've lived in London for the past couple of years because savory pies are so not an American thing." She took a bite, not even caring about how good it was, her hunger overtaking her. Though, to be fair, it was *fantastic*. "Okay, tell me about Sergio."

Callum started the car. "He's not there."

The food sank to her stomach like a rock. "What?"

Callum set his hand on the shifter, looking over his shoulder as he backed away from the curb. "But I know where he's heading."

She dropped her chin. "You might have started with that."

"I might have," he said with a ghost of a smile on his lips. "But it would have made my success less drawn out."

She shook her head, slugging his arm. Then she returned to the food. "How on earth did you find that out?"

Callum shrugged. "I just showed up, pretended I belonged there. Went up to a bloke about our age and talked for a while. I'm certain this bloke kept hoping someone would remind him of my name because he tried to play it off like he remembered me. Eventually, I asked him if he knew if Sergio had come. The party was just big enough that I blended but small enough that my guess that the younger crowd might know each other helped me."

"So he knew him?" Liddy tried not to think about how nauseating doing what Callum had done was to her. If the roles had been reversed, she would have probably frozen at the doorway and learned nothing.

Callum nodded and pulled out onto the street. "He said Sergio had already left. That he's taking a tour up to Arenal for the next couple of days and had to cut out early from the party."

"Wait—what? He really is a tour guide? What else did you find out?"

"Not much. I didn't want to seem overly suspicious, though it occurred to me at one point that maybe a blunt approach might be more effective. But if I had tried that and it backfired, I wouldn't have found out anything."

"But . . ." She didn't want to seem ungrateful.

But that's not a lot to go on.

They knew he was going to the Arenal Volcano—which was a large area, according to the guidebooks she'd looked at. Who knew where he would be? Searching for him would be like looking for a needle in a haystack. And Sergio *definitely* wouldn't have the wedding dress *with* him if he was guiding a tour. So even if they found him, it might still be days before they could get the dress back—if they were lucky.

"How are we going to find him?" she finally asked, her excitement level waning.

"I have no idea." Callum rubbed his eyes, his face appearing drawn. *He's probably just as tired as I am.* "But it's something."

Liddy finished the rest of the empanada in silence, her stomach churning. Something. Next to nothing. "So are we going to Arenal?"

Callum frowned at her. "No, I thought we'd go back to the hotel. Figure out our next steps and get some sleep." He cleared his throat. "If Sergio is taking a tour group to Arenal today, he's probably going to be there for at least a good portion of tomorrow, if not more. It's about three hours from here on a winding, mountainous road that takes tour buses forever. Any tour leaving tonight would get there past sunset, so I doubt they'd leave the area again right away."

"And how many tours do you think go out there daily?"

"Dozens," he answered soberly.

"Callum, the *only* thing we have on our side right now is time. How long does it take to get from the beach back to Arenal?"

"Probably three or four hours."

"Right. So if we leave tomorrow morning, we might come in a day late and a dollar short again. We should go there tonight. In the meantime, if you'll lend me your phone, I'll start googling the name Sergio and tour guides and Costa Rica and see what I can find."

Callum turned his head slowly toward her, then pulled back toward another curb. "Are you mad?"

Oh, I should have expected this.

"What, are you dying to get back to your comfortable floor?"

"No. But I am—" Callum ran his fingers through his hair. "I'm tired, Liddy. It's been a lot the past couple of days. We don't have a plan or a place to stay in La Fortuna—that's the town where Arenal is located. If we drive straight through, we'll be there by like eight. I don't have my laptop or my mobile phone charger, and I need to get some work done—which I already told you. We have no clothes or even toothbrushes. We can't keep going like this without some plan."

"And we can't just afford to lose whatever we gained by coming here today—which isn't really that much."

Crap. I didn't mean to sound like such a bitch.

Callum frowned. "Not much is still better than nothing."

"Look, I'm sorry. You're right. You're tired, and so am I. It's been a long day. I haven't eaten that much except fruit and empanadas and this cake." She took a bite, then her eyes widened. *God, that's incredible.* "What the hell do they put in these cakes? Crack? That's insanely good."

"I told you." He smirked.

"But seriously, Callum, I'm not trying to be ungrateful. I just . . . don't want to give up now. I know it's nuts. And, honestly, I know you don't do 'nuts.' I don't really do nuts. But somehow, it's been working for us the last two days. So maybe we should keep going and see where this takes us."

Strangely, even though she'd been talking about the situation with Sergio and the dress, she couldn't help but feel an energized subtext to her own words.

Let's see where this goes between us.

Callum gave her a grudging look. "Fine. But I'm stopping somewhere for a proper meal at some point." He dug out his phone and unlocked it, then held it out to her. "Don't use all the battery. We're already down to one phone between the two of us, and we need my GPS."

Liddy had already opened the browser. *Thank God.*

She hadn't realized how much she missed being plugged in until she'd been forced to go without. "If it's all right, I'm going to call Elle real quick. Tell her we won't be back tonight."

"Sure, but I don't have Elle's phone number stored in my contacts."

Her thumb froze over the touchpad. *Dammit.*

Callum raised a brow. "You don't know your own sister's phone number?"

"Does anyone memorize numbers anymore?" She scowled.

"I know my sister's."

"I doubt your sister had to change her phone number on account of being internationally famous," Liddy shot back. "What about Quinn?"

"He's in there somewhere."

Liddy typed in her brother-in-law's name and then dialed. He answered after the first ring. "Cal, where are you?"

"Actually, it's Liddy. I lost my phone yesterday, so I'm borrowing his. Is Elle around?"

"No, but she's been looking for you. Your mother has been, too. Kyle said you had some sort of trip planned today. A couple's horse-riding adventure?"

"Yeah . . ." Liddy darted a glance at Callum. She hated to lie to Quinn. He was one of the sweetest guys she'd met. But she couldn't start telling *everyone* the truth, no matter how much she trusted them. "It's been great. But we've zipped on over to see Arenal Volcano, and hopefully, we'll be back sometime tomorrow. I just wanted to let you guys know."

"That sounds fun. Erhm—just . . . be careful, of course. And we'll see you when you get back."

Is Quinn upset?

He said nothing, and she didn't want to ask.

Liddy had promised to run interference for Elle, after all. *Help her find a caterer. Shit.* But Taryn and Hunter should be there by now. They would help.

She didn't want to dwell on it, but guilt pooled in her throat regardless.

She quickly googled the most reasonable search she could come up with: "Sergio guide Costa Rican tours Arenal." As the search came up, Callum pulled the car over again.

"What is it now?"

"A pulperia. I'm going to grab some water bottles for the road, maybe some snacks, and some toothbrushes and toothpaste while I'm at it. Want anything else?"

She shook her head. "I'm good."

He was gone a moment later, and she watched as he crossed the street and went up to the window on the side of a building. Unlike the other convenience store, this one didn't have an obvious entrance, and he started talking to a lady at the window instead. The rain continued, and Callum ducked closer to the building to stay out of a stream of rainwater from the roof.

She glanced back at the search results.

Sergio is more common of a name than I realized. She even found a Costa Rican tour company titled after some guy named Sergio, but it wasn't the one she was looking for.

She rubbed her eyes, a wave of tiredness hitting her. Was she being too demanding?

A notification popped in from the top of the screen.

Isla: *All right, I've given you enough time to call me back. What the hell is going on?*

Liddy pushed the notification away, trying not to snoop, and went back to the browser. Another one dinged almost immediately.

Isla: *If you hate this woman, why are you pretending you're dating?*

This time, Liddy stared at the words, unable to tear her eyes away.

"Hate this woman?" she whispered, her heart giving a throb.

Clearly, Callum had had enough time to tell *her* something. *Including the fact that he hates me.*

Tears stung her eyes, her throat tightening.

Why should this hurt? I would have said the same thing two days ago.

Exactly. Two days ago.

Not today, after they'd been through—

The door to the car squeaked open, and Liddy swiped the notification away, her cheeks burning. Callum sat and slipped a small, red-striped bag into the back seat. He glanced at her as he started the car. "You okay?"

"Yeah—" Liddy swallowed hard, not wanting the tears prickling in her eyes to spill out and give her away. "I'm just . . .

tired, too. Probably not feeling so well on account of that pepper. Maybe you're right. Maybe we should just go back to the hotel."

"After I bought you a toothbrush and everything?" Callum grinned, then let out a slow sigh. "No, you're right. Finding Sergio is important, and this feels like the wiser thing to do. And I *have* earned the damn holiday. Camden Enterprises won't collapse without me. Maybe I need something—or someone—to force me into poking my head above the surface occasionally."

She stared at the browser on his phone, her breath still shallow, trying to recover.

I knew he hated me. This isn't anything new.

She just hadn't known he was so good at pretending.

Or maybe she did. Maybe *that* was what had bothered her all along about Callum. How he could so easily go from charming and flirtatious to cold and indifferent—like the first day she'd met him. She'd never been able to reconcile his two sides. The past two days had made her think that maybe her first impression had been the right one after all, but—no—this was all the confirmation she needed.

He's an exceptional liar when it's convenient.

It's probably what makes him such a cutthroat businessman.

"Fine, whatever you want to do," she whispered. She scrolled mindlessly as one of her tears hit the screen, unable to process the words from the search result.

Callum glanced over again and saw her crying. "Liddy, it's going to be okay. I promise. You know, Google searching might get us further than you expect. We should have probably tried to do that but, to tell you the truth, I wasn't convinced that anything Sergio told you, including his name, was true. And honestly, I doubt he has the dress with him, especially if it's a hiking tour. But . . . we can try."

I have to stop thinking about that text from Isla.

Lydia winced. "God, what if that's true, though? Who knows, you could have walked into that baptism party and asked for Sergio and—just look at these search results. *'Sergio is the BEST.'* There are tons of guys named Sergio, probably."

She held the phone out to him in frustration.

Callum's eyes flicked to the screen and then he did a double take. "Wait a second. Isn't that him?"

Liddy yanked the phone back toward herself. She'd inadvertently hit the "images" results when she'd turned the phone over and . . . *there he is.*

Sergio's handsome face smiled back from a photo, a snapshot taken by some tourist who had posted it to a review site, a parrot on his arm.

Holy shit.

She clicked the review for a company called *Aventuras y Escapes: Adventures and Escapes, Costa Rican Private Tours.*

Her fingers tightened around the phone.

"Oh my gosh." Glee pushed its way through her misery as she looked back at Callum. "I can't believe it. I can't believe it actually worked. Or that he told me so many true things about himself."

Callum threw his head back and laughed. "He's got to be the dumbest thief in history."

"This is unbelievable." She stared at the picture. "What do I do now? We know the name of the company he works for."

"Call them. I'll talk to someone there if they're open and see if we can't get a better idea of the itinerary for the trip Sergio's leading right now. Maybe we can say we missed the tour bus and are trying to catch up or something."

For the first time, this ridiculous plan seemed to be sort of brilliant.

If it had been anyone but Callum, Lydia would have wanted to hug him again.

But it was Callum Scott. A man who was excellent at pretending and lying.

A man who hates you.

Lesson learned: *guard your heart and that way, it won't ever be broken.*

CHAPTER FOURTEEN

As the police officer's blue and red lights clicked off behind them, Callum tried to keep himself from grinding his teeth.

They'd been pulled over for speeding on a mountainous winding road draped in thick fog, with no visible speed limit posted.

The worst part of it was that Callum had been so sure he was going to drive off a cliff that he'd been taking it easy. All the other cars on the road had passed him.

Yet . . .

"Motherfucker. My luck is shite right now," Callum muttered, his temples throbbing.

They'd managed to get away with bribing the officer. So instead of getting a ticket, Callum had forked over any remaining cash he and Liddy had, and now they were on their way. He'd have to withdraw and exchange more when he had a chance, but they were in the middle of god-knows-where right now, and dusk had fallen.

Even their momentary celebration over finding Sergio's

employer had been met with disappointment—the tour office they'd called was closed for the night. Who knew if they would be open on Sunday? But fortunately, there appeared to be an office in La Fortuna, so maybe they could drop in tomorrow.

"Battery on your phone is at ten percent," Liddy said in a soft voice as they started driving again.

Callum reached over and glanced at it. He'd asked in the pulperia where he'd stopped for toothbrushes to see if they had iPhone car chargers, but he'd been out of luck there, too. Now he wished he'd stopped at the *Mas X Menos* grocery store he'd seen while they'd been in Tibás. He might have had a better chance there. The red light of the battery level taunted him.

"Can you put it on airplane mode?" Liddy asked.

He shook his head. "I need the GPS." He pressed the button for the direction list. They were shoddy, at best. He tried to memorize them, keeping one eye on the road, then powered down his phone.

"I feel like we just went back in time or something."

"Travel disasters have a way of humbling you like that."

"You're not kidding. This has been the trip from hell."

Even though she was agreeing with him, something about her tone sounded . . . *off*? She'd been less than enthusiastic since leaving Tibás, especially after calling the tour company had produced nothing.

"You feeling all right?" He didn't want to pry. She'd been in tears when he'd asked before.

Maybe I was too harsh about wanting to go back.

"I'm just hungry. Tired. The cake and empanadas were good, but I need an actual meal."

He scanned the road.

Nothing in sight. Just more mountain road, more fog, an occasional cow, lots and lots of green . . . all quickly fading to darkness.

He wanted to be off this road before dusk dwindled, taking any semblance of light with it. There weren't any guardrails between the narrow road and sheer drop-offs. How locals didn't have more disastrous car accidents, he didn't know. The speeds at which some cars and tour buses passed him made him feel like he was eighty years old, hands death-gripped at nine and three.

"I'm hoping we get to La Fortuna soon. It feels like we should have been there already." The GPS had said they had about a half hour to go before he'd turned it off.

Silence settled between them, feeling heavier like it had when they'd driven from the airport rather than on their more comfortable trip this morning.

He made a few more turns, trying to focus his tired eyes despite the dense fog around them. Was it always this foggy up here? He'd been to Arenal a few times before, but mostly he remembered how carsick the drive had made him.

This wasn't like driving on the coast where he'd spent more time.

"What I wouldn't give for a good curry right now," Liddy said, rolling her shoulders back.

Callum smiled. "Now who sounds English?"

"I think I've more than proven my bravery to try foods from other cultures. And I live in London. There's curry everywhere. I get takeaway to the office at least twice a week. Especially if I'm working after hours."

"So you're the infamous curry feaster. I knew someone was bringing it in."

"Yet you never thought to get up and look to see who it was?"

"What was I supposed to do? Grab a fork and go sniffing? You don't think it'd be strange if I showed up in your office suddenly—for no reason at all—other than to inspect your takeaway?"

"True. But maybe it's better than the opposite where you hole yourself up in *your* office like the wizard of Oz."

"You know, you're not the first person to call me the wiz at work."

She laughed to herself, shaking her head.

"What?"

"Nothing." She giggled again. "It doesn't matter."

"No, seriously, what is it?"

"You know what they say about you, don't you? That the reason Callum Scott has no heart is because he gave it away to the Tin Man."

He grimaced. *No, haven't heard that one.* "What about my brain and courage?"

"Both are debatable."

"Then I'll have to work harder at the lack of heart thing. Make them too scared to question the other ones."

She studied his face. "You don't care what people say about you?"

I care what you say about me.

Where had that thought come from?

"Why should I?" He turned down a road that appeared to be part of the main one.

"That's lucky for you. I sure as hell care what people say about me. Especially at work."

"Maybe you care too much."

"And maybe you care too little." She sounded abrasive.

Maybe we both said more than we needed to. Or not enough.

He snapped his head toward her. "What has caring about what people think of you ever gotten you, Liddy? You're adventurous. You are. I can tell. But you hold back. The same way you do at work when we have meetings and I ask for suggestions. Maybe one of your suggestions might make things better for everyone, but you don't. Whether it's because you don't like me or you like to fit in, you keep your mouth shut."

"You don't know me—"

"And I think I finally know why. Because when you were growing up, people told you that you *couldn't* do things. I don't know who—maybe your parents, your classmates, your doctors. I'm not sure. It sure as hell wasn't your granny, and I can't imagine Elle in that category either. She started a dance school for kids with disabilities, for Christ's sake. That shows how she feels about the matter."

"Callum, stop."

He shook his head. "No, because you know what, you deserve better than what you're letting yourself have. You knew you were smart, so you worked hard and landed an incredible job out of university. Then because you're adventurous and brave, you hopped on a plane and moved to a new country. But you have to stop caring so much about what people think of you. Wouldn't it make you feel better to just tell them to fuck off? For once?"

"I'm more than happy to tell you to fuck off."

Ha. Serves me right.

He'd crossed the goddamn line again. Hell, if the roles were reversed, he'd tell her to fuck off, too. Callum cleared his throat. "I didn't mean—"

"To play armchair psychologist to my life? Really?" Liddy crossed her arms, visibly agitated. "Don't you *dare* bring up anything that I confided in you and use it against me. At least I try with people. You can say all you want about not caring what people think, but that's easy when you won't let anyone get close enough to hurt you. Your ex cheated on you with your best friend, so, of course, the solution is to shut everyone on the planet out."

Anger flared through him. "That's not something—"

"Something you want used against you? Yeah, I get it. Asshole." She shook her head, seething. "You even shut your own mother out, Callum. You shut the world out and then sit high and mighty in your corner saying, 'I don't care what any of them think.'"

Callum gripped the steering wheel tighter. Up ahead, a red sign glowed like a beacon from the fog. *Soda La Libertad*, it read. Thank God, somewhere to eat. He pulled the car into the gravel lot. Only a few other cars were in front of the small, shabby building, but he didn't care. He needed to get out of this car right now.

He turned the car off.

"You even shut your own mother out, Callum."

Shut my mum out? Nothing could be further from the truth.

She tossed me away as if I wasn't her flesh and blood. I mean nothing to her.

"My mum? Do you want to know what she said to me when she found out about Sophia? Do you want to know why I want nothing to do with her, Lydia?"

His heart raced. He'd never told anyone this. Not. A. Fucking. Soul. "I asked her to choose. It was either her or me. Surely, my own mother wouldn't want to betray her only son, right? My mum might have been Sophia's mum's best friend, but she was *my mum*. And she said, 'Callum, how can you ask me to make that choice?' Me. Her son."

He swung the car door open. "She made her choice, Liddy. It just wasn't me."

He slammed the door.

She was out her door a second later. "Callum—"

"Don't. Discussion's over." Callum could see by the expression in her eyes that his truth had affected her. But then she schooled her features and took a deep breath.

"What are we doing here?"

"You said you were hungry. This is a restaurant. A soda, to be exact." He gestured at the sign.

She scanned the exterior of the one-story pink-and-yellow breeze block building. "Are you sure it's safe to eat here?"

He shrugged. "Safe enough. I'd stick to bottled drinks, though."

"That's reassuring." She came up beside him, tension hanging thickly between them.

"It's local. Sodas usually have good food that's cheap. I was mainly suggesting you skip anything that might have unboiled water in it because water can be a source of illness for foreigners."

He glanced back at the car, wishing he'd brought some painkillers for the pain in his leg. That would have been a good thing to buy when he bought toothbrushes.

Although, his physical pain seemed secondary right now. He was more . . . aggrieved. She'd been so combative, and he hated how that conversation in the car had gone.

Though maybe it's good for me to remember what she thinks and believes about me.

He'd been letting himself get too comfortable. A reality check had been necessary.

They went inside and sat at a picnic table, where a middle-aged woman approached with some menus. They both ordered steak sandwiches and Coke, then Callum settled into his seat, scanning the interior.

Lydia was quiet, her gaze fixed downward. He'd tried and failed to comfort her, if she needed comforting at all, and now here they were. But the tension grew so uncomfortable that it almost choked him. "Look," he said after a few minutes of nauseating silence. "I'm sorry. I shouldn't have snapped. Or brought up anything from your personal life. You're right, I don't know you. And I'm sorry."

She rubbed the backs of her arms. "I'm sorry, too."

There. They'd both apologized.

Now why don't I feel any better?

Their food came quickly, and they ate in silence, neither of them trying again to bridge the ever-widening gap between them. Not surprisingly, they finished their food in almost record time, each of them swallowing their sandwiches in about five minutes.

The server brought the check at Callum's request, then he pulled out a credit card and handed it to her. He sighed wearily, sipping his Coke. Coming to La Fortuna had been a terrible idea, and he wished he'd been more adamant about returning to Samara. But hopefully, they could find a place to stay quickly enough.

The server returned a moment later. "Rechazaron la tarjeta."

Card was declined.

What?

Callum blinked at her, trying to understand more clearly. He had funds in his bank. He pulled out another card. "Try this one," he said in Spanish.

The woman nodded and went back to the corner of the room.

She returned a few minutes later. "La tarjeta no pasó." *The card didn't go through.*

Callum stared at her in disbelief.

Then it hit him.

"No, fuck. No." He covered his eyes with his hands.

"What's going on?" Lydia's alarmed voice broke through his racing thoughts.

"I forgot to call the bank—and my credit card companies—and tell them I was traveling internationally. My cards won't process."

How could I have been such an idiot? But he knew how. He'd spent the night before his trip getting sloshed. Even what little packing he'd done had been about twenty minutes before he'd left for the airport.

Lydia's eyes widened. "I don't have any cards on me. Or cash—we gave the cop the last of my cash."

What the hell are we going to do?

Heat crept up his neck as he turned toward the server's awaiting stare. "My cards are frozen because I came from England," he explained in Spanish, his heart beating unusually fast. He pulled out his mobile phone. "Let me just call the credit card company. Or get online. See what I can do."

The woman didn't look amused by his story. She nodded but didn't return to the kitchen. No doubt she was wary that he and Liddy would get up and leave without paying.

Callum turned on his phone. *Relax. It'll be fine.*

His phone turned on, and a sickening six percent now showed on his battery life. How had he dropped battery so fast?

Then he looked for bars of service.

Nothing.

He searched for Wi-Fi.

Nothing.

"Are you getting through?" Liddy's tone was anxious.

"No." Callum shut his phone off again. With his phone searching for service, it would kill whatever remaining battery he had left. He looked up and held Liddy's gaze. "You don't have any money?"

"I was going to exchange more at the airport, but then Elle's dress was taken." Liddy's face had paled.

The server was back, a man with her this time. Sweat broke out on the back of Callum's neck as he explained the situation to them both. "As soon as I can get somewhere with mobile phone service," he finished, "I can get online to my bank and get my cards working again. And then I come back here and pay my bill. I promise."

The man shook his head. "Tienen que dejar los pasaportes." *You have to leave your passports.*

Callum turned toward Liddy, his gut bunching. "He doesn't believe we'll come back. He wants us to leave our passports to be sure."

"Are you fucking kidding me?" Liddy hissed. She gave Callum a stern look. "I am *not* leaving my passport. It's currently my only form of identification."

Callum's mind raced. "Okay. How about I leave my passport, but my girlfriend can keep hers?" he asked the man.

The man considered Callum's words, then nodded. "Pero cerramos a las ocho. Y estámos cerrados mañana." *But we close at eight. And we're closed tomorrow.*

Callum reached into his pocket, then stopped short. "Goddammit." He looked up at Liddy again. "He agreed we could just leave one, but I can't leave mine. I can't drive without it here. We could get stopped again. And we'll probably need it to check into a hotel, too. So unless you can magic up a credit card once I get it going, I'll need my passport."

Liddy's face drained of color. Letting out a defeated sigh, she reached into her bag and pulled out her passport. She slid it across the table to Callum. "I didn't forget to call my credit card company," she said with irritation. "But now that reminds me, I need to cancel mine and haven't had a chance to do it."

"I'm sorry." Callum took her passport and held it out to the man, explaining the situation further. He wrote his name and mobile phone number on a napkin. "We'll be back as soon as possible."

They left the restaurant, and Callum swore. *This couldn't get any worse. What the fuck are we going to do?*

Complicated was an understatement.

One thing's for sure. Liddy will never forgive me.

CHAPTER FIFTEEN

THE CAR SHUDDERED.

Liddy drew in a sharp breath as Callum slowed to a stop on the side of the road.

"What happened?" she asked, sitting straighter. She'd dozed off and now her brain was thick with exhaustion. More civilization was taking shape in the form of random houses on the roads. But nothing that looked like a town yet.

Callum was staring out the windshield, unmoving. "We ran out of petrol."

"What?" She nearly sprang from her seat. "What? How? Why didn't you stop?"

"First of all, because I haven't seen a petrol station. But also, how am I supposed to pay for petrol?"

Oh my God.

How in the hell were they supposed to get to La Fortuna now?

Or a hotel?

Or get back in time to retrieve her passport?

Liddy focused her bleary eyes on Callum. "So are we . . . spending the night in the car?"

"I guess." Callum leaned his seat back and stretched out. "I'm officially out of ideas."

Liddy looked around the cramped space. Her back had been killing her for hours now, but she had said nothing, not wanting to bring up her condition again. "I cannot spend the night in this car."

"Well, what do you propose we do? Abandon the car and walk to La Fortuna? We're having a fucking amazing time, Liddy. I can't think of anything terrible that might happen, like our car being stolen, if we leave our rental on the side of the road."

"All right, all right, don't yell at me." Liddy massaged her temples, trying to think. "Did you check your phone? Maybe you have service now. You might start by seeing how far away we are. Or we could go to one of these houses and see if someone could give one of us a ride to a gas station if we're close."

Callum didn't answer. But a few seconds later, he pulled out his phone and turned it on. He waited a few minutes, then breathed out. "I have five percent battery left."

She let out a shaky sigh. "Please work," she whispered out loud.

A few seconds later, Callum said, "All right, I'm on the bank app. This shouldn't take long."

He couldn't see it in the darkness, but her fingers were shaking.

If this doesn't work, we're so screwed.

"It went through." The relief in Callum's voice was audible as he continued to tap. "GPS says . . ." He sat up then and tugged his seat back up. "We're only a half a kilometer away." He released an incredulous laugh. "It's like two more turns."

"Oh my God. Thank God." She sank her head back. "And a hotel?"

"I'm going to send my sister a message right now. Tell her to book me a room at Tabacón. It's the best-known hotel in this area, so not only will there be signs everywhere if my phone dies, but everyone will know how to get there." Callum clicked through his apps.

Liddy froze as he logged on. She hadn't told him about the notifications she'd ignored. Maybe he'd just think they'd come in while the phone had been off . . .

Callum said nothing as he tapped out a message. Then he shut the phone off again. "Done," he breathed out.

"So now, what do we do?"

"Well, we are in a manual. We can pop it in neutral. If I push this damn thing, will you steer it?"

"All the way to a gas station? For a half a kilometer?"

Callum raised his palms. "Have any better ideas?"

She didn't.

She hadn't driven a car in over a year and never a stick shift, so as she climbed into the driver's seat, a nervous feeling crept up her back. What if they got going too fast—like down a hill or something?

"It's going to be fine, Lid," Callum said, his voice calm as she glanced out the open window. "Put the indicators on. You never know. Maybe someone will stop and help."

She laughed, feeling slap-happy. "Do you think this is just like a terrible dream or something?"

"It probably is for you. Getting stuck with your arsehole boss in a country known as paradise to everyone else while you free-wheel in a dead car after the day from hell? No wonder we almost ripped each other's heads off before we got something to eat."

We sure did. For many reasons.

Liddy was still so deeply angry about what Callum's mom had done. No wonder he was so hostile toward her.

"I asked her to choose. It was either her or me. Surely, my own mother wouldn't want to betray her only son, right? My mum might have been Sophia's mum's best friend, but she was my mum."

Who chooses someone over their own flesh and blood? Their own child? Liddy had only ever seen loving sacrifice in her own family, so it was unfathomable what Callum's mom had done. And Sophia seemed to be okay with that as well. *Cow.* But Callum wouldn't want Liddy to talk about that.

So she focused on slowly steering the car, both fearful and excited. As she came to the first turn, she almost cried. A bright neon sign glowed in the distance. *A gas station.*

"Callum! A gas station. Up ahead." She could hardly contain the rush of emotion swelling within her.

As they drew closer, the legendary Tico helpfulness arrived, too. A group of men from the gas station came over and helped Callum push the damn SUV the rest of the way.

She almost kissed the ground beside the pump.

She smiled, feeling unusually better as Callum climbed back into the car. Maybe it was the promise of a potential hotel waiting not too far away. She didn't even care that there wasn't a chance she'd get her passport back today—or tomorrow, for that matter.

She just wanted a soft bed and a pillow.

THE ROOF of Liddy's mouth was parched as she woke, trying to reorient herself.

She turned on the bed, stretching, and her hand bumped

against Callum's shoulder. She drew it back, startled, then glanced at him.

Oh, yeah.

They'd arrived at the hotel shortly after getting to La Fortuna, both so exhausted that they could barely stand straight. In their possession was one backpack full of fruit, two toothbrushes and toothpaste, a dead cell phone, a couple of his credit cards, and his passport.

When they'd found out the hotel had given them a king-sized bed, she hadn't even bothered to object to Callum sleeping in the bed.

The fact is, he earned it.

And they'd both been asleep within minutes. He'd fallen asleep before her, in fact.

She climbed out of the bed now, feeling dirty and gross in the clothes she'd worn the previous day. Not that she had anything else to change into, but she'd seen a gift shop near the resort lobby, and they had some clothes and bathing suits for sale there. And the bathroom had two fluffy bathrobes.

She went into the bathroom and turned on the shower, hunting for the complimentary soaps and shampoo. Thank God Callum had wanted to book a well-known place. Even though she hadn't minded the rustic charm of *La Hacienda*, a little luxury felt incredible after their day yesterday.

Steam soon billowed over the top of the shower door, and she stepped into the stream of water, relaxing in the heat.

Given the ridiculous situation that had brought them here, drama today seemed inevitable. She'd better get in as much pampering while she could.

She took her time in the shower, even shaving her legs, before stepping out and wrapping herself in a robe. The sheer act of cleansing made her feel more balanced, as though it stripped away some of the awfulness from the day before.

She towel-dried her hair, then combed her fingers through it, leaving it loose and down her back. Unready to get back into her clothes yet, even if it meant Callum seeing her in a robe, she tied the knot on the robe tighter and stepped back into the room.

The scent of freshly made coffee filled the room.

Callum was awake, but he wasn't the first thing she saw.

He'd gotten out of bed and pulled back the curtain to their room, flooding it with light. On the patio that hid behind the curtain, the outdoor world they hadn't bothered to peek at the night before came into view. Arenal, the tall, conical-shaped volcano, graced the sky like a sleeping giant, completely unobstructed from cloud cover.

The sight stole her breath.

She watched the majestic volcano, her heart thudding in her chest. People from all over the world came to see this magma-filled crater, and she'd read in the guidebooks that it was notoriously difficult to see it this time of year.

It hadn't been something she'd come to Costa Rica thinking she'd get the chance to visit because Elle's wedding plans took priority, but here she was—and she'd practically stumbled here by accident.

This is breathtaking.

Movement from the patio caught her attention, and Callum shifted into view beyond the sliding glass door. He'd gone outside with a cup of coffee, and the sight of him made her blink.

He wore an undershirt and boxer briefs—what he'd slept in. She'd been so tired, she hadn't cared. But now she got a good look at him, realizing she hadn't seen him in short sleeves. Every other shirt he'd worn had also been a long-sleeved, lightweight fabric.

He had a half-sleeve of tattoos on his left arm, three-quarters on his right. One was various symbols devoted to different countries: Costa Rica, the US, England. A mix of flags and artwork. The other had what appeared to be some soccer-related symbols. She didn't know too much, but she recognized crests she'd seen her friends wear jerseys for before.

Which made sense. He'd been really into football. Inked it on his body.

Maybe it was why he didn't wear short sleeves, which was a shame.

A body as toned as his deserved to be admired. Taut, well-built muscles on his arms, broad shoulders that boasted of chiseled muscle, then tapered to his waist, and an ass and legs that made it clear he never skipped leg day.

God. He's beautiful.

She bit her lip, feeling a little unsteady.

Admittedly, she had dated little, but there had been the occasional date in college, and those guys had definitely been boys. And in London, the few men she'd gone out with were her age . . . but none looked anything like this.

Callum was *manly* in a way she didn't even know how to verbalize. Nothing about him hinted at physical awkwardness. *He probably knows exactly what to do with those hands.*

She averted her eyes as a flush went through her.

She'd been staring at Callum with a major case of lust for the last minute.

And he appeared to have noticed.

He opened the door and stepped through. "I made coffee if you want some." He nodded toward the in-room coffee maker.

"That would be amazing." *Why am I suddenly self-conscious about being in this robe?*

She went over toward him as he poured the coffee. "Did you sleep well?"

"Like a rock. There's sugar and powdered milk."

Liddy shook her head. "Black is good." She took the cup from him. "Slightly more comfortable than on the floor, huh?"

Callum's lips tipped upward in a smile as he stepped back. "Yeah, just a bit. It made the whole hassle of the day yesterday almost worth it." He tilted his head back toward her backpack, which was open on the table. "Though I hope you don't mind, I stuck some of the fruit into the mini-fridge and had some, too."

"I think I could plow my way through a fruit fest this morning," she said with a smile.

That feels like a lifetime ago somehow. Maybe it's the combination of jet lag and how long yesterday was. Going to the farmers' market had been her favorite part of the day—not that there was really a contest for anything else.

"Can I ask you a question?" Callum said, dropping back and sitting on the edge of the bed.

She sipped the coffee, the warmth of it making her feel instantly at ease. "Sure."

Callum lifted his phone, which was still plugged into an outlet. He'd snagged an iPhone charger from the hotel's lost and found at the front desk. Apparently, phone chargers were high on the list of forgotten items.

"Did you see my sister's texts come in yesterday while you were searching for hits on Sergio? They're time-stamped from around that time."

Liddy froze in place. *Oh crap.*

He'd caught her.

Shit, he's going to think I was snooping. She nodded, wordlessly.

"Why didn't you say something?" he asked flatly.

"Because . . ." Liddy took a deep breath. "Because I already knew you hated me, Callum. We never tried to pretend we liked each other—until maybe yesterday—and it's just too complicated, really. I don't *want* you to pretend you like me. I'd rather just lay things on the table and be honest with each other. Things are going to change between us when we get back to London, I'm sure. There's no way to go through what we've gone through without it changing the dynamic in some ways, but—"

"I don't hate you, Liddy." Callum clasped his hands, leaning forward.

She furrowed her brow. "But—"

"Isla and I haven't discussed what's happened since I arrived." He drew a sharp breath. "Look, she called me yesterday while we were at the church. My mum told her I'd brought a girlfriend—Quinn's sister-in-law—and she was a bit confused. She's my sister and one of the few people I talk to about personal things, so she knows I don't have a girlfriend. I made some offhanded comment about how you'd probably believed I hated you before this trip. But I don't hate you. Especially not . . . after the past couple of days."

Wow.

I can't believe he brought this up.

Yet he seemed sincere. *Honest.*

She sipped her coffee, holding the mug in both her hands, her elbows tight to her sides as though she was protecting her chest with the cup. "So . . . what? You like me now?" She raised one brow.

"Yes, I like you." Callum smirked. "Even though you can be a pain in the arse. We almost ended up sleeping in a broken-down car on the side of the road because of your ideas yesterday."

"That is *not* entirely my fault."

"You should have seen your face last night when I told you I was giving up and going to sleep."

Instead, he pushed the car over a quarter of a mile for me. To get us to a hotel.

When he was already exhausted.

Liddy was amazed at the difference in the man in front of her. He wasn't the jerk she had believed him to be.

"I like you, too, Callum," she admitted, smiling behind her coffee cup. "Maybe against my better judgment. But still, I like you."

"So long as you also haven't fought against your family's expectations and the inferiority of my birth by rank to come to that conclusion." Callum tilted his head to the side, giving her a once-over.

He's teasing me.

And I know that line . . .

"*Pride and Prejudice*," he filled in, since she was clearly struggling.

"Oh! Right." She laughed loudly. "Except in this case, that would make me Darcy."

"Not the worst character in literary history to be compared to. He comes around nicely." Callum stood and winked. "Unlike that Lydia character you seem to dislike so much."

I might swoon, which is ridiculous.

"So I took the time to look up the hours of operation for Adventures and Escapes—the tour company Sergio works for—today. And it looks like they're closed because it's Sunday. But given that he probably got into town late last night like we did, it might be a safe assumption that whatever tour he's guiding will be here all day into tomorrow. Either way, we can't go scouring for that tour in a place as big as this. And even though I agreed to come here, I don't know if I can take another day of craziness."

Callum went over to the clothes he'd thrown over a chair and shook out his pants. "We're stuck here until tomorrow anyway because we have to get your passport back from that soda. Would you be opposed to waiting to resume our search until tomorrow, when we can actually talk to the people at the tour company?"

She considered his words. They'd done so much to get here, but now they were just going to pause?

But why does the idea feel like relief?

Because she'd pushed herself like crazy the past couple of days. She needed a chance to recharge. "So we would . . . what? Just hang out here?"

"The room rental comes with admission to the hot springs area of the resort. And there are restaurants and the town to explore. If you're feeling up to it, we can do something more adventurous during the day and a night hike later. You can still hear the volcano at night even though the lava trails aren't visible like they were when I was a kid. But it's still a fascinating hike."

She chewed her lip. "I feel a little guilty. We're both supposed to be here for Elle and Quinn, and we've sort of run off."

"If Elle knew what you were doing to try to make her wedding go smoothly, there's no way she'd be mad at you. Besides, hadn't they written in one of those many wedding emails that the whole point of going a week before the wedding was for all of us to sightsee?"

True.

And she could use a break from chasing the wedding dress thief. They'd hit a snag in their search for him as it was.

"All right. Let's take the day to explore. But I'm going to need clothes and a bathing suit. I can pay you back if you don't mind lending me the money."

"Sounds good. Not that I'm worried. I know where you work." He cocked a smile at her.

I slept in a bed with my boss last night.

Yeah, no big deal.

And she was spending the day with him, just sightseeing. After they'd admitted to liking each other.

But liking each other wasn't any huge admission. This wasn't grade school where saying *"I like you"* meant you were halfway on your way to being a "couple" and sharing snacks at recess.

"Oh, this is a spa, isn't it? Maybe I could book a massage or something. Or we could get a couple's massage and split the cost."

"You know, if I hadn't been driving for twenty million hours straight, I'd laugh. But that's not sounding so horrible now that you mentioned it."

She smiled, feeling oddly excited.

A day of indulging and pampering would be amazing.

Even if she couldn't quite shrug off the sisterly guilt.

CHAPTER SIXTEEN

"This is so not what I had in mind when I agreed to stay for a day of pampering and relaxation," Liddy said, looking down at the waterfall over the edge of the jungle canyon.

Beside her, Callum wore the same rappelling gear she did. "You'll be fine."

The idea had been Callum's: go do something adventurous and sporty for the first part of the day, then spend the afternoon at the spa like Liddy wanted.

She'd grudgingly agreed, but mostly because he'd done a lot for her the day before.

Now that she was here, she completely regretted it.

She glanced at the carabiner on her rappelling gear's belt. *Is this thing supposed to keep me safe?* The waterfall rappelling company had outfitted them after they'd arrived. Their guide, Carlos, had assured her several times that it was perfectly safe.

"Who's ready to go down?" Carlos asked just then.

There were eight of them, in total, with Carlos and his assistant, José, a spry Costa Rican teenager who'd already shown off his impressive rappelling skills and now waited at the bottom.

"She will," Callum said, giving Liddy a nudge.

"No, no—"

"Perfect, a volunteer." Carlos gave her a wink. "She can test the ropes. Make sure they're not fraying too badly."

Everyone else in the group laughed.

Liddy turned and gave Callum a wide-eyed stare. "This is not making me feel better."

"Aquí, negra." Carlos pulled her over toward him. He tapped the top of her helmet. "You're going to get a little wet, so I hope you don't melt, okay?" Then he helped her get strapped on and into position.

Liddy's hands started shaking in the large orange gloves they'd given her. She looked up at Callum as Carlos brought her closer to the edge of the canyon.

Is this really happening?

She was about to jump from the top of a perfectly lovely waterfall and descend via a rope, hoping it would hold her.

"Callum, I'm going to kill you."

He knelt beside Carlos. "You don't have to do it if you don't want to—"

"I don't want to." She clung to the rope, not breaking eye contact with him.

"But if you just let go and do it, you'll find yourself at the bottom of that waterfall, Liddy. The only thing holding you back is you. Nothing else can stop you."

She nodded, shivering slightly. Her feet were already getting wet in her tennis shoes, as water sluiced down her legs. "Thanks, Coach," she said, a nervous laugh leaving her.

"Okay, here we go," Carlos said. "One, two, three!"

She didn't know quite how he'd gotten her started, but she was on her way down in an instant. Not a free fall. Just . . . a well-paced descent down the side of a waterfall, her feet scraping against the stone every few meters, then going farther.

She focused on the dark rock in front of her. How many times had these tour companies taken people down these ropes and falls? They did it every day.

I'm going to be fine.

She would be better than fine.

I'm rappelling down a waterfall. In the middle of the jungle.

Like she was an explorer or Lara Croft or something.

Maybe it was crazy, but she was doing it.

And she'd never felt more alive.

As she reached the bottom, José reached for the harness at her back and pulled her to safety. He unclipped her with a wink, then helped her step to the side of the rope. She stepped back, her body reeling as she sank into the pool at the bottom of the cascade.

I did it.

She wanted to dance. To jump. To do a victory leap.

Callum was on his way down next, and she laughed as she looked up at him. The harness that went around his thighs up to his waist was making his well-formed backside seem particularly, erhm, *nice*. Granny was right. He had a fantastic ass.

And he looked incredibly hot coming down that rope, even with the goofy helmet on.

How many times had Miranda talked about how hot Callum was? Liddy had thought so at first, of course, but the more she'd been on the receiving end of Callum's coldness, the less attractive he'd seemed.

But now . . .

No wonder women loved firemen and soldiers. More men should come down ropes and poles on a regular basis.

He reached the bottom with a grin and stepped toward her. "See?"

She hadn't intended it, but she threw her arms around his neck as he came closer. He caught her around the waist.

"I can't believe I just did that," she said breathlessly, not caring that they were both wet and their T-shirts clung to their skin.

"I can." His arms were tight around her, holding her close.

Why does this feel so amazing?

Maybe it was the euphoria from just having gone down the canyon, but—*no*. That wouldn't cause her heart to speed up like this. Or for her body to have this reaction, like she wanted to sink her lips against his.

As she pulled back, she fidgeted and tried to calm the bubble of nerves spilling through her. This wasn't like when she rappelled.

This was something different. Intoxicating and full of promise.

The fact that he'd brought up that whole conversation with Isla was . . . not what she'd expected from him. He could have ignored it. Wonder if she'd seen it and let her stew.

But he cared enough to mention it.

He didn't want me to think he hated me.

That has to mean something, doesn't it? Does he feel it, too, or is this just in my head?

The moment ended, and they both watched as the others rappelled down the beautiful waterfall. Then they continued their journey into the mountains. Each time Liddy had to rappel down a canyon, it became easier. Like she was chipping away at a part of herself—*fear, maybe?*—and leaving it at the top of each cascade.

"What has caring about what people think of you ever gotten you, Liddy?" Callum's voice rang through her head. He'd been passionate during their argument. And while she hated that he'd gotten close enough to play armchair therapist and piece

apart the wounds that made her tick, she also couldn't help admitting the truth to his words.

She'd tried so hard, for so long, to project herself as a *strong, confident, independent woman*. And maybe she'd pretended well enough that it was working, but that didn't mean she was daring. She was simply doing a good job with things she *knew* she could do well. She didn't take chances on the things she wasn't sure about.

I've been way too cautious.

But if she was honest, what surprised her most was the fact that Callum was so right. Callum had observed her from a distance all this time. *And has understood me better than perhaps I understand myself.* She'd process that later, though.

They approached the final part of the trip, a long zip line that would lead them back to the place where the tour bus was parked.

As she and Callum got closer to the platform, she looked out at the Costa Rican wilderness that opened up before them beyond the tree line where they stood.

The day was perfect, the crystalline sky without a cloud in sight, the sun shining brightly on the mountainsides. Save for the zip line, she could almost pretend no civilization existed here.

She wished she could stay here forever.

"So Miss Expert Canyoner. You ready to glide down a mountain on nothing but a cable?" Callum jerked his chin toward the woman from their group that had just left the platform on the zip line. She glided down, her feet held out in front of her as she barreled over treetops toward the other side.

Liddy felt pinpricks of excitement. "It looks like a wild ride," she said, then turned toward Carlos. "Can he and I go together?"

"Yes, you can go side by side. Race each other."

She queried Callum with a look. "You want to?"

"Feeling frightened again?" A teasing smile hung on his lips.

She shook her head. "No. I just . . . I don't know. I know I may have protested, but I appreciate you forcing me to do it. It's been one of the best experiences I've ever had. And I want to do this part together."

Callum held her gaze, then he nodded. "But you know—you didn't need me."

She rolled her eyes. "Yeah, I got it, Coach."

He laughed, then balled his hand into a fist and gave her a playful tap on her bicep. "Go get 'em, Slugger."

Liddy shook her head with a laugh as she climbed on the platform and readied herself to ride down the zip line. How could her opinion of Callum be changing so quickly?

She was more than enjoying his company—and in some ways, that scared her more than jumping on a zip line. *Because this version of Callum Scott is addictive. And the speed of this affection is a little terrifying.*

Terrifyingly fast.

The wind rushed her face as they jumped off the platform, the zip line giving a bounce as she started forward.

Then again, maybe fast is just what I need.

CHAPTER SEVENTEEN

WHOEVER INVENTED couple's massages had clearly not gone to one with someone as sexy as Liddy.

Callum tried not to stare as the massage therapist drew back the curtain separating them while they'd both been disrobing.

And while the idea of getting rubbed down by expert hands had been appealing when Liddy had suggested it, he hadn't given thought to the fact that they'd both be naked on beds beside each other. Sure, there were warm sheets, but if he rolled over now, he'd be pitching a tent.

He lifted his head and snuck a glance at her. She was face down, the massage therapist working on her leg, which was bare up to her glutes, the sheets tucked between her legs.

Nope, got to look down again.

Was this what all couple's massages were like for men? Because this wasn't entirely relaxing. Sure, it felt good to have the massage therapist rub away all the kinks in his shoulders, but he wasn't thinking about that.

He was thinking about Liddy. *Naked.*

And he was horny as fuck.

This went far beyond the platonic *"I like you"* from this morning.

Every fucking thought of her now was sexual.

Callum squeezed his eyes shut.

She didn't have to wear an ounce of makeup to be beautiful. When she'd gotten out of the shower in that bathrobe this morning, it'd nearly undone him. He'd been keenly aware of her in the bed during the night. No wonder she hadn't wanted to share a bed with him at *La Hacienda*.

I have to force myself to think about something else, or I'll never be able to leave this massage table.

He tried to zone out, listen to the spa music, and the birds in the surrounding trees. The spa at Tabacón was outdoors, in the middle of the jungle, surrounded by the hot springs the resort was famous for. The constant rush of water nearby made it feel like he was floating in a river near a waterfall.

He took a deep breath, channeling his mother's chants. She'd tried and failed to get both of her children into yoga, though Isla had admitted to him last year that she'd started doing hot yoga occasionally. Sophia, on the other hand, had loved it. Maybe because her mother had loved it, too.

Thoughts of Sophia and his mother did two things. First, thank God, it calmed his raging libido. *Nothing subdues a hard-on than thoughts of your mum and cheating ex.* But it also reminded Callum of the argument he'd had with Liddy the day before.

"You can say all you want about not caring what people think, but that's easy when you won't let anyone get close enough to hurt you."

She wasn't wrong, though.

He had done that.

When was the last time he'd let anyone get close?

He'd put a moratorium on all relationships after his breakup with Sophia five years earlier. He wanted nothing to do with anything like that again. Sure, he'd been young and foolish, thinking that *his girl was different*. And in university, when his mates had been out there enjoying themselves, he'd been saddled by the commitment of a long-term, long-distance girlfriend he'd had since he was a teenager.

What a dumb fuck I was.

Since then, he'd been happy to dodge all attempts at relationships. The beginning stage of attraction, when everything was carnal and lust heightened the experience of sex, was the best part anyway. He had no desire to stick around for anything that went beyond that.

The result was that Liddy was the closest any woman had ever gotten recently.

And she'd seen through him in an instant.

Which was why he needed to be cautious. He couldn't mistake the first connection he'd made with anyone in years as genuine feelings. That would just be foolish.

He blanked his mind eventually, and by the time the massage ended, he'd been able to relax into it. Liddy had booked some sort of waxing package, so she went off with another therapist to a room while he got back into the robe and flip-flops they'd provided him at the check-in to the spa.

He'd grabbed a T-shirt, board shorts, and sweatshirt at the gift shop while Liddy had picked up a dress and a few bikinis. She'd hesitated in front of the racks of swimsuits, but they hadn't carried anything else. Then she'd grabbed a T-shirt. "I'll just use this as a cover-up," she'd said.

Now, as he went back to the changing room and pulled on the board shorts and T-shirt, he could practically visualize her in one of those bikinis. He had no doubt she would look fantastic in them.

Yet she still feels the need to hide.

Her condition hadn't twisted her visibly—whatever treatment she'd received had taken care of her external appearance as best as possible—but it had clearly left her with insecurities. And he hated that for her.

Callum waited for her on a bench just past the entrance to the spa, watching as couples strolled through the adults-only area of the hot springs. This was a romantic getaway, for sure, which was probably why it felt so dangerous. They might have to go back to pretending to be a couple when they got back to Samara, but they weren't one.

And it's all feeling blurred.

After about thirty minutes, Liddy came out of the spa, wearing her T-shirt, her bikini bottoms peeking out past the hem. "You didn't have to wait for me," she said with a smile.

She looked refreshed, her cheeks pink and flushed.

"What else was I going to do? Go down the slide into the pool by myself? Grab a pina colada at the swim-up bar?"

"Oh, that sounds good. We'll have to do that." She glanced through the winding pathways that led to the springs. "But I'm dying to get in the hot springs. What about you?"

"Your wish is my command, my lady."

"Thanks, Coach."

He chuckled. *If anyone else called me Coach like Liddy is doing, I'd probably want to deck them. But it's . . . cute when she does it.* Also worrying that he liked it so much.

They left their few belongings in lockers near the springs, but the T-shirt stayed on. He tugged at it. "You going to get this wet? It might weigh you down a bit."

Liddy squirmed. "I don't feel comfortable without it."

He crossed his arms. "Have you ever worn a bikini?"

She shook her head, biting her lip. *She has to stop doing that. It makes me want to do it.*

"Okay." He fought through his thoughts. "Then why not now? You're somewhere you don't know anyone—except me—and I promise not to look at you if you prefer."

She laughed. "You're going to spend the whole time at the hot springs with me but not look at me?"

He put his palms up. "If that's what it takes for you to be comfortable."

She shook her head, then said, "All right, fine. But I'll be nice. You can't look at me until we get in the water. And I'll walk behind you." She tugged the shirt up. "Turn around."

Dutifully, he turned. *Now what have I gone and promised?*

She disappeared, stashing the shirt in the locker, then returned. "You know. I'm not sure if I trust you," she said from behind. "Why don't you keep your eyes closed until we're in the water?"

"How the hell am I supposed to get to the water?"

Her hand slipped into his. "I'll guide you."

This feels like trouble.

And not because he couldn't see where he was going. But because each time he touched her, he wanted more.

Liddy's hand tightened against his as she tugged him forward. "It's an unobstructed path. You'll be perfectly safe. I'll just lead you over there and get in, and then you can get in after me."

"Question." He really shouldn't ask, but she was making it impossible for him not to wonder, given her worries about being seen in a bikini.

"What?"

"Are you a virgin?"

Her fingertips reflexed, just slightly. "Um . . . no."

"But you don't like anyone to see you naked, right?" He was increasingly aware of her proximity, the softness of her hand against his.

"You'd be amazed at what you can do with the lights off."

"So you've never let any man look at you?" They were closer to the hot springs now. He could feel it from the humidity that hung in the air, the sound of the rushing water drawing ever nearer.

"Callum Scott, these are not the sort of discussions you and I are supposed to have. You know I can turn the tables—like . . . ask you your favorite position. If you like lots of foreplay or just jumping each other—"

"Hot and heavy is infinitely preferable because it usually means foreplay isn't necessary."

Liddy paused mid-step, which caused a break in their hand holding. "Wait, Callum—"

But it was too late. He'd already stepped from the path, straight into the blazing hot water. The temperature would have been tolerable, but he was unprepared for a sudden dousing, and his foot slipped against a rock as he went tumbling into the shallow pool with a splash.

Oh, fuck me.

Callum tried to keep water out of his nose by blowing out, his eyes popping open almost involuntarily. Bubbles surrounded his face as he came back up, dripping.

Liddy watched him, open-mouthed, from the nearby path, a mixture of horror and amusement in her expression. "Are you all right?"

Only a few people were in their vicinity, but he was certain he'd been seen falling into the water like a fool—if by no one else, by Liddy. He sat, knees popping out of the water, as he did a mental check. His hip was a little bruised, but otherwise, nothing felt abnormal. "I think I mostly smashed my dignity."

Liddy laughed, and his gaze focused on her.

She's . . . incredible.

And he absolutely hated anyone who had made her feel otherwise.

She caught his stare and gave him a scolding look as she rushed into the water. "You're not supposed to be looking at me. You promised."

"And you promised to lead me safely. Look where I am." He gestured around him. "A completely inglorious entrance into a bloody hot spring."

As she submerged herself, she scooted past him. Callum reached out and caught her hand. "Let's go this way."

He led her to the deeper part of the pool, then followed the water upstream, climbing over rocks to get farther away from other people.

Maybe it was the fact that they were in the hot springs, or perhaps it was because the resort was supposed to be a romantic getaway for couples, but the setting was idyllic. Public but intimate. They found a small pool that didn't have room for more than the two of them, a cascade of water coming down black rock surrounded by lush green ferns, orange and red parrot flowers, and purple orchids. The beautiful part of Costa Rica he'd largely forgotten.

As they climbed in, they were only inches from each other. *Inches from possibility.* "Come here, you gorgeous woman."

She turned toward him sharply, her eyes widening, and he pulled her closer, spreading her palm flat against his. His thumb stroked the inside of her palm, and she glanced down toward it, a blush spreading on her face. Her luscious lips were pink. Droplets of water dripped from her long, dark hair, cascading over her shoulder.

Electricity seemed to crackle through his fingertips as he touched her.

I want to hold her.

All of her.

Everything he wanted to tell her was suffocating him.

But he had to.

"You are so beautiful, Liddy. And I'm sorry if I'm crossing some boundary by telling you, but I couldn't live with myself if I said nothing. Whoever hurt you enough to make you feel like you had to spend your life hiding . . . I wish I could find every single one of them and punch them in the face. You aren't lacking in any way. You're sexy and hilarious. And, God, any man who sees you and doesn't want to touch every inch of your flawless body is blind."

Liddy slid her arms around his neck, her lips tantalizing close to his as she scooted forward in the water. "Liar," she whispered, her eyes locked with his. "But you've got some lines, Callum Scott. I'll give you that."

Her lips dropped to his with gentle but firm pressure, and his breath caught. His heart thudded faster.

I could lose myself to this woman.

But he didn't care about that right now.

He closed his eyes, his mouth slanting over hers as he returned her kiss.

A sweet, hungry kiss that made him want to mold his body against hers.

Slow down.

But he couldn't. Instead, his hands slipped around the smooth skin of her waist. He barely convinced himself to keep them safely there when she moaned softly, her mouth opening to his. As her tongue darted into his mouth, then collided against his own, he slipped his hands up her back, tangling his fingers into the hair at the nape of her neck.

God, this feels fucking amazing.

Pulling back, he leaned his forehead against hers, releasing hard, panting breaths. "Is this okay?"

His gaze dropped to where her breasts were tantalizingly

close to his chest. Her heart was beating so fast that he could see her pulse on those fucking incredible mounds of flesh as they rose and fell with each breath.

She nodded.

That's all I need to know.

The pool was surprisingly deep, up to their chests. A small ledge by the cascade provided a seat for the two of them, but Callum tugged Liddy and then lifted her onto it. He edged closer and slipped his hands onto her thighs.

A smile crept into the corners of her mouth, and she settled a hand onto the back of his neck as the other dug into his hair, tugging him closer. "More than okay," she said.

Their mouths collided with another kiss, this one hotter and more intense than the first. Callum felt himself losing what fragile grip he still had on rational thought. He wanted to taste her, to feel her breasts against his palms.

He groaned, his heart slamming into his ribs as he tugged her closer so that she could feel the hardness of his cock. Her thighs parted, legs wrapping around his waist as he breathed raggedly against her lips. "Fuck, Liddy. You're making it hard to think straight."

She leaned her head back as his lips trailed down her cheek to her neck. Her lips grazed his earlobe. "Right back at you."

He kissed her neck, pausing on that soft spot where her pulse throbbed just below her jawline.

We won't be able to come back from this.

And I don't care.

But she might care and feel used later if he didn't scale back. Like he'd played her with compliments he didn't mean.

The last couple of days had been confusing enough. Taking anything to another level would only make that worse.

Someone clearing his throat made them break apart, arms still around each other. A worker from the resort was nearby.

"We don't recommend staying in the water longer than fifteen minutes at a time," he said with a friendly wink, then continued on his way.

Callum settled his hands back on her thighs, putting some distance between them as he straightened.

Liddy released a choking laugh. "I guess that's our warning. God, I'm so embarrassed."

He smiled, then reached for her hand. He kissed the back of it, doing everything in his power not to pull her right back into his arms.

I want to fuck her.

But I have to stop.

Instead of kissing her, he breathed out slowly, then hopped up on the ledge beside her. He kissed her shoulder, still holding her hand, then pulled her to rest against his chest. "So maybe coming to Arenal wasn't the worst decision in the world."

She rested her head against his shoulder. "I'd say it's been perfect. You know—except getting here and all."

He chuckled, trying not to think too much about the obstacles they'd gone through to get to La Fortuna.

Obstacles that might still exist when they left the bubble of this place.

But for now, there was no way in hell he would let it ruin what they'd found here. *Connection.*

And that had been something missing in his life.

CHAPTER EIGHTEEN

"ARE two ice cream cones too many?" Liddy asked as she leaned against the glass counter, looking at the flavors displayed.

"Not in my book," Callum said with a shrug. "Life's too short to skip ice cream."

Today *had* been a day of doing whatever she damn well *wanted*. "I'll take both," Liddy said, her fist enclosing over the sample spoons as she turned to meet Callum's awaiting stare.

Callum smiled, then translated her order for the woman working behind the ice cream counter.

She tried not to stare at him as he spoke in Spanish. *He's so sexy.* Something about seeing him talk so effortlessly in another language was incredibly alluring.

And he kissed me.

That tongue had been stroking hers. Those lips had been soft and pliant as they'd ravaged her mouth.

Ravaged. Now I sound like I'm in a regency romance.

But still. It had felt like ravaging. She'd had sex that had been less intimate than those kisses.

And she wanted more. So much more.

He'd backed off after the resort worker had given them that gentle warning, so they'd spent the rest of the time indulging in the offerings of the resort—hanging out in the thermal pools for a while, enjoying the swim-up bar, and spoiling themselves with an incredible dinner at the restaurant. After, they'd walked to La Fortuna to an ice cream shop named POPS that Callum had recalled from childhood as being his favorite.

They finished ordering, and Callum paid while the woman behind the counter handed Liddy two ice cream cones—she'd opted for a sorbet called a *nieve* that was soursop flavored and incredible. And she'd also gotten a flavored bright pink one that was Callum's favorite—*kolita*—which he'd explained was named after a red syrup used to make snow cones.

"I think I've died and gone to ice cream heaven," Liddy said with a grin.

"If heaven is double-fisting ice cream, I'm in." Callum carried his banana split away from the register.

"You and your banana split. You're such an old man. I swear that's what my father orders when he gets ice cream."

"Don't knock it, it's amazing. Also, I'm not the one holding two ice creams like a toddler."

That's true. "I might go back for one more." She grinned, then slowly licked the side of the ice cream cone. "I love ice cream."

He groaned slightly. "That's ridiculously unfair."

She smiled, feeling daring.

This is fun.

Teasing him seductively was quickly becoming her favorite activity.

She'd always been so much more restrained with men, but she'd gotten used to expressing her thoughts with Callum and no longer felt that hesitation.

I really like him, too.

"So you ready for that nighttime hike?"

"A nighttime hunt for tree frogs at the base of a volcano? Who wouldn't be excited?" she said in a teasing voice. Then she grinned. "I have to admit, we probably did everything in the wrong order. Because I'm not sure a night hike will top the rest of the day."

Truthfully, she'd built up more anticipation for what would come *after* the hike anyway—when they'd both go back to the hotel room tonight.

After their kiss at the spa, she couldn't help thinking that tumbling into a bed with him tonight might lead to something.

She wanted to see where it went, but her stomach was a knot of nerves.

More than anything, she wished she could talk to Elle about him. *I need my sister's advice.*

Thoughts of Elle made her gut roil. She'd fully intended to call Quinn all day and give him an update on the change in their plans again—but then she'd held off. If Elle or anyone else wasn't thrilled with her absence, she didn't want to know about it. Not right now. She couldn't go anywhere until she got her passport back anyway.

But even if she couldn't talk to Elle, she needed to talk to *someone.* Miranda or Kyle would both help her figure out her thoughts. But without her phone, she couldn't do either.

"We definitely did it in the wrong order. I think I'm ready for a nap. Or it's jet lag."

She held his gaze. "We could just ditch the nighttime trek and go back to the room."

He raised a brow. "Is that what you want?"

"Yeah, I'm pretty tired." *And way too interested in finding out where this might go to hike at night looking for tree frogs, no matter how cute they are.*

"I'm up for whatever you want to do," Callum said in a tone that gave nothing away.

They finished the ice cream, then headed outside, where dusk had given way to the night. "It's crazy to me," Liddy said as they started toward the car. "All the people who live around here are just totally chill living at the base of a volcano. Maybe I read too much about Pompeii when I was a kid, but that would terrify me."

"Arenal was active when I was younger. At night, especially, you used to get amazing pictures of the lava trails. And honestly, living near volcanoes is just a way of life down here. There are six active ones and several dozen dormant ones. My grandmother used to talk about the year that Irazú in the Central Valley erupted. Said ash fell from the sky for months, ruining crops—but my grandmother focused mainly on the effect it had on her hair and clothes."

Every time Callum spoke about his knowledge of the country—or the food—he got a slightly different expression on his face. The first time, he'd been so pessimistic that Liddy had glossed over it, but the negativity had been disappearing. And in its place seemed to be something else she couldn't quite put her finger on.

"You know, for someone who hasn't visited in years, and who seems a little cynical about the country, you sure know a lot."

The corners of his mouth turned up just slightly. "I'd forgotten how much I knew about Costa Rica. I spent my whole life visiting every summer. Some of that experience was bound to rub off on me."

"Including your love of soccer?" She glanced at him cautiously. He'd brought that part of his life up so quickly, leaving no room for questions, but she couldn't help but wonder about it and who'd he'd been. The idea of Callum as an athlete rather than a businessman was strange. *Of course, he has the body of an athlete instead of a businessman.*

Callum was silent, as though considering what he should say. "The thing abou—"

"Liddy?" a deep male voice called.

What the hell?

Only a few feet away and coming toward them was Sergio.

Liddy's gut dropped, and she stepped back. Callum set a hand across her, blocking her ever so slightly with his body.

Sergio looked from Liddy to Callum, then back again, and smiled excitedly. "Liddy, this is *maravilloso*. I tried to call you for days. But it looks *como si el destino* brought us together again, *verdad?*

"How dare you?" Liddy managed, barely finding her voice. "I've been looking for you! You stole my sister's wedding dress. And now you're, what? Pretending that the last time I saw you it wasn't when I asked you to watch something valuable to me? I-I don't even know how you can stand there—"

"Stole it?" Confusion filled Sergio's face, and he stepped back. "No, no, no. What?"

What?

Is he really going to play it like this?

Revulsion filled her throat.

Callum approached him, and Liddy felt the relief of not only his presence but his stature, too. He was taller than Sergio by several inches and physically intimidating. "Where's the damn dress, Sergio?"

Sergio raised his hands but checked over his shoulder as though looking for an escape. "Let me explain—"

Grabbing him by the shirtfront, Callum backed Sergio against the closest building with force. "Yeah, you better explain. You have no idea what you did to Liddy by taking that dress from her—"

"I didn't take anything!" Sergio's voice was choked. He appealed to Liddy with wide eyes. "I thought airport security would contact you. Get the dress back to you. And I am not the person who was trying to bring marijuana into the country."

Uh . . . what?

Liddy marched up to him. "What are you talking about?"

"The dogs. They came up to me when you were in the bathroom." Sergio breathed heavily, sweat beading on his forehead.

If she wasn't so angry, she'd almost find his reaction comical. He looked terrified. *Not the flirtatious man I met on the plane.*

"Security took me away, held me for hours," he continued. "They found a bag of marijuana in the dress bag."

Blinking at him, Liddy tried to process what he was saying. She set a hand on Callum's forearm, urging him to back off. "I'm not sure I'm understanding—"

Callum's hold on Sergio released somewhat, but not entirely. "He's lying to you, Liddy. Why would he admit the truth now?"

"I'm not lying." Sergio appealed to Liddy with a helpless look. "I tried to call you and make sure you had gotten your dress back since you were gone by the time security released me. It was many, many hours. I left voicemail messages."

"Howler monkeys stole my cell right after I got to the hotel." Liddy stared at him, unblinking. As unbelievable as it sounded . . . *a part of me wants to believe him.* Not just because she had really liked this guy. She was past that now.

But because—why would he approach her here in La Fortuna?

. . . or give me his real name and job?

And something like voicemail messages could be easily

confirmed—if she'd had her phone. She turned toward Callum. "Can I borrow your cell phone?"

"Why?"

"I'm going to call my voicemail. See if he's lying."

Callum gave her a disbelieving look. "You're not seriously buying this load of rubbish, are you?"

She almost smiled to herself. For whatever reason, she loved his British accent right now.

Focus, Liddy.

Getting distracted by how much she liked Callum was not ideal right now. "I think it would be a good idea to check."

Callum backed off from Sergio and pulled his phone out, unlocking it. He kept his gaze firmly fixed on Sergio and handed the phone to her. "Don't even think about going anywhere."

"I'm not," Sergio said, adjusting his collar. "I've done nothing wrong, though."

Liddy's fingertips shook as she dialed her number, noting almost immediately that Callum didn't have her as a contact. *Why would he, though? It's not like he's ever had a reason to text or call me.*

She punched into her voicemail, feeling sick.

Her voicemail was full.

She had messages from Elle. From her mother. Miranda. Rebecca. Two from Kyle.

And three missed messages from Sergio, as well as someone from the airline, letting her know her bag had been found and was at the airport waiting for her to pick it up.

Liddy squeezed her eyes shut, trying to process everything. "Let him go," she said in a nearly breathless whisper to Callum. "He's telling the truth."

Callum's brow furrowed. "What are you saying?"

"The airline called. My bag is at the airport."

"I told you I did not take it."

Callum ignored Sergio and searched her gaze, stepping closer to her. "But . . . you don't smoke, do you?"

Because I'm too much of a Goody Two-shoes, is that it? She shook her head. "No, it's not mine. I have no idea how pot ended up in my bag. I mean, I barely even had the bag. I picked it up from Logan on . . ."

Logan.

Her eyes darted to Callum, and he seemed to reach the same conclusion as her, his eyebrow quirking.

"I'm going to kill Logan," Liddy breathed, massaging her temple.

Logan had stashed pot in the garment bag?

Oh my God.

No wonder he wanted to see the dress.

That little prick.

And if Sergio hadn't been caught with the bag, Liddy would have ended up in security for hours, trying to explain why she was coming into the country with illegal drugs.

"I'm going to call Logan," Callum said, his voice rough as gravel. *He's seriously annoyed.*

As Callum took a step away to call Logan, she turned to Sergio. "I am *so* sorry." She came closer to him, seeing a red mark on his neck from where Callum had shoved him. "So, so sorry. I don't even know how to begin to apologize to you."

Sergio held his hands up. "It's okay, it's okay." He set a hand on her forearm, his light brown eyes searching hers. "Were you here looking for me? You were supposed to be in Samara, no?"

She nearly squirmed. Not only had she caused him to be detained by security, then she'd basically stalked him, and Callum had handled him roughly. "I—"

The corners of his mouth turned up in a smile. "I can't

believe you found me here. That's impressive. And monkeys stole your phone?" He chuckled. "I should have warned you. They will take anything in those areas near the beaches. Sneak into sodas and bars and steal food, too."

How is he not angrier?

"You're not mad at me?" Liddy asked, baffled by his response.

"No, no, of course not. I mean, it was . . . eh, *inconvienente* . . . what happened at the airport, but mostly I was worried because you said it was your sister's expensive wedding dress. Although, did you think I would then take it on a tour with me? That thing weighed more than my overnight pack, Liddy." He laughed at his own joke.

"No, no. I just thought if I found you, maybe I could convince you to give it back. I didn't think you would have it *with you.*"

He smiled. "You thought I might be a nice thief?"

Yes, I stupidly had thought that. Which now seems insane.

His hand slid down her forearm and squeezed hers. "I'm really glad you found me again."

"Yeah, it was Logan," Callum said, coming back to Liddy's side. "He says he'd forgotten he put it there—gave me some nonsense about how he'd picked up the dress from the tailor and then stopped by his friend's for the marijuana and left it in the garment bag."

Liddy's cheeks warmed.

She released Sergio's hand, her palm breaking out in a clammy sweat. *This is so awkward.* Avoiding Callum's gaze, she cleared her throat. "I don't even know what to say, Sergio. Yes—um, I was looking for you. Because I assumed you stole the dress since I came out of the bathroom, and you were gone. Which I'm so sorry for. Again."

"I think you said that already," Callum said in a low voice.

Maybe you should apologize, too, Callum, she wanted to say. But Callum was still staring at Sergio with disdain.

"It's fine. Relax. You're here for a vacation, yes? This is the land of Pura Vida." Sergio glanced over his shoulder. "Listen, I'm taking a tour group back to San Jose tomorrow, but after that, I have a few days off. Why don't I come to Samara and take you to see some things?"

Liddy felt the weight of both men's stares on her.

Yikes. After everything I accused Sergio of, turning him down seems awful.

But Elle, Mom, Kyle, and everyone else had sounded . . . *annoyed* in their messages. And those messages were sent before she'd told Quinn she'd lost her phone. It'd already been another day since then.

"I-I've spent a lot of time away from my family already," Liddy explained. "I don't know how much more time I can take away from them. I want to make things up to you, and I know we talked about meeting up, but—"

"Okay, well, how about I just come and take you to dinner? There's a good bar in Samara for dancing, too." Sergio winked. "You know, to make things up to me."

Liddy searched Sergio's handsome face.

He would come all the way to Samara just to take me to dinner?

She felt terrible saying no.

He'd been put through, frankly, *a lot* on her behalf. Not to mention her unjust hatred toward him. And if Logan hadn't *left a fucking bag of marijuana* in the dress bag, she would have probably made plans to meet up with Sergio during this trip. She never would have spent this time with Callum.

She felt equally terrible saying yes.

Because she *had* spent this time with Callum. And something had started that she hadn't expected.

If she said yes to Sergio, how on earth would she explain going out with Sergio when she'd already told her family that she was dating Callum?

And how can I accept a date from Sergio after that kiss with Callum?

Feeling as though she would buckle under the pressure, she blurted out, "All right, that would be good. I'm at *La Hacienda Tropical*."

"Perfect." Sergio smiled again, not bothering to look at Callum. "I'll find you there. Let's say Wednesday night? I can call *La Hacienda* and leave a message."

"Make it Tuesday. I have the rehearsal dinner on Wednesday."

He nodded and gave her a wink. "I have to go, *bella. Buenas noches.*"

She watched him go, her stomach feeling like lead. Surely, she could think of a way to get out of the date. Then she turned toward Callum, breathing out as her face flamed. "I didn't know how to tell him no," she said, still unable to look him in the eyes.

"I noticed," Callum said flatly.

Oh no. Callum is going to think I still like him.

"Callum, I don't actually intend to go out with him."

Callum's jaw was set in anger, his expression stony. "You know what, Liddy? It really doesn't matter. You're free to do whatever you want."

"But—"

Callum stepped back. "I'm serious. It's fine. Sergio is right. You should enjoy yourself right now. That's what today was all about. Just enjoyment, nothing serious. I'm just relieved we know where that dress is and are done chasing Sergio." He cleared his throat. "I think jet lag is catching up with me, though, so are you ready to head back to the room?"

Liddy searched his face.

He's already closing himself off.

Moreover, he'd implied that he hadn't seen their flirtation and kissing as anything real. He may as well have said they'd just been messing around.

And maybe that's all it was to him.

He flirted with me once in London, then turned it all off like a spigot.

Maybe Callum was just that capable of emotional detachment. He'd proven over the years how indifferent he could be.

Hurt ebbed near her heart. "Yeah, I think so."

CHAPTER NINETEEN

The inside of the car had gotten hot once again as they'd gotten closer to the coast, and Callum leaned into the rush of wind coming from the driver's side window. He adjusted his sunglasses, frustration seeping through his fingertips as they got closer to *La Hacienda*.

The last few days had been a whirlwind, none more frustrating than the night before when they'd gotten back to the room at Tabacón. Sleeping in a bed with Liddy again had been painful because he'd wanted to curl his arm around her waist and draw her into his body, which kept betraying him with images of their kiss in the hot springs.

And Sergio had clearly confused her.

He wanted to be angry with her but—*fuck*. She'd wanted that wanker first.

All right, so maybe he turned out not to be a wanker, but still . . .

And now that Liddy had learned Sergio was everything she'd hoped he would be and Elle would get the dress back, everything would go back to the way it had been. They still had to pretend they were dating, but that was easy enough.

A relationship with one of his employees wasn't an option and this would all end neatly, with no messy emotional drama.

Just how I prefer it.

Except, as he glanced at Liddy, who looked unexpectedly tanned and tropical in the dress she'd bought from the hotel, her hair pushed back by her bandanna, but long and flowing over her shoulders, he wanted to stop the car and kiss her until she understood she should be considering a date with him and not that nitwit Sergio.

But if I have to convince her of that, then there's nothing for me to say.

He would never beg a woman to choose him. Never.

And anyway, what was there for her to choose? They'd shared a kiss. A good one. But that didn't mean anything else was on the table.

I don't have feelings for her.

Not that Sergio is probably looking for anything either. He lives in Costa Rica.

Though he had come from London . . .

He had to stop thinking about this.

"I still feel like we should have gone to get the dress this morning," Liddy said as they pulled into Samara's main street.

Callum blinked away his convoluted internal debate, then flicked his gaze at her. The beach was right off the main road, glistening in the morning sun, and she looked like she belonged here. He, on the other hand, felt more awkward than ever in his touristy Pura Vida emblazoned T-shirt from La Fortuna.

"I have to go out that way anyway to pick up Isla this afternoon. It would honestly be a waste of four hours if we went now, and it would make more sense to arrive with Isla at this point. It'll be fine. Now that we've rescued your passport, you may even arrange with the airline to have me pick it up for you if I take it."

"You don't think I'm going to get arrested for bringing pot into the country, do you?"

Callum shook his head. "They probably just confiscated it and gave Sergio a stern warning. Who knows? They let him out, and they wouldn't have done that if they were worried about drug trafficking. Besides"—he nodded to the beach— "Samara may not be as big of a hippie, pot-smoking town as Tamarindo or some of the other beaches on this coast, but it has its fair share of lawbreakers. The police will let it slide as long as it's not flagrant or excessive."

"I'm still worried. And still going to kill Logan. What did you tell him when you asked him if he had left pot in the bag?"

Callum shrugged. "I asked him if that's why he'd said his mum wanted to see the dress, he admitted it was, and I told him that Isla found the bag while she was packing. I explained we didn't tell him we didn't have it because we didn't want his mum to be worried and asked for him to be discreet."

Liddy winced. "I feel bad for all the lies your poor sister is going to have to keep track of on our behalf."

Her comment produced a laugh in him, the first real one he'd had all morning. *Isla lives for this crap.* "I wouldn't worry about that. You're going to like her. She's about as easygoing as it gets. But she does like having the inside scoop on everything."

Now why did I say that? What difference does it make what Liddy thinks about Isla?

"She sounds great." Liddy looked down at her hands, clasping them in a gesture that Callum was starting to realize was a non-verbal cue of when she felt insecure.

He cleared his throat. "Look . . . Liddy. I know the past few days have been *different*. But I don't regret anything that happened, and I don't think either of us should. And maybe the good thing is that we finally settled what happened a couple of years ago when we met. Not have that continue to poison our professional relationship."

"I guess that's true," Liddy said, a smile at her lips. It didn't quite meet her eyes, though. "But just in case you're worried, I fully intend to keep my end of the bargain with you. I know things are tough for you with your mom, and I'm sure having Sophia here is awkward, so I'm happy to do my share. I mean, by now most of my family probably thinks we went off to be alone and have our own adventure, so that should help."

Callum had no doubt of that. "If only they knew the truth. You deserve the sister-of-the-year award after that disaster."

Liddy rolled her eyes, settling into her seat more. "Except it was my dumb ass that created this mess."

"Not really. More like Logan. Speaking of which—you don't still have any of those hot peppers from the market, right? Because I could think of a use or two for them with Logan."

"Oh God, I never want to smell one of those again. I think I may never even *try* hot peppers again. We'll think of something to punish Logan, though."

Callum breathed out, releasing the knot of tension that had been building in his chest during the drive. *Why does this feel so natural?* Talking to Liddy had always been anything but. Three days of forced and continuous contact had made that vanish completely.

Not talking to her is the difficult thing now.

They pulled into the drive for *La Hacienda*. Funny how it didn't bother him to be here nearly as much as it had the first day he'd arrived.

He glanced over at her as he parked the car. "Are you going to find your family, or do you want to sneak by the room first?"

"Room, please. I need a hairbrush, at minimum." She made a face. "I'm also a little worried my family might be furious with me when I show up. I mean, in some ways, we should probably try to act like a relaxed, sexed-up couple who just had a mini honeymoon, but I'm worried that might piss them off if they're mad."

Sexed up . . .

Callum tried not to react.

Instead, I have blue balls.

Sleeping on the floor tonight would be a relief in some ways.

He didn't respond as they got out of the car, but she slipped her hand into his as they started toward the room. She winked at him. "Showtime?"

He laughed. "You're dedicated to the ruse. I'll give you that."

"I owe you. I fully intend on repaying my debt to you now so that you can't lord it over my head when we're back at work."

Funny how all that made him do was think about how much he'd love to bend her over his desk . . .

He released a slow stream of air from his lungs. *Get it together.*

They started through the lush walkway, passing the office as they went. Callum didn't glance at it, but no sooner had they gone by the door than it opened, and his mother came out—as if she'd been watching through the window for him.

"You're back!" she said with a friendly smile. She approached them with a few quick steps. "You'll never believe what I found in the garden last night." From her pocket, she produced Liddy's mobile phone.

Liddy's jaw dropped. "You found it?"

"I've been looking for it every day," Mum said with a laugh. She held it out for her. "I hope it still works. The battery was dead, so I plugged it in for you."

Liddy took the phone, then let go of Callum's hand and

hugged her. "Thank you so much for looking. I'm so grateful. I can't tell you how relieved I am to see this. Even if it doesn't work anymore. Oh—my gosh, my credit cards. I was going to cancel them today, too."

"I can't believe you haven't already," Callum said.

"Oh hush. It's not like I've had a ton of access to modern technology." Liddy pulled away from his mum.

A look of surprise registered in Mum's eyes, then she squeezed Liddy's hands. "Of course, mi amor. Happy to look out for you."

Callum tore his gaze away. *Does she really think I don't know what she's doing?*

Mum had been trying to find a way back into his life for a while now. And now she thought she had found a new way—by showing love and acceptance for the "new woman" in his life.

To hell with that.

Mum sniffed as she stepped away from Liddy. A timid expression crossed her face, and she shifted, clasping her hands. "I'm just happy you're here. How is your family enjoying *La Hacienda?* They are all so nice."

She seems nervous.

Liddy smiled sweetly. "They love it. It's wonderful. Thank you so much for being such a lovely host."

And Liddy called me the liar. He smirked to himself.

"We should get going, though." Liddy gestured back at the path. "We really didn't mean to take off for a couple of days, and I'm sure my family is wondering why I disappeared."

"Of course. Hasta luego," Mum said with another broad smile. She reached for Callum as he passed her, coming up with only air instead. "Come visit me, Callum. I would love to talk to you."

"I know." His curtness almost made him grimace. *Be nicer.* He didn't want to sound like such a dick and turned toward her. *Especially not in front of Liddy.* "Maybe once Isla is here, we can have a family lunch or something." Isla would be a good buffer.

Mum's eyes shone. "That would be wonderful."

Liddy was practically dancing as they continued walking toward the room. "I cannot believe your mom found my phone. That was so amazing of her to keep looking for it."

"She tries to be a good businesswoman." Callum repressed the urge to sigh. *And she's great at manipulating.*

Liddy gave him a sidelong glance. "You know, I know it's none of my business, but it really seems like she wants to be in your life. That's not nothing. And she's your mom. Maybe it would be worth having that talk with her and hearing her out. Even if you still feel the same way about things—and you're totally within your right to be hurt about her continued relationship with Sophia—it might be good for you."

. . . and there. That's exactly what Mum wanted.

Callum shook his head and gave a sardonic chuckle. "Now I see why she's trying to butter you up. See how well it's working? If we really were a couple, her pressure on you would be enormous. Whatever her motivations, it's manipulative, Liddy. Just like she's always been."

"I haven't seen her try to convince you to give Sophia another chance—"

"That's because we've barely been here. Trust me when I tell you I know what I'm talking about. You only know the side of her she wants you to know."

"I'm not trying to question that but"—she set a hand on his arm—"you don't seem like you're happy with the way things are either."

The last thing he wanted was to be further irritated with her. She meant well. Probably even thought she could give him some insight into this that he didn't already know. But spending three days with him hadn't made her an expert on his life. He resisted the impulse to say anything to that effect. Instead, he turned to her and said, more emphatically, "Trust me."

She faltered in her step. Then she started forward again without looking back. "Okay. Sorry, I didn't mean to be pushy."

He caught her hand in his. "It's fine. If anything, I like it when you're pushy. Reminds me of the girl who made me flip a coin with her for a damn guidebook."

Liddy looked over her shoulder, her wide eyes making it clear she hadn't expected him to bring that up.

Her fingers tightened against his. She couldn't possibly know the effect her touch had on him.

I have to stop touching her.

And the more he thought about her telling Sergio to come out here for their date, the moodier and more pissed-off he became.

"Do you ever wonder what would have happened if you hadn't turned out to be my boss?" Her voice was low, as though she was making a great deal of effort to speak cautiously.

"I guess that depends on whether you would have called me." But that wasn't entirely truthful, either. In fact, he'd never been more thankful that she'd been his employee. She would have been just another woman from his past by now. *Or worse, I would have hurt her.*

As a member of his staff, she'd been safe from that. *Safe from me.*

They rounded the corner of the path that opened to the swimming pool, and Callum nearly stopped. If they'd wanted to go back to the room sight unseen, they couldn't have picked a worse time. It appeared everyone who had come to the wedding and was staying at *La Hacienda* had gathered around the pool.

"Liddy!" A woman with long gray hair waved her arms as

she rushed toward them. She moved with a slight limp, her yellow dress a bit wrinkled. "You're back!"

"Hey, Mom." Liddy left Callum's side. "Oh, wow, I didn't expect everyone to be out here right now."

"We tried to get in touch with you. It's a welcome brunch now that almost all the wedding guests are here. You know your sister's wedding is in three days." Liddy's mum gave her a scolding look.

"I know, Mom." Liddy cleared her throat, a visible flush creeping up her neck. She turned and practically yanked Callum over to her side. "I didn't have time to introduce you the other day, but this is my boyfriend, Callum Scott. Callum, my mom, Brenda."

Whatever Liddy's mum might think about the two of them taking off the past few days, she said nothing as she held out her hand for Callum. "Nice to meet you. Quinn's been telling me so much about you. Your mother, too—she's a lovely lady."

"Yeah, I've known Quinn practically since birth," Callum said, ignoring the comment about his mother. That his mum would tell Liddy's mum anything about him was oddly disconcerting.

And it also occurred to him that—though he and Liddy had shared a lot with each other the past few days—the gaps in what they didn't know about each other were huge. They should have probably taken the time to cover the basics.

Note to self for later.

"Well, I hate to tear you two lovebirds apart, but you'll have plenty of time to spend together later, I'm sure. Elle had a few questions for you, Liddy." Brenda was already leading Liddy away. Liddy gave Quinn a helpless look over her shoulder, her backpack slung over her arm.

Given Isla and Quinn—and their mothers—had already remarked on their absence, he probably couldn't escape right now, no matter how much he might want to. Hating his touristy shirt and feeling more awkward than ever, Callum trudged toward the Camdens.

Mason was the first to see him and turned away from where his girlfriend, Rebecca, was applying sunscreen to his cheeks. "Mate, you're back." He held out a hand toward him. "I heard you did some sightseeing, you tosser."

Rebecca gave him a shy, clearly uncomfortable smile. She still wasn't used to being around him in social settings. And Liddy's harsh words about the way he treated his employees rang through his ears. "Hi, Callum. Liddy come back with you?"

This was the part of this arrangement that he should have expected. The one where it meant lying to the people they both knew and worked with. He nodded in Liddy's direction. "Her mum grabbed her right as we got in."

"And did you have a pleasant trip?" Rebecca raised a brow.

He stiffened. *Did Liddy tell her anything?*

The subtext to her words seemed to imply she knew something more about why they'd left *La Hacienda.*

Callum choked back the impulse to ask her. The more people who knew about their arrangement, the higher the chance his mother or Sophia had of finding out the truth. And then Mum would become even more relentless about not only him talking to her—but talking to Sophia, too. "A bit of a disaster, really. We ran out of petrol, got pulled over for speeding . . . among other things. But it all worked out in the end."

I need to check with Liddy and find out who—if anyone— she's told about our deal. He'd asked for her discretion but hadn't outright told her not to say anything to anyone. But maybe he should have. Mason was too close to Quinn. Given that Logan already knew more than he should, Callum felt as though he stood on shaky ground.

Quinn picked that moment to approach them, a mimosa in one hand. "Cal, it's good you're back, mate." Quinn clapped him on the back and leaned in closer. "Next time you decide to steal away with the maid of honor, you might give me a bit of a warning."

"Is everything all right?" Callum scanned Quinn's face.

"Erhm." Quinn cleared his throat. "It's all fine."

"Quinn!" A petite blond woman with a tight bun, dressed in a business suit and yielding an iPad, came striding up just then. "Ah, there you are. We need you to sit at the head table with your bride for the welcome brunch photo." She didn't wait for Quinn to respond and turned toward Callum. "Hi, I'm Kat. And you would be?"

"Oh, Kat, this is Callum Scott," Quinn said with a polite smile.

"Oh! The missing groomsman." Kat tapped on her iPad. "Excellent. So glad you've returned. Just remember, we're going to need you on the bus today at two o'clock at the latest. Try not to get lost, all right?"

Who the hell is this woman?

Callum gave Quinn a curious look, then glanced back at Kat. "Actually, I have to pick my sister up from the airport in Liberia today at four."

"Your sister?" She tipped her face down at the iPad again. "Ah, yes. Isla Scott. No, darling, don't worry. I already have someone else assigned to that task. Everything is completely under control now. See you at two," she said with a stern look, then practically prodded Quinn. "Come along then, Quinn."

Someone else is going to pick up Isla? Dammit, that will complicate things with retrieving the dress.

Callum raised his brows as his friend was helplessly dragged away.

Mason filled the space where Quinn had been. "That's the

wedding planner Mum surprised Quinn and Elle with yesterday."

Callum nearly groaned. *Oh no.*

He searched the crowded pool area for Liddy. He should have noticed before—this event was over the top for *La Hacienda*. A long buffet table, featuring an omelet station and what appeared to be a personalized crepe and waffle station, was set up in the most open area of the pool, blocking the path to the beach. Cocktail tables, complete with fresh flowers and long tablecloths, had been set up around the pool, and the wooden lounge chairs that normally occupied the space were mostly pushed out of sight.

He found Liddy. She stood beside Elle, who wore a thin-lipped smile.

Liddy met his gaze, then grimaced.

The situation was clear enough: Quinn's mother had staged a coup.

CHAPTER TWENTY

Liddy waited until Kat had scurried Elle away for a photograph to make a beeline for Taryn and Hunter, Elle's best friends, who stood in front of the crepe station. "Liddy!" Taryn said, pulling her in for a hug. "Come here, girl. I am so happy to see you. You look amazing."

Liddy hugged her back. "I can't believe it's taken this long for me to actually see you on this trip." Even though Elle's friends had always been Elle's friends, they'd become a part of the Winnick family over the years, and Liddy felt as though she knew them almost as well as her own friends.

Taryn tossed her long black hair over her shoulder. "I hear you've been gallivanting about the country with a hot new man." She scanned the pool area. "Which one is he?"

"Um. Callum . . . he's that one." She nodded toward him, where he stood with Mason and Rebecca—who kept looking over at Liddy expectantly, as though to say, *"Get over here already."*

"Nice work," Taryn said with a wink. "He's a ten."

Hunter leaned back just then, holding a steaming hot crepe

on a plate. "Oh, which one is he? We've all been curious to find out the secret man's identity."

Liddy glanced around. *We?* Her aunts and uncles and closest cousins were all here, so that could literally be anyone she was related to. Her love life had never been a topic of conversation before—let alone under the microscope—so this was getting embarrassing.

"The tall one with the tats over by Mason and Aiden," Taryn whispered loudly.

Hunter made an impressed face. "Oh, he *is* a ten."

"Don't be too obvious." Liddy swatted him. "He's my boss, and he's standing next to my coworkers and the CEO of the company I work for."

He wiped mock tears from his eyes. "I'm so proud. Little Liddy, all grown up, screwing her boss. It's enough to warm my cold, dead heart. By the way, if you were trying to keep it a secret from your company's CEO, you should'a picked someone a little less close to the Camden dons."

I should have seriously thought this fake relationship through better.

But, focus.

"Okay, but seriously, guys, I leave for two days, and what the hell happened while I was gone? Who is this Kat lady, and why is she walking around like she's in charge? Elle seems really, really upset, but she keeps saying she's fine."

Taryn grimaced and aimed a look at Hunter, who was digging into his crepe. "Oh, this crepe is good. There's like a whole crepe menu. This one is called the *Italiano* and has mozzarella and basil . . ." Hunter cleared his throat. "But I digress."

"No, that's my point." Liddy pointed to the crepe. "What happened to the homemade Costa Rican breakfasts? What's this whole spectacle?"

"Welcome breakfast."

"Brunch," Hunter corrected.

Taryn made a face. "Elle wanted to do a welcome dinner for friends and family the other day, but on Saturday, I was talking to the countess"—she gestured toward Quinn's mom, Ellen, who appeared dressed for a garden tea—"and she said something about how she had a friend who had a daughter who was a 'world-class wedding planner,' and the next thing we know, Kat showed up yesterday morning and took over."

"How world-class can she be if she flew here at the last second?" Liddy asked.

"I think Momma Camden might have hired her a long time ago without saying anything. I'm not sure."

"Or she doubled her rates. You know, as super rich people do." Hunter shrugged.

A wave of guilt washed over her. Elle had mentioned that welcome dinner. *And I completely forgot about it.*

I never should have stayed at La Fortuna.

I never should have gone on a wild goose chase for Sergio.

If she had just stayed here and been patient, Callum's mom would have found her phone—which had turned on, though Liddy hadn't been able to inspect it—and she would have found out the truth about Sergio. The entire trip had been pointless.

Except that I got closer to Callum. Who had barely talked to her all morning.

Dammit, dammit, dammit.

"This is all my fault," Liddy breathed, frustration bubbling. "Elle told me how much fuss her mother-in-law was making about everything. If I'd been here, I could have just put my foot down and told her to relax and enjoy her son's wedding—but you know Elle, she'll never stand up to her."

Taryn shared a sympathetic look. "Liddy, I don't know that you could have done much. But if it makes you feel better, Kat seems well-intentioned. She has a whole excursion planned today for all the guests to some butterfly and orchid sanctuary while she makes some adjustments to the accommodations, and then tomorrow, she's shifting us all over to The Four Seasons for the rehearsal dinner and wedding. The only reason we're not going sooner is because we're still waiting on Jasper to fly in tomorrow, and Kat didn't want to risk that the officiant would wind up at the wrong place."

"The Four Seasons?" Liddy's jaw dropped. *And an excursion?* She still needed to go get the dress from the airport.

"Isn't that Quinn and Elle's favorite hotel chain? They met at one, didn't they?" Taryn asked.

"No, that was the Ritz Carlton," Hunter interjected. "And technically, they met in a closet at Georgetown."

"But that's not the point. The Four Seasons isn't what Elle wanted. I'm sure it's beautiful and luxurious. I read amazing things about it in my guidebook. But she knew it was an option and didn't pick it." Liddy frowned, then looked toward her sister, who stood in front of a tropical photography backdrop with Quinn while a photographer took their picture.

Ugh, cheesy.

She winced. "Elle wanted something like this place. She's not the best at always speaking up for herself, and she asked me for my help, but then I left and—" Liddy rubbed her eyes. It's funny how, between the two of them, Liddy was the "assertive one." Maybe she was—with things that weren't intensely personal to *her*. "And now I come back to a Four Seasons wedding and omelet stations and *all this*."

Hunter slowly lowered his fork from his mouth, then wrinkled his nose at the crepe. "So you're telling me I'm enjoying traitor crepe?"

"It's fine, just eat it." Taryn rolled her eyes at him. "It's already been paid for and made."

"I can't eat it. It violates my principles." Hunter set the plate down on a nearby cocktail table.

"Well, what are we going to do?" Taryn asked, drawing closer to Liddy. "Elle didn't tell me any of this. Do you think maybe she's relieved on some level?"

"I doubt it. I'll talk to her. If I can get her away from that damn wedding planner." She glanced back toward Callum. *And I need to talk to Callum and find out what to do about getting the dress.*

"Okay, well, you know you can count on us for anything," Taryn said with an emphatic nod.

"Operation Sabotage the Momzilla has begun." Hunter placed his hand out toward them both, palm down. "All for one . . ."

Liddy and Taryn just stared at him with raised brows.

"You know, you two aren't any fun," Hunter said with a shake of his head.

Liddy left them and started toward Callum, her neck tight with tension.

This just keeps getting worse and worse.

She'd almost reached Callum when Rebecca intercepted her. "Oh no, you don't. Liddy Winnick, what on earth am I hearing? Mason says you've been dating Callum for months and you didn't tell me?"

Her words were almost a relief. *At least that means Miranda hasn't told her anything.*

But it was also only a matter of time until Miranda and Rebecca compared notes, and then Rebecca *would* find out. "It's a bit more complicated than that." Liddy squeezed her hand. "But I'll tell you everything when I have a chance."

"I thought you hated Callum," Rebecca hissed, sidling up to her.

"Well, there's a thin line between love and hate."

Rebecca grabbed her arm, jerking Liddy to a stop. "Are you telling me you're in love with him?" She raked her fingers through her dark hair. "Oh my gosh, you must be, considering you just went away with him for days." Then she gave Liddy a softer look and smiled. "Honestly, good for you. And for him, too. Callum is rough around the edges, but I don't know, once I started dating Mason, I got to know a different side of him. He's come to a few of the Camdens' parties."

Funny how Rebecca had that insider's perspective on the Camden family now—one that Liddy had thought she shared in. But really, she didn't. She was one step removed. The sister of the "in-law."

It must have been a hard line to walk, going along with Liddy and their friends' complaints about Callum, probably feeling as though she'd be ostracized from their group if she revealed her departure from their viewpoint.

The realization had the double-sided effect of making Liddy want to confide *more* in Rebecca—yet . . . it might not be the best timing right now, too.

"I'll find you on the excursion later. We can sit next to each other or something on the bus. I just need to steal Callum away for a minute." Liddy blew a kiss at her, then hurried over to Callum's side.

"Hi." She slipped her hand into Callum's and nestled against his arm, doing her best to look like a doting girlfriend. "Can we talk for a minute?" Then she glanced at the person Callum had been speaking to—Quinn's father, Arthur.

Arthur nodded a hello at her. "Hello, Lydia. So good to see you."

A pang of guilt went through her gut. She liked Quinn's father. She liked his mother, for that matter. They were kind and welcoming. Maybe not like her own crazy and loud family —she'd done her best to evade Granny, who was chatting loudly in the center of a group of her uncles—but still wonderful people.

But that doesn't mean they get to take over my sister's wedding.

"Good to see you, too." She stepped back from fawning over Callum, though.

"I was just telling Callum that it was such a lovely surprise to hear that you two are attached. Callum has always been one of our favorites."

"Well, he's obviously one of my favorites, too. Is it all right if I steal him away for a few minutes?" She tugged at Callum's hand.

"Of course." Arthur smiled broadly, shaking his head as they turned away. "So lovely."

Callum's eyebrows drew together, and Liddy practically yanked him toward the path that led to her room. "What's going on?"

She pulled out her room key. "The wedding has been taken over, that's what. Quinn's mom brought in some outside planner who's trying to move everything over to The Four Seasons for the wedding."

"Do Quinn and Elle know?"

"Of course they do." Liddy shot him a look of disbelief. "But have you met them? They're both so nice and polite that neither of them has spoken up against the takeover. For God's sake, Callum, they *nearly didn't get together* because they both share that tendency to keep their mouths shut when they shouldn't."

"But if they won't say anything, then isn't it better if we just all go along with the new plan?"

"No." Liddy scowled at him. *Fuck, no.* "Quinn and Elle picked *La Hacienda.* Maybe they didn't realize it would be as rustic as it is, but also, I know my sister. This is completely up her alley. She just can't relax enough to enjoy herself, which she should be able to because it's her wedding. And I'm not going to let the countess of . . . whatever Quinn's title is, take over the wedding."

She unlocked the door and pulled him into the room. As she shut the door, she caught the amusement in Callum's gaze. "What?"

Callum smirked. "Nothing."

"No, tell me. What is it?"

Callum shrugged, crossing the room and flipping on some lights. "I just like this side of you."

That's the second time he's said something like that today. Callum clearly liked women who weren't wallflowers.

He dropped onto the bed as though they were still sharing one. "What's your plan?"

"Well, that's why I need your help." Liddy dropped her bookbag. She wanted to shower and change after their car trip, but this was more important. "You know this place. You know the types of things they'd enjoy doing." She thought about what Hunter had said. "I want to sabotage the takeover. Let's start with this excursion thing. I don't think Quinn and Elle were hoping for butterfly sanctuaries, do you?"

Callum discarded his flip-flops and leaned his forearms on his knees, clasping his hands. "Probably not."

"Great. So I need some ideas for things they *would* enjoy. That and a bus. I'm thinking we could tell whatever tour bus we book to pick everyone up at one, and then you and I go around and tell everyone the time's been changed. Hopefully Kat will be too busy breaking down this brunch that she won't find out. By the time we're supposed to meet at her excursion pickup, we'll be long gone."

"And the point would be?"

Ugh, do I have to spell everything out for everyone?

"That Quinn and Elle have some real fun and relax. To get Quinn's mother off her high horse and to just see how magical this place can be if you let yourself enjoy it—like I did when we went to La Fortuna. Maybe once they all realize how much fun the wedding could be here, Elle and Quinn will feel like they can speak up."

A few seconds ticked by before Callum bowed his head. "You don't need me. You need my e—Sophia. She handles everything like that around here. And unlike my mum, she's young and probably goes out. Does more interesting things than lead yoga sessions."

"Oh." *Shoot.* "You're right. She probably does have a lot of connections with local tours." Liddy approached him and sat beside him. She didn't want to seem selfish, especially considering how much she had asked of him. "Would you ask her?"

Callum kept his gaze straight ahead. "To be clear, is this a new favor or just an extension of the old one?"

She laughed, then looked over at him and saw his deadpan expression. "Wait. You're serious?"

Is he still mad at me over the whole thing with Sergio?

"Callum . . . you know I'm not actually planning on going on that date with Sergio, if that's what's bothering you."

"You can date whoever you want. That's none of my business."

Oh my God, he's so infuriating.

His choice of words is interesting, though.

Just like when she'd told him his family issues were none of her business.

Enough of this.

"So we're just going to pretend that kiss in the hot springs never happened? Is that it?" She stood, prickles going up her spine. She wished there was more room to pace in here. "You're angry. I get it. But I refuse to believe you didn't feel anything or that it was some sort of casual peck to you. I'm not going to keep skirting around this when an honest conversation could solve this tension between us."

"What would you like for me to pretend it was? Four days ago, you couldn't stand me, Liddy. That's the truth. And another truth is that it *was* just a kiss. Nothing more. I'm not looking for a relationship. I don't do them."

Oh, ouch. She took a quick breath, realizing her mistake as embarrassment shimmied its way through her. *This is why I shouldn't have said anything.* She crossed her arms. "I didn't say I was looking for a relationship, either, did I?"

"Then what should it matter if you go out with Sergio? You liked him before you thought he was a thief, right? And now he's not. Sounds like a straightforward decision in my book." Callum leveled his chin with her.

Wow, he really doesn't give a shit, does he?

He didn't need to spell it out any more clearly.

"All right, fine. I'll go." She narrowed her eyes at him. "Glad we had this talk. Now are you going to help me save my sister—and your good friend's—wedding? Or do I have to do something in return to make you pretend to be a decent human being and help me again?"

"I don't know. I kind of like the idea of you owing me. Could come in handy." Callum went over to his suitcase and peeled off his shirt, with a comfort level that had clearly come in the last few days. He flung his used shirt into the corner of the room, his well-muscled back taut and rigid with tension.

Asshole.

Pulling out a short-sleeved, button-down shirt, he put it on, then turned back toward her as he buttoned it. "But I'll help. Even if it means going and asking for the help of the person I was hoping to avoid."

Anger surged through her. "Don't worry, you're such a peach. I'm sure she feels the same way."

Callum's eyes flicked toward hers, and his lips drew to a line. "I'll find you later and let you know what Sophia comes up with." He strode past her, irritation in his every movement, then went out the door.

Unexpected tears pricked her eyes.

"I'm not looking for a relationship." His voice rang through her head.

Stupid, stupid, stupid.

That was so stupid of me. Of course, he's not. And even if he was, he's not looking for someone like me. He's too busy letting events that happened forever ago continue to wound him.

She pulled out her rescued cell phone and swiped it open. Relief flooded her as her home page picture—one of Elle, Kyle, and Liddy at Christmas—swam before her watery eyes.

She swiped the tears away.

God, I am so mad at Callum.

And myself.

Kissing him at the hot springs had felt so natural, so easy. Then Sergio had come along and Callum had completely shut down. Gone right back to putting up all those walls he'd had when they'd arrived.

She didn't need this. Didn't need to get involved with someone like Callum. But she was also fooling herself if she pretended not to have some level of emotional investment in him now. He was pushing her away, but she'd gotten too good of a peek at what was underneath all that armor.

And dammit, but I give a shit about him.

Her phone rang, and she looked down at the incoming call. *Miranda.*

Swallowing the lump in her throat, she swiped to answer the call. "Hey, how's it going?"

"Oh, you sound terrible. Did I wake you?"

Liddy sniffled. "No . . . you just caught me having an awful moment."

"Oh, sweetheart. What happened? Did the dead soul we know as Callum Scott strike again?"

Ugh. Liddy rolled her shoulders back, then went over to her bag and pulled out a bottle of pain meds. After the last few days, she needed some relief. The massage had helped a ton, but even her tailbone hurt from sitting so much.

"It's nothing like that. Well, not exactly. He's . . . *different* from what I thought. I spent the past few days in a car with him and got to know him and, I don't know, Mir—"

"Oh my God. You've gone and developed feelings for him, haven't you?"

"No. I mean . . . gah, I don't know." She sucked in a breath, then filled a glass of water at the sink. Swallowing her pills, she set the glass down and scanned her own reflection in the mirror.

He made me feel so beautiful. So wanted.

"Did something happen?"

Liddy chewed on her lower lip, then turned away from the mirror. "We kissed. And it was amazing. Not like a peck, but this really sexy, incredible kiss. And you can't tell anyone. Promise me you won't tell a soul."

The silence on the other line was oddly disconcerting. "Callum kissed you?" Miranda said at last. "Were you drinking or something?"

"No, nothing like that. He's been really, I don't know. *Different.* Mir, he helped me scour the whole countryside for the guy I thought stole my sister's dress. And we ended up at these hot springs and went waterfall rappelling and got a couple's massage, and then it just happened while we were at the springs. And it was such a good kiss." Liddy's throat tightened. "But now that we're back at the hotel where my family is, he's acting like it was nothing. He still wants us to go on pretending we're dating, but this is just getting too complicated emotionally."

"That's because Callum is a fucking arsehole, Liddy," Miranda snapped, her vitriol surprising Liddy. "He's using you when it's convenient. Sure, he'll shove his tongue down your throat, but then he'll turn the whole thing around and make it like you're the slut who was just asking for it."

Uhh . . . what?

"I honestly didn't mean that. He's a lot nicer than any of us give him credit for—"

"Did he tell you he almost had sex with me the day before you two flew to Costa Rica?"

The air in the room seemed to dissipate, her gut dropping. "What?"

"Yes, Liddy. I ran into him at a pub, and he was sloshed. We snogged for a while, then *he* had the audacity to treat me like I was a whore that had come on to him. Like he's got a golden prick, and I just couldn't stay away. He completely humiliated me."

A sick feeling stirred in her stomach.

Callum and Miranda?

Miranda was still speaking, but Liddy's ears had started ringing, and she blinked, numbly, as she sank wearily down to the tile floor.

So much for drawing a hard boundary at members of his staff.

This shouldn't hurt. Callum had been clear. The kiss had been meaningless to him.

And just like that, we're right back at the same dynamic we've had from the beginning. He dishes out actions or words that cut deeply and shrugs his shoulders, claiming it isn't personal.

But it was personal to me.

That kiss had been the definition of personal. Intimate.

And apparently, she was just one more woman who he kissed and had zero interest in.

Liddy drew a sharp breath. "Mir, I've got to go."

"Oh . . . are you all right?"

No, I'm not.

"Fine. I'm fine." She was mostly trying to convince herself. "I mean, it's nothing. We had some deep conversations, and I thought I had seen another side of him. But I was obviously wrong."

"I'm honestly shocked the bastard tried something like this on you. But don't feel badly. Callum is persuasive. That's why he's so good at his job. He finds weaknesses and exploits them."

Liddy shook her head, thinking of their kiss in the hot springs. "He told me I was beautiful," she whispered, her heart clenching. "Said that he wanted to find anyone who'd ever made me feel like I was less and punch them."

Miranda was silent for a few beats. "Wow, he really said that?" Miranda's voice grew angrier. "He's such a sod, Liddy. I'm sorry."

"I really have to go." Liddy said another goodbye, then hung up, holding the phone to her chest.

I should have known Callum was nothing more than a manipulative faker.

. . . but then why had it felt so real?

CHAPTER TWENTY-ONE

LATIN MUSIC POURED through the office as Callum opened the door and he slipped through. Through the open doorway that led to the back room, he saw his mum sweeping the floor of the kitchenette that they used to make the morning breakfasts. Sophia sat near the counter, eating from a plate of *gallo pinto*.

They both stopped quickly as Callum came through the doorway to the back room.

Mum set the broom against the wall and smiled. "Callum. You're not at the party?"

"Obviously not."

Sophia rolled her eyes. "Same old Callum." She nodded toward a plastic food storage container on the counter. "*Gallo pinto?* We have a lot left over that your mum made this morning."

The thought unsettled him. "They didn't tell you they were doing this breakfast instead of the included one?"

"Ah, not until this morning," Mum said and smiled pleasantly, nonetheless. "Not that I blame them. The breakfast looks beautiful. *Muy elegante.*"

"You know the Camdens, Mum. They like their posh creature comforts." *Which is why agreeing to help Liddy with this plan feels foolish and pointless.*

"It's been so long since I visited their house . . ." Mum shook her head, blinking away the memories. "That feels like a different lifetime."

"It was probably twenty years ago." Callum scanned his mum's face.

He knew little about his parents' divorce or why they had fallen apart as a family. He'd long suspected his American stepmother had played a role—Dad had quickly moved to Connecticut after the divorce—but Callum had never cared to ask. But his parents were good at co-parenting and hadn't spoken disparagingly about each other, and given his mother's Latina tendency to speak her mind, he probably would know about it by now if it had been an affair.

"Listen, Liddy wants me to see if I can find some tours and a bus that might come today and pick up all the wedding guests." He checked his watch. "In two hours."

"In two hours?" Sophia exchanged a look with Mum. "I don't know if that's possible. What's the rush?"

Callum hooked his thumbs into the belt loops of his shorts. "It's Liddy's last-ditch effort to help everyone here have a 'magical and fun time' and stop the Camdens from moving the whole wedding to The Four Seasons tomorrow."

Mum gasped. "They're leaving?"

Shit.

He hadn't meant to be so imprudent.

But the Camdens should have told Mum.

Maybe they were waiting until after everything was confirmed before they did. Or maybe Liddy was right—Elle and Quinn hadn't completely signed off on the new plans yet and there was still time to turn things around.

His voice was softer as he said, "They might be."

"But your girlfriend said they were having a good time." Mum set her hands on her hips.

"They are, Mum. I just think maybe the Camdens are less of the 'unplug and commune with nature' types and more of the 'serve me my cocktails on my beach lounger' types. And you know how Arthur had that stroke several years ago. I don't think they've gone on many holidays since then."

Mum teared up. Without another word, she scurried away from the office, the door slamming behind her as she wiped tears away.

Fantastic.

Just what I needed.

Sophia was quiet as she stood. She moved over to a clean stack of plates and then uncovered the *gallo pinto*, spooning it out onto a plate. Approaching him, she held out the plate. "I guess we should try to help your girlfriend. If she's the only one trying to help us, anyway."

"It's not personal, Sophia." He took the plate from her. "I didn't say I wanted this."

She rolled her eyes. "Then throw it out. It'll get thrown out anyway if no one eats it. But it used to be your favorite, and you haven't had your mum's cooking for a while, so you may as well have some."

He hated that she was right. Grabbing a fork, he dug in and took a bite. The taste transported him instantly—like so many foods had the last few days—to easy days. Better days. Mornings of *gallo pinto* and surfing. Days playing football. Nights that included sneaking bottles of *Imperial* beer and kisses with the girl he'd thought would be the love of his life.

The thought of it made him feel sick.

Reminded him of other things, too.

Of being in so much pain that he couldn't see straight.

Of losing the contract that had promised him three million pounds and a place in the international football league.

Arduous days and nights, having to practically relearn how to fucking walk again and years of physical therapy.

And the one bright spot in his life becoming the deepest hole of darkness he'd ever experienced.

Goddamn Liddy for making me do this.

"Can you help me?" he asked, setting the fork down. He couldn't look at Sophia.

"Yes. There are some good new tours in town. I think horseback riding for the older couples—the horses are gentle—and maybe four-by-four jungle treks for the younger crowd. Dividing the group will make it easier for an afternoon activity on such short notice. Then everyone can meet back up and go on a sunset catamaran party cruise and see dolphins." Sophia slid a laptop over from the counter and opened it.

"Maybe something other than horse riding, too? In case there are people with physical disabilities. Arthur Camden had a stroke several years ago, so I'm not sure if he'll be up for riding a horse."

"Ah, yes, and the grandmother, too."

Callum smirked. "I'm fairly sure Granny will opt for riding in a UTV. Driving it, if she can."

Sophia clicked a few keys on her laptop. "A wild macaw tour in Punta Islita maybe?"

"That could work."

"I'll set it all up. What time do you want the tour bus here? And how do you want to pay?"

Oh fuck. Payment.

He gritted his teeth. He hadn't gotten this far in the planning with Liddy. She probably hadn't even thought about how expensive it all would be or that the extremely wealthy

Camden family didn't have to blink twice to order something like a butterfly excursion and pay for everyone.

He could go to Liddy and tell her about it, but he'd been an arse. The conversation from the room had made him want to put a fist through a wall. The conflict inside him was sufficient torment.

But the hurt that had flashed on her face was enough to make him want to do some form of penance.

Not to mention, Liddy probably couldn't afford it, and he couldn't very well go to Quinn or the Camdens.

Callum sighed and dug a credit card out from his wallet. "Here. Put it on this."

Sophia gave him a skeptical look, then nodded. "You must really like her," she said with a shake of her head.

Like her? How could I not? But Lydia Winnick would always deserve more than Callum could give.

"I do."

Sophia took the credit card. "Callum. Tía wouldn't want me telling you this, but . . . things at *La Hacienda* haven't been going well lately. The bigger hotel chains in Guanacaste have been making things harder for us smaller places."

Sophia shifted her gaze out the door to where his mum had gone. "So we're thinking of selling. She had high hopes for this wedding, especially because the Camdens are an important family and Elle Winnick is a famous singer. Thought it would be good on the website. That's why she's so upset."

Selling La Hacienda?

Callum met Sophia's gaze. He didn't want to take pity on her, but he also couldn't help it.

They'd both been children when his mum and her mum, who he'd called Tía Carmen, had bought this place. Nothing had been here. But property had still been cheap, and they'd had a dream. The first night, they'd all camped out near the beach in a tent.

And as a child, he'd been just as excited as his mum. Isla, too.

"I'm not sure a pseudo-celebrity wedding could turn things around that much, Sophia. This place is run-down, even for a place boasting rustic charm."

"I know that." Sophia gave him a sad smile. "But that didn't stop Tía from hoping. You know how much she loves it here. And it's one of the few things she has left."

The pang of guilt that went through him was visceral despite his immediate rejection of it. *Is this why Mum wants to talk to me?*

He could see her doing something like that. Asking him to step in and help save the business. Or even Isla—even though his thespian sister barely scraped by.

"Mum can't expect Isla or me to bail her out if that's what she's hoping."

Sophia gave him a hard look. "No one's suggesting that. I was just explaining to you why she's upset. You know, you used to be a nice person. Someone who didn't turn his back on the people he loved."

"Well, a certain woman I loved ruined the whole concept of love for me. So there's that."

Sophia gave him a look of disbelief. "And does your girl-friend know that? That you're just this . . . this loveless man? Because you might want to tell her before she moves halfway across the world for you and then gets treated like dirt—even though she does everything for you and tries to take care of you. But no. You couldn't appreciate it because you were too angry about never being able to play football again. You didn't care about any of the good things you had left in your life."

She raised her chin defiantly. "I'm not justifying what I did,

Callum, but I was twenty-three years old, and I was in London, alone—completely alone. And the only people I saw were your friends. How could I have time for anything else when I was so busy taking care of you? Because even though you were there, you *weren't*. The person you were? He didn't get his leg broken. He got his spirit crushed. Destroyed. *He* was gone. He *is* gone. You're not the man I loved, and you never will be."

For someone who didn't feel she was justifying her actions, that diatribe certainly sounded like justification to Callum. *And to think she'd once asked for forgiveness.* From the moment Quinn had told him about the wedding here, Callum had known this confrontation would have to happen, and it seemed Sophia believed he was incapable of love. Callum couldn't really disagree with her. She wasn't asking for forgiveness now, and neither had his mum, so it seemed he was justified in his mistrust for a woman's heart. *They are fickle.*

Once her words would have wounded him to the deepest part of his heart. Now they fell off the armor surrounding it like arrows hitting steel.

"Are you done?" he asked calmly. He was *done* with this conversation.

Her face reflected her fury. "Not even close. But what does it matter? You treat people like luxuries you can throw away. And someday you're going to learn that you could have had everything you really wanted if you weren't such a coward. You only have yourself to blame for being a miserable bastard."

"Fantastic. Just let me know when the trips are booked. You can bring the credit card back to my room later."

Then he left, restraining the urge to flex his fist as he walked.

She knows nothing about me now.

But why, when she'd been calling him a coward, had Liddy's face flashed through his mind?

CHAPTER TWENTY-TWO

"Scoot it, buddy. You get to spend enough time with my sister," Liddy said as she got to the bus seat that Elle and Quinn occupied.

Elle threw her a warm smile, one that didn't speak of any anger or resentment.

God, she's such a good person. Elle hadn't even said a thing to her about her mother-in-law's takeover of the wedding or Liddy's disappearance for a few days—and if Liddy knew Elle, both were probably bothering her.

But she wasn't the type of person to hold onto that and get resentful.

She'd just . . . let go of what she had wanted.

"I thought the bus would be bigger," Elle mused, then glanced back at the other bus parked behind them. "But I have to admit it's nice that all the older crowd is taking the other bus." Taryn and Hunter divided the group, gently nudging the parents and their ilk into the second bus.

"We got to keep all the young'uns together," Granny

chirped from the seat beside the driver. She checked the mirror. "Leo's back there with them, though, right?"

Liddy held back a laugh as Quinn moved to another row, and she sat beside her sister. She'd let Kyle and Granny in on Callum's and her sabotage plans—partially because she knew they'd be mad if she didn't and partially because even with Taryn and Hunter's help, they needed a small miracle to pull this off and keep Kat from finding out.

That was what Kyle now oversaw, in fact. He'd been assigned to monitor Kat and make sure she didn't get anywhere close to the tour bus loading area—and that Quinn's mom didn't talk to her.

"Granny, why'd you bring a man along if you weren't planning on spending time with him?" Liddy asked with a shake of her head.

Granny puffed out her cheeks. "It's more fun that way. Plus, I need someone to dance with at the wedding. And he's not a half-bad dancer when he's got a few drinks in him."

Quinn gave her an affectionate smile. "I'd have danced with you, Granny."

"No, no, no. You need to save it for the bride. And for baby-making later. I'm putting the request in right here, right now for great-grandbabies sooner rather than later. If Brenda's bad luck continues, my great-grandbabies could have a good twenty years to get to know me."

"What on earth do you mean?" Elle asked, looking shocked.

"Oh, you know. No woman wants her mother-in-law living till one hundred. Brenda's pretty good at not having things go her way, so I think my chances of living that long look swell." Granny grinned mischievously.

"To Granny," Callum said, catching the tail end of her comments as he climbed aboard the bus, a cooler of beer in his hands. "Long may she reign."

Liddy looked away from him.

"He's a smart one," Elle whispered in Liddy's ear, giving her a playful pinch on the forearm. "He knows how to butter up the matriarch."

"Yeah, he's great," Liddy mumbled back, her throat clenching at the words. *Irredeemable bastard.*

If only he'd get on the other bus with Leo.

She didn't have to wonder if Callum would sit next to her. He avoided her gaze and instead sat with Quinn and his brothers.

Elle looked from Liddy to Callum, then frowned. "Trouble in paradise?" She raised a brow.

So much for being a happy couple.

Elle wasn't the only one who had noticed either. Rebecca, who had been sitting with Mason, gave her a curious look, then slid into the empty seat beside Liddy. "You okay?"

"I'm fine." Liddy put on a brighter smile. She *had* felt better until Callum had gotten on the bus. She'd done her best to avoid Callum, asking Taryn and Hunter to finalize the plans for the excursions with him, and had gone back to the welcome brunch. Spending time with her family had done wonders for her aching heart.

Because that was the only way to describe how she felt.

Callum's indifference to her now, after the past few days they'd spent together, was much more painful than his initial brush-off had been two years ago. She'd shared things with him she'd never told anyone.

And if she hadn't had that conversation with Miranda, maybe she would have been able to swallow her pride and understand that he needed her friendship, even if he hadn't given that impression at the hot springs.

But now I know better.

Elle leaned over and slipped her hand into hers. "You

know, I can still have Quinn cut him from the wedding party if he hurts you," she whispered.

"I'm fine. It's fine. Just a long morning." Liddy nestled her head against Elle's shoulder.

God, I so desperately want to talk to my sister.

Elle would give me good advice.

But she'd made a deal with Callum, and he'd kept his end of the bargain. The proverbial deal with the devil, it turned out.

"Did you dye your hair so that you two would look different?" Rebecca asked, tilting her head. "Because I swear it never occurred to me how much you look alike until seeing you next to each other now."

A wave of affection came over Liddy. "Sort of. Elle's a natural blond. I started that way, but my hair gradually got darker over the years, and I didn't have time to get highlights before I left London, so I just went with box dye to match my roots."

"Next time, you should tell your boss to give you some time off to get your hair appointment in," Elle said a bit more loudly. "Ahem. Liddy's boss."

Callum checked over his shoulder at Elle. "All she has to do is ask if she wants time off."

Yeah, because you're so approachable.

Hunter, Taryn, and Kyle clambered aboard the bus, shutting the door behind them as the bus carrying the older crowd started past them. "Go, go, go!" Kyle told the bus driver. "Right now!"

Liddy turned to look toward *La Hacienda*. Kat was running toward the bus, her iPad bouncing against her chest as she ran.

Oh shit.

The bus lurched forward, with Taryn and Kyle holding onto the backs of seats while Hunter pitched forward onto Granny.

"Hello, handsome," Granny said with a gleeful laugh.

"Hello, gorgeous," Hunter returned with a wink.

Quinn and Elle gave Kyle confused looks and then looked back at *La Hacienda*. "Was that Kat?" Quinn asked.

"Cat? I didn't see a cat." Taryn squeezed in beside Rebecca, then gave Liddy a thumbs-up.

"Everyone got on?" Liddy asked Hunter as he plopped down in a seat.

Hunter gave her a thumbs-up.

Rebecca leaned toward the window. "Is something going on?"

Callum dug into the cooler. "Who wants a beer?"

Several hands shot up into the air.

With everyone else sufficiently distracted by the beer, Elle frowned at Liddy. "What in the hell is going on?"

"Okay, don't get mad. I might have kidnapped you. And all your wedding guests."

"It wasn't just Liddy," Taryn chimed in. "So if you get mad, don't blame her."

Liddy appreciated Taryn's show of loyalty, but she also didn't want Elle's friends to take the blame for this.

Quinn turned and knelt on his seat. "What do you mean, kidnapped?"

"Look, Elle. Quinn." Liddy reached out and squeezed Elle's hand. "I know you two. You didn't come all the way to Costa Rica for butterfly excursions or The Four Seasons. And I know you didn't pick this beach and this place by accident. So . . . I just figured I'd give you a little taste of the adventure you *came* here for."

"Meaning?" Quinn's expression was blank as though he still couldn't follow.

"Meaning we set up some alternate plans for the day. We're going to go on four-by-fours through the jungle trails while the parents and their friends go horseback riding or wild macaw viewing, and then we're all going to go on a sunset cruise on a catamaran. Surprise," Callum said, handing Quinn a beer.

Elle's lips parted with shock. "Are you serious?" Then she looked down at her long sundress. "I am *so* not dressed for a UTV."

"Are you mad?" Liddy asked with a grimace.

"Are you kidding? This is amazing." Elle's eyes shone. "I'm so excited."

Quinn lifted the beer toward Callum. "This is brilliant."

Liddy relaxed in her seat. "Oh, thank God. I was so worried that you'd be worried about Quinn's mom getting mad."

"Oh . . ." Elle's smile froze. Her eyes darted to Quinn's. "Oh, babe, do you think she will?"

"That's the beauty of it," Callum cut in before Quinn could respond. "She won't even know that Kat didn't set this all up until she gets back tonight."

Hunter lifted a backpack. "I stole all the old people's phones except Leo's. Granny said he could be trusted, so I figured it would be good to have one person we could keep in touch with. Told the rest of them it was an unplugged excursion. Kat won't be able to reach your mom."

Quinn looked from Hunter to Callum. "I-I guess it'll be fine, then. Besides, it doesn't matter. If this is what Elle wants to do and it makes her happy, I don't see what difference it makes."

Sweet Quinn.

Her sister knew how to pick a good man. *Meanwhile, I just seem to keep crushing on men who make me feel like dirt.*

Taryn seemed to know what Liddy was thinking. "Lucky woman, that one." She nodded toward Elle. "Everyone needs a Quinn in their life."

Rebecca grinned. "Mason's a good catch, too."

As Quinn shook his head and sat, the group resumed their chatter, making it easier for Liddy to talk to Elle. "So I take it you haven't told Quinn you absolutely do not want to do a wedding at The Four Seasons, and that's why Kat's running the show now?" Liddy stared at the back of Quinn's head. "Because you know he'd support you if you told him. I don't think he'd be afraid to stand up to his mother."

"Yeah, but why cause the drama?" Elle's gaze darted out the window. She looked back at Liddy with a taut smile, then sighed. "No, it's not what I planned or wanted, but clearly, this means more to her than I thought it would."

"It's your wedding, Elle. Yours and Quinn's." Liddy scooted closer to her. "I'm sorry I left. I know you needed my help, and you've been really stressed, and I didn't want to leave you with that. It's just . . ."

God, this would be so much easier if I'd just told Elle the truth from the start.

"No, I get it." Elle gave her a gentle look, swiping some tears from the corners of her eyes. "You needed time with Callum. It totally makes sense. Especially during those first few months of dating, when you're walking on the clouds, and everything is perfect. I totally understand."

I don't deserve how good she is to me.

Her words also made Liddy's heart give a painful lurch.

Elle might understand what that was like, but Liddy didn't. Her relationships had always been disastrous. No one had ever made her feel that valued. *That loved.*

And Callum made it clear he's not interested in doing that either.

At moments like this, Liddy truly hated their ruse. She needed her sister. She wanted to be honest and talk to her about the feelings she'd developed—the unrequited feelings. *But I can't and probably never will be able to.*

This time, she couldn't stop the tears that slid onto her cheek. She turned away so Elle wouldn't see her crying and swiped the moisture away. *Elle does not need my drama on top of everything.*

Rebecca caught her eye, then leaned over toward Taryn, whispering something in her ear.

A moment later, Taryn stood and pushed her way between Elle and Liddy. "All right. My turn with the bride."

Rebecca pressed a tissue into Liddy's hand. "What's going on?" she mouthed.

If only she could be as honest about this with Rebecca as she'd been with Miranda. She needed a friend who was here, not back in London.

And even though Liddy had sworn Miranda to secrecy, the fact remained that she was uncomfortable with one of her friends knowing the truth but not the other.

Then again, she and Callum had discussed an exit strategy for when they got back from the beach. Maybe implying things were rocky wasn't the worst idea.

"I just . . . you know how Callum can be. Hot and cold." She twisted her lips. "And when it's cold, it's cold."

Rebecca grimaced. "I hoped that wouldn't be the case. How'd you two get together in the first place?"

Um. We really should have talked about this. "Late night at the office one time. One too many glasses of scotch."

"Oh my God, have you had sex in his office?" Rebecca hissed, her eyes sparkling. "I would be so afraid to do that with all those windows."

Liddy tried not to visualize it. *Or think about how weak in the knees that makes me feel.* "Loads."

"Raarr. I'm so proud." Rebecca wrinkled her nose, then became instantly more serious. "But really, Liddy. If he's not always making you completely happy, don't put up with it—

even if he's our boss. He's handsome and probably has a lot of money by now, but you deserve to be completely, blissfully happy. And you know you can count on those of us who love you to have your back. Go and get what you want and deserve. Want some?" She held out a beer.

Liddy nodded, then sat back, her eyes darting toward Callum. She sipped the beer he'd handed back to Rebecca.

Rebecca's talking as though I'm the sort of girl who knows how to do that.

And maybe if Callum hadn't been so assertive himself, she would have tried. Because that kiss they'd shared had made it clear she wanted Callum, even if it was just raw sexual desire.

Then again, Callum hadn't eliminated that as a possibility.

He'd just said he didn't want a relationship.

She contemplated the thought for a minute, then sighed.

Yeah, no.

She wasn't about to get involved with Callum sexually. Especially not after what Miranda had told her. That would just be stupid and complicated. Not to mention the fact that she didn't think she was capable of emotionless sex.

But, then again, why shouldn't she just have fun? She couldn't complain about gatekeeping if she was the one doing it to herself, could she?

"Oh, by the way," Taryn said in a low voice, then dug into her bag she had belted around her waist. "The woman from the front desk asked me to give this to you." She handed Liddy an envelope.

Liddy frowned, then opened the envelope. A stack of neatly folded papers was inside. She tugged them out of the envelope, and when she opened them, a credit card tumbled onto her lap.

Callum's.

Then she checked the papers—and her heart froze.

Holy shit.

She hadn't even asked Callum how these alternate plans had been paid for. In her distress, she'd just asked for it to be done and sent him on the errand without giving two thoughts about the logistics.

He paid for it?

The total for all these people to do tours for the day was close to ten thousand US dollars.

She nearly fell back in her seat.

But . . . why would he pay for something like this?

Maybe that was why Quinn's parents had picked a butterfly excursion.

How was she ever going to afford this?

Refolding the papers, she stuffed them into the envelope, along with Callum's credit card. She didn't want to make a big deal of it now and have Elle and Quinn find out how much this was costing them.

Because she needed to pay Callum back. And soon.

I don't want to owe him anything else.

CHAPTER TWENTY-THREE

"Outta the way!" Granny called, her ATV bouncing on the path.

Liddy jumped off the dirt path, dodging toward a tree as a four-by-four with Granny and Kyle went roaring past them. Granny was in control, to no one's surprise, and one of Liddy's cousins hooted at the sight.

Liddy grinned. Much as she hadn't expected to enjoy this, especially considering that a bumpy jungle path might further aggravate her pain level from the past few days, being around family members she hadn't seen in years made this place feel like home.

They didn't have to be in Nashville for that. Wherever her family was, she was home. Whether it was in London when they came to visit her or Quinn's fancy estate for Christmas.

Granny pulled to a stop and dismounted, taking her helmet off. "Who's next?" she called out.

The tour operators laughed and high-fived her.

"I think I want to grow up to be Granny," Hunter whispered beside Liddy.

"Don't let her hear you. She'll get a bigger ego than she already has," Elle said, relaxing back into Quinn's arms. Her eyes scanned the group that waited for their turn on the vehicles. "Liddy, you and Callum going?"

Liddy stiffened. "I'm not sure—"

"The correct answer would be yes." Granny tossed the helmet toward her.

Liddy caught it, the sound of her hands smacking against the plastic cap echoing around her. She didn't dare look for Callum. "Really, Gran—"

"Liddy, Liddy, Liddy . . ." Granny started chanting, orchestrating with pumped fists toward her cousins who soon joined in.

Liddy rolled her eyes as the Costa Rican tour operator extended his hand, inviting her toward the vehicle. "Granny . . ." she tried, shaking her head. But Granny and her cousins were too loud for her to be heard. She threw her palms up, then went toward the operator.

Her cousins cheered, then Granny turned toward Callum and started, "Hot rod, hot rod, hot rod . . ."

God, this is so embarrassing.

Callum handed his beer to Aiden, then winked at Granny. He seemed to be in a surprisingly good mood as he sauntered toward Liddy. Unexpectedly, he swept her off her feet and carried her onto the ATV, setting her down on the passenger seat behind the main operator seat.

He's so smooth. Fucking charmer.

That only seemed to goad Granny further.

"Kiss, kiss, kiss . . ."

Callum quirked a brow and turned toward Liddy. She gave him a hard look. "We don't have to."

He leaned toward her, setting both hands on either side of

her face as he closed the distance between them. "We're a happy couple, remember?"

She almost glared at him, then raised her hands to his jaw. He lowered his lips to hers with firm but gentle pressure, and she closed her eyes.

I hate that I love the way he tastes.

Her body almost instinctively curled into his as he slipped his arm around her waist to a chorus of hooting and hollering. His breath was warm against her mouth, the barest hint of his tongue sliding against her lip like a promise.

He pulled back, then set his forehead against hers. "Good girl."

Asshole. "Don't good girl me," she gritted through her teeth, managing a smile despite the surge of anger coursing through her.

The tour operator was by their side, though, giving Callum instructions as she settled back into the seat. Her cheeks burned and the warm pool of desire that had ignited in her core at that kiss only made her more furious. It wasn't the first time she'd felt betrayed by her body, though, and it wouldn't be the last.

Callum might affect her, but he didn't have to know that.

The tour operator instructed Liddy to settle her arms around Callum's waist and then they were off, tearing through the bumpy trail and away from their group. Some of the other members of their party were ahead of them on the trail, but they were nowhere to be seen. The tour company only had four ATVs, which meant they'd all had to take staggered turns.

Mud shot up from the tires as Callum took a sharp turn, and Liddy buried her cheek into his back, shielding her face. "You okay?" Callum called back toward her.

No.

She didn't want to be enjoying the rush of the ride.

Or how she loved being this close to him.

This close, she could smell his shirt and body wash, which had some manly spice in it that made her want to take a deep breath.

Or that she could feel every ridge of muscle of his taut abs against the backs of her forearms.

But then she visualized him kissing Miranda, and she almost threw up.

I can't do this.

"Stop!" she called into his ear. Callum slowed, then pulled to the side of the path.

Disentangling herself from him, she hopped off the vehicle and moved away, trying to catch her breath.

"What happened? Are you hurt?" Callum followed her, his face written with concern.

"I'm *fine.*" She rubbed her temples, trying to clear her thoughts.

"You're clearly not fine. What hurts?"

"I'm fine," she repeated, turning away from him.

I will not cry in front of him.

Callum took her elbow. "Liddy, what happened?"

She shook her head, clenching her jaw.

Fuck it.

She turned toward him. "You. You happened, Callum. I know, I know. I brought this upon myself by agreeing to this ridiculous ruse in the first place, but I thought that I'd gotten to know you over the last few days. I shared things with you I've never told anyone, and not because I thought we were heading toward a relationship—don't worry, I know you're not inter-ested, you made that clear enough—but because we maybe, at least, were being honest with each other. Maybe even becoming friends. And then I find out that this is just the way you are. You screw around with women's heads and then act like it's their fault for liking you."

His eyes narrowed at her. "Because I told you that you were free to go on a date with a man you're clearly interested in?"

"No, because you kissed Miranda just days ago. She told me all about it."

He removed his helmet slowly. "Miranda? Miranda Kaster?"

"Yes, *that* Miranda. Fuck, Callum, did you think she wouldn't tell me? That I wouldn't find out that this is just your . . . *I don't know*, sick pattern of behavior?"

Callum crossed his arms. *And, dammit, why do his arms look so good when he flexes them like that? Fuck, no. Not going to think about that.*

"You mean the woman who threw herself at me when I was stumbling home drunk?"

"That's not how she tells it."

"That's because she was enraged that I turned her down. And, yes, I kissed her," Callum snapped, his eyes burning with fury. "Or rather, I allowed the kiss to happen after she initiated it. Allowed her to shove her hand down my pants aggressively. Is that what you want to hear? But I stopped it right after that and told her that nothing would ever happen between us."

Liddy squeezed her eyes shut. No, she didn't want to hear that. Didn't want to think of Miranda's lips on his, her hands on him. "So you're telling me you had nothing to do with it?"

Callum raked his fingers through his hair. "Look, I have never pretended to be some sort of fucking prince like Quinn. Even my ex says I'm incapable of love. And yes, I have slept with *plenty* of women that I have no intention of ever seeing again. But I've never once been dishonest about it. Not once. And I sure as hell have never had to throw myself at someone like Miranda Kaster just to get a snog and then laugh at her for being gullible. That's not how things work for me."

She swallowed hard. His words fell like stones into the pit of her stomach. She'd known, of course—that first day she'd met him he'd mentioned several women—but it hadn't affected her before. His sex life was his business.

I don't want to know about it.

But now, it was eating her alive.

"Yeah, you're a real saint," she muttered, digging her nails into her palms.

Callum held her gaze. "I never said I was."

"Then why . . ." She took a few deep breaths, trying to gather her thoughts. *Why are you so upset, Liddy?* "Why did you pretend you gave a shit about me? Why kiss me and then tell me it meant nothing? It was a good kiss, Callum. I was there."

"I do give a shit about you." Callum stepped back. "And it *was* a good kiss. But did it ever occur to you that the whole reason I've made my intentions clear is that I don't want you to get hurt? I know we have to pretend for the sake of this dating ruse, but I shouldn't have kissed you at the hot springs. It blurred the lines of reality."

"Right. Because you like definite boundaries." Liddy hugged her arms to her chest. "Except when it comes to me. And Miranda. And—"

"And no one else," Callum growled, his irritation palpable. "Miranda was a mistake. A stupid, drunken slip that shouldn't have happened *after she came onto me* and you—"

"Another stupid mistake that shouldn't have happened, right?" She leveled her gaze at him.

"It's not the same thing," he said coolly.

"How is it not?" She hadn't noticed before how hot and humid the air was, but now with her increasing anger, she was finding it hard to breathe. A beautiful rain forest like this wasn't the right place for this sort of argument. She was supposed to be having fun with her family. Not squabbling over whether Callum was as much of a schmuck as he appeared.

"It's. Just. Not." Callum pulled the helmet back on his head.

"That's not good enough."

"It's going to have to be. You getting back on or should I send someone to come pick you up?"

She set her hands on her hips. "There are only two options, Callum. Either you are exactly what Miranda suggested and you don't care about anything or anyone but yourself—"

"Or?"

She glared at him. "Or you're telling the truth. And if that's the case, then you're just pushing me away because that kiss made you feel something you didn't want to feel. And then the second Sergio came around and threatened your fragile ego, rather than man up and admit that you might actually *want* to cross the line with me—smash all your stupid boundaries—you just tucked tail and ran."

Callum's lips pursed, then he settled back onto the ATV. "Think whatever you want, Liddy. It makes no difference to me."

She balled her hands into fists.

She wanted to punch him.

But then, as she tried to calm her racing heart, she considered his words. *His version . . . of sorts.*

"I do give a shit about you. And it was a good kiss. But did it ever occur to you that the whole reason I've made my intentions clear is that I don't want you to get hurt? I know we have to pretend for the sake of this dating ruse, but I shouldn't have kissed you at the hot springs. It blurred the lines of reality."

At least he wasn't claiming he'd faked his attraction to her. She'd *felt* it.

But he was still quick to walk away.

So he didn't hurt her.

Or so he thought. She was having a hard time wrestling through her anger, hurt, and now indecision.

Had Miranda just spun her a tale to encourage Liddy's hatred of Callum? Because if Liddy was completely honest with herself, she did find it easier to believe Callum's version of the story than Miranda's.

But why? Miranda's my flatmate. We've become good friends over the last two years.

But Liddy *had* gotten to know Callum. And option two made more sense.

"Why would Miranda exaggerate—or even lie—about what happened between you? She's my friend. And she said you two almost had sex." *God, the words almost hurt to get out.*

"Maybe she's not the friend you think she is." Callum squinted at her, revving the engine with a twist of his wrists.

She set her hands on her hips. "What's that supposed to mean?"

Callum gave her a withering stare. "Forget it. You want to believe her and think the worst of me, go right ahead. It's nothing."

She wedged herself in front of the ATV. "There's no nothing now, *Cal.*" She flung the nickname bitterly. "What the hell do you mean?"

He rolled his eyes. "I mean that while your *friend*, Miranda, was busy trying to seduce me, she insinuated we should go back to my place because her flatmate had a crush on me. Which— I'm not saying I believed her—makes her a terrible friend, wouldn't you say?"

A fresh wave of humiliation flushed through Liddy's body.

A crush?

Miranda wouldn't really have told Callum that, would she?

. . . except Miranda had said those same words to Liddy frequently enough.

Oh, I'm going to be sick.

Miranda had made her sound like a pining schoolgirl *to Callum.* And given that Liddy had kissed him since then . . . *my God, what must he think? That I've just been secretly infatuated with him this whole time?*

She covered her mouth and Callum's expression softened. "Like I said, I didn't believe her. I don't consider Miranda particularly honest."

I'm going to kill Miranda for telling him that.

She stiffened, slowly lowering her hands. "To be clear, I haven't spent the last two years secretly hoping—"

"I know. You've been completely professional. And I never considered the possibility of our . . . *friendship* taking a turn like this."

Then that's it. We're friends. Nothing more.

He couldn't be clearer if he tried.

That didn't mean she had to forgive his casual dismissal of her, though.

She climbed back onto the vehicle, desperate to get back to the comfort of her family's presence. She wanted to hate him, but mostly she just hated that he'd gotten to her.

She glared at the back of his head and leaned forward. "You know the one thing that you keep forgetting to ask in all this?"

His shoulders were taut. "What's that?"

"Whether I'd ever want to have a relationship with *you.* And the answer is no, Callum. So maybe get off your high horse for once and for all, okay?"

CHAPTER TWENTY-FOUR

"This was a bloody brilliant idea," Quinn said as he sat beside Callum on a deck chair, squinting into the orange glare of the sun. "Well done. I don't think I've seen Elle so happy the entire time we've been here."

The catamaran trolled in the water, the sea calm as they glided through it, party music streaming from the speakers. Callum sipped his beer, noticing the tingle of a sunburn on his cheeks. "It was all Liddy's idea. I can't claim any credit."

"Yes, well, she claims you're the one who deserves the praise, so one of you is lying or you're both humble—which I know isn't true of you." Quinn smirked, clearly somewhat drunk.

Ha. Quinn wasn't the first to accuse him of arrogance today. It seemed to be a theme.

Quinn nodded toward his parents, who stood on the deck, arm in arm, admiring the sunrise. "Even my parents seem to be enthralled."

"Costa Rica has a way of doing that, if you let it," Callum

said noncommittally. He knew the charm, of course. He understood why tourists fell in love with the "Pura Vida" lifestyle and the different beat of life. It beckoned to the tired masses who spent their days toiling in cubicles, to those who had never experienced a soda café on the beach or the sand between your toes.

Life as it should be.

Unless you'd been here too much, like Callum had, and then you knew the other side. The side where families still experienced disharmony, where crime still marred perfection, where you accepted that days of football weren't a career. Where dreams ended and bills still needed to be paid.

"We should move here," Quinn announced, unsurprisingly.

How many times have I heard people say that same thing? Callum pushed his sunglasses up the bridge of his nose. "You think so?"

"If I can run Sperare from Nashville, there's no reason I can't run it from here," Quinn mused. The nonprofit organization he ran for disabled children had flourished in the past couple of years despite his move from London to be with Elle. "Though, I suppose Elle would miss her children at Heartbeats."

"This does have the right pace of life for a couple of do-gooders." Callum cracked a smile.

"Could you imagine? Sitting in a hammock every morning, drinking the best coffee in the world? Delicious, fresh food. A beach just footsteps away. It's heaven on earth, I tell you. The sizable ex-pat community here proves how wonderful it is."

Maybe it was an opportunity to bring up the whole wedding issue that Liddy was so concerned about.

"If that's the case, why are you moving the wedding to The

Four Seasons? Why not stay here in Samara, where Elle wants to be?"

He didn't have to tiptoe delicately around the subject. Quinn was one of his oldest friends.

Quinn gave him a blank look. "What do you mean? Is that what Elle said?"

"No, but now that Kat has arrived, it seemed to Liddy that what Elle wanted was being . . . overlooked."

Quinn frowned. "Elle seemed thrilled when my mum offered to fly Kat in here and take some of the stress of the wedding off her. Things weren't coming along as smoothly here as we hoped."

Oh.

Could Liddy have gotten it all wrong?

Quinn stood quickly. "Let me talk to Elle. I don't want—"

"No, no." Callum put out a hand to stop him. "I don't think that's necessary. Liddy was just worried. You know—sisterly instinct and all. She wants to make certain everything is perfect for you both."

Fuck it all. This was why it was better not to intrude on things like this. He was here to stand at the end of a row of groomsmen, drink, and nothing more.

Quinn continued to appear torn.

"Really, mate, there's nothing to worry about. You know how women can be," Callum babbled, trying to think of a way to change the topic. "I don't pretend to be an expert in knowing how to keep one happy, let alone a bride trying to manage a wedding. I'm amazed you tried to do things at my mum's place to begin with."

"I remembered how much you always loved it when we were boys. I have to admit, I may have been insanely jealous at the thought of your holidays here. And it's exactly as you described, you know. No wonder your mum wanted this."

That's something I don't want to think about.

Fortunately, he was spared from having to answer Quinn as the song switched to one of Elle's most well-known country hits. The group on the boat gave a wild cheer. Quinn left Callum's side to wrap his arm around Elle's waist, then pulled her in for a kiss.

The moment turned into an impromptu dance for the happy couple, with everyone watching around them, and Callum dropped to the back of the group. He was happy for Quinn. He truly was. Quinn and Elle were a perfect match, and their love was so obvious to everyone who knew them. They deserved this sunset-draped, romantic celebration.

Hell, knowing them, there were probably dolphins nearby, ready to spring out of the water and make it a fairy-tale moment.

Then from the corner of his eye, he saw Liddy wipe a tear from her cheek. She was smiling, watching her sister and Quinn, but her gaze lifted and met Callum's.

A thunderclap sounded through his heart.

She broke eye contact, turned, and strode away from the group, going around the side deck away from them.

Callum hesitated.

What good can come from following her?

Their argument in the jungle had eaten him alive all afternoon.

Yet he couldn't stay away.

He found her standing there, facing the sunset, the wind gently fanning the locks of hair that cascaded around her shoulders.

She's so beautiful.

Instead of speaking, he came to her side and set his hands on the handrail, leaning his forearms on it. The water sparkled below, like gemstones giving one last show in the fading light. "Arguments with me aside, was it a good day?"

She sighed. "Arguments with you aside . . . it was . . . so much fun." A smile hinted at her lips, but her eyes were still sad. "I've been meaning to tell you all afternoon . . . but thank you, Callum, for making it all happen. And paying for it. I don't know why it completely skipped my brain that we'd need to pay for this all up front, but I'm going to pay you back."

He gave her a quizzical look. "How did you find out?"

"Sophia gave Taryn the receipts—and your credit card—to give to me." Her eyes bored into his. "You didn't have to do that, you know. It's a lot of money."

He shrugged. "I live alone and never go on holiday—as you so correctly pointed out. I can spare it. You don't have to pay me back."

She stared at him without speaking for a moment. "Yeah, but it was my idea."

"Quinn and Elle are my friends, too, you know. We'll just call it a wedding present."

"Oh my gosh, no one gives such expensive wedding presents."

"Well, the Camdens do."

Liddy laughed lightly. "I guess you have me there." She drew in a deep breath, then sighed. "I'm just happy to see Elle happy. She went through a lot before Quinn. Had to kiss the proverbial frogs . . . and then she found her prince."

Was that what she was tearful about?

Something told him that Liddy had only ever kissed frogs before.

Including me.

"Liddy . . ." He set his hand on top of hers, but she forcefully pulled hers away.

"No. No, you don't. You don't get to kiss me and tell me

lies. That you think I'm beautiful, and all that bullshit you spewed in the hot springs, and then tell me it's all meaningless the next day. Even if I believe what you said about Miranda, that's not how this works, Callum. We were never friends. And we're sure as hell not going to be after this."

Her words caught him by the throat. He'd pushed her away and pushed hard.

But she believed him?

That was surprising.

And he shouldn't care that she was pushing back.

But I do.

He reached for her again, but this time, he turned her by the shoulders to face him. She deserved something honest from him, especially after the way they'd sparred today. Her tears told him she wasn't as unaffected by him as she'd tried to claim after their last argument. She'd put on a show of bravado because he'd hurt her pride.

I'm such an arse.

His hands cupped her chin, and he searched her watery gaze. "You're right, we can't be friends. I *do* like you. But trust me when I tell you, you don't want to get mixed up with me either. Because the side of me you dislike so much? That's a part of me, too, Liddy. And you won't be safe with me, no matter how much I like you. I'll just end up hurting you in the long run."

"Oh, so what? Am I supposed to just thank you?" Her gaze was hard. "Well, *thank you*, Callum. For saving me from you. Because—what—I'm so damaged I need you to look out for me? I'm so grateful."

She tried to pull away, but something in her words stung. Callum's jaw hardened, and he edged her closer to the wall of the cockpit. Pressing her back against it, he dropped one hand to her waist, skimming the soft skin that showed in a sexy cutout on her dress. His thumb and forefinger held onto her chin, and he pushed his hips closer to hers.

"You think I haven't thought about stripping you down before, Liddy? You're fucking gorgeous. You need a man to tell you that you spent your whole life pretending to be the ugly duckling when you're the fucking swan princess? Fine." His fingertips brushed her jawline before digging into the hair at the nape of her neck as his lips dropped to her ear.

His heart pounded as he felt her breath grow shallower, heard the soft catch in her throat as the hardness of his length pressed against her.

What the hell am I doing?

I want her so fucking much.

"Any sane man would give his left nut to be with you because you're a goddess. You're smart and sexy, with a sass and wit that drives me wild. But you deserve more than just *any* man. And more than a madman. And maybe that's why I kissed you. Because you drive me insane."

I have to stop this.

Her soft lips caught the edge of his jaw, melting his resolve.

She thinks I can be reformed. That there's something good about me. And she needs to know there isn't.

"You deserve *everything*. And I can't give you that." He turned his face toward hers and descended on her lips with force in a raw, punishing roughness that was nothing like their kisses the day before.

But she seemed to match him, breath for breath, each hard stroke of his tongue met with equal force. Her hands wove around his neck, fingertips digging into his hair and pulling. Her teeth sank softly against his lower lip, then harder still, and he groaned.

Blood seemed to rush through his ears, his head light as he deepened the kiss, his hand moving up from the safety of her hip toward her breasts, his hand palming her soft curves. He wanted to find someplace below deck and strip her down, watch those blue eyes widen with pleasure as he took her—

A crack of thunder startled their mouths apart.

Liddy drew a deep breath, still panting. "Was that thunder?"

Even though his body screamed at him to continue, Callum stepped closer to the railing and looked toward the shore. Instead of the relatively cloudless vista of sunset and water, threatening clouds bloomed over the shoreline. He looked toward the deck.

He hadn't realized how visible he and Liddy had been to anyone watching their kiss, but that wasn't something he could worry about now.

The music on the catamaran had stopped, and the crew, who had been handing out ceviche and cocktails, were now handing out life vests.

"Looks like a storm is coming this way." Callum took Liddy's hand and tugged her forward. "Let's go."

"Why would they keep us out here if a storm was coming?" Liddy asked with a hint of fear in her voice.

"It's Costa Rica during the rainy season. There's always a storm coming."

The festive and relaxed mood had changed as they reached the deck. A light sprinkling of rain had already begun, the wind picking up. A crew member handed them life vests immediately as Callum scanned the deck for Quinn's mother.

She was among many of the guests who were attempting to squeeze into the cabin area, which wouldn't fit them all.

She doesn't look happy now.

Fuck.

He finished pulling on his vest, then checked Liddy. Her face was anxious as she held onto a nearby rail.

A bright burst of lightning followed another crack of thunder, and the sky opened up. Rain battered them, and Callum pulled Liddy away from the rail, bringing her closer to the center of the deck. He wrapped his hand around a handrail, bolted into a seating area, then tucked her into his arm.

Regardless of that kiss, she didn't hesitate to sink against him, shielding her face from the rain and salty waves as the catamaran headed back toward the shore.

Liddy lifted her face slightly as another couple sat beside them—Quinn and Elle.

"Wow, that came in fast," Elle said in a loud voice, then reached over and squeezed her sister's knee. "You doing okay, Lid?"

"Yeah, I'm just worried about you." Liddy set her hand on Elle's. "This is not what we wanted for you guys."

"It's the weather. You can't control the weather." Elle shook her head, swiping rain from her eyes. "Honestly, it wouldn't be that bad if it weren't for the fact that so many older people are on this boat. Your mom is going to be livid," she said to Quinn, gripping his hand.

Funny how I had that thought, too.

Quinn's gaze darted to Callum's face, then he looked back at Elle. "Don't worry about my mum. It's our wedding. She can be out of her comfort zone for a few days."

"Yeah, that's easy enough to say. She adores you. I'm just the daughter-in-law, and she'll blame me." Elle shook her head. "Maybe Kat's right about doing the wedding inside rather than tempting fate and doing it on the beach. The weather is too unpredictable this time of year." The ship yawed to the left, and Elle held onto Quinn, who held her close.

Liddy lifted her head from Callum's chest and exchanged a look with him.

She didn't have to say anything. He knew what she was

thinking from the troubled look in her eyes. This might have been a fun idea, but they hadn't considered the risk—that it would only put further doubts into Elle's mind about her wedding plans.

In which case, Liddy is going to feel like we failed.

CHAPTER TWENTY-FIVE

Liddy slammed her hand on the handle of the shower, shutting off the water, and shivered.

This day has been a total disaster.

They'd got back on land after a harrowing trip in the storm, at which point several of the guests had been seasick from the rough waves, including both her parents and Quinn's dad. Once on shore, Kat had been the hero of the hour, waiting with beach towels and dinner for all—delivered to the comfort of their rooms, of course—and a deep, scathing frown for Liddy.

She'd given Liddy an earful about going rogue and not keeping her in the loop with plans, treating her practically like a toddler, then squirreled Elle away for "pampering and planning."

And Elle hadn't answered any texts since.

Kat probably took her phone.

Liddy ignored the dinner Kat had brought in and went to take a shower, only to get doused with freezing water halfway through shampooing her hair.

Which, frankly, tracked for this trip.

Liddy stepped out of the shower and dressed in her pajamas, then towel-dried her long hair. She would give anything to be at her apartment right now and make a cozy cup of tea. Read a book. Fall asleep on the pages.

At this rate, she would need a vacation from this vacation.

She opened the door to the shower, then pushed her way out to find Callum sitting in the sole chair in the room, staring at his phone. He gave her a wry glance. "Penguins?"

Liddy looked down at the fuzzy gray pajama pants, which featured cartoon penguins sliding down hills in the snow. "They're my favorite animal."

And I never intended for you to see my pajamas.

"Very cute." Callum put his phone away and stood. "So bad news. My sister arrived here a bit ago. I haven't seen her yet, but apparently, she couldn't get the wedding dress. Despite the call we made where we explained the incident, who was going to collect the dress, and your permission, the airline wouldn't release it to her. They will only give it to you with your passport."

"Are you serious?" Liddy groaned.

Just one more thing to do tomorrow.

"We'll figure it out." Callum grabbed a few things from his bag. "If nothing else, we're still partners in crime." He headed into the bathroom, then shut the door behind him.

Liddy stared at the closed door. Since that kiss on the boat, they'd seemed to fall back into the easy camaraderie they'd formed over the past few days.

Not that a hot kiss solves anything.

The water started, and she drew a breath, then stepped forward to warn Callum.

Then she stopped short, a smile coming to her lips.

A yelp, followed by a *"Holy fuck,"* came from the bathroom.

She suppressed a giggle, then went over to the bed. Turning on the light on the bedside table, she grabbed a book from her bookbag and sank against the pillows, her back aching as she did. She winced, trying to stretch her shoulders back.

Probably from the ATV.

The day hadn't been *all* bad, though. She'd always wanted to go four-wheeling and had never attempted it. She'd been scared that it might hurt her back, but once she'd been there, she hadn't wanted to make a big deal out of it either.

She could still picture the smiles on Elle's and Quinn's faces as Granny had ridden past them all.

And somewhere on her phone were photos of a toucan and some sloths they'd seen.

The boat ride had been amazing until the storm, and she was convinced ceviche was her favorite appetizer—ever.

Plus, that sunset.

Combined with that kiss.

She'd spent the rest of the evening feeling weak in the knees every time she thought about it. Callum was good with words when he wanted to be—and even better with his mouth when he kissed.

But I'd better not think about that right now.

Settling onto the bed, she opened the book and laid on her left side to read, facing the wall. She'd barely started reading when the door to the bathroom opened, and Callum strode out. A moment later, the towel snapped against her backside, stinging, and she cried out with a laugh. "What the hell was that?"

She turned to see Callum standing a few feet from the bed, his wet hair sticking up in several directions, towel slung over his shoulder. He had shorts on but was shirtless, a few drops of water still clinging to the rigid muscles of his torso. A grin was on his handsome face. "That's what you get for not warning me the water was frigid."

She grinned and gave a scoffing laugh. "Who doesn't check the water temperature before they get in the shower?"

"Someone who's expecting it to be already warmed up." Callum leaned past her and grabbed the empty pillow. "And I'll take that for my comfortable floor bed, thank you." He glanced at the sheets she'd already crawled under. "Do I get a blanket tonight, or should I resign myself to a wet towel?"

She grimaced, glancing at the hard tile he'd slept on the first night they'd been in the room. He hadn't protested or even asked for a different arrangement, but the guilt was there regardless.

She scooted over closer to the wall, pushing her pillow. "You can sleep in the bed. I'm not going to pretend we haven't already shared one."

"What about our body parts being close together?" Callum asked, laughter in his eyes.

Considering your tongue was down my throat today . . .

Liddy threw him a glare. "Do you want to sleep on the bed or not?"

Callum tossed the pillow back down beside hers. Climbing on the bed, he swung his legs onto it. He laid back, head on his pillow, then shifted to his side, leaving a respectable amount of space between them.

Which must be hard in a full-sized bed.

She glanced at her book, then shut it. "Will you put this on the nightstand?"

Callum retrieved it, glancing at the spine as he set it down. "*Every Piece of Me?*"

Great. Here comes the commentary. "Yeah, it's a romance."

"The half-naked man on the cover gave it away." He smirked, then shut off the light. "So that's what you enjoy?"

"Among other things." She rolled onto her back. The room was mostly dark except for the faintest moonlight from the crescent moon. The curtains wouldn't have helped if it was a full moon.

"So what other things? Elves and fae or shifters?"

What?

She glanced at him and laughed. "You read romance?"

"I read nonfiction. But I'm *aware* of what's popular." He leaned closer and said in a mock whisper, "Contrary to popular belief, I'm actually not an ogre who never leaves my office cave."

"Yes, if I remember correctly, there seemed to be quite the parade of girlfriends in your life when we first met."

"Playthings, not girlfriends." He set his arms behind his head. "And if we're being completely honest, I haven't gone on a date in months. The sheer boredom of it has made it less appealing recently."

She choked out a guffaw. "I'm not sure I can sleep in a bed with any self-respecting man that calls a woman a plaything."

He shrugged. "I never claimed to be self-respecting. Or decent. You keep making assumptions about me, and I keep telling you I'm no good."

She shifted closer to him. Whatever body wash he'd used was intoxicating. *Sort of like him.* "You know, if we're going to continue to pretend to date for the next few days, we should probably learn some basics about each other—things our families would be surprised our significant other didn't know."

"Like your love of penguins and smut?"

Reaching over, she flicked his ear.

"*Ow.* It's true, you know."

"And you like . . .?" She prodded, but he didn't answer, so she continued, "What do you read?"

"History books."

"What era?"

"I'm boring. World War II."

"And your favorite animal?"

"Sloths, actually."

"They are pretty cute. Maybe I should change my favorite to sloths."

"Not unless you want me to tease you for lack of originality."

His weight shifted on the bed, and his thigh brushed against her, sending a shiver up her skin. "Did you just scoot closer to me? Knowing two things about me isn't that much, Romeo."

"I'm falling off the damned bed, Liddy." He released a long sigh. "But anyway, I never cared for the industry standard of 'what's your favorite movie/song/color?' We're beyond that."

"Still, it would be useful information. Also, it would be *Saving Private Ryan, Daydream Believer*, and turquoise."

"Stop feeding me answers you think will make me fall in love with you. No woman loves *Saving Private Ryan*."

She poked him in the ribs. "I do. It was the first movie my dad and I watched together, just the two of us. And I love it because of that. What are yours?"

He shook his head, then rolled onto his side, propping his head up with his hand. "I have no idea. I can't remember the last time I watched *any* movie with my dad. If I ever did. Also, those questions wouldn't be what I'd ask you on a date."

She didn't dare turn to look at him even though he was clearly staring at her in the darkness. *Thank God for the dark.* He would be able to see her blush traveling into her face with his nearness. She was incredibly aware of that—and the fact that he was still shirtless. She kept her hands at her sides, breathing shallowly.

He doesn't need to know how much he turns me on.

"What would you ask me?"

"I'd ask . . . what's the one thing on your bucket list you could do *right now,* and what's stopping you from doing it?"

She liked that. Liked that his question was deeper. With his talk of "playthings" and being clearly anti-relationship, it worried her that maybe he was just as shallow as he claimed, and she was trying to fool herself. She stared at the ceiling, then smiled. "I think . . . I'd say skinny-dipping and . . . what's stopping me is the fact that I just got in bed after being cold and wet, and I don't really want to get wet again."

"Are you telling me that skinny-dipping is actually on your bucket list?"

She tried to poke him again, but he caught her hand this time. "It's *my* bucket list. You can't make fun of it. And yes. You'll find my list is probably more normal stuff. What's on yours? Ménage à trois? Climbing Mount Everest?"

"Ménages à trois are overrated. And not Everest—I have zero interest in spending an ungodly amount of money for a sherpa to do most of the work." He pushed back the covers and cooler air hit her. "But come on, get up. Let's go."

She leaned down and reached for the covers, but he held them back. "What are you doing?"

"I'm making you go skinny-dipping."

No way.

"I don't think so." She grabbed the covers and this time, tugged them farther away.

Callum stood and stripped the top sheet, then, as she squealed, he scooped her into his arms. He set her on the floor slowly, and she came to the tips of her toes, her arms wrapping around his neck like it was the most natural thing in the world.

Oh God, are we really doing this?

Because she had a feeling she knew what he was up to.

Her confidence in that fact had only grown with the kiss on the boat earlier. With that knowledge came a sense of power.

Callum wants me.

So he's doing everything to avoid intimacy.

Her lips skimmed his jawline, traveling down his neck as his hands slipped around her waist, pushing up her shirt and settling against the bare skin on the small of her back.

His breathing had gone shallow, and she didn't have to see that piercing gaze to know he felt *desire.*

Raw, fiery lust surged through her, making her core lurch and tug, her underwear growing wetter by the second. "We don't have to go outside," she whispered, and her hand traveled down, settling on his chest. His skin was hot, searing her palm and making her suck in a breath. His nipples had gone hard, his chest taut with tension. "It's not going to keep us so busy that this won't happen, Callum."

"Let's just go outside, Liddy. Knock something off that bucket list." His low voice had a rough edge to it that she hadn't heard before.

I'm right.

He's trying to tempt me with something else I want . . . to keep me away from him.

Despite that, one hand had traveled up her bare back ever so slightly, his palm sending goose bumps up to her shoulders.

"What are you so afraid of?" She stepped back and pushed her penguin pajama pants off her hips, trying to quell the quiver of her own stomach. A T-shirt and underwear were no less revealing than that damn bikini she'd had to wear the day before, but this was different.

His rejection could undo me.

But with each breath, her fear seemed to slip away.

He hadn't moved. She went back toward the bed, her fingers shaking as she reached for the bedside table. Then she flipped on the light, the orange glow spilling through the small room.

"You wanted me to strip down." She reached for the hem of her shirt.

Callum drew a sharp breath. "Don't."

"Or what?" She teased him by raising the hem slowly, revealing her flat belly, the very edge of her breasts. His intense, dark stare followed her movement, his gaze hard as steel.

"Or I'll kiss you so hard that we won't just end up panting on the side of a boat, but completely naked, with you screaming my name as I take you." He stepped closer to her as though he couldn't stay away. "And I can't promise it'll be ever anything more than that, Liddy. I'll wreck your heart, and I won't be sorry."

She almost smiled.

He's conflicted because he cares.

Of all the fucking things I didn't expect, it was that Callum Scott might truly care about hurting me.

His words made her want to sink back and melt against the bed. "You're going to ruin me, is that it?" She arched a brow and licked her lips. "The thing is, Callum, if you don't care about me, then why are you warning me? Why are you stopping yourself?"

His eyes were dark as he stood only inches away, obviously willing himself not to touch her. "Because I know who I am. I'm never doing another relationship. *Ever.* I will ruin you. And I won't like it. But it still won't stop me."

The hardness of his words, the threat of potential heartbreak, seemed to feel strangely. . . like a challenge.

Tantalizing. She shivered, feeling more daring and fun than she ever had—even when jumping off canyons and plunging down a zip line. Wilder than she would doing something like skinny-dipping.

This is fun.

And there was something in that rawness, that honesty, that made her feel like she was the one in control here.

"Maybe I want to be the woman that you try to stay away from but can't. Or maybe I don't even care. You think I can't handle you?" She forced herself through the fear his words were supposed to bring and stepped closer still. "I don't want to handle you. I want to fuck you. And I don't want you to apologize for wanting me."

He drew a breath through his teeth as though her words were a gut punch, and his hands dropped to her hips, grasping her so hard that she was certain he'd leave a mark. "Liddy, I'm warning you—"

She splayed her hands on his chest, her face only inches from his. "Let's be real, Callum. Even if you had gotten me outside tonight, jumping in that ocean naked, you think I wouldn't have pulled you into the water with me? And then we'd be right here." Her lips brushed his lower lip. "And then I'd just be a different sort of wet."

He groaned, then crushed her with a bruising kiss, his arm wrapping around her waist, pulling her tightly against his hips, the hardness of his length thick against her.

"I don't treat the women I fuck like the women I work with," he growled as though it was taking everything in his power to convince himself not to do this. His lips were on her neck, his arms still cradling her against his hips.

A heavy feeling built in her breasts—longing to be touched —and her clit throbbed as pressure and wetness flared between her legs. *God, I want him.*

I want to be the woman he fucks.

This whole trip, Callum had seemed determined for her to challenge her perceptions of herself. Set herself free.

And this. This he holds back on.

She wanted to be fun. *Wild.*

"You promise?"

That seemed to be enough for him. He returned his lips to hers, slanting his mouth over hers with a scorching kiss.

Oh God.

His tongue.

God, the taste of his tongue is incredible.

His hands pushed beyond the waistband of her underwear, cupping her ass and grazing lower. She wanted to push back against his hands, feel his fingers slide behind her, but his palms cupped her ass, then pressed her hard against him.

"Fuck, Liddy. Told you I wanted you. You're so fucking beautiful."

Electric energy sizzled its way up from her core.

And his hands.

She didn't doubt for a second that Callum had much more experience than she did. But he didn't make her feel like that.

Not bent.

Not broken.

Not imperfect in any way.

He makes me feel like a fucking goddess.

His hands left her ass, then pulled her shirt off in one fluid move, and she gasped as his lips left hers briefly. Pushing her onto the bed, he stripped the underwear off, too, and then lay her back. Eyes dark, deep unreadable pools of desire, screaming how dangerous he was. *And I want that danger.*

He's the most danger I've ever felt.

And it made her feel alive.

She watched as he pushed his pants down, her eyes dropping to that long, hard length—*God, he's big*—and she swallowed. His eyes never left her body, watching her lips, her breath, her breasts. Gaze sweeping to her legs, his knee pushed between her knees and parted her for his view.

She shivered in the cool, humid air, her breath falling fast. "Touch me," she rasped.

Those full lips, still wet from kissing her, curved in a smile as he leaned over her, then flipped her onto her stomach.

And then she gasped.

She'd never let anyone see her like this. Heat burned her eyes as his hands skimmed the surface of her back. He crawled onto the bed behind her, lips dropping right between her shoulder blades.

It would have been sexy *even if* she didn't know exactly what he was doing.

The scar she'd hated so much. That she'd been so ashamed of . . . his lips trailed down it, nearly making her body spasm with the soft sensation.

His hands cupped her ass again, this time his fingers dipping lower, pushing between her legs and inside her as she moaned, her legs coming together reflexively.

"Let go, beautiful. Let me in. You want this? Don't hold back."

She released a shattered breath, her body trembling as he pushed one finger, then two, deep inside the slickness there. "Yes . . ."

I want him to fill me. I want his cock inside me.

Callum pulled back, then rolled her gently onto her back. His hands rested on either side of her shoulders as he leaned over her, his mouth catching hers in a kiss once again. "You're like a fucking delicious feast, Liddy. I don't know what part of you I want to taste first."

Why does everything sound sexier in his smooth, cultured accent?

With his tongue diving deep into her mouth, his hands cupped her breasts, his thumb and forefinger rolling her nipples, then pinching, hard.

She groaned into his lips. "More."

He smiled, then dropped his lips to one nipple. Taking it gently into his mouth, he sucked, and her stomach clenched, her hips thrusting up against his.

"Oh my God, Callum."

Her fingers were in his hair, tugging at it, her body aching for more.

He repeated the process with the other nipple, until they'd become hard and wet, pliant with his kisses, the peaks cold in the absence of his warm mouth.

I've never been this wet in my life.

He knelt between her legs again, rubbing her clit with the tip of his cock, and *oh God, more, oh God.* She panted, hips arching, longing to be filled by him.

"Grab my cock, baby."

And something in the nickname made her want to put him in her mouth. But she did what he ordered, wrapping her fingers around his thickness, a deep pulse surging through him at her touch.

"Fuck. I want to take you hard, Liddy. I can't be gentle right now."

"Please, Callum."

A smile hinted at his lips, then he reached for his pants, still on the bed, and fished out a condom from the pocket.

She grinned. "For someone so determined not to do this, you came prepared."

He is huge.

The thought of him pushing that length inside her was nearly undoing her.

"Just because I don't think it's a good idea doesn't mean I wasn't wanting you with every fiber of my body." He rolled the condom on, then edged closer, his thumb stroking her clit. Her body spiraled with every stroke, her legs trembling as he pushed the tip of his cock closer to her. He held her hips, his eyes locked with hers.

"Tell me you want me."

A gasp left her as that rhythmic stroke of his thumb continued. She was dizzy with desire. "Yes, Callum, I want you. Oh God. Yes, more . . . *more*, please."

He leaned over her, then pushed inside her, slamming his full length into her body with a feral groan as she cried out. *Oh my God, he's fucking inside me, and it's incredible. . .*

His touch hadn't let up, either, and she writhed as he pulled back, then pushed again, somehow going deeper as she jerked her hips against him. "God, *Callum*."

"Say my name, baby. I want to hear you."

"Please fuck me, Callum. Fuck me hard."

The tension in her body felt like a string ready to snap as her hips rose to meet each thrust of his hips. "I'm going to fuck you, baby. And not just once. I want to fuck until we both can't walk tomorrow. Say you're going to fuck me."

Her body seemed to float above her. "*Yes.*"

"Come for me, baby."

With the sensation of bursting into a thousand shattered pieces, her body broke free, an orgasm ripping through her as she cried out. He was relentless, driving her higher and higher through the orgasm until her legs clamped against him, and she screamed. "Fuck, Callum."

Then as she floated back to earth, he grabbed her hand, setting it at the base of his cock. "Squeeze me."

As she did, he moaned, heat surging through her hand as he poured himself out, his orgasm throbbing inside her. She gasped, then closed her eyes, spent, her body still tingling.

Exhilarating.

She'd had sex. She'd never *fucked*. Not like this.

Not with someone who made her feel like this either.

Callum pulled out and the fact that she suddenly missed his warmth was startling as he rolled to his side on the bed. As they both caught their breath, he looked over at her. "Good?"

She smiled, a wave of happiness rolling over her.

I just fucked Callum.

What on earth happens now?

"Eight out of ten. Would fuck you again."

He raised a brow. "Only an eight?"

"If I give you a ten, it leaves no room for improvement. And I'm a big believer in achieving perfection."

He closed his eyes, and she could see his pulse on the skin above his heart.

"That's because you're perfect, Liddy."

His words were surprisingly gentle.

And stung.

She didn't want to think about his warning. That this was just a physical thing, nothing more.

Because, dammit, I really like him.

"I'm not perfect. But you know what I am?" She rolled over and looked at him. "Hungry. Like really, really hungry. Know anywhere we can get food close by?"

He checked his watch. "Almost ten . . . maybe, but it'd be a drive." Then his eyes lit, growing almost . . . *mischievous?* "Actually, get dressed, sexy girl. I have an idea."

CHAPTER TWENTY-SIX

Fuck me.

What the hell did I just do?

Breaking into his mum's office had been the last thing on his mind tonight, and—honestly—it was nothing compared to the cataclysmic event that had led to it.

I fucked Liddy.

And not a romantic, holding hands sort of fucking.

Thoroughly fucked. Hard. Fast.

But as he stared across the small table in the office at her, where she was thoroughly enjoying the leftover *gallo pinto* he'd reheated in the microwave for her, he knew one thing.

I'm in trouble.

Not because of work, because, *goddammit*, that was complicated enough. He'd definitely dipped his pen in the company ink, and it wasn't just some coworker either. Liddy Winnick was practically family to the Camdens. The Camdens were as loyal as they come, but if there was any choice between Callum and Liddy, she'd win, no contest. They weren't down here for a getaway with the Winnicks, a big jolly holiday.

They were down here because Quinn Camden, heir to the Camden estate, title, and fortune, was marrying Elle Winnick. That made the Winnicks closer than even their business partners.

And he wasn't in trouble because Liddy was glowing in post-coital bliss—which she was. *Fucking glowing*. She looked radiant and beautiful. She'd worn just one of his long T-shirts and flip-flops, as though she didn't have a care in the world if anyone saw them wandering around the hotel property *looking like they'd just had sex.*

She'd been wild and free.

Hadn't cared about being a fuck and not a thing.

If anything, it'd made her even bolder.

She was bold, outspoken, smart, loyal, kind, and funny. Even her score of an eight had made him laugh. *And that's rare for me.* He had told her he was bad for her. He had warned her. Yet she'd risen to what had seemed like a challenge. And he was terrified that he would hurt and ruin her.

I'm in trouble because I care about her.

No question.

He wouldn't have broken into his mum's office for just anyone.

Wouldn't have traveled all over this country for anyone.

Wouldn't have spent almost eight thousand pounds trying to help save Elle and Quinn's wedding . . . *for anyone else.*

From the moment he'd met her two years earlier, he'd known she was trouble.

And once he'd found out who she was, he'd put that wall up. Kept his distance.

And now she'd broken through as though that armor had been paper thin.

Seeing her happy, though, that had been his undoing.

How can I go back after this?

"This might be the ultimate comfort food. Mashed potatoes and chicken soup have nothing on this," Liddy said, licking the spoon. She smiled. "Though that ice cream we got in La Fortuna might give me wet dreams for years to come."

His gut clenched.

He wanted to kiss the dirty words right off those luscious lips. "Keep talking like that and I'll have to drizzle myself with ice cream."

She set the plate to the side, then left the table, coming over to where he had leaned back against the counter. She set her hands on either side of the counter, then kissed his jawline. "Go on."

Her fingers teased at the waist of his mesh shorts, sending shivers up his skin.

She's insatiable. Callum interlocked his fingers with hers, staying her before she could take it further. "You're going to get yourself in trouble that way."

Squeezing his fingers, she let his hand go, then slipped her hand down the waistband. "What if I want trouble?"

Her lips collided with his, effortlessly, magnetically, her tongue diving into his mouth as her hand stroked him. All thought went out of his brain except that damned word *trouble* pulsing with each caress.

She's trouble.

"I don't have a condom here," he whispered as she pulled away.

She smiled, then pulled her shirt off. "We don't need one."

Oh fuck, those tits. He needed to add that to the list of things to do with her. "We don't?"

Full, with rosy-pink nipples that were hard already. "I'm going to have my way with you, Callum. First, I'm going to kiss you." She pushed those perfect tits against his shirt front and he groaned, hands reaching for them.

"You make me feel free," she whispered against his lips. "I want to kiss you hard, fast, and—*oh* . . ." she moaned as he pinched her nipple. "God, yes, more."

He rolled her nipple hard between his fingers, then dipped his head to kiss the other one. Her throat rested against the top of his head and she released a whimper. "And then I'm going to take your cock in my mouth, suck you until you come in my throat . . . oh, *yes* . . ."

Trouble.

He squeezed her tit hard, and she groaned again. His tongue flicked her nipple, his need for her overtaking him at the sound of her pleasure.

"And then we're going b-back . . ." she panted as he moved to the other nipple. "Back to the room and you're going to fuck me, bare, until we can't walk."

Everything about this woman was surprising. Even her ability to talk dirty and still look like a perfect angel.

I'm fucked.

She drew her hair back, pulling it into a hair tie around her wrist, then knelt in front of him. Pulling his shorts off his hips, she took his length and licked him.

Drawing him into her mouth, she stroked him with her tongue, twirling it around him. Her hands connected with her lips, taking him deeper.

My God, this woman.

He panted, any ability to think gone as she worked her magic, taking him deeply, rhythmically, with all the skill and confidence in the world.

Until he groaned.

Fuck.

Trouble.

He was coming. In her mouth.

His fingers were tight on the top of her head.

Click.

He could barely process what was happening until the back door to the kitchenette was already open.

Mum and Isla stood there, blinking.

Isla—*God love her*—slammed the door shut again.

Liddy pulled away, scrambling for her shirt as Callum turned from the doorway, bare-arsed, then reached for his shorts.

"Shite," Callum said, yanking his shorts up. He glanced at Liddy, who had somehow pulled the shirt on already—albeit inside out.

She stood, red-faced, then covered her face. "Oh my God, your mom."

From outside the door, Callum heard Isla cackling. "Can we come in now, lovebirds? Or is there still sex going on? I wouldn't want to interrupt before Callum gets his happy ending."

"*Callate,*" Mum hushed in Spanish, her voice sounding farther away. "Jesús! Nunca lo hubiera creído." *I never would have believed it.*

Holy fuck.

Callum drew an embarrassed Liddy into his arms as Isla opened the door again. *No getting around this one now.*

His sister strode in, a grin on her face. "Mum decided to take a little walk." Isla tossed her hair—dyed red—over her shoulder, then came up to Liddy, hand outstretched. "I'm Isla. Callum's sister."

"Liddy," she managed.

"Oh, *you're* Liddy. Nice to put a face to a name." Isla wrinkled her nose. "You don't have to be embarrassed. I've seen loads of breasts before. And you have nice ones—I should know, I work in theater. Everyone's half-naked part of the time backstage. And as for that peen"—she gestured toward Callum

—"Mum used to have us take baths together when we were kids, so I've seen that, too."

Callum rubbed the back of his neck, not sure if he should be more embarrassed for Liddy, who still looked mortified, or for the outrageous behavior of his sister. "Nice introduction, Isla."

"Well, we may as well acknowledge what's what. Though, from the looks of it, you're—what? Lovers? Callum wasn't exactly clear on what was going on."

Liddy cleared her throat. "Um, why don't I go back to the room? Let you and your sister catch up?"

Callum nodded. "See you soon."

Liddy gave Isla a polite smile. "Nice to meet you, Isla."

Isla watched Liddy go and then arched her brow. "Damn. I was hoping she'd be spunkier."

"She's plenty spunky, you just embarrassed the shite out of her."

Laughing, Isla gave Callum an impressed look. "Wow, you must really like her. Defending her and everything. Clearly, she's more than just a good lay."

"Watch it, Isla." Callum hardened his gaze against her.

Yet she's not wrong.

"If this was the first time I'd walked in on you, Cal, it would be different. I wouldn't have a yardstick to compare to. You were quite an arse to that poor girl who yelled at me when I stopped by your flat that night Charlie broke up with me. I believe you yelled right back and then tossed her out."

"This is a totally different situation." Callum went over to the sink and turned it on. He splashed water on his face, cooling his skin.

"Yes, you like this woman. That's the difference." Isla came up beside him and put her arm around him. "I'm so proud, big brother. You've finally opened your heart up to love again."

Callum chortled. "I do *not* love her." He turned and narrowed his gaze at her. "Things are just complicated with her because of Mum and Sophia. I told Mum we were dating to keep her from spending every waking hour trying to convince me to get back with Sophia while I was here." *Although, I am absolutely certain Sophia has never shared Mum's optimism about us. Sophia's words were clear.* "But she's a colleague and Quinn's future sister-in-law—"

"And you're clearly intimate." Isla crossed her arms and turned her back to the counter. "Was this before or after you arrived?"

"After. And after I spent the last few days trying to help her track down Elle's wedding dress—we thought it was stolen— only to find out that it was at the airport all along."

Isla smiled. "Oh, big brother, you have no idea what you're doing, do you? You must really, really *like* her." She reached over and pinched his cheek. "You're so cute when you're a real person with feelings."

Her words were like a blow to his gut, and his chest tightened.

He knocked her hand back. "Stop it."

She ignored him and squeezed his side. "Callum and Liddy. It's cute. Has a nice ring to it. And if you wanted to convince Mum that you're involved, you did an excellent job there. She might be at the house bleaching her eyeballs."

"Probably praying to God that somehow lightning strikes Liddy dead, more likely."

Isla draped herself on his arm. "Oh stop. I swear, Callum, if I have to spend this entire trip hearing you whine about how terrible Mum is, I'll shoot you myself."

Seeing an opportunity to shift the conversation away from Liddy, Callum took it. "Did Mum tell you she's thinking of selling *La Hacienda*? Sophia said business isn't going so well."

Isla's demeanor changed in an instant. "Wow, she brought you up to speed faster than I thought." She chewed on her lower lip. "I knew," she admitted to his hard stare.

"Mum told you she was struggling?"

"She probably would have told you—you just refuse to talk to her. Or to me about her. When was the last time we talked about Mum? You rarely let her name pass my lips."

That's true.

Then as he'd expected, Isla said, "I want to buy it. But I don't have the money. So I was thinking maybe you could lend it to me—"

"Absolutely not."

"Callum, this is Mum's dream. She built this place with the love of her life, and you, what, just want to see it die?"

Callum frowned, her words hitting him hard.

Love of her life?

"What?" He gave Isla a confused look. "What 'love of her life?'"

"Carmen." Then Isla scanned his face, horror coming into her expression. "Are you telling me you . . . didn't know?"

"Didn't know . . ."

Isla covered her mouth. "How could you not know? Oh my God, big brother, I never imagined you were *this* naive."

He was quickly putting the pieces together, but less quickly than he should have for something that should have been more obvious. "Mum and Carmen . . . were best friends." His words sounded empty, even from his own lips.

"They were a couple, Cal. Mum left Dad to be with Carmen."

"S-she . . . cheated on him . . . with Carmen?"

Isla nodded.

What. The. Fuck.

Unfiltered rage curled through his veins.

All this time, he'd thought Dad was the one who broke up their family.

But Mum?

And *La Hacienda*—and everything they'd built here—had been based on that betrayal.

A sick feeling crested through him.

No wonder Mum hadn't batted an eyelash at Sophia's cheating. *It takes one to know one.*

Although, that wasn't really all it was either. His mother considered Sophia an actual daughter. *Because she's Carmen's daughter.* She had literally been like a goddamn daughter to Mum for more years than he'd known.

"How can you make me choose?" Mum's words make far more sense now.

Callum raised a hand to his throbbing temples. "I need to sit." He stumbled toward the chair at the table and sat, unable to think straight and feeling sick.

How could his mum never have said anything? How could she have been so happy to see her son in a relationship with a girl she viewed as her own daughter? He felt incestuous as fuck. The whole thing was sick.

Everything he'd ever known about his mother was a lie.

A mixture of emotions played on Isla's face. She was clearly flabbergasted but also. . . *sad?* "I can't believe you never knew," she said softly. "Didn't Sophia ever say anything?"

"Sophia?" *Good God.* She'd known about it, too? Callum raked his fingers over his scalp. "Carmen got so sick right after we'd started dating. Sophia never wanted to talk about her. She'd just start crying. Then she died, and it was even worse."

"I guess that makes sense. You weren't here that often after you went to university, anyway. And you were a kid before that, really."

He scanned Isla's face. "It's hard to believe you have a relationship with Mum after all she's done. She's even worse than I thought, Isla. She destroyed our family. Cheated on Dad. Encouraged my relationship with someone she thought of as my *stepsister?*"

"I know." Isla set her hand on his. "And I get it, I do. I get why you're mad. But she's also our mum. And the way I see it, I can either have a mum and accept that she's human and imperfect or I can cut my family off and be lonely and miserable like you. And this is my home. I don't want to lose it. Not when I could save it . . . if you'd help me."

"It's not my home. And in my case, Mum has spent the last five years whitewashing the same sort of betrayal that she dealt out, telling me I should forgive and forget. Making me feel like I was less important to her than the daughter of her bes—*her partner.*"

Isla fidgeted in her seat. "Maybe it's not Sophia that she's eager to have you forgive, Cal."

Callum stood. "It doesn't matter. I don't forgive her. Not for picking Sophia and especially not for picking Carmen. And I have no interest in saving her little dream here, no matter how attached to it you are." He gestured toward the office. "So don't ask again."

He left Isla there, his blood boiling.

Veering off the path to the bungalows, he made his way down toward the beach, stopping short when he came to a clearing in the jungle.

He drew in a deep breath, the sweetly scented, humid air filling his lungs that they had been desperately deprived of.

Goddammit.

He didn't want to hurt Isla. She was the person who mattered the most to him. The one constant in his life.

But it had all started here.

All the hurt.

Confusion.

Betrayal.

Being a scared nine-year-old kid who no longer had a home, no longer had a family altogether in the same place at the same time. Who shuttled from one place to the next, never feeling like any place was his.

Rootless.

He sat on the path, drawing his knees in as he wrapped his arms around his legs.

And I'm just supposed to forgive all that?

Mum's dreams had destroyed his life.

He caught sight of one of the scars on his leg.

And then this place destroyed mine.

CHAPTER TWENTY-SEVEN

"Morning, gorgeous." Callum's voice was husky as Liddy woke up, still tangled in his arms.

She murmured a response, then sunk her head back on the pillow, barely feeling like she could move. Somehow, though, Callum's hand roved up her thigh, skimming hungrily.

"I'm still asleep." She laughed as his fingers found her swollen clit. He was hard already, and she shifted her legs open as she curled her ass into his erection.

He pushed his way inside her effortlessly, like he hadn't fucked her six—*or was it seven*—times throughout the night. Thank God she'd still been taking the pill, even during this crazy trip. They'd ditched the condoms after the first time.

She groaned in pleasure. His hand held her breast as she pushed back against him, enjoying this. She'd never experienced spooning and fucking simultaneously, but it was easy and lazy, just what she needed for early morning sex.

After that incredibly embarrassing episode in his mom's office the night before, she wasn't sure what sort of mood Callum would come back in. She'd gotten her answer when he'd walked into the room later, climbed straight into bed, and buried his face between her legs.

That orgasm was a ten out of ten. But she hadn't told him that.

They hadn't talked much but, somehow, something seemed different in him. And then they'd kept coming back to each other throughout the night, clinging to each other.

He's spent more of the night inside me than out, she thought with an amused chuckle.

And with each touch, with each time they came together, she knew one thing clearly . . .

I like Callum.

Except she couldn't.

He didn't want that.

He wanted someone to fuck and leave.

And, shit, I still have that date with Sergio tonight.

And have to get Elle's dress.

She wasn't sure what she was going to do about either.

Right now, though, it didn't matter. Right now, her legs trembled as her body came closer to coming.

He thrust harder now, up into her as his fingers refused to relent on her clit. "That's so good, babe . . ." she murmured, pushing back to meet each thrust.

So good.

"Oh God, Callum."

"Say it."

She turned her face and pressed a breathless kiss to his mouth.

"You fuck me so good, Callum."

"Yeah? You want more?"

"Yes . . ." Her body was in a full-out spasm now, each thrust, each stroke bringing her closer to bliss. "Fuck me. Fuck me good, babe. I want to feel you come inside me."

He groaned, releasing his load, and the sensation made a spasm rip through her core, bringing her to the edge. "Say it, baby."

"I'm coming for you, Callum. It's so good . . ." She could hardly get the words out now, her moans louder than she intended. Her breath came in short pants of pleasure, heat burning her face, making spots dance in her eyes.

Then she relaxed, her core unclenching as she came down and settled back in his arms.

I could lie in his arms forever.

She swallowed nervously, the thought pulsing through her brain clearly enough.

Callum was right.

He'd told her he was going to ruin her.

And I could fall for him. Hell, it would be so easy to pretend this is the start of something more long-term.

His breath was soft on her neck, and she shivered, then disentangled herself from him. She needed to clean up.

Get up.

Much as she wanted to stay here, the more she considered doing that, the more afraid it made her.

She stood, then kissed his cheek. "I'm going to shower. Hopefully, there's some hot water this time. Then maybe I'll go out, see if I can find Elle and talk to her before Kat gets ahold of her."

"If you change your mind, I'll be here getting some of the sleep I didn't get last night."

"Whose fault is that?" she teased.

He slapped her ass as she scooted past.

This.

She wanted this.

Playfulness.

Morning sex.

All of him.

She pushed the thought away.

She showered and got dressed, and by then, Callum really had fallen asleep again. Then she slipped out the door quietly, the early morning light soft as it filtered through the canopy. The howler monkeys were at it again, but she smiled at them.

At least I got my phone back.

Then she wrinkled her nose, feeling guilty. When she'd vented to Miranda about Callum the day before, she hadn't been entirely generous. She wished she could take it back. And now that she'd slept with Callum, it would leave her in a precarious situation with her roommate. Miranda wouldn't be thrilled to hear that Liddy had not only chosen to believe Callum's version of what had happened but then she'd also slept with him.

But that was a problem for later.

Maybe the monkeys knew what they were doing by taking my phone.

She hadn't gone far when she spotted Kyle on a lounge chair by the pool. He waved when he saw her.

"You up already?" Kyle asked, surprised.

"Yeah, I'm looking for Elle."

"She's on the beach. Morning yoga. I'm waiting to escort Granny and Mom down, too."

Liddy cringed. If Elle was on the beach, then that was where she had to go.

But if she's doing yoga, that means Callum's mom will be there, too. She wasn't sure that she could look Callum's mom in the eye ever again.

"You're a good brother, you know that?" Liddy said, sitting beside Kyle. "Taking care of Granny, babysitting Kat . . . you basically do anything that's asked of you."

Kyle offered her a warm smile. "Well, if you haven't

noticed, I'm one of the few single people here, which makes my schedule more flexible. And definitely the only single one in our family, unless you count you, which I don't because I saw a certain guy kissing you on that catamaran yesterday."

"You saw that?" Liddy's eyes widened.

Kyle rolled his eyes. "If you were going for discretion, you could have picked a spot that wasn't in plain view of anyone on that back deck." He winked at her. "So I guess things went from fake to real somewhere on the road?"

"Not exactly." Liddy clasped her hands. She should feel happy. And some part of her *did* feel like she was floating on the clouds. Probably the part of her that remembered a night of the best sex she'd ever had. "It's just a . . . vacation fling. We'll end it back home."

"Back home . . . in London?" Kyle gave her a confused look. "And what the hell do you mean, a vacation fling? You're Liddy. The good one. You don't do flings."

"Yeah, I know," she breathed out. "I do terrible relationships with stupid guys and get my heart broken." She rubbed her knees. "So I've decided to turn over a new leaf and just have fun."

Kyle stared at her, his eyes unamused. Then he shook his head, tearing his gaze away. "Goddammit. You're going to make me punch someone on this trip, aren't you?"

What?

She loved that Kyle was so fiercely protective of her but where was this coming from?

"What are you talking about?"

"I . . . I-I don't know how you can sit there and say that with a straight face, Lids. Answer me this: who wants this to be a vacation fling? Him or you?"

Oh.

She drew a shallow breath. "Him."

Anger flashed in Kyle's eyes. "Right. Because . . ." He stood, clearly struggling to sound calm. "Because he's a stupid guy drawing you into a terrible relationship. And he's going to break your heart, too."

Why do his words ring so true?

Because I'm scared. Scared I'm going to get hurt.

And yet . . .

This is what I want.

I want to be with Callum, even if it's just for this trip.

She'd tasted him. Slept in his arms. She couldn't go back now.

"Kyle." Liddy stood and took both of his hands. "I know it sounds crazy, but I'm going into this with both eyes open. I know what he's offering, and I know what I can handle. So just give the guy a break, will you? For my sake? He's been great and really sweet the last few days. He even paid for all those excursions yesterday." *Kyle doesn't have to know about our arguments.*

"Amazing how sex messes up people's ability to think straight," Kyle said in a flat tone. He glared at her. "And don't deny it."

"Deny what?" Granny's voice came from around the bend. She walked right beside Mom with a bounce to her step.

"Deny me the opportunity to watch her do yoga," Kyle shot back. "Looking beautiful this morning, Granny. You, too, Mom."

Mom rolled her eyes. "You don't have to compliment me, Kyle. I'm not a compliment whore like Fran."

Granny gave her a side-eyed glare. "No, you're just a regular old whore, am I right, Brenda?" Then she cackled and continued down the path with Kyle.

"You're really going to yoga, Liddy?" Mom looked surprised as Liddy fell into step beside her. She made a face.

"Sorry. I'm not trying to discourage you. I know you can do much more now since your surgery. I just forget sometimes. My friend Linda—you remember her son, Jalen? Severe allergies. Even though he's been out of the house five years, Linda still checks labels everywhere she goes."

Liddy sighed, her eyes skimming the palm trees bent low over the water near the beach. The small group on the shore chatted as they rolled out yoga mats on the sand. "It's fine, Mom. Yeah, I'm going to yoga. I need to talk to Elle."

"About what?" Mom held onto Liddy's arm as she descended the last steps toward the beach. Hard to believe that just a few years earlier, Mom hadn't been able to move around without a walker after her accident.

"I just want to make sure she's okay. I know Quinn's mom really mixed things up by bringing on that wedding planner and trying to change the wedding to The Four Seasons."

"Elle seems happy with the changes, honey. I wouldn't bother her with that."

Liddy searched Mom's face. "Does she, though? You know how Elle is, Mom. She doesn't like making waves."

Mom squeezed Liddy's forearm. "Liddy, I don't want you to take this the wrong way, but the only person I've seen causing waves lately is you. Look"—Mom gestured toward the group peacefully stretching on the beach—"everyone is fine. Relaxed. Happy. You're the only one who seems out of sorts." She winked at Liddy as they reached the sand, then released her arm and continued forward.

Liddy hung back, Mom's words making the hairs on the back of her neck rise.

Am I really the one causing drama?

On the one hand, Mom was right—several people were on the beach, relaxing into yoga poses. Elle was there, a smile on her face, her blond hair swept back into a messy bun. Quinn's mom was close by, wearing a hat and a loose white cover-up. Rebecca and Taryn and Hunter were among the yoga group, along with several of the Winnick cousins.

Quinn and his dad appeared to be fishing on the beach with his brothers and Liddy's dad. Even Leo was there with them.

A content, peaceful scene.

Liddy hugged her arms to her chest, feeling oddly like an outsider.

This was her family.

Her people.

The one group she should fit in with.

Yet most of the time she'd been here, she'd been on the outside. Because of Sergio and the dress and *Callum.*

Too many lies.

She'd never been so unable to speak freely with her sister.

And even Kyle, who knew the truth, wasn't exactly happy with her or Callum.

She stepped forward, and then her mom's voice rang through her head. *"You're really going to yoga, Liddy?"*

Tears stung her eyes.

Maybe she'd always been the outsider.

The one who'd held them back.

How many family vacations had never come to fruition because of her spine and her expensive medical care?

Not to mention the times that her parents had declined opportunities because "Liddy won't be able to do that."

Elle *did* seem fine with the changes Kat had made. She didn't seem mad at her mother-in-law. And Elle had also asked Liddy for her help with the wedding plans that were falling apart, but she'd been so busy trying to track down Sergio that she hadn't provided it. *Of course Elle turned to someone else.*

"I'm the problem," Liddy whispered. She didn't need Elle

to say what a letdown she'd been. She'd been too busy with her own things. *How can she not resent me?*

Liddy turned to go.

She nearly ran straight into Isla.

"Whoa, lady." Isla jumped back, then laughed. "We have to find less interesting ways of meeting." She reached for Liddy's hand and smiled. She was gorgeous, just like Callum, and equally magnetic. "I feel like I completely embarrassed you last night, by the way. And I probably shouldn't even bring it up, but I wanted to apologize."

"No apology necessary." Isla's warmth was enough to get Liddy over the embarrassment anyway. Despite not knowing Isla, it was clear she was Callum's opposite. Or maybe more accurately, Isla was more like the side of Callum that he only showed in private.

"So my brother seems smitten with you," Isla said, linking arms with Liddy and tugging her back toward the beach. "Which is wonderful because he needs a good woman. He's spent the past five years only going out with the most inane women on the planet because they're the only ones who would put up with him."

Funny how Isla, who Callum rarely talked about, also seemed to be the person he'd allowed to know him best. "I don't think smitten is the right word."

"Well, it's clearly more than lust." A hint of a dimple showed in Isla's left cheek as she spoke. "Lust is something he's able to control. I get the feeling he's not quite in control when it comes to you." She stopped, gesturing toward the group doing yoga. "You going to join in?"

Liddy tried not to overthink Isla's bold words. "I'm not sure. I have a rod in my back. Scoliosis since childhood."

"There are plenty of yoga poses you can do despite that.

Why not get my mum to help? She's good with that sort of thing."

Something else Isla had in common with Callum. Her determination not to let Liddy get out of anything easily.

Callum had said she'd like Isla, and he was right.

"Oh, just do it, Liddy." Rebecca, who was beside them, tossed a yoga mat over. "You'll be fine. It's yoga, for goodness' sake."

"Who's this?" Isla asked.

"Isla, this is Mason's girlfriend, Rebecca. And a good friend of mine. And this is Callum's sister," Liddy said, introducing them.

Isla unrolled a yoga mat for Liddy, then waved her mom over.

"Mum, can you adjust things for her as you go? You know, for her back?"

"Por supuesto," Callum's mom said with a smile.

"Oh—um, Señora—" Liddy had forgotten what Callum's mom had asked her to call her.

"Lety."

"That's right." Liddy's heartbeat ticked up in speed. "I just wanted to apologize about last night—"

"No, no, is okay." Lety set her hands on Liddy's shoulders. "You love my son, yes? I understand."

Love? Liddy grimaced to herself. *Or something else.* She'd certainly *wanted* her son. Been *having fun* with her son. "Well, I still feel bad."

Lety winked. "We are all young once." Then she scrambled back to the front of the group, ready to start the class.

"I'm still completely embarrassed," Liddy told Isla.

Rebecca lifted her head. "And why's that?"

"My mum walked in on Liddy and Callum banging in the office last night—"

"Isla!" Liddy hushed her with a look.

Rebecca gave Liddy an impressed glance. "This is a whole new side of Liddy I didn't know."

Liddy flung a handful of sand toward her. Rebecca dodged it, laughing. "You two better keep it down before it becomes a whole new side of me that everyone else finds out about."

"To be fair, it's the only side of you I've ever known." Isla unrolled her mat and then glanced up. Her expression changed, and Liddy followed her gaze.

Sophia had appeared on the beach, a yoga mat under her arm.

A look of dislike flashed in Isla's eyes, then she blinked it away. Isla's gaze darted to Liddy. "You going to be okay?"

"Why wouldn't I be?" *Other than the fact that Callum's ex is a gorgeous, tanned Latina who looks like she belongs here while I don't.*

"You know, the whole 'ex my brother was still hung up on five days ago' thing," Isla whispered and braided her hair swiftly. "I can understand why you'd feel uncomfortable around her."

Still hung up on?

The words dropped to the pit of Liddy's stomach.

Was Callum still hung up on her?

A familiar feeling of insecurity crept over Liddy as Sophia approached the group, then got ready to join them.

But, then again, what difference did it make?

It wasn't like Liddy and Callum were an actual couple.

The insecurity was natural. She couldn't compete with *that.* Sophia was lithe and bendy.

The thought of Callum's hands on Sophia's body made her shudder.

No reason to be jealous.

Except for the fact that I do give a shit.

. . . because I'm involved with him now.

Feeling stuck but more awkward than ever, Liddy followed in the yoga session, making halfhearted attempts at the poses as Lety came over to check on her from time to time.

I don't belong here.

Elle did.

Elle was graceful. And next to her was Taryn—a trained, professional dancer.

What was it that Callum had said? That she viewed herself as the ugly duckling?

She wanted so badly to believe Callum's words, but she hadn't gotten through the challenges that life had thrown her way by lying to herself either. She would never be like her sister or the other women around her. They had no idea what it was like to have a body that did what it wanted, rather than what *she* wanted.

The yoga session was anything but relaxing.

With each second that passed by, Liddy felt a familiar, defeated numbness enclosing over her.

What am I even doing here?

Everything was too confusing. Too complex.

Whatever she was feeling for Callum. Her fears for Elle's wedding day.

Kyle's warning had shaken her in a way she hadn't wanted to admit. Was she risking her heart foolishly?

Callum's words rang hollowly through her chest as she dropped into child's pose, trying to ignore the grit of sand beneath her forehead on the mat.

"Because I know who I am. I'm never doing another relationship. Ever. I will ruin you. And I won't like it. But it still won't stop me."

He'd nearly promised he *would* hurt her. So how would she stop that?

In his arms, with their bodies intertwined, it had been too easy to forget that he didn't want her. That he would call her beautiful and sexy, but then walk away when this was over.

And the thought of that made her heart ache, a low, pulsing, dull pain in her chest.

And then there was Elle's wedding. She had meant to support Elle, make sure she was happy. And she thought she had been . . . *but* . . .

"The only person I've seen causing waves lately is you."

Was Mom right? *That I'm the one causing all the issues here?*

As the session wrapped up, Liddy rolled her mat up slowly, then dumped it in the pile. If Elle was happy, then that was all that mattered. And right now, Elle looked happy. The total opposite of what Liddy felt. Was she just assuming Elle was miserable because of how she was feeling herself?

She started to walk away, but Elle saw her and came toward her. "Hey! I didn't know you came out here until the end. You should have come and hung out with me. I miss you."

"Everyone wants to be next to the bride," Liddy said with a shrug. She clasped her sister's hand. "Anyway, I got to hang out with Rebecca and Isla."

"Isla?" Elle searched the group on the beach for her. She stepped closer to Liddy and lowered her voice. "Did she bring my dress? I really need to try it on."

Umm.

How am I going to explain this?

"Well, actually, I think the airline rerouted it to the other airport . . . but it's coming," Liddy stammered. "Should be here today."

Elle's face fell. "Are you serious, Liddy? God, at this rate, I just should have had Logan bring it."

Ouch.

"I'm sorry, Elle," Liddy said, her throat tight.

Elle's eyes softened. "No, it's fine. I'm sorry, too. I shouldn't have snapped. It's just that I've been fielding some questions from Kat about when the dress will be here."

Liddy reached for Elle's hand, everything she wanted to say on the tip of her tongue.

Elle, I know I messed up. I lost the dress. I haven't been here for you when you needed it, and I've been lying about Callum and me. And don't you think you'd be happier in the long run if you stayed in La Hacienda?

But what would that accomplish?

It would just bring her sister more stress.

Maybe the best thing to do right now, no matter how much guilt she felt about it, was to let it go.

"Look who we dragged out of bed," Aiden said from behind them, and Liddy and Elle turned to see Aiden and Callum approaching. Logan was steps behind them, a soccer ball under his arm. "Any of the ladies fancy a game of football?"

Liddy met Callum's eyes, her heart giving a *thump* at the sight of him. She'd thought he was sexy before last night, but now her whole body seemed to be aware of his presence. A smile played at his lips as he exchanged a look with her.

I'm in serious danger of becoming addicted to that smile.

"You're in a good mood for someone who got dragged out of bed," Liddy teased.

Aiden wrapped his arm around Callum's neck, then ruffled his hair. "Cal wouldn't miss football, eh, mate?" He let him go, giving him a shove toward Liddy. Then he winked and jogged toward his other brothers farther down the beach.

"I am not playing soccer," Elle said with a shake of her head. "Knowing my luck, I'd get elbowed in the face and wind up with a black eye for my wedding."

"You're playing?" Liddy asked, searching Callum's face.

Does he even play anymore? A career-ending injury didn't mean he couldn't play recreationally. But he'd spoken about the end of his football days with bitterness. "Are you—"

"I'm fine." Callum set his hands against the small of her back, tugging her against him. "If you can do yoga, then I can play football." Dipping his mouth to hers, he caught her lips in a sultry kiss. He dragged his mouth to her earlobe. "I missed you."

She laughed, her face warming as she stepped back. *This feels so real.*

"Oh, you should have seen my Callum when he was a boy," Lety said, coming closer to them, pride beaming on her face. "All the kids would play on the beach. But he was the best." She touched his cheek, turning his face toward her. "Carmen and I would sit and watch you get all the goals. We were so proud."

Callum stiffened. "I honestly don't give a fuck if Carmen was proud. I didn't do it for her," he gritted out.

Yikes. That was harsh, even for Callum.

His mom dropped her hand. "I only meant—"

"Mum, don't embarrass him," Isla called from a few feet over. "Liddy knows from experience Cal is the best at everything he does." She winked at them.

"Isla, por Díos," Lety muttered.

Even Liddy knew what that meant. Her thoughts had been identical. She glanced around to see who might have overheard. *Oh God. Isla.* Liddy was going to kill her. *She's having way too much fun with this.* But she had defused the tension between Callum and his mom.

What Liddy hadn't expected though, was how Sophia would be staring at them all. She hadn't acted jealous at all over the course of this trip, but the look on her face now was . . . *sheer dislike.*

CHAPTER TWENTY-EIGHT

Had Sophia overheard Callum?

He appeared to be occupied by his mom and their standoff. Maybe Lety had scolded him about the scene in the office the night before.

Either way, neither of them seemed to catch Sophia's hostile glare.

Then Sophia noticed Liddy's stare and her expression cleared instantly, a pleasant smile returning to her lips. She sidled over toward Liddy. "Are you going to play fútbol with the men? You should."

"Liddy rarely plays contact sports," Elle said, and Liddy raised a brow. She'd almost forgotten her sister was quietly observing everything going on around her. Elle's voice held a protective tone, and not in how Mom usually tried to discourage her from doing "dangerous" things.

Had Elle seen Sophia's look of dislike, too? Liddy tried to catch Elle's gaze, unsuccessfully.

"You really don't have to, Lid," Callum said in a low tone, taking her hand.

"I'll play," Isla announced cheerfully. She tied her hair up and bounded over toward the group, leaving a trail of prints in the sand. If Liddy had any doubt that she'd been purposely trying to lighten the air between her mom and her brother earlier, she no longer did. Isla was clearly used to playing the peacemaker.

This time, Isla's antics didn't seem to affect the strained group, who paid her little attention.

"You should let your girlfriend play, Callum." Sophia raised her chin, squaring off with Callum. "Unless you think she can't keep up with you."

Is that a dare?

Why was Sophia purposely trying to rile up Liddy—or Callum? She must have heard him mention her mother and grown defensive.

"Maybe she's standing right here and can speak her own goddamn mind without your interference," Callum said in a cold, stern tone.

Callum's mom looked tense as she glanced between Sophia and Callum.

Liddy shifted her weight, feeling only slight comfort from Elle's presence. Her gaze flitted to Isla, whose words earlier came back to her.

"... the *ex my brother was still hung up on five days ago.*"

Was this why Callum had wanted to pretend to be dating? Not because he worried about his mom's interference but because he wanted to make Sophia jealous? There certainly seemed to be *tension* between them, that was for sure.

"I *can* play, but I don't want to," Liddy said in a quiet voice. Her gut roiled as she turned to go, and Callum's hand tightened against hers.

"Stay," he said, stepping closer to her. His eyes searched

hers, a piercing intensity to his gaze. "Please. I enjoy seeing you here."

He didn't lower his voice or say it in a way that only she could hear, but it somehow still made her feel as though he couldn't care less who was around and listening to them.

God, I wish I could fully believe he means that. That it's not all just a show for his mom or Sophia or whoever.

But that would also mean believing that he could feel more for her than he did. And he'd been clear that would never happen.

Liddy held his gaze, then nodded. Isla unwrapped an orange sarong from her waist. "Here, you can sit on this. These are my favorite things to carry onto the beach. They're practically sand proof."

Liddy thanked her for it, then spread it out onto the sand a little way off from where Quinn and his brothers had gathered and were discussing the boundaries of the "soccer field." She sat, then Elle popped down next to her. "What was that about?" Elle hissed, resting her weight back on her hands.

"What?" The mixture of emotions in her heart was becoming almost too much to process.

"I-I don't know. But something's off. Between Callum and his mom and you and him and Sophia. Even Isla was hopping around acting nervous."

Liddy focused her attention on the beach, where Mason was setting up a few fallen coconuts on either side of the playing field to mark off the goals. Callum had joined the men, along with Isla, Taryn, Rebecca, and a couple of their female cousins. As Callum laughed at something Mason said, Liddy envied his composure.

But that's Callum.

Emotionally disconnected and unavailable.

Cool under pressure.

Meanwhile, I'm sitting here feeling like I'm fraying at the seams.

Not because she couldn't handle a sexual relationship with Callum where he promised nothing but the thrill of right now. *Right? I can do that.*

It was fun. Exciting. Sexy as hell.

And *terrifying.*

Callum peeled his T-shirt away at that moment, revealing his muscular frame, and Liddy felt her mouth go dry. Would she ever be able to look at him at work again without remembering his taste?

And he looks so fucking good in a suit, too.

"You look like you could eat him," Elle said with a quirk of her brow. "Man, Lid. I mean, I didn't know you were so into him." She ducked her chin. "Now are you going to tell me what that was all about?"

"Sophia is Callum's ex-fiancée, that's all," Liddy whispered. The game started, and Callum sprinted forward onto the sand, his muscular frame quickly overtaking Quinn, who was doing his best to hold onto the ball.

He dodged forward, getting one bare foot on the ball, then swiped it away from Quinn in a blink with fast, fancy footwork.

God, he's beautiful.

And clearly good at this.

Which doesn't surprise me, his past career aspirations aside. Isla was right. Callum was good at everything he did.

"That's all?" Elle gripped Liddy's elbow. "That's huge. Quinn never told me that."

"They broke up five years ago. I mean—" She steadied her breath as Callum kicked the ball and it went sailing through the goal. *I never knew I could get so turned on by soccer.* "Quinn probably knows about it. But he doesn't know that it didn't end well between Sophia and Callum—she cheated on him—and Callum never told Quinn."

"Oh, wow. That's awful. I wish I had known." Elle's gaze was fixed on Quinn. "I can't believe he didn't—"

"Is this seat taken?" Sophia's voice came softly.

Liddy glanced up at her, the rising sun making it hard to see her shadowed face.

Seriously?

"Um, no." She scooted closer to Elle, who'd tensed.

Sophia settled down beside Liddy but sat on the sand rather than on the sarong. She smiled at the game. "It's good to see Cal playing again. When I last saw him, he swore he'd never touch a ball again."

"He's amazing," Liddy said, surprised at how genuine she sounded. Partially because it was true—Callum was amazing at the sport. Quinn and his teammates were struggling to keep up.

"I just wanted to apologize." Sophia sifted some sand between her fingertips. "I wasn't trying to pressure you to do anything you didn't want to do. My apologies."

Elle grazed Liddy's elbow ever so slightly, as though to offer the reassurance of her presence, and Liddy smiled to herself, grateful for her sister. Whether or not Callum was hung up on Sophia, he'd spent the night in bed with Liddy. The past few days with her, in fact. And that wasn't *nothing* either.

And you have no right to be jealous anyway. She wasn't in a cat fight for Callum's feelings, after all. That would only end badly for her.

"You don't need to apologize," Liddy said with a breezy smile. "All you did was ask a question."

Sophia stopped fidgeting with the sand, then nodded. She looked over Liddy's profile toward Elle. "Speaking of questions, your planner told me you are all leaving today? I just wanted to confirm since you paid in advance. If no one is here, I can refund you the money and try to rebook some rooms."

Elle cleared her throat. "No, that's unnecessary. I mean, of course, feel free to rebook the rooms once we leave, but you don't have to refund us. Quinn and I don't want to do that to you all."

Liddy shielded her eyes from the glare of the sun against the sea. Her guilt at Elle's words ebbed closer now. Her sister and Quinn had paid for everyone's stay at *La Hacienda*. Even if it wasn't as expensive as whatever Quinn's mother had planned, they would still lose money over it.

Because I should have stayed when Elle asked for my help.

"What time do you think you will check out?" Sophia asked, smoothing her hands over her bare, tanned legs.

"I'm not sure." Elle pursed her lips. "I can check with the planner. Do you need us gone by a certain time?"

Hopefully, Sophia doesn't hear the hostility in Elle's tone like I do.

Liddy drew her brows together. After all, they had a right to be here if the rooms were paid for.

"By three would be perfecto." Sophia smiled, clearly missing the point of Elle's inquiry. "I just want time to turn the rooms over before—"

A soccer ball whizzed between Sophia and Liddy, nearly hitting Sophia. Both Liddy and Sophia let out startled cries, springing back as the ball tumbled harmlessly onto the sand behind them.

Then Liddy whirled back in the direction the ball had come from. Callum jogged toward them, his stride relaxed. "Sorry about that." Callum stopped in front of Liddy. "The ball went off my foot the wrong way."

She could practically see the smirk in his eyes. *If he kicked it, he did it on purpose.* "Yeah, well, try to be more accurate, Mr. Scott."

Callum bent down and scooped her into his arms. His chest was damp with sweat, his skin scorching to her touch. He kissed her hard.

Just for show.

It's just for show.

But her heart was slamming against her ribs.

She pulled away and tipped her lips to his ear. "You better not be kissing me to make your ex jealous," she whispered.

"What ex?" Callum's lips grazed her earlobe. "I'm kissing you because I *want* to kiss you. Kicking the ball over here was just my excuse to sneak away to kiss the most gorgeous woman on this beach."

Her legs were unsteady as he set her back down again. Liddy caught the approving expression on Elle's face as she stared at Callum.

It shouldn't matter to me if Elle likes him for me.

But she also wanted her to.

She wanted Callum to fit with her crazy family. To show him off to her parents and aunts and uncles. They'd all been whispering about "Liddy's new man" this whole trip.

She looked over her shoulder. Sophia had disappeared.

Elle nestled her head against Liddy's shoulder. "I like seeing you happy."

Liddy murmured a response, letting them slip into silence as they watched the game. With the sea sparkling in front of them, and the sound of family laughing, it was so easy to push away the troubled thoughts that had plagued her during yoga.

But a voice at the back of her head wouldn't stop chattering either, reminding her how quickly things could change—*will change . . . when I return to London.*

CHAPTER TWENTY-NINE

Quite possibly the best thing about getting so sweaty playing football on the beach had been the shower with Liddy afterward.

Callum stretched his shoulders back as he pulled a fresh T-shirt over his head. His leg hadn't ached while playing today, which was a satisfying reminder that his daily weight training was helping him.

But that satisfaction wasn't what bubbled near the surface right now.

He knew this feeling.

Not that it was unfamiliar or that he hadn't felt this way during the past five years . . . it was just *different*.

He was happy.

Lydia exited the bathroom, wearing a summer dress, her wet hair twisted up in a clip, light makeup—not that she needed it. She was naturally pretty, and the hours spent in the sun this morning had given her a healthy, tanned glow. She set her makeup bag on the bed, her gaze falling on his board shorts. "You going swimming?"

"Kyle asked me if I could help him work on surfing for a while."

Her face registered surprise. "Kyle?"

"What's that look for?"

She glided toward him, slipping her arms around his waist. "Nothing. But he might also test you. Kyle's not exactly a fan of our arrangement."

"What part of our arrangement?"

"The one where we're having a vacation fling against our better judgment."

Callum grinned, resting his chin against the top of her head. *It's amazing how easy it is to slip into her embrace.* She fit in his arms perfectly, and when he was near her, he wanted to be touching her. The sweet scent of her coconut shampoo wafted toward him. How long had it been since he'd appreciated the soft, feminine side of a woman? Or slept in a woman's arms? His nights with most women usually ended shortly after sex.

Whatever he'd risked by letting her get close the night before, by bridging that gap between attraction and a physical relationship, he no longer cared. Incredibly stupid as it might be, he'd deal with the consequences later. His rigid sense of self-control was furiously trying to break into his thoughts, but every inch of him wanted her in his arms.

"I'll be on my best behavior around your brother, I promise. Give him no reason to think any worse of me."

"Hmm." She stood on her tiptoes and brushed a kiss to his lips. "You may not be able to do much. If some sexy, relationship-averse womanizer was banging your sister, you might want to have a word with him, too."

Ouch? Also, she was right.

"Womanizer?" Callum quirked a brow.

"Can you really deny that one?" She searched his gaze with laughter in her eyes.

"Fine. But also, Isla's a grown woman. I trust her to make her own decisions about her relationships."

"That's very levelheaded of you." She grinned and dropped her arms. "I also don't believe you for a *second*. My guess is that Isla is the one person on the planet you'd drop everything for. So even if you trust her judgment, it doesn't mean you want her around someone you think will end up hurting her."

He pursed his lips. Funny how well she seemed to know him.

Her words found an unexpected mark, too.

Hadn't he warned her the night before that he'd hurt her?

God, what am I doing?

The muscles in his arms flexed, and he released her.

"I should get going. Before your brother thinks I'm cowering."

She grabbed a striped canvas bag from beside the bed and slipped her sunglasses on top of her head. "I'll walk out with you. I think I'm going to hang out by the pool for an hour, then come back here to pack before we all have to leave here."

Callum gave her a sympathetic look. "Are you giving up your plan to change Elle's mind?" As much fun as they'd had since the previous night, they hadn't talked about any of the important things that were affecting them both since then either. They still needed to get the damn wedding dress today.

And then there's the whole matter of Sergio, which he foolishly hoped wouldn't even come up again. He wasn't about to ask, that much was certain. Not after their last discussion about it.

"Yeah." Liddy sighed, then grabbed a wide-brimmed hat. "I don't want to make things more stressful for Elle. It was probably already too late when I made the excursion plans yesterday, but I didn't want to accept it. Letting go of what I might want may not be easy, but it's the best solution."

Callum joined her by the door, taking her hand when she offered it as they walked outside. Once again, he felt the sharp twang of guilt at her words. How often did Lydia let go of what she wanted to keep things amiable?

He'd seen her do it at the office frequently enough.

And during this trip.

Walking hand in hand with anyone was an odd reality for him. He'd never spent a lot of time holding hands with Sophia. Their relationship had been built on summer friendships and, later, holidays and breaks from university. The lengthiest amount of time they'd spent together had been when she'd come to help him after his accident. In some ways, their failure as a couple had been predictable. He'd been young, and they were childhood sweethearts.

Up until recently, she'd occupied a place in his memory that brought with it dislike and resentment.

But today when he'd looked over on the beach and seen her, he'd truly felt nothing toward her. His father had once told him that the opposite of love was indifference—a telling thing coming from someone who'd been a master of indifference for most of his life.

And since his breakup with Sophia, he'd used that lesson as a guide for how he handled relationships with women.

The sound of a splash drew him from distant memories. Hunter and Granny were in the pool, while Leo prepared to cannonball. *No wonder Granny likes him.* Either that or Leo had realized he needed to do better to keep up with the spitfire.

Kyle waited for him on a lounge chair, along with Isla, who'd done him the favor of grabbing his old surfboard from his mum's house on the property.

Across from them on the other side of the pool were a few

other people Callum didn't know—some of Liddy's extended family—and Elle and Quinn with most of Quinn's family.

"I guess everyone decided to move up from the beach." Liddy wrinkled her nose. "So much for getting any reading done." She released his hand. "Have fun with my brother."

"There she is." Elle got up from her lounger and came toward them. She grimaced. "Kat is asking me about the wedding dress again."

Bollocks. Maybe a surfing lesson would have to wait.

"Liddy!"

Oh. Fuck. This moment keeps getting worse.

Callum stiffened as he followed the direction of the voice.

Sergio.

He stood near the path that led to the office and waved at Liddy. Sophia was beside him.

Several heads turned toward Sergio.

Oh shit.

What in the hell is he doing here now? Worse still, had he told Sophia why he was here?

"Who is that?" Elle asked as Sergio started toward them. Thief or not, Callum still didn't like him. Especially not with the way he was looking at Liddy.

Dammit.

Liddy turned and looked at Elle. "Um, he's, um, a friend of mine."

Sergio reached them, smiling. "I hoped I would find you." He leaned down, then greeted her with a kiss on the cheek. "You look beautiful."

Elle arched a brow.

Think fast, Liddy. Right now. Get Sergio out of here. He wished she could read his stare.

"I'm Sergio," he was already saying, holding out a hand toward Elle.

"This is Elle, my sister," Liddy said.

By now, curiosity had driven Quinn toward them, who came over to join them.

"Ah." A light lit Sergio's eyes. "The bride."

"Everything all right?" Quinn asked, pausing beside Elle.

"Yes, I'm just here to take your sister out later," Sergio said with a smile, then slipped his hand on Liddy's shoulder. "But I came early, to surprise her. The rain yesterday caused a mudslide on the highway, and I wanted to be sure another accident wouldn't prevent us from getting to know each other better." He squeezed Liddy's shoulder.

Redness crawled into Liddy's face as Elle and Quinn swiveled questioning gazes toward her.

Callum snuck a look at Sophia.

She watched them intensely, with no obvious intention of walking away just yet.

"I—um. I can explain," Liddy started.

"Did you get the dress back?" Sergio turned toward Liddy.

"Dress?" Elle crossed her arms.

"I'm so sorry about the mess with it all. Liddy was guarding that dress with her life before security came and stole me away, though. She's a good sister," Sergio said.

"Yeah, the best," Elle said sarcastically. Her gaze nearly skewered both Liddy and Callum.

Sophia had stepped back, but her expression seemed to show she was rather enjoying this.

Fuck it. He had to tell Sergio to keep his mouth shut before he said anything else, even if it meant exposing the truth about Liddy's and his fake relationship to Sophia.

"Mae, suave un toque. Ellos piensan que nosotros somos una pareja. Por favor no diga nada mas," Callum said quietly. *Hold on. They think we're a couple. Please don't say anything else.*

Sergio gave him a baffled look. *He didn't know I spoke Spanish, clearly.*

"No, I want to hear what he has to say, Cal." The spark of anger in Elle's eyes was unmistakable. Liddy shrank back.

"Um—" Liddy pulled away from Sergio and grabbed Elle's arm. "Can I talk to you? Alone?"

"Actually, no." Elle's eyes flashed. "I think Quinn will probably be interested in hearing whatever you have to say. I sure as hell am." Her face reddened. "What in the hell is going on, Liddy?"

The jig is up.

Liddy squirmed. "Callum and I have something to tell you."

"Can we take this to the beach?" Callum asked, glancing at Quinn with a pleading look. He was distinctly aware of Quinn's family watching the scene unfolding with curiosity.

Liddy was red-faced and already speaking, "So Sergio and I met on the plane ride from London, and I mentioned to him I had your dress. We got to talking and exchanged numbers, but after I got my bags, I needed to go to the bathroom and asked Sergio to watch the dress. And then I thought he stole it, only he didn't."

Elle's brows drew together. "I'm not following any of that."

Sergio cringed sheepishly. "I didn't know you hadn't told them, Liddy. I am so sorry."

Callum kept his gaze trained on Quinn. They were attracting attention. And given Logan's involvement in all this, he doubted Quinn would want the whole thing handled indiscreetly. "Please. Let's just go farther down the beach, at least."

Sergio, who'd irritatingly had his arm on Liddy's shoulder, pulled away. "I'll wait up by the office. Pardon." He gave Liddy a sympathetic look, then started back the way he'd come.

Sophia smirked at Callum, then followed Sergio.

Now's her chance to ask Sergio anything she wants. But he wasn't about to leave Liddy's side to save face.

Elle and Quinn hadn't moved.

So much for being out of view.

Callum came closer to Liddy, who appealed to him with glossy eyes. "Let me try to summarize, if I can. Liddy brought your dress with her. Before we'd got all our bags, Liddy went to the bathroom. When she came out, Sergio, who'd been holding the wedding dress, had vanished. Turned out Logan had left a bag of marijuana in the dress bag and a security dog detected it."

"Logan?" Quinn repeated, then shot his brother a hard look.

Fuck. From the way that Logan shrank back, even at the distance, it was clear Logan knew what they were talking about.

"Okay." Elle pushed a strand of hair behind her ear. "Where is my dress, guys?"

"At the airport." Liddy stepped closer to Callum.

Isla stood cautiously from the lounger, looking worried. Everyone around the pool was staring at them.

Elle palmed her forehead. "I have no idea what's going on. Why would you lie to me about Isla bringing the dress? And the whole thing about you forgetting it, Callum?"

"We didn't know Sergio hadn't stolen it," Liddy said in a soft voice that was barely audible. "I thought he did, and Callum covered for me—in exchange for me pretending we were dating."

"What?" Elle's voice was sharp. She gave Callum an accusing glare. "What the fuck?"

Quinn cringed and set a hand on Elle's forearm. "Maybe we should go down to the beach."

Thank you.

"And let them both just get out of the tangled knot of lies

they've been telling?" Elle looked like she was halfway between bursting into tears and throwing punches. Hopefully people would assume it was just about the dress, for now, if they'd overheard that bit.

Quinn set his arm around her. "I think we should hear them out. Preferably in a place that doesn't involve everyone else around us. I'm not thrilled with these revelations"—he gave Callum a hard look—"but I don't want to introduce any unnecessary drama to our wedding either."

Elle clenched her jaw, then nodded. Without waiting for any of them, she stormed down the beach, away from the people at the pool.

"You'd better have a really good reason for all this," Quinn said to Callum angrily, then followed Elle.

Callum reached for Liddy's hand. She looked miserable. "It'll be all right." He squeezed her hand but didn't let go. *She deserves my full support.* She hadn't gotten into this mess on her own. He wasn't going to leave her feeling alone.

"That's easy enough for you to say," Liddy muttered, her stress visible in her expression and the rigidity of her movements as she walked away from the pool area. "You *wanted* to lie to your family. I didn't."

Harsh—but also true.

When had he grown so comfortable with deceiving the people he cared about?

Maybe it had happened in degrees.

Quinn was quietly comforting Elle as they approached them on the beach. Elle, who'd turned away from them, looked over and her gaze settled on Liddy and Callum's joined hands. "I thought you two were just pretending."

Liddy dropped his hand, as though stricken.

"Elle, look. I'm sorry." She swiped a few tears away. "I really am. I didn't want to lie. I just—I was so worried about you because you were so stressed, and then when I lost the dress, I didn't want to give you more to worry about."

"But why pretend you were dating?" Elle crossed her arms. "That's the part I don't get. What does one thing have to do with the other?"

"It's my fault." Callum wished so badly he could shield Liddy from Elle's anger. *This must be killing Liddy.* "Almost all of this is my fault. I overheard Sergio on the phone telling someone where he was going to be on the day after we arrived. But rather than give Liddy that information, I bribed her into pretending to be my girlfriend to put an end to my mum's harassment about me getting together with my ex."

Elle searched his face, her cheeks red. "God, you know, I always thought you could be a selfish prick when you wanted, but you had the good sense to draw the line at your friends. Seriously, Cal? You pulled this with *my sister*? What sort of person does that?"

Quinn grimaced beside her.

Not that I should expect to rely on Quinn's support right now. I deserve their anger.

"It's not Callum's fault," Liddy said, shifting her weight onto her back foot. "Yes, he suggested it, but I'm the one who lost the dress and assumed Sergio had stolen it. Callum didn't need to help me, and he went to a lot of trouble to help me find Sergio afterward. Like *a lot*. We basically got stranded in the middle of the country without any money, out of gas, no cell phone—plus some restaurant owner held my passport as a guarantee when we couldn't pay the bill."

Quinn's brows drew together. "You must be joking."

"Wait, that's where you guys went? To find this Sergio?"

Callum nodded. "Liddy did everything in her power to get that dress back for you, Elle. I fully accept that I've behaved like an arse. But please don't hold her responsible. She only ever wanted to do right by you."

Elle stared down at the sand, appearing torn, her shoulders bunched. "Telling me—and Quinn—the truth would have been the best way to do right by me. Not only is it incredibly insulting to find out you've both been lying to us, but I *was* hurt by the way Liddy took off, too. With no explanation."

Elle met Liddy's eyes. "I told you I needed your help, and then you just left. And now I find out you were lying too?" Elle's eyes shone with tears. "I *really* didn't expect that."

Liddy took a step forward, then hung back. "I'm sorry, Elle. I felt—feel—horrible. The whole time, all I wanted to do was just tell you the truth, but after that initial lie, everything happened so quickly and then I felt like I owed Callum . . ."

Tense silence hung between all four of them.

How could he ever come back from this? Elle might forgive her sister, but him?

I brought this upon myself.

Elle swiped tears from her cheeks and Quinn slipped his arm around her shoulder, hugging her against him. Shaking her head, Elle looked from him to Liddy. "So all that kissing and hand-holding—that was just for show? To *lie* to us?"

"Not really. Callum mainly wanted to just get his mom to leave him alone."

"I don't remember Cal's mom being on that catamaran when you guys were making out," Elle remarked dryly. She held up a hand, abruptly. "You know what? Don't answer. I really don't care. It's gross, but you all do whatever you want. How do I get my damn wedding dress?"

Pain flashed across Liddy's features. "We have to go to the airport in Liberia to get it. The airline will only give it to me. But we can leave right now and get it in Callum's rental car."

"No, we're going to go with you." Elle glanced back at Quinn. "I need my dress, and honestly, I'll feel a lot better if I can be there to make sure there isn't another issue." She checked her watch. "I'll meet you by the parking lot in five minutes."

Without waiting for a response, Elle walked toward the hotel steps.

Liddy looked stricken. "I don't think she's ever been so mad at me before."

Quinn reached over and squeezed her shoulder. "It'll be fine. Once the shock wears off, she'll let it go."

Liddy drew a sharp breath. "Yeah." She didn't look comforted, though. "You won't tell anyone, will you, Quinn?"

Quinn offered a kind smile. "You know you can count on me for discretion, Liddy."

Liddy nodded then glanced at Callum. "I'll meet you by the car. I need to find Sergio real fast and talk to him."

Sergio. What might he have told Sophia by now? Or his mum?

This is going to get even messier, fast.

Callum watched as Liddy started up the stairs, feeling Quinn's intense stare.

"I fucked up, Quinn."

"Yeah, I'd say so." Quinn crossed his arms. He didn't sound pleased, but wasn't overtly angry, either.

I can work with that. Then again, they'd been through twenty-nine years of friendship at this point. He hoped they could survive this hiccup.

"You're sleeping with her, aren't you?"

Callum clenched his jaw. Quinn might forgive his lack of judgment when it came to this—and the lies—but he would not as easily forgive this. Callum gave one curt nod.

"Goddammit, Cal." Quinn turned away for a second, his hands flexing. "Elle loves me. And she's trying to be patient with you because of that. But I swear, if you hurt Liddy, you and I won't be able to come back from that. She's my sister now. And I know how you are with women. I'd like to think you'd know better than to risk our friendship over a holiday fling with someone I care about."

Damn.

Yes, if I'd been a decent man—a decent friend—I would have stayed away.

And he'd tried. He'd done his best to stay away from Lydia Winnick.

He'd spent two years ignoring her. Maybe not for the sake of his friendship with Quinn but still. That respect had been there.

And now he'd fucked up beyond belief.

"But I swear, if you hurt Liddy, you and I won't be able to come back from that."

Years of friendship . . . and he'd royally fucked that up, too.

"May I be so bold as to ask if you have any intention of continuing a relationship with her after you both return to London?" Quinn gave him a hard stare.

Callum shook his head.

The honesty of his own answer made his heart squeeze painfully.

She deserves better than what I can give her.

"Then you need to end this. Right now. Whatever it is you're doing with Liddy cannot continue. She's not like you. And she'll get hurt, you know it. For everyone's sake, end it now, before this gets worse."

Quinn brushed past him as he left Callum alone on the beach.

Callum was only here because of his friendship with Quinn.

". . . I know how you are with women. I'd think you would know better than to risk our friendship over a holiday fling with someone I care about."

And now Callum may have screwed that up beyond repair.

And Elle was right.

I took advantage of Liddy.

Threatening gray clouds had moved in while they'd all been speaking and he watched them, a dark feeling crossing over him. He had no idea how to proceed with her right now or what to even think. The truth was out to Elle and Quinn, but others were still under the impression he and Liddy were a couple.

And especially after last night, explaining that we aren't might only cause Liddy more pain and embarrassment.

He could go on, pretending they were a couple. Sleeping with her. *But Quinn has asked me not to.*

I have to end it.

Before she gets hurt.

Hopefully right now the damage would be minimal. They'd fucked but she'd said she was prepared to handle that. To be a fling and nothing else.

A light rain started.

I never should have touched her.

Lifting his face toward the sky, he closed his eyes.

He'd spent plenty of time in the rain in England, of course, but the rain here was different. Warm. Cleansing.

I have to end this.

Before I ruin everything.

He hoped he wasn't too late to make things right. But what if he was? Quinn had flat out told him that their friendship was over if Liddy got hurt. And Liddy was right—he didn't have the luxury of many friendships. Not anymore. Quinn had been a good friend over the years, one he'd needed.

And once they got back to *La Hacienda* tonight, he'd do what needed to be done.

If Liddy had thought the car ride from the airport had been uncomfortable, it paled compared to the trip she was taking right now.

The tension in the car was thick, rigid. Nearly impenetrable. Elle was barely talking, which only made Liddy feel worse, and she could feel her sister's eyes boring into the back of her neck. Confessing to lying had never been part of the plan—and now Liddy felt increasingly stupid for having lied.

And that was on top of the awkward, two-minute conversation she'd had with Sergio, where she'd tried to tell him she wasn't dating Callum but her family thought she was, while trying to come up with a way to explain their date wouldn't be happening.

God, I feel horrible about all of it.

A rainstorm had broken out as they'd left *La Hacienda.* Now rain poured down the windshield, the wipers moving as fast as they could. At Sergio's advice, they'd taken the coastal road, which Callum had informed them would take longer. But apparently a mudslide had taken out part of the main highway with the storm the day before, which was why Sergio had shown up early. He'd been worried he wouldn't make it on time and leave Liddy waiting for him.

Because I should have canceled the date with him before today. Or never agreed to it.

"I have to go to the bathroom," Elle announced from the back seat, her arms crossed in irritation.

I can't remember the last time I saw Elle so angry. It was expected, though.

Callum's gaze flicked into the rearview mirror. They'd already stopped twice for that purpose and had only been on the road for an hour. If Callum was frustrated at the delay, he didn't show it, and Liddy imagined he must feel bad about all this.

But then again, what do I know about his feelings?

Callum seemed to try his best not to *have* feelings. Whatever emotions he did display were more like reflexes.

"You want to stop right now?" Callum asked.

"Sorry, mate," Quinn said apologetically.

"I heard that," Elle said, crossing her arms. "Don't apologize to him. He doesn't need an apology. I'm pregnant and I have to pee. That's not something you should apologize for."

Right. The pregnancy.

Quinn grimaced and looked back at his wife. "Darling, I'm not apologizing for you having to use the facilities."

"Yes, you are. And honestly, if I have to stop every five minutes, then that's how it's going to be. Callum's a big boy, he can handle it."

Yeesh. She'd never heard Elle be so rude like this. But Elle was also angrier than Liddy had witnessed in a long time.

"I'm not sure there's a place for us to stop right now, Elle," Liddy said gently. They were in the middle of nowhere, surrounded by jungle, and it was raining. "But there might be a town soon?" She looked hopefully at Callum, then added in as cheerful of a tone as she could, "At least we have GPS and phones this time."

ELLE STARED AT HER, then looked at Callum. "So was anything that you two told me the last few days true? Anything? You're not a couple—but you went above and beyond to convince us you were. And I still don't really get why Callum forced you to pretend you were dating. So . . .?" She arched a brow.

She's really furious.

And I hate this so much.

"This isn't Liddy's fault," Callum said, speaking to Elle through the rearview mirror. "It was *my* idea to lie, *my* idea to buy some time while we tracked down Sergio. She wanted to tell you the truth, but I thought it would be more stressful for you. Sophia and I broke up years ago and, because my mum has always loved her, she didn't take the news well. I didn't want to give her any reason to attempt a reconciliation."

"So you're just a liar." Elle held his gaze for a moment, her eyes narrowing. Then she glanced at Quinn. "Did you know this about him?"

"I think Callum and Liddy were trying to make the best of an unpleasant situation," Quinn said, gripping her hand. "Though obviously it would have been preferable to just tell us the truth."

Liddy gave Quinn a guarded look. He'd been kind throughout this all—which wasn't surprising—but he also risked irritating Elle, which wouldn't be good.

"Preferable? That's putting it mildly. I can't decide who I'm more frustrated with—Callum for manipulating Liddy the way he did or Liddy for not trusting me *and* letting Callum make a fool out of her and using her for some . . . duplicitous vacation fling."

Liddy stiffened. *A fool out of me? That's a bit . . . much.*

Then annoyance rankled her. Stressed or not, hormones or whatever it was, Liddy was also sick of tiptoeing around her sister, feeling like she couldn't have a conversation with her.

The car slowed and Liddy looked over at Callum. He nodded at the road, which had disappeared from view. Instead, the path of the dusty inland road, a river flowed toward the sea, swelling from the rain.

"What the hell?" Liddy asked.

Callum grimaced. "I should have known this would happen. I've had to go through the rivers on this road before and avoid it in the rainy season—but usually October is the worst time for this, not June."

Quinn leaned forward from the back seat. "You mean to tell me this happens on a regular basis?"

Callum stopped the car. Rain pounded on the windows. It was so bleak.

Elle peered through the windshield. "Where's the road gone?"

"The river swelled and went over it. We have to go through it to get to the other side," Callum said, his voice unusually quiet.

"Through the river?" both Elle and Liddy said nearly simultaneously.

How is that even possible?

Callum shrugged. "It happens during the rainy season. We should be fine, but I'm going to wade out there, make sure it's not too deep."

"Wait, what?" Liddy set a hand on his shoulder. "Isn't that dangerous?"

For some reason, a smile curled at the corners of his lips as he met her gaze. "It'll be fine. There's an umbrella in the back if you want to help hold it over Elle so she can . . . relieve herself." He nodded toward the trunk area.

"Let me go with you, mate," Quinn said as Callum opened the door.

"Please don't get killed and leave my baby fatherless," Elle said, a hint of anxiety in her voice.

Quinn winked at her, then stepped outside.

As both men walked forward in the rain toward the swollen river, tense silence settled between Liddy and Elle.

Liddy gritted her teeth, then said, "Listen, Elle, I'm sorry. I really am. I didn't mean to cause you more stress."

"I just . . ." Elle studied her. "None of this is like you. What are you trying to prove? And to whom?"

Good question.

Why had she felt the need to prove so much lately?

She didn't have an answer for that. "You know, why don't I get that umbrella and get Quinn to help you. I'll see if Callum needs anything, that way you don't have to worry about your husband drowning on top of everything else."

Something unreadable flashed in Elle's eyes, then she nodded.

Liddy couldn't get out of the car quickly enough.

She hurried over to Quinn and handed him the umbrella. Callum was already wading into the river, his back to them. "Why don't we switch?" Liddy said as brightly as possible.

Quinn gave her a look of surprise, then squeezed her shoulder. "It's going to be all right."

As Quinn went back, Liddy stared at the gushing brown water just a few feet away. She took a few cautious steps into it.

.   .   .

AFTER THE TENSION of the morning, standing in the river with rain dripping down her face, soaking her shirt was . . .

Relief.

More than anything, she wanted Callum to tell her everything would be okay. That *they* would be okay. Not that there even was a "they." But with their fake relationship exposed to more people, it all felt so close to being over. Just when they'd barely gotten started.

She splashed out into the water and grabbed Callum's hand. "Wait—"

He turned toward her. "What are you doing?"

"I don't know. You were just standing there and . . . I just wanted to be here with you. I don't know why."

He smiled sadly. "God, you're so beautiful. You know that? Especially when you're fearless."

Her stomach roiled. *Why does it feel like he's going to push me away again?*

She grabbed his hands, interlacing her fingers with his. "Thank you, Callum. For everything you've done this week. I'm sorry Elle is mad at you, but I just want you to know—I'm not. And I don't care what she or anyone else thinks."

He raised a brow. "Is that so? What about Sergio?"

"Ugh, don't remind me. Hopefully he got the hint and went home." She didn't want to rehash that stupid argument right now.

Liddy shook her head, trying to clear some of the rain from her face. Feathery strands of hair stuck to her cheeks. "Why does stuff like this keep happening to us? We're seriously going to drive through a river in our car? This is like the Oregon Trail or something."

His fingers tightened on hers. Leaning down, he kissed her forehead, then her lips with gentle pressure. "My life was nothing short of boring before you came into it, Lydia Winnick."

Then he tilted his head toward the car, his heart wreathed in a turmoil he didn't dare display. "And yes, we're going to drive through the damned river." He held her hand as they started back. "The water is just at my knees. We should be fine. In theory."

"In theory?"

He grimaced. "Unless we drive into an area of the river that's deeper than I can see. Then the engine will flood. And with the water moving like this, it could push the car out to the sea."

She grasped his hand tighter. "What?" She looked warily back at the rapid flow. "Um, maybe I shouldn't ask but are there any creatures I should be worried about out here?"

He gave her a rueful smile. "Crocodiles. Snakes. But I doubt we'll encounter them."

She squealed, then yanked him back toward solid ground.

Elle and Quinn were quiet as they got into the car, and Liddy didn't meet Elle's gaze. Muttering a silent prayer, her fingers tightened around the seat belt as Callum put the car into first gear and crept toward the river.

"I can't believe we're doing this," Elle breathed.

Quinn scooted closer to her sister and held her hand. "It's fine. Callum wouldn't do this if the water was too deep."

"But you can't just drive a car through a river." Elle stared out the window as they pushed slowly into the water.

"Happens all the time here," Callum said dryly.

The front two wheels were in. Liddy looked out the side mirror as the back tires left what was once the road.

Slow.

Steady.

Her heart rate surged. She breathed out slowly, focusing on

the path forward as Callum kept going. Not that there was an actual path.

Keep going.

He rolled the window down and stuck his head out. She didn't have to ask what he saw. The water level was rising up the side of the car.

Dangerously high.

Elle looked horrified. "Oh my God. What happens if the water goes too high?"

"The engine floods," Quinn said, squeezing her knee comfortingly.

"And then?"

"Then we push the car to higher ground and wait for a tow," Callum said in a matter-of-fact way, as though he hadn't just told Liddy the other potentially hazardous possibility.

A phone rang and Liddy glanced back to see Elle take hers out. "It's Kat." Then Elle's face looked stricken. "Oh man, she's going to kill me. We were supposed to be going to The Four Seasons today."

"You don't have to answer it," Liddy said. "She'll be fine."

Elle gave a strangled laugh. "Who are you, and what have you done with my sister? The Liddy I know respects and *loves* schedules."

"Schedules be damned. We have a wedding dress to rescue."

They were in the middle of the river now, and Liddy held her breath. Of all the men in the world, she wouldn't have expected her boss—who looked so good in a business suit and managed his team of twenty-five so professionally—to also be someone she had complete confidence in during an adventure like this.

But I do.

All four wheels seemed to lift off.

Fuck, no.

Elle might not know what was going on, but Callum shifted in his seat, giving Liddy a worried glance.

"Cal . . ."

They were still gliding forward in the water.

Seconds ticked by, lengthening in her ears with her pulse.

Liddy set her hand on his shoulder.

Hit the ground. Hit the ground.

Then a bump, and the front tires hit land again.

She breathed out, her heart rate slowing.

"Did we . . . float?" Liddy asked, meeting Callum's eyes.

"Float?" Elle's jaw dropped open.

Callum cringed. "Just for a second. But I have to warn you—this isn't the only river we have to cross on the coastal road."

"Oh my God." Elle squeezed her eyes shut. "I don't even want to wear that damn dress. It's long-sleeved and fluffy, and I just didn't want to hurt Quinn's mom's feelings, but I hate it." She huffed, her knuckles white. "Are we going to die trying to get a dress I don't even want to wear?"

Seriously?

They were on land now and Callum pulled the car to safety, then stopped it. Turning around, he arched a brow at Liddy.

We've been killing ourselves over a dress Elle doesn't even want?

If it hadn't been so damn ironic, she might just have cried. A smile played at Liddy's lips, and then she threw her head back and laughed. "You've got to be kidding me."

Her laughter seemed to be contagious because Elle started laughing, wiping her nose tearfully. "I don't—I don't know why it took me so long to say anything." She met Quinn's eyes. "I don't want to wear that dress, Q. I don't."

Quinn smiled, a tenderness in his gaze that Liddy only

hoped someone would look at her with someday. "Then don't wear it."

Hallelujah. A tight feeling choked Liddy's throat. Maybe it had taken Elle a bit too long to come around and admit it, but . . . *I was right.* And Liddy had finally broken through to her sister, too. Maybe it had been her speech while Callum and Quinn had been outside of the car, and maybe it had been the emotional river crossing—but either way, *thank God.*

Then Elle squeezed Quinn's hands, turning in the seat toward Liddy. "I'm sorry. I've been a jerk to you. And Callum. And you're right. The Four Seasons is beautiful but not what I wanted. I want to get married on the beach we picked. Even if there's no music and the food isn't from a Michelin-starred restaurant."

No need to make Elle eat humble pie.

"Does anyone really feel full after eating at those places, anyway? They give these unsatisfying, tiny portions," Liddy said, snickering. "I swear the last time you and Quinn took me to one of those places, I went home and ordered a pizza because I was still hungry."

"It's true." Elle dug in her purse for a tissue.

"And, the fact is, you're already married. You may as well do whatever you want. It's not like the countess can raise an objection to you two being married during the ceremony."

"She wouldn't anyway," Quinn said wryly. "She loves Elle."

"I'm sorry I was so mad. I'm sorry. You're right about everything, Lid, and you're the only one who even tried to tell me."

Liddy sniffled. "I wish I could hug you right now."

Elle laughed lightly. "There's just one problem." Elle swiped through her phone. "This rain seems like it doesn't want to let up. The forecast for the next few days is awful, including the morning of the wedding." She held up the weather app she'd opened. "See? Kat showed me this yesterday."

Liddy took the phone and swiped through the app. "There's a window tomorrow evening that doesn't look too bad."

"The wedding's on Thursday, though." Quinn shifted in his seat.

"But everyone's already here, aren't they? Why wait? If I've learned anything on this trip, it's that everything you're expecting can change in an instant." Liddy's eyes settled on Callum's.

His jaw tensed.

"I mean . . . I guess we could do the wedding tomorrow night." An excited look came over Elle's face. "Q—what do you think?"

"I think that whatever makes you happy is exactly what I want."

Liddy smiled. "I have an idea of how we might make everyone happy. Including Kat. Just leave everything to me, okay?"

"Uhh . . ." Callum squinted at Quinn.

Quinn just gave a low chuckle, shaking his head.

"I hate to be a bother," Callum said, clearing his throat. "But are we still going to the airport?"

Elle sniffled again and shook her head. "No. You know what? Forget it. Let's just leave the dress there, and Liddy can pick it up on her way home. I'll just tell Quinn's mom that it didn't arrive, and she'll have to accept it. It's the best way to let her down gently."

Now who's the liar? Liddy didn't dare say anything, though. "Let's go back to Samara."

"Perfect." Callum turned the steering wheel. "All we have to do is cross the damn river. Again."

CHAPTER THIRTY-ONE

CALLUM HAD NEVER BEEN so glad to see *La Hacienda* before —if only because it meant a chance to get out of the car. His clothes were also still wet, and even though Elle seemed calmer now—and Quinn, by extension—all Callum wanted was to grab his laptop, go to a café, and lose himself in everything he'd missed at work for the past few days. He'd be woefully behind when he returned.

Funny how the desk job he'd once dreaded had become a lifeline.

If anyone had told him when he was still dreaming of playing football that he'd find comfort in the routine he'd carved out now, he wouldn't have believed them. For a moment today, even, he'd had that spark of nostalgia come hurtling back as he'd run on the sand, skillfully dribbling the ball.

A glimpse into a life he'd forgotten. His family nearby, a land he'd loved as the literal ground beneath his feet, friends laughing . . . and a gorgeous woman watching him with a look that had tempted a passionate kiss from him.

And now that woman headed up the path toward the bungalows, feeling more out of reach with each step she took.

Quinn and Elle had hurried away to find Kat and explain the change in their decision about the wedding. If they were going to pull off the wedding being here tomorrow afternoon, they would need Kat's help and expertise at this point.

But Quinn's warning and request that Callum end things with Liddy weighed heavily on him.

This shouldn't be hard.

But why am I dreading it so much?

He hurried to catch up with Liddy, but as they reached the pool area, he slowed, going rigid. Sergio stood under the safety of their bungalow porch, out of the rain.

Damn.

I guess he didn't give up so easily after all.

Sergio straightened, his smile at Liddy faltering as his gaze flicked toward Callum. Liddy paused, then checked over her shoulder.

The guilt on her face was clear enough, but why should she feel guilty? He'd told her he didn't care if she went out with Sergio.

Then why do I want to punch him for still being here?

Liddy still hesitated, and Callum caught up with her. "Looks like your date is still here," he muttered, a taut smile on his lips.

Liddy didn't answer. "Hey, Sergio." She grabbed Callum's elbow and dragged him under the shelter of the porch. "Can you give me a second? I need to change and talk to Callum."

"Of course." If Sergio thought this situation with Callum was strange, he said nothing as Liddy pulled Callum into the bungalow. *Then again, she probably already explained that we're not dating.*

. . . and who knows what Sergio told Sophia.

As Liddy closed the door to the bungalow, she pushed her hair back behind her ear. "Listen, you have nothing to worry about. I'm going to tell him I can't go."

Any relief he might have felt at her words was quickly drowned out by the echo of Quinn's voice. "... *if you hurt Liddy, you and I won't be able to come back from that.*"

The words felt like sandpaper scraping his throat as he forced out, "You *should* go. Nothing has changed between us."

Liddy held his gaze. "You don't mean that."

Being cruel to her now wouldn't make Quinn less angry with him. He weighed his words carefully. "Liddy, I'm in over my head. I'm not like you. You have loads of family—who you have a relationship with—and friends. Ones who aren't furious with you for interfering with people they care about. We had fun, but we also agreed this would end."

He brushed her cheek with the backs of his knuckles. "A few more days of this would have been incredible, but the result would still be the same. It's better if we part ways now, before one of the few friends I do have starts believing I'm as rotten as everyone else seems to think."

"I don't give a damn about what Quinn and Elle think about us." She grabbed his hand. "Stop worrying about that. I don't *want* to go out with Sergio, Callum. It's that simple. I'm having fun *with you*. I ..." She let out a short, frustrated breath. "Please. Just don't push me away because of something like Quinn being mad at you. I'll talk to him myself. He can't hold you responsible for the two of us getting involved. I'm a fucking grown-up, as ridiculous as it sounds to say."

If only it were that simple.

Callum dropped her hand. "I'm going to shower and then pack my things. Fortunately, I still have a room I can stay in. And chances are my mum already knows we're not a real couple, so I should probably clear things up with her." *Even if that kills me.*

"Callum, don't do this." Liddy's eyes shone with tears.

Goddammit.

She was going to get hurt. He'd warned her. And there was no way around it now.

I have to.

He stepped back, steeling himself to be as matter of fact as possible. "We can tell everyone we had a fight. And you dumped me, which makes the most sense."

He almost wished for her anger and irritation, but she raised a brow. "And why did I dump you?"

"Does there have to be a reason? You yourself told me how many people believe I'm an arse." He shrugged. This wasn't really a good time to bring up that disagreement from yesterday, but it made sense for their story—at least for anyone from London. "Only a handful of people—and possibly Sophia and my mum, since Sophia was there when Sergio arrived—know about our arrangement. I'd rather not have to go through the hassle of telling everyone about our ruse."

Liddy flinched. "And this is what you want?"

No.

But that didn't matter.

"I think that will be the easiest thing to do." He grabbed a fresh shirt and jeans from his bag. "Have a good time with Sergio."

He crossed the room and shut the bathroom door, flipping on the light switch.

The bathroom smelled like Liddy's coconut shampoo, reminding him of their shower earlier that morning.

"Fuck it all," he muttered, then locked the door, willing himself to stay inside.

He set both hands on the vanity, then leaned against it, staring at himself in the mirror.

Why is it taking every ounce of willpower I have to do this?

He hated this.

And then Sophia's words played through his head. *"You only have yourself to blame for being a miserable bastard."*

Miserable. Funny, that term.

What was it that Isla had said to him the night before he'd come down here?

"You're miserable. And I can't remember the last time I saw you truly happy."

I was happy this morning.

While Liddy was mine. Even if it had been temporary.

Until Sergio had shown up and everything had gone to hell.

This shouldn't be so difficult.

He turned the faucet on and splashed water on his face. That he was having such a hard time doing this was unnerving and incomprehensible. Sure, he'd known Liddy for two years now, but how had she possibly managed to get under his skin this way in just a few short days?

He'd had plenty of casual flings. They'd been forgettable, no matter how good the sex had been.

That wasn't the sum total of his experiences, though—he knew the other side. A committed relationship. A fiancée.

When that had ended, though, he'd been angry. Moving on from Sophia to other women had felt easy enough, and he'd told himself it was easy not to miss her after what she'd done.

But the idea of not having Liddy in his arms again . . . was a strange additional torment.

He shaved his face, then peeled the wet clothes from his cold, clammy skin. A shower did little to break the deep chill permeating through his muscles.

Once he'd dressed, he left the bathroom.

Liddy was gone, of course, as she should be.

Good.

She went with Sergio.

Even on the slim chance that she hadn't, it didn't matter. He had to stick to the plan.

His belongings didn't take long to gather, considering he'd barely spent time in the room. As he finished packing his bag, a knock came from the door.

"Open up," Isla called from the other side.

He suppressed a groan. As much as he loved his sister, he'd been looking forward to slipping away from here for a while.

Callum opened the door, and Isla breezed through without waiting for him to ask her inside. "I've been looking for you," she said, then plopped down on the unmade bed. She wrinkled her nose at the state of the sheets. "Wow, you had some fun last night in here, didn't you?"

He crossed his arms. "Is there a point to this?"

"Aiden was looking for you. Apparently, the wedding planner is going mad trying to pull some last-minute wedding for tomorrow together, and Aiden thought it would be good to remove some guests from the hotel—throw Quinn an impromptu stag night. He needs all the groomsmen."

Callum frowned. "And he couldn't just call me?"

"You haven't been the easiest to call *or* text this trip." Isla rolled her eyes, then her gaze landed on his bag. "Oh no. What's happened?"

"Nothing's happened."

She hopped down from the bed and barged right into the bathroom. A moment later, she emerged, a triumphant look on her face. "None of your stuff is in there. Which means you must have packed it."

"I'm going to stay with Mum the rest of the trip, that's all."

She raised her brows. "What happened with Liddy, Cal?"

"Besides Elle and Quinn finding out about our fake relationship? Ah yes, there was also the part where Quinn asked me to stay the hell away from his sister-in-law."

"That's ridiculous. He has no right to interfere in your love life. Unless he thinks you're just planning on . . . wait." Isla stepped closer to him, searching his face. "You weren't just using her as your scratching post, were you?"

"We had sex. It was never going to be anything else. I ended it."

Isla squared her shoulders. "Cal, I love you. So please take this in the best way possible when I say what the fuck are you even thinking? You clearly *like* this woman."

Her words hit close to his chest.

"I like plenty of women."

"I'm going to punch you, big brother." She glared at him. "You're out of your mind. The first woman who comes into your life in years that might actually make you happy, and you're going to run away lamely because Quinn doesn't like it? God, I thought you were more of a man than that."

She crossed her arms. "This isn't because of Sophia, right? You're not still harboring on to some—"

"For Christ's sake, Isla. I'm not going to have that conversation with you again. I am not, and haven't been, remotely concerned with Sophia in years. Hell, if we're being honest about the whole damn thing, I think I stopped loving her before we even broke up."

Isla blinked at him. "Then why have you made Mum's life so impossible about it? Because she wounded your pride?"

"Don't you get it, Isla?" He shook his head, raking his fingers through his hair. He'd never really verbalized this to her.

But then again, I never knew all the pieces to the puzzle until recently.

"*This place* was one of the few places where I felt I

belonged, even if it wasn't like you belonged here. Or Mum. But when Sophia and I broke up, it was made crystal clear to me how much I didn't belong. I understand why now better. Mum went right on having her relationship with the *daughters* she *raised* here. Her son was always disposable."

Isla blanched. "You don't really believe Mum cares more about Sophia than you, do you?"

"She's more than proved it."

Isla came closer to him and slipped her hand into his. "I don't believe it. But I understand why you would feel like that." She squeezed his hand. "But, Cal, none of that makes any bit of difference with Liddy. You're being a complete arse by letting her go. Don't you think you deserve a bit of happiness after all you've gone through?"

A bitter chuckle left his lips. "What have I gone through that I didn't bring upon myself? Quinn doesn't want me near Liddy because I've shown him my true colors. I wouldn't want me near her either, if the roles were reversed."

Her eyes softened. "You're not a bad guy, Cal. So you've made mistakes. We all do, you know. Liddy doesn't seem to care, and what's more, I think she sees the good in you, too."

"Liddy doesn't know me. I've spent the last two years making sure she never had the chance to."

Isla's mouth twisted. "Maybe that's the problem, then. You're scared. You don't want to believe she could possibly like you because it makes it easier to push her away if she doesn't." She poked a finger into his chest. "Knowing you, I'd say you're also too scared to trust that she'd continue liking you the closer she gets."

Callum stepped back, his throat tight. He felt exposed, and he didn't like it.

Enough.

"I should go find Aiden." He checked his phone. Sure

enough, he had a few missed texts. "Do me a favor, will you? Can you take my bags up to the house? I'd rather not talk to Mum—or Sophia—right now."

Isla set her hands on her hips.

A disgusted look came into her expression. "You want to keep walking away from any possibility of happiness? Then do it yourself." Pushing past him, Isla left the bungalow.

Callum stared at the space she'd vacated. *Great. Another person irritated with me.*

He slipped the bag strap over his shoulder and exited back into the rain. Isla being upset with him would only make staying at his mum's house more awkward. Maybe he should see if any other local places had accommodations. Elle had said that some family members who hadn't been able to stay at *La Hacienda* had trouble finding a place to stay nearby, but right now, any other place—no matter how far—seemed preferable.

For now, though, he didn't want to make any more waves as the irresponsible member of the wedding party. He'd just leave his bags in the office and come back for them later.

He hurried toward the office, not thrilled to get rained on again, then slipped inside.

The sound of paper rustling caught his attention before he saw Sophia nearly leap away from the counter.

A man Callum didn't recognize—maybe an American from his appearance—leaned against the counter. He jerked his chin up in surprise, then gave Callum a curious look.

Why does this feel like déjà vu? She had that guilty, *just caught* expression written on her face and she lifted trembling fingers to her waist, smoothing out her dress. "Callum. What are you doing here?"

"Friend of yours?" the man asked Sophia. *Definitely American.*

Callum raised a brow. *I don't even care. Whatever she was doing, it isn't any of my business.* He said nothing, then pushed past her toward the kitchen. Even if she was co-owner, he was still the other owner's son. That came with some privileges. He dropped his bags in the kitchen, then headed back toward the main door.

The man had slipped out. *Probably a lover.* Maybe Sophia didn't want his mum knowing she was getting it on in the office during work hours.

"I'm leaving some things in the kitchen. I'll be back for them later," he said over his shoulder, not bothering to look back at Sophia.

"Wait . . . Callum."

He paused, clenching his jaw. *Can this day get any worse?* Turning, he shoved his hands into the pockets of his jeans. "Yes?"

"I—" Sophia muttered a curse under her breath in Spanish. "I wasn't expecting so many people to still be here. Your friends are staying here for the rest of the week, yes?"

Is she embarrassed? I've seen her in a more compromising situation than this.

"I believe so." He nearly rolled his eyes. "And it's fine. I won't say anything to Mum, if that's what you're worried about."

She nodded, her lips drawing to a line. "Thank you. And I did the same. I didn't tell her anything I overheard this morning."

He nodded. This wasn't a conversation he was interested in having.

As he turned, Sophia said, "What happened? If you don't mind me asking."

"I do mind, actually." Callum gave her a sharp glance. He wasn't about to discuss Liddy with her.

The corners of Sophia's lips twitched, her gaze unreadable. "Thank you, Cal. For making this so easy for me."

"Was I supposed to?" Just the day before, she'd practically ranted about how their breakup had been his fault.

She shrugged. "It doesn't matter. Goodbye, Callum."

This time, Callum was only too glad to escape back outside. Funny how when he'd been young, he went out of his way to find moments to be with her. Now, she just felt ordinary.

Even if their conversations weren't fraught with tension, he didn't know what he would have to say to her anymore.

It had been so long since he'd really *talked* with any woman, though. Maybe that was why he couldn't get Liddy out of his head. Everything with her had been unexpectedly effortless. They could talk about anything, even if it was about the fruit in a market or work.

Stop thinking about this, for fuck's sake.

He'd come here for his friend. *Nothing more.*

CHAPTER THIRTY-TWO

Liddy lifted her head as Isla and Hunter came into the small office of *La Hacienda*, plastic shopping bags in hand. She frowned at the sight of rain still battering the outdoors, then shifted some of the fabric she'd been cutting on the floor, so Isla would have a path to walk through.

"Did you find something?" Taryn asked, hopping up fluidly from the floor. She reached for the bags.

"Four options I think will work," Isla said, then rolled her eyes at Hunter. "And two dresses that Hunter insisted 'would be sexy as hell' but I'm not sure are wedding dress appropriate."

Hunter gave an unapologetic shrug. "I know my girl. Is she back from the spa with the moms? I want to see what she thinks."

"Not yet," Kat said, poking her head in from the other room. "She should be on her way in twenty minutes, though."

Gotta love Kat for being on schedule.

Even though changing plans once again must have added a lot to Kat's plate, Liddy was surprised at how well the woman had rolled with the changes. She'd taken charge, of course, but

Liddy didn't mind this time. Elle needed someone who had connections and knew what to do to pull this off.

The reception, Liddy and Elle had decided on the car ride back from the failed dress retrieval, would be on the beachfront right where they'd done yoga that morning. Kat would bring in a dance floor and a long table and chairs—which were on their way here from where she'd ordered them.

And when Liddy had described an idea for the reception to Kat, her eyes had immediately lit up. Liddy had no idea where she'd gotten drapery fabric from so quickly, but it had arrived by the bolt a couple hours later, forcing them to have to cut it to the correct size while Elle went out for some much-needed pampering. Quinn and the groomsmen, on the other hand, had gone out for an impromptu stag night. The women had plans to crash the men's party after they got some wedding work done.

Which I'm dreading. Liddy didn't even want to think about seeing Callum right now.

The office was the only space big enough for the rest of the bridal party to work together, so here they were. Rebecca also volunteered to help since Mason was occupied with his brothers.

"I should check on the men. Make sure they're done with the tasks I gave them," Kat said, checking her watch. "And if they are, we can all probably take a break for the night. It's late, and the big day is upon us! I'll still need a few helping hands tomorrow, though."

"I'll help. I don't have to be with bridal hair or makeup," Rebecca said, coming in from the other room with her arms loaded with fabric. "What do we still need to do?"

Thank goodness for Rebecca. She'd been such a calm, steady presence the entire time.

"There's so much." Kat appeared red-faced. "I have trucks of flowers and dinnerware coming in. The caterer I'd found can't accommodate us here, so I'm talking to one of the local restaurant owners to see what we can manage locally. Honestly, I'll probably be up all night." She twittered a bit as though the craziness of this wedding was catching up to her. "But that's the biz. And I wouldn't have it any other way. It'll be perfect."

She grabbed an umbrella and hurried out of the office.

Hunter raised a brow. "Am I the only one who gets the impression she's trying to convince herself of that last part?"

Liddy smoothed her hands on her knees, then used the wall to help herself stand. Her back was really aching now—between the work they'd done today and not having taken it easy on herself the last few days. *Not to mention a night of sex.*

She needed pain meds, but she didn't want to say anything and cast doubt on her ability to push through this for Elle.

"It will be perfect, Hunter. Because even if the tables and chairs and flowers don't arrive and we have to walk down to one of those sodas on the beach to eat dinner, it's all going to be fine."

"Yes. That." Taryn gave Liddy an impressed look. "Elle mentioned you've found a new sort of let-it-ride attitude down here. That's just what this wedding needs."

"Let it ride or take a ride?" Rebecca gave an impish smile.

Isla gave Liddy a cautious look as Liddy's face warmed. Somehow, Liddy got the feeling Isla already knew about Callum's decision to abruptly end . . . *whatever it is we were doing.*

"We all know you're talking about sex, ladies," Hunter said in a flat tone.

Taryn came over to Liddy and slipped her arm around her shoulders. "This is practically my little sister, y'all. You leave her kitchen blow jobs out of the conversation."

Liddy's jaw dropped. "Oh my gosh!" Her gaze went from

Isla to Rebecca, and then she covered her face. "I can't believe you told them."

Good lord. How many people are going to find out about that?

Taryn squeezed her shoulder. "Don't worry, your secret is safe with me. Now Hunter, on the other hand, has a big mouth. So I would highly recommend keeping a babysitter on that one when he starts drinking around your family."

"I do not need a babysitter." Hunter raised his chin. "And can I help it if I'm just proud of this carefree, bold—and happy—version of our Liddy?"

She smiled as brightly as she could, then knelt to fold the cut drapery fabric. Once again, she wasn't telling people everything about Callum, but this time, it was because it would hurt to say anything.

She wanted to close her eyes and pretend it was still last night when she'd actually been as happy as Hunter believed.

Happy . . .

She was happy in some ways . . . Elle was finally getting the wedding she'd wanted.

The dress was no longer an issue, and—best of all—she was no longer hiding secrets from her sister.

Trying to pull the wedding together for tomorrow evening had forged a bond of camaraderie with everyone here, no longer leaving Liddy on the outside.

. . . and then there's Callum.

When she'd seen him in that river earlier today, there had been a moment when her heart had squeezed so hard that she'd just jumped in that water after him.

And when he'd turned toward her and kissed her, she'd felt something in his kiss that she hadn't before—even with all the passionate kisses they'd shared.

He'd kissed her like he cared about her.

Was that enough? To know that maybe he'd cared enough to let her go before she got hurt?

Because I don't want to be the woman who became carefree and bold because of the man in her life.

She wanted to be the woman who had come to this place and found her confidence *because I deserve to be confident.*

Callum had been a part of that, of course. Thinking differently would be foolish.

And so had Sergio. Even when she'd told him their date wouldn't be happening, he'd called her beautiful and told her to look him up if she changed her mind. Even after everything.

Hell, he drove hours to come see me today.

But it wasn't as though men had never complimented her. Wanted to sleep with her.

Callum might have encouraged her to jump off the top of the waterfall, but in the end . . . *I was the one who jumped.*

Granny might have shoved her ass out the door to go surfing . . . *but I still did it.* She'd face-planted, but she'd done it.

Nothing this past week had gone according to plan. And she hoped she'd learned something from it.

"Well, ladies, I don't know about you, but I am ready to consume ridiculous amounts of alcohol and get this party started," Hunter said, interrupting her thoughts as she finished folding the fabric.

"I don't know that I have anything to wear," Liddy said, standing and straightening with a grimace. All she wanted was to go back to her bungalow and crawl into bed, but she wasn't about to ruin Elle's last "single" night.

"Don't worry." Hunter winked at her and reached into the shopping bags he'd brought back. "I picked up a couple of sexy little numbers for my girls while I was shopping. Yours is yellow. And it'll definitely get you laid again." He handed Liddy a silky golden yellow dress.

"Wow, that's gorgeous, Hunter."

"I know." He turned and gave Taryn a grin. "And now that Quinn's friend Jasper is here, Taryn, you have someone to hook up—"

"Can it, Hunter." Taryn shoved him. "Let's meet back here in like fifteen minutes. Elle should be back by now."

"Want to share an umbrella?" Rebecca asked Liddy.

"I'd love to." Liddy started toward the door, then startled as Rebecca pulled an umbrella from where it'd been propped against a wall in the corner of the room. Together with a couple other umbrellas, it had covered some bags sitting there, which Liddy instantly recognized as Callum's.

Liddy's heart gave a painful lurch.

He really did leave the bungalow.

She'd been doing her best to avoid thinking about it, but seeing the bags there made it hard to breathe.

Wow. Why does this hurt so much?

A part of her had been stupidly hoping he'd change his mind. Or that things could return to the way they'd been this morning.

Rebecca watched her closely. "You all right?"

Liddy avoided her gaze, trying to think of a suitable response as they stepped outside. Sharing an umbrella put them closer proximity wise. *And besides, I trust Rebecca.*

"Callum and I had a fight," she said at last. In some ways, it was true. It'd been less passionate than that, really. Callum had that defeated, emotionless mask on his face again. And she'd been too frustrated to argue back. Especially when he'd been trying to tell her to go out with Sergio, as though it was nothing to him.

"Another one?" Rebecca grimaced. The lights on the path cast deep shadows on the walkway and Isla had warned them earlier to watch out for frogs, which sometimes came out on the paths. Liddy kept her gaze down, using that as an excuse not to look at Rebecca.

"We butt heads easily." Another truth. Lying by omission might be easy enough.

"I have to tell you something. Miranda sent me a message earlier today."

Oh.

Liddy's pulse slowed.

Shit. Now I really feel like a jerk. "I was going to tell you, Rebecca, I just—"

"Then you know?" Rebecca gripped her arm. "Oh my God. I've been wrestling with whether I should tell you. I hated for you to find out from me, but I also couldn't stand the idea of you being cheated on." She furrowed her brow. "Did Callum tell you?"

Just what did Miranda tell her?

It sounded as though Miranda had simply divulged that Callum had kissed her. Her next breath came more easily. *Thank goodness Miranda didn't say anything more.*

"He did." Liddy hugged the dress Hunter had given her closer to herself as a sprinkle of rain hit her forearm.

"I can't believe he'd do that." Rebecca shook her head, anger flickering through her face. "You deserve so much better than that. He's such an—"

"Actually, he's not," Liddy breathed. She'd had enough confessions for one day, but Callum didn't deserve this. *I can't do that to him.*

"We're not really together." She didn't want to tell Rebecca all of Callum's private matters, but maybe there was a good compromise. "We hooked up on this trip. And I promise— there's a reason I didn't tell you the truth. It all seems dumb in retrospect, but Callum wasn't dating me when that incident with Miranda happened."

Rebecca was silent for a few beats. "I . . . um. All right, then."

Liddy bit her lip, feeling more awkward than ever. "I'm sorry, Rebecca—"

"You don't owe me an apology. If you say you have reasons, I believe you. That's enough for me."

Unexpected tears burned in Liddy's eyes. "Really?"

Rebecca laughed lightly. "Of course, I fully expect you'll eventually tell me those reasons—when you're able to."

"I will."

"All right." Rebecca slowed as they drew closer to Liddy's bungalow. "You're my friend, Liddy. The only thing I worry about is that you're putting yourself in a position to get hurt, not who you might sleep with. I will say, it doesn't make Callum look good—for him to snog with Miranda days before this. My gut tells me Miranda likely wanted something more to come from that and she's smarting over it, but Callum showed some serious lack of judgment. Though I suppose we all knew he was a knave."

"He's not, though." Liddy stepped under the porch, away from Rebecca. "Really. He's . . . sweet, if you can believe it. Surprisingly thoughtful. And getting to know him has been the best part of this trip."

"Getting to know him or having good sex with him? There's a difference, you know."

Liddy smiled. "Both were great. But I meant the non-sexual one." Liddy looked over her shoulder toward the darkened bungalow. "But too many people found out the truth about our arrangement, and it's over now. He's ended it."

"And you don't want it to be." Rebecca searched her face. "Right?"

"Yes."

"Did you tell him that?"

"He didn't give me a choice." Liddy rubbed her fingertips into the small of her lower back, where a dull ache was forming. "I really like him. It feels as though there could be something worth exploring between us. But I think he's scared to let it go anywhere."

Rebecca practically snorted. "Of course he is. He's an emotionally stunted man-child. Look, at best, we can hope that men stagnate somewhere in adolescence, but Callum appears to have been served his trauma early, given the way he's internalized it all . . ." She grinned. "Don't mind me, I've been inhaling true crime specials with loads of psychological analysts."

"I can tell."

Rebecca shook her head. "But that's not the point. The point is, *everyone* has been talking about how clearly captivated Callum is by you, Liddy."

Captivated?

Stupid hope. It flared within her despite her best effort.

"It was all part of the act."

"I doubt that. Callum isn't that good of an actor. And neither are you. You both seem to really get on well."

We do get along . . . in some ways. "Callum made it clear he's not the relationship type."

"Hmm, that's funny. Mason told me Callum's ex-fiancée works here."

Liddy furrowed her brows, trying to follow Rebecca's train of thought. "Yes . . ."

"Callum Scott was *engaged* before, Liddy. And when he was young, obviously. Which means he's absolutely the relationship type. If he proposed to someone before, it's because he wanted a happily ever after. He's probably a goddamn bleeding-heart romantic who will spoil you to death—once he lets you in. Problem is, you let him shut the door."

Was it possible? Did I let him?

He didn't give me a choice, really.

Then again, she hadn't pushed back—not when it came to ending this early anyway. She'd pushed for sex. "He told me we could only ever have a brief, physical relationship. He never opened the possibility of anything else—and I said I could handle that."

"Oh please, Liddy. He's known you for two years. If all you were was some girl he'd met and went home with, this would be a different conversation. I *promise* you that whatever rationale Callum used to go into this, it wasn't done lightly. He's probably been interested in you for a while."

For a while?

A tiny lizard darted up the porch post, and Liddy watched it, her pulse speeding as she chewed her lower lip, considering Rebecca's words. *He asked me out two years ago. Before he knew who I was.*

She still had that damn guidebook they'd flipped for. Every now and then, she'd come across the number he'd scrawled on the back page. And if he hadn't ended up being her boss, she would have called him.

She'd never expected Rebecca to be this encouraging— especially after admitting to lying to her. But then again, maybe Liddy had never understood that this was how real friendship worked.

Liddy searched Rebecca's face. "What are you saying?"

"I'm saying, if you two make each other happy, don't let Callum's stupidity stop something that could be good for you both. Go kick down the damn door. And I highly suggest you do it in a yellow minidress."

CHAPTER THIRTY-THREE

THE ENERGETIC BEAT of loud Latino music filled the air. The rain had stopped for long enough that Callum and the other groomsmen were barefooted on the wet sand of the beach, smoking celebratory Cuban cigars that Aiden had brought. The bar was an open-aired place, right at the edge of the water.

"Dammit if I don't feel old tonight," Quinn said, sitting beside Callum on a long palm whose trunk had bent perpendicular to the sand before jutting out over the water. He stared at the cigar in his hand. "It's amazing how little appeal these have for me."

Callum chuckled. He'd snuffed out his own cigar against the trunk minutes before. "We are almost thirty. Nearly halfway to the grave. And soon enough you'll have an infant, you poor sod." He kept his voice low, as Quinn's brothers were close enough to hear.

"God, that's terrifying, isn't it?" Quinn leaned back, then fell right off the other side of the trunk.

He must have had too much to drink already.

Throwing his head back with a laugh, Callum held out a

hand to help him stand. "No need to be dramatic about it. Unless you want the bartender to cut you off early."

Quinn took Callum's hand and righted himself from the awkward position, then dusted himself off. "Yes, please. I don't want to spend my wedding day hungover. And Mason seems hell-bent on getting all of us sloshed."

"How about this? Every time he asks for a shot, I'll take yours. He'll have fun with that once I can barely stand."

"Brilliant." Quinn set his hands more firmly against the trunk again as he sat. "Oh bugger, I dropped the damn cigar in the sand."

Callum shrugged. "I won't tell Aiden if you don't."

"Have I told you how incredibly useful you can be, Cal? If you weren't screwing my sister-in-law, you'd be my favorite groomsman."

"I heard that," Mason said, plopping down on Quinn's other side. "What did the rest of us do to earn your scorn?"

"Apparently, it's a lethal combination of whisky, cigars, and . . ." Callum looked at Quinn to finish.

"The illegal drugs our brother Logan left in Elle's dress garment bag." Quinn nodded with a flop of his head. "Security nearly stopped Liddy for it."

That was a discreet way to put it.

Mason gawked at Logan, who stood in conversation with Kyle, Aiden, and Jasper.

Jasper, Quinn's former flatmate who would officiate the wedding, was in the middle of a loud, clearly hilarious story. He'd always had a commanding presence and the ability to keep most people laughing, which was why Quinn had probably chosen him for the role. But in the absence of moonlight on the unlit beach, Jasper's dark skin and choice of dark clothing made him hard to see, making him seem like a disembodied voice.

"Logan. Did you really try to get some herb into the country?" Mason hollered at Logan, his hands cupped around his mouth.

Logan gave him a chagrinned look. "Do you have any idea how incredibly boring it is to live at Littleton? What else am I going to do?"

"You're talking with the only other people in the world who know *exactly* how boring it is to live at Littleton, you dimwit." Quinn stood with a shake of his head.

Aiden snorted. "He has you there, little brother. We all shared your misery as children. Not all of us were given the luxury of constant adventure and jet-setting to paradise like Cal." He puffed on a cigar as he approached them. "Not sure how you ever chose London over this place, I have to admit," he said to Callum. "Even the rain the last few days is far superior to our dreary months at home."

"You know what I find the best way to deal with rain?" Mason set his hands on his knees and stood. "Alcohol. I'm going to get another round for us."

Callum grimaced as Mason went off toward the bar. He'd better drink water if he was going to drink two shots for every one that Mason proposed. A numb buzz already vibrated through him. *The things I do for my friends. Drink their shots.*

Give up my woman.

He stiffened. *His woman?* Where had that notion come from?

And yet, the bitter feeling that came with the thought didn't wash away with either shot of whisky that Mason returned with.

He'd just thrown back the second shot when a cheer broke out in the bar. Glancing over his shoulder, he peered into the dimly lit space.

Isla led some of the women and Hunter through the bar,

Elle at her side. Elle had a small white veil clipped to her head, along with a white "Bride" sash around her dress.

A few steps behind her was Liddy.

Callum's stomach clutched at the sight of her.

Fuck me, she's sexy.

Maybe it was the alcohol, but he wasn't sure if he'd ever had such a raging sense of lust sweep over him. She wore a tight yellow minidress, her hair swept half up, the rest of it cascading in waves down her back.

Isla had already spotted them out on the beach, and she gave a playful wave, then redirected the group of women toward the bar.

"Do you think they're here to check on us or torment us?" Quinn asked, watching Elle with a grin.

"Torment, absolutely," Mason said, staring at Rebecca.

Kyle made a face. "Anyone else want to go shoot a round of pool?"

Callum's gaze flicked back to Liddy. If she'd seen him, she hadn't bothered to turn and glance his way. She didn't look unhappy either. *Maybe the date with Sergio went well.* Her smile as she chatted with Isla was carefree. *Beautiful.*

He gritted his teeth and forced himself to look away.

"Should we say hello?" Mason asked their group.

Quinn was already heading that way.

Callum smiled to himself. Stag night or not, Quinn was unapologetic about his desire to be around his wife.

But if Callum was going to survive the next few days with any grace, he'd have to do a better job of keeping his distance from Liddy. He hadn't told anyone about their breakup yet, but he doubted he could hide how miserable he felt about the whole thing while at Liddy's side.

"I'll shoot some pool," Callum said to Kyle.

They left the others and headed toward the lone pool table

in the bar. Unsurprisingly, the cues seemed slightly warped—a likely effect of humidity. He picked the two straightest ones while Kyle racked the balls.

Handing Kyle the cue, Callum sized up Liddy's younger brother. He knew they were close in age. If Liddy hadn't dyed her hair, all the Winnick siblings would look alike. "Sorry about the surfing lesson earlier today, mate." Callum rubbed some chalk on the tip of the cue. "We can try again later in the week if you'd like."

Kyle studied him. "It depends."

Callum drew his lips to a firm line. *Great.* He knew where this was heading. "On?"

"How much you care about my sister."

Callum leaned his torso toward the table and lined up the cue ball. The ricochet of the break sounded off the sides of the table and he watched as the balls rolled to a stop. "Stripes." He lifted his gaze and met Kyle's eyes. "Well, I ended things this afternoon, so that probably doesn't bode well for our surfing lesson."

To his surprise, Kyle's reaction was unreadable. "Huh. Why exactly?" He moved to the other side of the table.

"Why what?"

"Why did *you* end things?"

Better to answer truthfully. "Because she deserves better than me."

Kyle laughed sardonically, then bent to line up his shot. "Obviously. But is that what she wants? Or are you just trying to prove how undeserving you are to make yourself feel better? She's had a lifetime of people making decisions for her based on what they think is best for her, you know."

Callum jerked his chin up. "What?"

Kyle shrugged. "Look, Callum, I don't know you. But of course I'm going to assume you don't deserve my sister. She's one of my best friends. And she's a good person. But clearly, she sees something in you." He struck the cue ball, sinking one of the solids into the pocket. "Unless you think she's just not capable of making her own decisions."

Callum's mouth nearly dropped open.

Bollocks.

Say what you want about the Winnick siblings, but they're a force.

Kyle quirked a brow at Callum, then leaned down and sank another ball into the pocket. "It looks like Liddy has caught someone else's attention." He hit the cue ball, perfectly executing a trick shot that sank two more balls. "I can finish this game in three more shots, by the way."

Callum's head swiveled toward the bar. A dark-haired man had sidled up beside her. Reflexively, Callum's fingers curled tight around the cue.

The sound of another ball sinking into the pocket made him wrest his attention back to Kyle, who still watched him with interest. Then he did a combination shot that sank two more balls.

Callum shook his head and set the cue on the wall rack.

He strode across the bar toward Liddy, ignoring any other thought that tried to push itself into his head. Maybe the alcohol made him reckless, but he didn't care. Liddy wasn't engaging with the man's attempts to get her attention, though she politely smiled, then shifted her body away, closer to Taryn. But Taryn was talking to Elle and not paying attention to Liddy.

Then the man set his hand on the small of her back.

Mine, arsehole.

Callum reached Liddy and stepped between her and the man. Setting a hand on her hip, he caught the faint look of surprise in her wide eyes as he leaned toward her, then dropped a kiss to her lips.

She stiffened against him for a beat, before her warm lips parted against his slightly as she returned the kiss.

Having spent the night in her arms, he knew that she was clearly holding back, but why shouldn't she?

Callum nearly groaned, though. It'd only been—what—eight hours since he'd kissed her. But he'd missed the taste of her mouth. The smell of her body. The feel of her curves under his hands.

God, I want this woman.

I need this woman.

She ended the kiss, then smiled, dragging her lips away toward his ear. "What are you doing?"

Claiming what's mine.

"Helping you," he answered in a low growl.

Being this close to her, it was all he could do to keep his hands off her.

She pulled back, then slipped her hand into his. Tugging him away from the bar, she pulled him toward the beach. He followed without question, not bothering to look back at the man who had been hitting on her.

They hadn't gone far—close to where he and Quinn had been smoking cigars—when Liddy stopped. She turned back toward Callum. "What the hell was that?"

He rubbed his eyes. "I didn't—"

"Didn't what? Think I could handle myself?" Liddy set her hands on her hips. "Or did you change your mind about us?"

"No—I . . ." Callum gritted his teeth. "Couldn't stand the thought of him hitting on you."

"But you sent me off to go on a date with Sergio." She crossed her arms. "And, before you ask, I didn't go. I'm not going to have sex with you and then go out with another guy four hours later. I know you're used to a different standard of behavior from women, but that's not who I am."

I know. That's why I like you.

Her words brought him a relief he hadn't realized he needed, and he released a breath. "I'm sorry."

She stepped toward him, then slipped her hand into his. "I'm sorry, too. I shouldn't have left the room without making that clear. I was hurt by what you said about last night meaning nothing—then confused because I know that's what you want. You want it to mean nothing, and I told you I'd be okay with that. And I think we both know that you're right. I'm not okay with it."

She ran her thumb against the palm of his hand, tantalizing him with her touch. "But I also refuse to accept that it meant nothing to you, either. And I'm not going to let you push me away without getting a say in it, Callum. You matter to me. Whatever we are—it's no one else's business. And I don't mind telling Quinn that either."

He stared at her, certain he was hallucinating.

What? She'd apologized . . . to me?

She smiled, then she brushed her lips against his palm with a featherlight kiss. "When was the last time you let a woman actually take care of you, Cal? Was it Sophia? You don't have to do everything alone just because she hurt you. Or maybe it goes even deeper than that. I don't know and you don't have to tell me, but I refuse to be one more person who you shut out because you want to protect yourself. I won't hurt you. I promise."

His heart squeezed painfully in his chest.

Didn't I just tell her the exact opposite last night?

His loathsome words to her rang through his head.

He'd promised to hurt her.

"I don't deserve you," he whispered.

"Why don't you let me decide that?" She kissed the back of his hand, then released it. "We're only here for a few minutes and then Isla is taking us to another bar. But I'd prefer you be in one piece tonight when I get back to our bungalow, so for God's sake, don't get into a fight with anyone tonight. I don't want to kick anyone's ass if they punch you." She stepped past him, her fingertips brushing his hip as she leaned over and nipped at his earlobe. "Because I'm going commando. Kicking might not work out so well."

Oh . . . fuck me.

He groaned out loud, turning to reach for her and grabbing only air as she stepped farther away.

She grinned. "By the way, I found your luggage in the office and put it back where it belongs. See you later, Cal."

As she strode across the sand toward the bar, he had to restrain himself from the temptation of leaving the stag party early and tossing her over his shoulder on the way out the door. Not that she needed any masculine shows of strength.

A strange, strangled hope rose in his chest, and he swallowed hard.

Considering what he'd said and done earlier, she should have given up on him.

The fact that she hadn't put him in unchartered waters.

Because, for the first time, I don't want to be given up on.

CHAPTER THIRTY-FOUR

"Did you have fun tonight?" Liddy asked Elle, leaning against her as they walked arm in arm toward the bungalows.

"So much fun. I mean, it's probably less fun than you all had—you know, not being able to drink and all—but it was perfect. Way better than a silly rehearsal dinner."

"Good." Liddy stopped as the paths split by the pool. They had different walkways to take, and it was really the first time all night she'd been alone with Elle. She sighed, then hugged her. "I'm thrilled for you."

Elle held her close, settling her chin against Liddy's shoulder. "Lid, I'm sorry if I was a jerk earlier today. Or if I've been awful during the past few days. I'll admit I was jealous. You were spending so much time with Callum, and I've barely gotten to see you the last year and you see him every day." She pulled away, straightening. "But I'm so proud of you. You're so independent and amazing."

"Yeah, well, my sister set a high bar of achievement to look up to. Don't forget, I'm not the famous one."

"Ugh, don't remind me." Elle stepped toward her bungalow. "I should check to see if Quinn is back. Hopefully, the men didn't get him too wasted tonight. I don't need my mother-in-law . . ." She paused, then gave an exaggerated shrug. "You know what? I don't care. It doesn't matter."

Liddy laughed. "See? You're learning. Speaking of Quinn, though, can you do me a favor?"

"Sure. What is it?"

"Can you tell him that while I appreciate him trying to be a good 'big brother,' just let Callum and I figure this thing we've got going on together?"

A hint of a smile touched Elle's lips. "You've got it. Like I said, you're all grown up now."

"But I'll always need my big sis."

"And I'll always need my little sis."

Liddy hugged her one more time, then they parted. Liddy strolled slowly toward her bungalow, searching her clutch for the room key. There had been a break in the rain for the evening, but clouds appeared to be rolling over the stars again. Everything in the canopy of trees around the bungalows was damp and glistened with droplets. The monkeys and birds were quiet for the night.

A soft snore broke the silence as she reached the bungalow.

Callum was curled up in the hammock, one hand hanging over the edge. He didn't look entirely comfortable.

But he's here.

That filled her with a happiness that made her chest hurt.

Going closer to him, she squatted, then swiped her hand across his cheek. Lowering her lips to his, she kissed him softly. "Hey, sleeping beauty."

Callum blinked, then pushed his shoulders back. He smelled of alcohol, which didn't surprise her. *Just how drunk is he?*

"Didn't make it inside?" she teased as he sat up straight, almost dazedly.

"Not quite." Rather than get up, he reached for her and pulled her onto his lap, one leg at a time so that she was straddling him.

She relaxed into him as the hammock swayed slightly, wrapping her arms around his neck. "Miss me?"

"You have no idea." His hand had found its way up her dress and deftly unhooked her bra. "I've been waiting here for you for ages."

She chuckled against his jaw, sucking in a breath as his palms slid around to her breasts. "We're outside you know," she whispered. "Someone could see us."

"It's dark," he countered, making slow circles with his palms over her nipples. "And we can be quiet." His lips found hers, and he drank from her mouth with raw intensity. He tasted like whisky, not that she minded.

Her pulse was already speeding, her desire for him mounting.

"Are you drunk?"

"Just a bit." His hands left her breasts and pushed her skirt up.

"Liar. You're wasted."

"I promised Quinn I'd have his shots so he wouldn't be hungover tomorrow." He nuzzled her neck, his breath hot against her jawline. His fingers found the wetness of her entrance, and he sucked in a sharp breath. "God, you *weren't* lying. You're not wearing a stitch." His fingers traced against the slick, tender flesh there, and she gripped him tighter, hot lust surging through her.

"No foreplay?"

"Foreplay happened hours ago when you teased me. I've

been hard thinking about what I'm going to do to you ever since."

They relied on his balance and stability to stay on the hammock, but somehow it seemed to help the rhythm of his movements. Her lips parted over his, and she drew short, shallow gasps as he locked eyes with her, watching her with a fiercely intense gaze.

Somehow, he'd freed himself from his zipper and pushed his pants down. He slid inside her, still holding her gaze.

Oh, yes.

"Callum."

The way he watched her made her raw with hunger for him and her legs locked around his waist.

This is crazy.

Anyone could walk by. At any moment.

Her lips and face and ears were burning hot, her breath still mingling with his.

But I don't care.

I want him.

I want us.

"I can't let you go, Liddy." He closed his eyes, his forehead against hers. "I don't want to."

"So don't." Her lips skimmed his throat. "I'm right here. I'm not going anywhere."

"I can't."

He's not making any sense.

He crushed her in his arms, locking her hips against his, his hold so tight that she could barely do more than grind against him.

Then he didn't say anything else, and they were both lost to the pleasure, their bodies moving together in a rhythm that felt so natural, so perfect. And when they both came, his hold didn't lessen. He sank his lips into the crook of her neck, his heart pounding against her chest, his breath ragged.

His forehead pressed into her shoulder, and she could hardly breathe.

He was drunk, and that could be a part of it, but the way he held her fiercely also worried her.

"Callum, are you okay?" she asked, pulling back enough that she could draw a deep breath. "What's going on?"

He pulled himself out of her on a wince. With a gentle push of her knee, he brought her onto the hammock beside him, then lay back with her.

He didn't speak for a minute, the gentle rocking of the hammock and the creak of its ropes the only sound she could hear through the rain.

"My mother cheated on my father."

Oh.

Okay . . .

Did he just find out?

Maybe he'd talked to his mom at long last.

"Then . . . that's why they got divorced?"

"I'm sorry. I sound like a fool, I know. You just said earlier that you didn't know if something deeper had ruined me."

She cringed. He wasn't completely coherent and *that* she was certain had to do with the alcohol.

"That's not *entirely* how I said it but—"

"It turns out Sophia's mum was my mum's lover. Isla told me. Which, the more I think about it, makes it even more sick and twisted because it's like Sophia was my stepsister. That's why my mum couldn't choose between us. She views her like a daughter."

Oh, wow. Yeah, that would be a lot to take.

"But she wasn't *your* stepsister. You didn't know. You can't beat yourself up over that." Liddy interlaced her fingers with his. "Are you upset because you never knew your mom was . . . what, bi?"

"No." Callum shook his head. "No, that doesn't make a difference. It doesn't matter who she left for. Who she cheated with. The effect was the same. It blew up my life. My family." He cleared his throat. "I barely got to see my sister, except on holidays. I spent years wondering if I had something to do with their breakup. I thought if I had been a better child, my parents would have stayed together—they sent me to a boarding school. Almost as though they didn't want me around. Then years not having a real home. I still don't have a home. The last time I did, I was nine years old."

His words filled her with a profound sadness. She loved living in England, but she also knew that, no matter what she was going through, no matter how much she might not always see eye to eye with her parents, she could go home. Her roots were deep. And not because of the house where she'd grown up —her parents had sold that when Elle had bought them a better place.

But because of the people.

"Ever heard the expression 'home isn't a place'? That's what I've found, anyway. I'm home whenever I'm with the people I love the most in the world. Wherever that may be," she said in a gentle voice.

The hammock swayed in a breeze, then a light sprinkling of rain started again. They were under the cover of the porch, but the mist dampened her skin.

"Maybe . . . but I don't have that. The thing of it is that Isla does. Isla was miserable at the boarding school she was sent to, and Mum insisted to my dad that she come live with her instead. So Isla spent years here. And now my mum is looking to sell it because the business isn't doing well. Isla is sentimental and wants to buy it, and she doesn't have the money, so she wants me to lend it to her."

Her heart ached for him.

He had every reason to be angry and not *want* to lend his sister the money. Not that anger was serving him well.

"Would she be able to pay you back, do you think?"

"It's not that I don't trust her. I'm not certain she's aware of the extent of the changes that would need to happen to make *La Hacienda* profitable, though. Or that she has the personality to run this place—she's a dreamer, like my mum. But I also don't want her to lose the place she considers home."

She rested her head on his chest, tracing the outline of the tattoos on his forearm. The Callum that had inked his body in soccer team tattoos, she imagined, had probably been a different person. But what he'd told her also made her realize that he'd probably lost another sense of home and belonging when he'd lost his dream to play soccer.

And when he broke up with Sophia.

Which explains a lot, really.

His sense of worth had been shot down over and over again. His sense of place. And belonging.

She closed her eyes, listening to his heartbeat.

She'd struggled with belonging, too. *All my life.*

That was why she felt so unmoored today when she felt like an outsider to her own family.

He doesn't even have that.

"You know, Sergio actually mentioned something interesting to me earlier. He said he'd spent the time while we were away today talking to some American who's interested in buying the land. I didn't quite get that he meant *this land*, but that must have been what he meant."

Callum released a guttural sigh. "Shite. Then I don't have

as much time to decide as I thought if my mum is already lining up buyers. I don't want Isla to lose everything because of me."

This must be so heart-wrenching for him.

"I can't tell you what to do with your money," she said gently. "But I think you've spent a long time running from some of the people and places who made you what you are today. Your mom may not deserve a second chance or a relationship with you—that's up to you to decide—but sometimes facing the things that have made us feel like outsiders is the only way to move forward. You should face your fears and talk to her." She splayed her hand on his chest. "Like you made me face my fears, Coach."

He gave one light chuckle. "I didn't make you do anything. I simply suggested."

"True. But you helped me believe in myself. Helped me be fearless, and I'm thankful to you for that."

She reached up and kissed him, then rolled off the opposite side of the hammock. "Come, Callum. Let's go to bed."

She held out a hand for him.

Callum turned his head toward her, his eyes roving over her figure. He took her hand.

CHAPTER THIRTY-FIVE

R**AIN** in the morning meant the surf would be rough, but Callum still slipped out before sunrise and headed to the beach.

As he nabbed the surfboard that he'd set on the side of the bungalow, he wished he could grab a cup of coffee before going out there.

Or wake Liddy just to kiss her.

But he'd been afraid of what else he might say to her. He'd been drunk last night, and he definitely wasn't sure how to proceed with her.

He was in unchartered waters.

Callum tucked the surfboard under one arm, then carried it down to the beach. Predictably, the water was choppy, but the waves were good. If he hadn't gotten on that surfboard earlier in the week when Granny had insisted on those lessons, he might not have remembered how easily this could come back to him, though.

It turned out that climbing back on a surfboard was a bit like getting back on a bicycle.

He was in the cold water in minutes, paddling out beyond where the waves were breaking. Surfing and football. His childhood.

Coming back here felt like a strange time travel.

And it was more than just that. He hadn't lost an ounce of Spanish, even if he'd been out of practice with it. But he'd forgotten how much he loved the taste of tropical fruit and rice and beans. He'd forgotten the Tico people, with their kindness and easygoing charm—and their ability to set work to the side and enjoy life.

Simplicity. *My God, I forgot that.*

Friendship, too.

And worse—what it felt like to be in the arms of a woman who challenged him. Not only to do better but to *be* better.

The salt water stung his eyes as he tossed his board over a wave, then dove into it.

I once belonged to this ocean. To this land.

And now the only thing—the only person—I want to belong to . . . is Liddy.

He no longer felt as . . . alone. As if he had another person in his corner who cared for him even when he was an arse. He wasn't wrong when he said he didn't deserve her, but maybe, just maybe, he could work harder at that. At deserving her. Like a second chance.

He'd considered Liddy's words, too.

"But sometimes facing the things that have made us feel like outsiders is the only way to move forward. You should face your fears and talk to her."

It was time to move forward.

He had to let go of the anger that had consumed him.

As he burst through the surface, the breath he drew felt like freedom.

He rode a few waves, letting go of his troubles and clearing his mind. He lost track of time, and then, as the sky grew lighter, he headed toward the shore.

Finding his flip-flops off on the sand, he gathered them, sinking his toes into the cold, wet granules. Funny how things like this didn't change—he still loved the beach at this time of day, no matter the weather, just like his mother did.

Speaking of his mother, he had one more thing he needed to do this morning before heading into the wedding preparations.

He didn't bother to towel off yet, as it made no difference in the light rain, and he walked back up toward *La Hacienda*. Passing the bungalows and office, he took another path farther back, heading to the house his mum and Carmen had built here —the first structure they'd put on the land.

Mum's house was simple with three small bedrooms, a kitchen, and a living room. The peach paint on the walls was peeling badly, but still the same shade he remembered from all those years before.

Callum stashed his board and then shook the water from his hair. A light was on in the kitchen, and he went toward the fern-covered area his mother called a "patio," which had a door that led to the kitchen.

He tapped twice softly, hoping that it wouldn't be Sophia who was awake, then opened the door.

Mum sat at the kitchen table, wearing a robe. Her eyes widened. "Callum. What are you doing here?"

The guilt that passed over him was palpable. He'd told himself he was completely justified in staying away—and maybe he was—but Mum didn't exactly look as young right now. It could be the lack of makeup or the fact that her hair was in disarray. *Or the worn, tired expression on her face.* The light that had always twinkled in her eyes had faded.

He could picture her in this kitchen, singing and dancing.

Carmen nearby, laughing at Mum while she chopped green beans for *picadillo.* Or the two of them sitting at the table, having their afternoon coffee together while gossiping over biscuits.

Maybe I just didn't want to see what I should have known.

"Are Isla and Sophia awake?"

Mum shook her head. "Isla is sleeping." She sipped her coffee. "Sophia moved to a new house a few months ago. She's not here."

That was surprising. He'd assumed Sophia still lived with his mum.

I assumed a lot, it seems.

He stopped a few feet away from her. "Isla told me about Carmen. Who she was to you. That she was why you left Dad."

Mum froze, a shadow crossing her face. "I didn't know you never knew."

"If I'd been less innocent when it happened, I might have figured it out. The adults' bedroom and the kids' bedrooms. It just made sense. You were friends." He shrugged as he pulled out the chair in front of his mother. "I had no reason to question the narrative."

"I wasn't trying to hide it from you when you were older, I just—"

"You were. But that's not the point. The point is, I know now. And I also know why you didn't bat an eyelash when Sophia cheated on me. You viewed her as your daughter. And made excuses for her behavior." He should have grabbed a towel. His soaked bathing suit was making him shiver. Or maybe it was the nerves firing through his body. He'd known he needed to address this and approach his mum as an adult—but *doing it* was another matter altogether.

Tears filled Mum's eyes. "No. Callum. That's not true. I was mad at her—for a long time—for hurting you. But she also told me another side of the story. Of how cold you were to her. How angry you were all the time. How you treated her. And it reminded me of why—"

"Why you cheated?" Callum raised a brow. "Yes, exactly, Mum. You saw yourself in Sophia. And you know, maybe I was insufferable, but I was also suffering. And rather than talk to me, she crushed the only piece of my heart left. Betrayal isn't a solution to being miserable. It only makes the misery worse for everyone involved."

Tears escaped her eyes. "Carmen begged me on her deathbed—she made me promise I would always take care of Sophia. I couldn't break that promise."

"I was your son, Mum. What about the promise you made to me when you decided to have a child in the first place?"

"You *are* my son, Callum. You can't stop being my son just because you decide. You will always be my son, and I will always keep hoping you forgive me."

"Then start by admitting what you did. What you continue to do by choosing Sophia every day."

Mum wiped her cheeks and sank back in her chair. "What was I supposed to do, Callum? She owns this just as much as I do. And just like now, when she's insisting we have to sell, I don't have a choice because I don't own *La Hacienda* outright."

That's . . . not how Sophia had put it.

He tried to rack through his brain for the precise words Sophia had used when telling him Mum was thinking of selling *La Hacienda,* but he couldn't remember outright. "Wait. She's insisting you sell?"

Mum nodded tearfully. "She doesn't want to keep running the business. She says it's too much work, and we're barely surviving—but I never cared about making a big profit. As long as I was paying my bills, I was happy. She says it's not worth it."

Wait.

Sergio had said he'd talked to an American who wanted to buy the land.

And yesterday when I found her talking to an American man in the office, she behaved nervously.

She planned on selling, with or *without* Mum's blessing? Hell, she might even be planning on letting someone else buy her out and deal with the messiness of co-ownership.

That bitch.

And maybe it was too strong of a feeling, but the fact was, his mum wasn't a young woman anymore. If Sophia insisted on selling, Mum would be out of a job, a business, and a home. *Her home.*

"But . . . you've always been loyal to her." The idea that Sophia could turn around and do something like this to his mother, even after Mum had picked her over her own son, after working together for years, after *everything* made him so furious that he could hardly see straight.

Mum gave Callum a helpless look. "I never should have made her feel like she was more important to me than you. And now I've earned my punishment, yes? For everything. For leaving your father, for not breaking my promise to Carmen." She bowed her head. Tears shook her shoulders. "I'm sorry, Callum. I'm so sorry. I love you, I always have. I was selfish, though. I chose what was easy, even if it did not make me happy. I didn't want to lose *La Hacienda,* and I thought you would come around. I knew it would make me miserable in the long run. I knew I would end up alone and empty."

Quiet sobs shook her shoulders.

She looks frail.

Broken.

So human.

She's so . . . lonely, especially having lost Carmen—now that

I fully understand what she meant to her. Carmen had been dead for eleven years now. Mum had been alone ever since.

And Sophia was ready to toss her to the side—for money. Seemed that Sophia had deceived both him and his mum. Had she ever been someone they should have trusted? Even though he felt closer to Liddy and saw her as special, he wondered if he'd ever be able to fully let go of the doubt—that fear to trust— that still plagued him.

But I want to try.

Callum tugged at the wet hair on the top of his head.

Fuck.

He had no idea what to do.

"*I chose what was easy. Even if it did not make me happy . . .*"

Those words were haunting.

They might have been the most honest words his mother had ever spoken.

Maybe even the bravest.

He'd spent the past five years doing the *same damn thing.*

How many times have I chosen to do what I know will make me miserable because it's easier? Because changing what I've been doing means facing a different fear?

Liddy's face flashed through his mind.

He reached out and set a hand on his mother's shoulder.

How do we even go forward from this?

Can we?

He tried to think about what he'd wanted to hear all this time. What he'd needed to feel.

What had been missing in his life.

After Sophia had gone home from their breakup, he'd sworn to himself that he wouldn't let himself love *anyone* else again.

He'd closed himself off.

. . . and where had it gotten him?

No one had gotten close. No one.

. . . until Liddy.

That is why she terrifies me so much. Why I wanted to push her away.

Callum released a slow breath and then said in a ragged voice, "I love you, Mum."

Mum sniffled, her eyes red rimmed. "I know it's too late—"

"I don't know that." He pushed her hair back behind her ear, then tipped her chin up so that he could search her eyes. The skin of her cheek was softer than he remembered, the lines around her eyes deeper. "I'm not good at forgiveness. Or I haven't been. But it hasn't made my life any better either. I can tell you it's going to take work, Mum. We can't go back to that time when I held you on a pedestal as a child. When I thought you'd never hurt me. But if you're willing to put in the work"— he struggled to get the words out—"then so am I."

Mum let out a soft, breathy cry and nodded. Then she leaned over and flung her arms around his neck, sobbing against him.

Callum held her tight, his mind spinning.

He'd been born here. Lived here.

Turned his back on it all.

But so many times this week, he'd felt that tug of the familiar. The sense of knowing who he was by being here.

This was a piece of the puzzle of who he was. And without this piece, he couldn't be truly happy.

And it's Isla's home.

He pulled back from his mum and clasped her hands. "So let's talk a little more about what it's going to cost to save *La Hacienda*."

CALLUM LEFT his mum's house and headed toward the bungalow he'd been sharing with Liddy.

He didn't quite know what he was going to tell her.

I just have to see her before the day gets too chaotic.

He was still wet and cold from the time he'd spent on the beach this morning, but he smiled to himself.

Maybe Liddy would have enough time to take a shower with him.

"Callum." Aiden strode down the path toward him, an umbrella on his shoulder. "Glad I found you."

Interesting how he doesn't appear glad.

Had something happened to Quinn?

Aiden's face was serious, a marked difference in demeanor from the previous night when they'd been drinking at a bar together. Their dynamic had always been unique, to say the least. Aiden had gone from being the younger, sometimes annoying, brother of one of his closest friends to his colleague, then his boss and good friend. Besides Quinn, Aiden was probably his best friend, if he thought about it.

"Everything all right?"

"Not exactly." Aiden gestured down the path. "Care to have a chat for a minute?"

"Sure." Callum followed him toward one bungalow. Aiden held the door open for Callum, and Callum passed through.

No one else was inside, and Callum assumed it was Aiden's room—the bed was neatly made, something Callum had always seen Quinn do whenever they'd gone places overnight together. "Please." Aiden gestured toward the chair.

Callum took a seat, his brow furrowing as Aiden sat across from him on the bed. He chuckled. "Somehow I feel as though I'm in trouble."

Aiden frowned. "Well, you might be."

What?

Aiden dipped his chin. "I'll just come out with it. I spent the morning on the phone with the head of human resources at Camden. Apparently, a complaint was filed against you by one of your employees—Miranda Kaster."

Oh fuck.

"What was the nature of the complaint?"

"Sexual harassment."

"Listen—" The details of that drunken stupidity in the alley near his flat the day before the flight seemed less clear. "The whole thing was after hours, in a bar, once I was already drunk. I didn't initiate anything. She followed me home, practically threw herself at me, then tried to bribe me when I turned her down. We kissed, but it hardly went beyond that."

Aiden stared at him, and his brows drew together. "Good to know. If that's true, it certainly helps with context." He cleared his throat, his neck growing red as he rubbed the back of it. "That wasn't the complaint, though, mate."

If that's true?

Why the fuck wouldn't Aiden believe him?

Callum stared at him in disbelief. "What do you mean?"

Aiden leaned forward, setting his elbows on his knees. "She claimed that you've coerced Lydia Winnick to enter into some sort of sham sexual relationship. I think she used the word 'blackmailed.' And, unfortunately, she had texts from Liddy from the day of your flight down here together."

Aiden leaned across his bed and grabbed his phone. He swiped it open, then turned the phone toward Callum, holding it out for him to take.

Callum almost didn't reach for the phone. He didn't want to read the texts.

Because whatever is written there is just a sign that Liddy can't be trusted.

He didn't want to know that.

Didn't want to believe that the woman he was falling for could be so duplicitous.

But it's happened before, hasn't it? A woman you loved has betrayed you.

He hesitated, then took the phone.

Liddy: *I think our boss just sank to an all-time low.*

Miranda*: Oh . . . what now?*

Liddy: *Long story short . . . my sister's wedding dress was stolen. Callum knows where the guy who stole it is heading. He refuses to tell me where, though, unless I pretend to be his girl-friend. Apparently, his ex-fiancée is going to be at the hotel, and he doesn't want to show up alone.*

Miranda: *Stop. He did not.*

Liddy: *Don't worry, I told him to go to hell.*

He'd known Liddy and Miranda were friends and flatmates.

And he'd known Miranda had told Liddy about that foolish kiss in London.

But he hadn't expected this.

Maybe he'd been naive, but he'd assumed Liddy hadn't told Miranda about their arrangement.

Callum could barely look Aiden in the eye, his head pounding. "This says nothing about a sexual relationship."

"That part was apparently relayed by a phone call. Miss Kaster claimed Liddy said you were pressuring her into sexual relations."

Was it possible?

Think, Cal. Miranda is a liar. You know that.

Callum handed the phone back to Aiden, a stabbing pain searing through him.

Aiden searched Callum's face. "Is any of it true, Cal?"

Callum tried to calm his racing thoughts.

If Miranda knew anything about his sexual relationship

with Liddy, this could be nothing more than her attempt to get revenge. He'd turned her down and she'd been furious about it. He didn't trust Miranda *at all.*

Goddammit, Liddy.

Of all the people she could have talked to about this.

And this was precisely why he'd always been so careful about staying away from any woman he worked with.

"Liddy and I have a sexual relationship, yes." He hated to cause Liddy any embarrassment, but he wasn't talking to his friend Aiden right now. This was his boss, and his job was on the line. Anything less than the truth could have serious repercussions, especially now that HR was involved. "But I never pressured her or blackmailed her into sex. That . . . happened separately."

"And the sham relationship?" Aiden turned his phone off and set it on the bed.

"That's true." Callum rubbed his jaw. "Though—just so you know—the wedding dress was located. Security grabbed it because of the marijuana Logan left in the garment bag. And Elle and Quinn both know the truth."

Aiden didn't react. He folded his hands together, the silence between them tense.

"What would you have me do, Cal? I know you're on holiday and this isn't work-related, but HR knows about this. Miranda is clearly spreading this. We're facing an HR nightmare when we return. And Liddy will be dragged through it with you."

It was strange . . . *I should be angrier with Liddy.*

But I'm not.

Because he didn't believe Liddy had said what Miranda accused him of. *I know her better than that.*

He wasn't numb, either. Numb would have been bad, but the fact was that this wasn't Liddy's fault.

He had tried to blackmail her with the information about Sergio.

The fake relationship had been his idea.

And their first kiss in Mum's office was barely consensual from an HR perspective.

When they'd driven in from the airport, Liddy had no reason *not* to share things with her friend. Her choice of who she shared it with had been unlucky.

And then, laughter built in his chest, and he shook his head, covering his face.

It would come to this.

A meaningless, reckless kiss with Miranda Kaster was about to end his career.

And yet . . . he had to be honest.

This is on me.

CHAPTER THIRTY-SIX

Elle and Quinn swayed on the dance floor. The thousands of twinkle lights strung from wood beams installed around the dance floor gave the space a golden glow.

To Liddy, it looked like a fairy tale.

Everything had been perfect. Her sister's dress—a simple, stunning, and also sexy cream satin midi dress Hunter had picked—was perfect for the setting. And the groomsmen were barefoot, which Quinn had insisted on, to his father's horror.

Not that the Camdens had protested anything. Kat had worked her magic, and flowers cascaded from the center of the long main table, making the reception look incredibly elegant.

And, most importantly, Elle looked happy. Radiant.

Surrounded by her closest family and friends, in the arms of the love of her life.

Just like she wanted.

Liddy hugged her arms to her chest, standing off to the side of the dance floor. The day had been a complete blur from the moment she'd woken up. She'd been sad that Callum was gone already, but there hadn't been time to dwell on that as she'd rushed over to get ready with Elle, Taryn, and Hunter, who was serving as a man of honor along with the two women.

Between the nail salon, hairstylists, and makeup artists, and getting ready for photos as soon as the rain broke—she had done nothing but wedding day prep.

She'd barely even seen Callum, except during the pictures and ceremony, and then she'd practically melted at the sight of him looking so sexy in his linen suit. Quinn didn't pull it off nearly as well as Callum did—but he wasn't half Latino either.

But she'd had no chance to talk to Callum and he seemed to have vanished after dinner.

And the more time that passed without him, the more it hurt to be away from him.

Is he avoiding me again?

Last night, it felt like they were finally getting somewhere.

But maybe it was just because he was drunk and not thinking straight.

He'd come back to the bungalow, though. That had to count for something.

And we had sex again.

But he was gone this morning without a word.

She grabbed a flower from a nearby arrangement and plucked at the petals.

He loves me . . .

He loves me not.

Her lips twisted wryly.

The schoolgirl game seemed about as accurate a predictor of whether Callum cared about her as his behavior did.

"Why aren't you out there on the dance floor, young lady?" Granny sidled up to Liddy, hands on her hips.

Liddy smiled. "I'm going out there soon. Just taking it all in."

"You pulled it off, kid. It's spectacular. The best wedding

I've ever been to." Granny leaned over and planted a kiss on Liddy's cheek. "And believe me when I tell you I've been to a lot of weddings."

"Thanks, Granny. I appreciate your help with everything." Liddy held onto her arm. "Where's Leo?"

"Ah, he's out there dancing without me." Granny shrugged, patting her hand. "I saw you standing here looking all sad, and I thought I'd see if you were okay. Where's your man?"

"I don't know." Liddy's heart tugged in her chest. "And, honestly, Granny, he's not really *my* man. I'm not sure things will last too long after this vacation."

Granny's eyes twinkled. "Don't worry, kiddo, Kyle told me the whole truth. I know the little fibs you've been telling." Then she smiled more broadly. "But I *also* heard from Hunter that you might have been getting a little nooky in the kitchen the other day."

Liddy pinched the bridge of her nose. "Apparently, I can't trust anyone around here."

"Don't worry, your secrets are safe with me." Granny stepped closer to her. "Can I interest you in some unwelcome advice, though?"

I'm not sure if I want to hear it or not. Some things Granny said couldn't be unheard.

"I guess so."

"Good. Because I've been watching you the last week and you know what I think is troubling you the most?"

Liddy tried not to roll her eyes. "What's that?"

"I think you spent a long time seeing yourself one way. And while you had that brace on your back, everyone else could see it. So you tried hard to prove them all wrong. But now, that brace is gone. No one can see a damn thing different about you. And you're still stuck trying to prove to them—and yourself— that you're good enough."

Her words were like a gut punch.

"Make no mistake. You're good enough. But believing it starts with you."

Liddy swallowed hard, her eyes misting with tears.

Oh my God. She's right.

For her whole life, Liddy had been fighting against a disability that had suddenly become invisible to everyone but herself. And she was still the kid in the back brace, trying to prove she could *do* and *be* more, while never fully accepting it herself. While forgetting herself in the process.

Granny reached over and tugged the flower from Liddy's hand. "If a man's playing games, and if *you* have to pluck that flower to decide whether or not he cares . . . And don't tell me that's not what you were doing—I'm hard of hearing and live in a senior community, so I know how to read lips." Granny winked. "But if he ever makes you doubt he cares about you, he's not worth it. Because you're a damn amazing woman, Lydia. Don't let anyone treat you less than one."

She cradled Liddy's cheek with a soft caress, then started flapping her arms as she walked back onto the dance floor.

Liddy almost laughed, shaking her head as Granny found Leo and started dancing.

What on earth did she even mean?

The flower in her hands was sweetly scented, and she glided the soft petals along her lips. The petals she'd plucked and left on the floor haunted her.

He loves me.

He loves me not.

She lowered the flower, her heart getting tighter.

He wants me.

He wants me not.

Sleep with me today.

Forget me tomorrow.

Those were the rules, though, weren't they?

Callum had been clear. This wasn't going anywhere.

Tears stung her eyes.

Because I've done exactly what he hadn't wanted—I've fallen for him.

She didn't know if it was possible to fall in love with someone after a week, but she knew she'd never felt this way about anyone before.

But she'd known Callum for two years now, not just one week. Maybe not the way she knew him now. She'd spent a long time allowing her prejudice to cloud her perceptions about him. Looking back, she could admire the boss he'd been. That he'd always pushed her into jobs that challenged her.

She smiled to herself, remembering the first time they'd met. Every time she'd seen that guidebook in her apartment, she'd wondered what life in London would have been like if *that* version of him had continued in her life.

Now she knew better—he hadn't been ready for a relationship or to trust again. Definitely not then, and not now, either.

He might never be.

A set of firm hands encircled her waist just then, tugging her back. She knew the scent of Callum before she saw him, the familiar feel of his body against hers. She closed her eyes, leaning her head back against his chest as his lips brushed the sensitive spot at her jawline, right below her earlobe.

"Has anyone told you how ravishing you look?"

She smiled sadly, tears still wetting her lashes.

God, I really am falling in love with him.

"I was beginning to think you were avoiding me," she tried to joke, but her voice cracked.

Callum turned her to face him, searching her gaze. "Are you all right?"

"I'm fine." She managed a brave smile. "Just—"

Callum held his fingertips to her lips. "You really did think I was avoiding you, didn't you?"

She nodded, swallowing back tears.

"You are an angel for tolerating my behavior the past few days." His face grew more serious. "But we should talk."

Her heart fell.

Then he is going to end things again.

She'd tried to avoid thinking about that, but now that it was happening, she wasn't sure if she could do what she'd done last night at the bar again. How many times could she throw herself at him and let him reject her?

This wasn't the best place for a discussion like this, and the music on the dance floor was loud. She took his hand, then led him away, straight onto the beach.

They didn't have to go far to find quiet and privacy. She turned to him, trying to get the words out before she lost the nerve. "I know you said you don't want a relationship, and I get it. I'm not trying to push you into one. But I just can't keep doing this. You were right. I'm starting to have feelings for you, and if we keep doing what we've been doing the past few nights, I'm going to get hurt. Really hurt. Because I care about you."

She remembered Granny's words. "And I deserve better than being just another fling to you. I don't need to try to prove anything. Not to you or to myself. I don't need to be tough and flippant about caring about you because that's what you want. Especially if it's not what I want."

He released her hand and stepped back, his face sobering. "I know. And you're right, too. The fake relationship needs to end. We have to go back to our lives, and I don't date my employees."

Her stomach clenched.

Then that's it.

He doesn't want me for anything other than sex.

She swallowed, hard.

Oh God, I'm going to cry.

Holding her breath, she nodded, then moved to walk past him back to the party.

"Of course, I'm no longer your boss. So there's that."

He caught her hand, and she stopped, her heart slamming into her ribs.

She turned toward him slowly. "What?"

"I'm not mad, Liddy. I want you to know that up front. But Miranda Kaster went to HR about our fake relationship. She claimed I had blackmailed you into a sexual relationship."

Liddy gasped.

Miranda . . . did what?

She'd barely had time to even think about Miranda. "Oh, no, no . . . why would she do that? That's not what I told her." A sick feeling rushed through her. "Callum, I never said that to her. I was mad at you for kissing me and then telling me it meant nothing to you, so I vented about *that,* but I didn't say anything about having sex."

"I think this was her revenge because I turned her down. To me, not you. If anything, she probably wanted to get back at me for the both of you."

Guilt and hurt clawed through her.

Then fury.

"How dare she go to HR about this *for* me? I trusted her with this."

"I know."

How was he so surprisingly chill about this?

She wiped angry tears from her eyes. "Did you get fired?"

"I resigned." Callum shrugged as though it was nothing. "I didn't want you to have to deal with an HR circus when we returned. And since, as of twenty minutes ago, I'm the new owner of *La Hacienda Tropical*, I might be heading on an alternative career path anyway."

She blinked at him, mouth parting in shock.

"What are you talking about?"

"It's a long story. Suffice it to say, Sophia was pressuring my mum to sell. I decided to try to reconcile with my mum and buy Sophia out, but then I found out that the American man Sergio told you about? Sophia was going to sell her part of the property to him. He's an American investor and was going to sue my mum for the sale of the property through the courts. It would have forced my mum to sell. So I made a deal with Sophia that would be too good for her to refuse, so long as she accepted it immediately."

Liddy tried to process everything he'd said.

No wonder she'd barely seen him today.

He'd been busy.

"And all this happened today?"

"Unbelievably." Callum reached for her, tugging her closer to him. Taking her hand in his, he lifted her hand to his lips and kissed the back of it. "Liddy, I . . . can't lose you. I know what I said about ruining you, but the fact is, you ruined me. I can't return to London and pretend none of this ever happened. I'm falling in love with you. And it terrifies me. But the only thing that scares me more is facing a future without you in it."

She stared at him.

Is this a dream?

"You want to be with me?"

He smiled, and Liddy wasn't sure she'd seen this smile on Callum before. Except when he'd been eating his favorite ice cream . . . *when I'd noticed pure delight on him.* It was a good look.

"Yes. And for more than tonight. You challenge me and drive me mad, but you're also the woman who will hold my hand when I'm drunk and . . . I don't think I've ever met anyone as fiercely loyal as you." He dropped to his knees. "I'm begging you, Liddy. Be with me."

She laughed, then dropped in front of him, putting her arms around his neck. "You're ridiculous. Of course I will be. All you had to do was ask. But what about *La Hacienda*? Are you going to live here now?"

Callum held her face in his hands. "I'm the owner and the investor at this point. Isla is going to move here and run it with my mum. I'm going back home."

She searched his gaze. He wouldn't use that term lightly. "Where's home?"

"Home is wherever you are, Liddy Winnick."

She kissed him hard until they were both breathless.

Flash.

Liddy blinked, unsure, for a second, where the light had come from.

Then more flashes.

A photographer was taking their picture.

Then she heard a voice saying, "Did they just get engaged?"

The flashes had drawn attention from the wedding, and people were turning to see what was going on, craning their necks toward them.

Liddy and Callum exchanged a look, then started laughing.

"Show us the ring, Liddy!" one of her uncles yelled from the dance floor.

Wonderful.

She turned toward Callum . . . and kissed him like no one was watching.

EPILOGUE

One Year Later

THE BATHING SUIT-WEARING baby girl in Liddy's arms was cuter than any baby had a right to be, and as she stared at her aunt with a toothless smile, Liddy's heart melted. "Isn't she just perfect?" she asked Callum. "Almost makes you want one."

"I think we should get lots of practice on the *making babies* part," Callum whispered in Liddy's ear, wrapping his arms around her waist from behind.

Liddy snickered and handed Tara back to Elle's outstretched hands. "Hear that, Elle? My fiancé practically has baby fever."

Callum laughed, his arms tightening. "That is *not* what I said."

Elle set Tara on her shoulder, then bounced her in a way that seemed like a habit at this point. "All I can say is that you will never know how much time you had and wasted until you have kids. Right, Q?"

Quinn pushed his sunglasses back, squinting at them from the lounge chair beside the pool. His eyes were red rimmed with lack of sleep. "What?"

"Go back to your nap. It's not important." Elle blew him a kiss. She turned toward her parents. "But seriously, Mom, do you think you could take Tara to the beach for a couple of hours this afternoon so I could get some sleep?"

Brenda Winnick held both hands out for her granddaughter. "I'll take her whenever you want. Don't get to see my baby barely enough."

"You're over at the house five days a week, Mom," Elle said with a shake of her head.

"I'm the one who doesn't get to see my granddaughter," Quinn's mom piped up, coming up beside them.

Liddy turned toward Callum. "I think this is our cue to exit before the moms start a fistfight."

Callum grabbed their beers, and they slipped away together, heading away from *La Hacienda's* pool area.

The idea to have a family reunion at *La Hacienda* for Elle and Quinn's one-year anniversary had been Arthur Camden's. And while not everyone could make it, with most of the family not having had a chance to meet Tara, a surprising number of family members had come to the reunion.

"It's like the wedding all over again," Quinn had said with a rueful look when they'd arrived.

In some ways, it was. But *La Hacienda* had changed a lot, and it had also been an excellent opportunity for Liddy and Callum to check on the progress of the renovations.

The pool had been expanded, as well as the deck area for it. And all the bungalows had gotten a major facelift, including king-sized beds in all of them. Isla had hired Sergio as an in-house tour operator, and apparently, that was drawing more bachelorette parties to the site. Callum had also arranged for Kat to be their official wedding planner.

Elle and Quinn's wedding really had been the catalyst for *La Hacienda's* rebirth. Callum's mom still did yoga, and all the beachy, eco-friendly sweetness that Liddy had loved about this place was intact—especially the hammocks on the front porches of each bungalow.

Settling her head against Callum's shoulder, Liddy followed him toward the beach. "The weather's been really nice this year." She waved at Kyle, who was getting good at surfing. "Maybe we ought to find Kyle a nice girl. Do you know anyone?"

"He'll be fine." Callum snuggled her into his arms. "And, no. I had enough trouble finding a nice girl myself."

She pulled back and gave him a flirtatious grin. "You didn't call me nice when we were in bed this morning."

He set a kiss to her lips. "That's because I forgot how wild this country makes you. Not that I'm complaining."

She kissed him back. "That's because I love it here. It reminds me of where I fell in love with you. On that front porch where we had sex in the hammock. You were very drunk and very cute. I might have to get you like that later."

"Yeah?" He laughed, then took a swig of his beer. "I'll keep that in mind."

She watched the bright blue sea, the foamy waves coming closer toward their feet. She really did love it here. Not that they could move here anytime soon, but she didn't think she'd mind it if they did that eventually. She'd been promoted to Callum's position after he'd resigned the year before. Then she'd moved in with him since her roommate situation wasn't working out and fired Miranda, who had been, thankfully, discredited.

She smiled at the sense of satisfaction that still gave her.

Maybe the job did come with a bit of assholery. And she *was* too busy to consider moving anywhere for now. She was almost jealous of Callum's freedom from the grind.

Almost. But not quite.

She focused her attention back on Callum, who'd grown quiet beside her. "What about you?"

"What about me?"

"When did you know you loved me?"

He gave her a look like *why are we doing this,* and she poked him in the ribs.

"Probably when you passed out after eating that damn hot pepper. I knew then and there I'd never meet someone as stubborn as you, and I loved it."

She burst out laughing. She'd come as close to pushing that memory to the furthest recesses of her mind as she could. "Come on, that's not true. Tell me when."

"You know when I started falling in love with you, Lid."

"No, I don't." She stepped away and shrugged her shoulders innocently.

His expression softened, and he set his beer down in the sand. Then he reached for his pocket and took out his wallet. He dug out his license, then pulled something from behind it and held it out in the palm of his hand.

A quarter.

"I fell in love with a girl in a bookshop who asked me to flip for a guidebook." He searched her gaze. "But I couldn't have her. So I kept the memory of her instead."

Just when I thought I couldn't love him anymore.

"You kept the quarter?" She could hardly find the words.

"You left it on the floor where we were flipping it. I picked it up and tucked it away. Could never get rid of it."

She reached toward it with fascination, and he closed his fingers around it. He tucked it away again. "This one is mine. Get your own lucky quarter. You got the guidebook."

"You know it's going to be your guidebook, too, once we're married. The whole what's mine is yours, marital property thing?"

He shrugged, then reached for her hands. "The guidebook was always supposed to be yours anyway. I was buying it as a welcome book for you."

She shook her head. "All the crazy things we had happen to us. Hard to believe we spent two whole years missing the chance to be together."

"Maybe. But I don't think either of us were who we needed to be for each other during that time." He held her chin, then kissed her. "We weren't ready. Or I wasn't, at any rate."

That's true. But he'd come around nicely since then.

Their toes sank deeper into the sand as a wave came up and lapped at their feet. She kissed him again. "I love you, Callum. I love us. I'm glad you finally found your way back home here— I'll always think of Costa Rica as the place that brought us together."

"I love you, too, beautiful." He pulled her against him, steadying her upright as another stronger wave rushed against their shins. "I'm glad we're here together. My roots will always be here, but you . . . you're my home."

"And you are mine, my love."

She smiled, then kissed him with reckless abandon, ignoring the way they had sunk into the sand.

The tide must be coming in.

Maybe even a storm.

But they'd weathered storms before, alone and together . . .

If she'd learned one thing throughout the last twelve months, it was this:

Life wasn't always easy, but when you had the right person by your side, when you weren't trying to prove that you could handle everything alone, even the hard days couldn't overwhelm or defeat you.

NEWSLETTER AND NEXT BOOK

I hope you enjoyed Liddy and Callum's story! For some fun notes about what I pulled from real life (which was a lot, haha) check out the acknowledgements.

Thank you so much for reading; my readers really are what make this possible and I am so grateful for you! If you enjoyed this book, I'd love it if you took the time to leave a rating or review at your favorite book retailer. It truly goes a long way.

And if you'd like to stick around and see more of my work and see more of Isla and Aiden, check out the next book in this series, *One Time in Paris*, which will be available in September 2025!

Want to keep up with me and hear what's going on in my world? Join my newsletter on my website or Facebook Reader's group! I have freebies and giveaways, exclusive content and, of course, you get to hear all about upcoming book news, my life, and my small army of children.

ACKNOWLEDGMENTS

In some ways, I spent a lifetime researching for this book. I even stole a lot of travel misadventures from my own life for it—hah! Monkey theft, fording a swollen Costa Rican River in our SUV (just as scary as it sounds), traveling down harrowing mist-covered mountain roads without a GPS, forgetting to call the credit card companies . . . all been there, done that! (And it was my father who, in real life, swallowed a chili pepper and passed out.)

Being half-Costa Rican, I wanted not only to pay homage to a country that made me who I am (and where I was born, actually), but also to that feeling of being someone who has lived between worlds, never quite fitting in either. So a good person to start the thanks with for this book would be my mother, who as an eighteen year old, boarded a plane from San Jose, Costa Rica to spend a year as an exchange student in Spokane, Washington and ended up changing her fate as a result.

I also couldn't have written this book without the assistance of my cousin, Raquel, who was a great resource and who reminded me that this book would be much better written if I wrote what I knew.

Many thanks to Marion Archer, who helped make Callum and Liddy shine. Your edits always bring out the story I'm actually trying to write and I'm so thankful to call you my editor.

To Julie Simms, Amanda Coleman, Julie Deaton, and

Jayne Campbell—my wonderful team that helps bring these books to a shine!

Huge thanks to Patrick Knowles for the wonderful cover; I described what I wanted in one quick summary and you encapsulated my vision perfectly!

Last, but never least, to my wonderful kids and my extremely patient husband. Your love and support are everything to me.

ALSO BY ANNABELLE MCCORMACK

The Windswept WWI Saga

A Zephyr Rising: A Windswept Prequel Novella

Windswept: The Windswept Saga Book 1

Sands of Sirocco: The Windswept Saga Book 2

Whisper in the Tempest: The Windswept Saga Book 3

The Brandywood Small Town Romance Series

All This Time

I'll Carry You

Once We Met

Until Forever Ends

Ever With Me

Wanderlust Contemporary Romances

See You Next Fall

He Loves Me Knot

One Time in Paris (September 16, 2025)

The Route to You (December 16, 2025)

To find out the latest about my new releases, please sign up for my newsletter! I love hearing from readers and have some great offers lined up for my subscribers.

ABOUT THE AUTHOR

Annabelle McCormack spins you tales of epic historical adventure, heartfelt romance, and complex family dynamics with strong female protagonists to make things interesting. She is a graduate of the Johns Hopkins University's M.A. in Writing Program. She lives in Maryland with her badass husband, where she plays competitive rounds of chess with her five homeschooled young children.

Visit her at www.annabellemccormack.com or http://instagram.com/annabellemccormack to follow her daily adventures.

* 9 781960 883063 *